In her latest mystery, *A Dilly of a Death,* national best-selling author Susan Wittig Albert has crafted "more than just a whodunit . . . readers will relish this more-sweet-than-sour adventure." (*Booklist*) Lawyer-turned-herbalist China Bayles becomes immersed in a local mystery—and to find clues, she'll have to scrape the bottom of the pickle barrel . . .

China Bayles is in a pickle. The daughter of her best friend Ruby has turned up on her doorstep, pregnant and in need of a place to live. And her otherwise sensible husband McQuaid has announced that he's bored with teaching—he wants to try his hand as a private eye. His first client is Phoebe the Pickle Queen, owner of the biggest little pickle business in Texas. According to Phoebe, her plant manager is embezzling, and she wants McQuaid to "follow the money." Meanwhile, Pecan Springs is hosting the annual Picklefest—and this year, China and Ruby are on the planning committee, along with Phoebe. But just days before the festival starts, the Pickle Queen disappears. Some say she sold her business and split; others think the answer may lie with her missing boyfriend. It's up to McQuaid and China to search for the Pickle Queen—and for clues in a case that promises to leave a very sour taste.

"ONE OF THE MOST ENDEARING AND PERSONABLE AMATEUR SLEUTHS." —*Midwest Book Review*

"SUCH A JOY . . . AN INSTANT FRIEND."
—Carolyn G. Hart

continued on next page . . .

Praise for the China Bayles mystery series . . .

"[China Bayles is] such a joy . . . an instant friend."
—Carolyn G. Hart

"A treat for gardeners who like to relax with an absorbing mystery." —*North American Gardener*

"One of the best-written and well-plotted mysteries I've read in a long time." —*Los Angeles Times*

"Albert's characters are as real and as quirky as your next-door neighbor." —*Raleigh News & Observer*

"Mystery lovers who also garden will be captivated by this unique series." —*Seattle Post-Intelligencer*

"Realistic, likable characters." —*Chicago Tribune*

"Lively and engaging." —*Fort Worth Star-Telegram*

"Gripping." —*Library Journal*

"Entertaining." —*Midwest Book Review*

"Cause for celebration." —*Rocky Mount Telegram*

"The best." —*Booklist*

SUSAN
WITTIG ALBERT

A DILLY OF A DEATH

BERKLEY PRIME CRIME, NEW YORK

THE BERKLEY PUBLISHING GROUP
Published by the Penguin Group
Penguin Group (USA) Inc.
375 Hudson Street, New York, New York 10014, USA
Penguin Group (Canada), 10 Alcorn Avenue, Toronto, Ontario M4V 3B2, Canada
(a division of Pearson Penguin Canada Inc.)
Penguin Books Ltd., 80 Strand, London WC2R 0RL, England
Penguin Group Ireland, 25 St. Stephen's Green, Dublin 2, Ireland (a division of Penguin Books Ltd.)
Penguin Group (Australia), 250 Camberwell Road, Camberwell, Victoria 3124, Australia
(a division of Pearson Australia Group Pty. Ltd.)
Penguin Books India Pvt. Ltd., 11 Community Centre, Panchsheel Park, New Delhi—110 017, India
Penguin Group (NZ), Cnr. Airborne and Rosedale Roads, Albany, Auckland 1310, New Zealand
(a division of Pearson New Zealand Ltd.)
Penguin Books (South Africa) (Pty.) Ltd., 24 Sturdee Avenue, Rosebank, Johannesburg 2196,
South Africa

Penguin Books Ltd., Registered Offices: 80 Strand, London WC2R 0RL, England

This is a work of fiction. Names, characters, places, and incidents either are the product of the author's
imagination or are used fictitiously, and any resemblance to actual persons, living or dead, business
establishments, events, or locales is entirely coincidental.

A DILLY OF A DEATH

A Berkley Prime Crime Book / published by arrangement with the author

PRINTING HISTORY
Berkley hardcover edition / January 2004
Berkley Prime Crime mass-market edition / April 2005

Copyright © 2004 by Susan Wittig Albert.
Cover design by Judith Murello.
Cover art by Joe Burleson.

ISBN: 0-425-19954-1

Berkley Prime Crime Books are published by The Berkley Publishing Group,
a division of Penguin Group (USA) Inc.,
375 Hudson Street, New York, New York 10014.
The name BERKLEY PRIME CRIME and the BERKLEY PRIME CRIME design
are trademarks belonging to Penguin Group (USA) Inc.

PRINTED IN THE UNITED STATES OF AMERICA

10 9 8 7 6 5 4 3 2 1

AUTHOR'S NOTE

I would like to give special thanks to Steve Collette, owner of Goldin Pickle in Garland, Texas, and former president of Pickle Packers International. Steve showed me how pickles are commercially manufactured, gave me a glimpse into the pickle industry, and offered a couple of excellent plot ideas. He makes tasty pickles, too—every bit as good as those my grandmother used to make.

Thanks again to Bill, without whose many contributions none of these books would be possible. He doesn't make pickles, but he does keep the ideas flowing and the computers operating, and he makes Meadow Knoll an altogether delightful place to live, work, and grow herbs.

And speaking of herbs, China and I would like to remind you *not* to use any medicinal herb without first learning all you can about it. Like other medications, plants contain potent chemicals, some of which may trigger an allergy, cause unwanted side effects, or interact with other medicines you're using. So please, dear Reader, do your homework.

Susan Wittig Albert
Bertram, Texas
August 2002

Chapter One

Dill (*Anethum graveolens*) is a hardy annual member of the parsley family, native to southern Russia and the Mediterranean area. According to Prior's *Popular Names of English Plants*, its common name is derived from the Old Norse word *dilla*, which means "to lull" or "to calm." It was widely used to treat colic in babies, and every mother kept dill seeds handy to brew a soothing tea for her infants.

 "It was *tacky*," I said indignantly. "And none of her darn business."

"I'm sorry she brought it up, China." McQuaid pushed back the heavy shock of dark hair that had fallen across his forehead. "On behalf of my mother, I sincerely apologize."

"You can't apologize on behalf of your mother, sincerely or insincerely," I retorted, trying to stay irritated, trying not to allow myself to be distracted by the affectionate smile that lurked in my husband's slate-blue eyes. "She's got to do it herself, and she won't. Or rather," I added, reluctantly fair, "she can't, because she doesn't even know she was being hurtful."

"That's why I'm doing it for her," McQuaid said, with the air of a man who has irrefutably countered his wife's best argument and feels he has won the day. He picked up his cup and pushed back his chair. "More coffee?"

It was a rainy Sunday afternoon in Pecan Springs, Texas. The June sky was gray and weepy, the live oaks dripped, and raindrops dappled the silvery puddles in the grass around our house on Limekiln Road—not a pretty day, I suppose, by most people's standards. But since I have a couple of acres of garden to water, rain means I don't have to drag hoses around for a few days, so I'm always glad to see it. This rain was gentle and well behaved, too, which made it especially welcome. Undisciplined cloudbursts and rowdy gully washers are something else again. Five inches of rain in two hours is no gift to anybody, especially when you live in the Texas Hill Country, on the wrong side of a low-water crossing. If you take a chance, you may find your vehicle sailing downstream and yourself stranded in a cottonwood tree—if you're lucky. You may also find yourself dead. People do, all the time.

Rainy Sundays are good for serious indoor pursuits, and that's what was going on at our house. McQuaid and I were sitting over coffee at the kitchen table, pursuing a discussion of something that had happened earlier that day. Brian was in his room upstairs, pursuing his interests across the vast reaches of the Internet. And Howard Cosell was stretched across my feet, his paws twitching as he pursued rabbits across the landscape of his dreams, with an occasional muffled yip of alarm when he actually managed to catch one and had to figure out what to do with the mouthful of fur.

McQuaid went to the counter and picked up the coffeepot. "Well, I suppose you can understand why Ma keeps raising the subject," he said, comfortable now that he had made the apology. "She's got a certain investment in babies. After all, I'm her son. My kids are her grandkids."

He poured, added sugar, and stirred, while I eyed his profile. Tall, dark, lithe, and lean-bodied, with the shoulders of a college quarterback. Craggy face, twice-broken nose (once on the football field, once in a fight with a crazy drunk), a jagged scar across his forehead (a relic of an encounter with a doper). Not quite handsome, but close enough. And sexy. Ah, yes, sexy.

I pulled my attention back to the conversation. " 'My kids are her grandkids.' " I repeated. "That should be singular, shouldn't it? Your *son* is her grandson. That is, unless you've neglected to tell me about a chapter or two in your checkered past."

"Of course it's singular," McQuaid said. He opened the refrigerator and began to rummage among the leftovers. "You can't really blame Ma for coveting a few more grandchildren, can you? Her grandmother had a whole slew of them, thirty, or something like that, and twice as many great-grandchildren. Ma must feel like a pauper in comparison."

I shuddered. "Your mother's grandmother had ten children. She never heard of Margaret Sanger. Anyway, Jill is going to produce a grandchild in six months. That should take her mind off us. I sincerely *hope*," I added fervently.

"It probably won't," McQuaid said. "When Ma sinks her teeth into a project, she's like a coyote with a leg of lamb. The devil could goose her, and she wouldn't let go." He took out a plastic margarine tub. "What's this?" he asked, opening the lid.

"It's a dead frog," I said. "Brian is planning an autopsy." I added with a grin, "Probably wouldn't taste very good."

While McQuaid is contemplating his son's autopsy sub-

4

ject with some distaste, I'll take a minute to introduce us. Mike McQuaid—formerly a Houston homicide detective and currently on the Criminal Justice faculty at Central Texas State University—is my husband. We've been married almost two years now, after dating each other for a long time and living together for a while, on an experimental basis, to see if it would work out. We live about a dozen miles from town in a big Victorian house that a previous owner named Meadow Brook, and since the house site includes both a brook and a meadow, the name seems to fit. I've turned part of the meadow into a large herb garden, where I grow popular culinary herbs like dill, marjoram, and parsley, which I tie into fresh, fragrant bundles and sell in my shop and to the local markets.

Brian is McQuaid's fourteen-year-old son by his first wife, Sally, who drops into and out of our lives like a whimsical bad fairy. He's a smart kid whose current passions include spiders, snakes, lizards, and girls, not always (but mostly) in that order. He says he's going to be a biologist when he grows up, and judging from the live collections in his bedroom, I'd say he's already on his way.

Howard Cosell is McQuaid's crochety basset hound, who (in defiance of the fact that bassets are bred-in-the-bone rabbit chasers) would never dream of chasing a real rabbit when he's awake. He's a notably intelligent dog, but lazy; with regard to rabbits, he'd rather do an on-line search, preferably from his comfy basset basket beside the Home Comfort range in the kitchen.

And I am China Bayles, formerly a criminal defense attorney in Houston, now the owner of Thyme and Seasons Herbs and co-owner, with my best friend, Ruby Wilcox, of Thyme for Tea. And if you're thinking that dropping out of the career culture and moving to a small town is a come-down from something important, you're dead wrong. In my book, being my own boss and not having to deal with bad guys is a major upgrade. I am very happy with the way things have turned out—although at this very moment, I have to confess to being more than a little irritated by my mother-in-law.

My irritation began with our Sunday noon dinner with McQuaid's parents at their home near Seguin, a small community about thirty miles southeast of Pecan Springs. It was Mother McQuaid's seventieth birthday, and we were all gathered around the big dining room table to celebrate: Mother and Dad McQuaid, Jill (McQuaid's sister) and her husband, Pete, and McQuaid and I and Brian. When Mother McQuaid had blown out the candles on her devil's food cake, Jill lifted her glass of iced tea in a toast.

"Well, Ma," she said, "you're going to get one of your wishes, anyway." She looked around the table, smug. "Pete and I are having a baby—a boy."

I was startled, as much by the sudden envy that rose up at the back of my throat as by Jill's unexpected announcement. But I swallowed down the sourness and did my best to join in the yelps of delighted surprise and ecstatic hugs that went around the table. Jill is a couple of years older than McQuaid, which puts her in her early forties, and her mother was jubilant, having given up all hope that her daughter would get pregnant. I was pleased too, since I knew how much Jill and Pete wanted a baby and how hard they'd tried to make it happen. The whole thing would have been entirely delightful, if Mother McQuaid had not spoiled it with her next remark.

"Now it's your turn, China," she said, turning to me.

"You and Mike have been married for almost two years." She gave me one of her sweetly innocent smiles. "You're not getting any younger, you know, dear. Isn't it time you were thinking of giving Brian a little brother or sister?"

By that time, I had successfully dealt with my envy—which wasn't envy at all, just surprise. "No," I said, in a firm voice that carried a little farther than I meant it to. I smiled too, showing my teeth. "No, I don't think so." I was about to say more, but McQuaid hastily cleared his throat.

"Hey," he said. "What are we waiting for? Let's cut that cake!"

Mother McQuaid ducked her head with a hurt look, as if I had smacked her. "I don't mean to interfere, of course." Hand on bosom, she heaved a dramatic sigh. "All I've ever wanted is for you children to be happy. And our Brian is such a wonderful young man. It would be so much fun for him to have a sweet little—"

"Cut that cake, Ma," Dad McQuaid interrupted sternly, "before China throws it at you." Everybody laughed, some of us more loudly than others.

McQuaid shoved Brian's frog into the refrigerator and came back to the table, where he put his hand on my shoulder and bent to drop a gentle kiss in my hair.

"Hey," he said softly, "stop scowling, China. In case it's worrying you, I'm entirely happy with the current cast of characters. Just you, me, Brian, Howard Cosell, and the occasional dead frog." Another kiss, another pat. "As far as I'm concerned, a baby isn't an essential part of the package."

"You're sure?" I asked, with more than a little anxiety. We had discussed this issue at length before we decided to get married, because the statistics aren't very promising for women over forty, which includes me. I chose a law degree and a high-octane career over marriage and kids, and by the time I'd ditched the career, created a quieter life, and opted for marriage, my biological clock was about to reach the witching hour. Children weren't likely to be a part of the package.

But as long as I'm in confessional mode, I might as well go all the way. Even if I could get pregnant, I wouldn't want to. By the time a little girl was old enough for sleepovers, I'd be past fifty. I might just be able to handle that, but say that the baby was a boy. When he was old enough to drive, I'd be past sixty. Could I cope? I don't think so.

Of course, it's probably not politically correct for me to say this, because I have several friends in their early forties who would trade their souls for a baby. But while I'm perfectly happy to cheer them on in their efforts to be fruitful and multiply, I am also perfectly happy with my own situation. Selfish? Maybe. But I've lived long enough with myself to understand the importance of maintaining my personal space, my privacy, and my autonomy. I'm learning to carry my share of the marriage, and I'm even getting comfortable with being a mother to Brian. But a family of three is quite large enough, thank you, and I'm not in favor of upping the total. I hoped McQuaid meant it when he said he hadn't changed his mind about babies.

"Yep." McQuaid sat down, regarding me thoughtfully. "I'm sure we'd manage if a baby happened along, but we've definitely got enough on our plates. You have the shop and the tearoom and all your other enterprises, and I have—" He stopped, looking uncomfortable. "I've been meaning to talk to you about this, China."

I gave him a wary look, not exactly sure about the tone of his voice. "Talk to me about what?"

He turned his coffee cup in his hands, looking down at it. "About what I want to do. With my future, I mean." He cleared his throat. "Of course, it's *our* future, so you've got something to say about it. I don't want the decision to be just mine."

"What decision?" I was beginning to get concerned about the direction this conversation was taking. "What are we talking about? Another career change?"

This was not just a wild guess. McQuaid had already made one big change in his life—from cop to university professor. After a couple of years of teaching, though, he had begun to find his classes a little boring, while the slash-and-burn politics in his department was more un-nerving than street work. So he'd tried to bring a little ex-citement into his life by taking on an undercover narcotics investigation for the Department of Public Safety. The job had been more dangerous than he'd bargained for, though, landing him in the hospital with a bullet very close to his spine. He had survived, thank God, but with a permanent limp, a disability that meant he couldn't go back to police work even if he wanted to. Which, I was afraid, he did. Teaching was no longer much of a challenge, and he hadn't stopped hating the departmental politics. It was only a mat-ter of time before he decided on a new direction.

"Well, it's sort of a change." The corner of McQuaid's mouth quirked, and while his voice was flat, it held an un-dertone of barely suppressed excitement. "What I'd like to do is hang out my shingle. As a PI, I mean. By the end of the month."

"A . . . a private investigator?" I managed. I wasn't exactly surprised, because he'd always enjoyed investigative work more than any other part of being a cop. But the suddenness of it was jolting. The end of the month was almost here.

He looked crestfallen at my lack of instant enthusiasm. "It's not as prestigious as being a university professor, I'm afraid," he said ruefully. "And it's not going to pay as well, either. I'll teach the summer courses I'm signed up for, and I'll probably teach a course or two during the year, which will help out some. But I can't predict how much I'm going to bring in from the PI work. We'll have to watch our bottom line pretty closely."

"The prestige thing isn't a problem," I said. "Or the money, either." Pecan Springs's economy is based on tourism, and both the shop and the tearoom were doing reasonably well, for small businesses. The money wasn't coming in hand over fist, but there'd be enough to tide us over until he picked up the first few clients. I looked at him, loving him. "It's the other part that I worry about. Your safety."

McQuaid raised one dark eyebrow. "Well, if it's danger that bothers you, you can stop worrying, China. The jobs I'm looking for will be purely investigative—digging up information and putting it together. Solving puzzles is what I'm good at." Reminiscently, he rubbed the scar across his forehead. "I've had enough run-ins with bad guys to last me a lifetime. I am definitely not looking for more."

I took a deep breath. "That's easy enough to say. But behind that academic facade, you're still a cop at heart. You enjoy a piece of the action. If there's a challenge out there, you'll find it." I made a face. "Or it will find you."

"I don't think so." He was boyishly pleased with himself. "Anyway, I plan to be choosy about the kinds of cases I take on. If it doesn't smell right, I don't want any part of it." He paused, expectant, his dark eyebrows cocked. "Don't you want to know the name of my business?"

"Okay, I'll bite. What's the name of your business?"

"M. McQuaid and Associates, Private Investigations," he said, with a dramatic flourish.

I tilted my head curiously. "Associates, Sherlock?"

"I thought maybe some people might be put off if they thought it was a one-man firm. Anyway, there are several people I can count on to give me a hand if I need it."

"Absolutely," I said with enthusiasm. "There's me and—"

"No, no," he broke in hastily, before I could mention Ruby. "I'm thinking of people like Bubba Harris and Tom McConnell. They're both expert investigators." Bubba is the former Pecan Springs chief of police, and Tom is retired from the Texas Rangers.

I was tempted to argue with him. After all, my work as a criminal attorney has pulled me into plenty of investigations, some of them involving very bad guys. But the fact is that I don't have time for that sort of thing any longer. Between the herb shop and the tearoom, my days are fully occupied, and I devote my spare time to getting a life.

"All I care about is your safety," I said. "If you keep your nose out of trouble, I'll keep my nose out of your business."

He grinned. "Is that a promise?"

I nodded, and he put both his hands, large and warm and strong, over mine. Through his touch, I could feel his confidence, his excitement about this new chapter in his life. "So it's okay with you if I do this?" he asked.

"It's okay," I said, and squeezed his hands to show that I meant it. "Whatever you want is fine with me. As long as it doesn't involve making babies. And doesn't get you killed."

"That's good," McQuaid said, with evident relief. "Because I've already taken the exam and done the paperwork to get registered. With my law enforcement background, it was a piece of cake. I'm going to work out of my office here at the house, at least in the beginning. In fact, my first prospective client will be showing up"—he turned his wrist to glance at his watch—"in about ten minutes."

"Ten minutes!" I yelped. It was just like McQuaid to set everything up before he told me what he was up to. He protects his personal space almost as passionately as I do. "You were pretty sure of yourself, friend. What would you have done if I'd said I wanted you to stay at CTSU?"

He was not perturbed. "I was sure you wouldn't. And if you did, I was sure I could talk you out of it." He kissed his finger and ran it down the bridge of my nose. "I would use all my persuasive powers. You'd be putty in my hands. You wouldn't be able to resist."

"Probably not," I agreed equably, "but it might be fun to try. I'll resist, you persuade." McQuaid has always been able, ultimately, to persuade me, even when I hold back. And I had held back a lot, in the old days, for marriage (like children), wasn't high on the list of things I wanted to accomplish in my life. But McQuaid had been persistent, his pursuit surprising me, annoying me, confusing me, and finally, beguiling me. "This client of yours—who is he?"

McQuaid leaned back in his chair. "He's a she with nice deep pockets, always an asset in a client. She's Phoebe Morgan. Charlie Lipman sent her."

"Phoebe the Pickle Queen Morgan?" I stared at him. "You don't want to work for *her,* do you?"

"I won't know until I hear what the job is." He frowned. "Why? What's wrong with Phoebe Morgan?"

"If you don't already know," I said, "it's almost impossible to tell you."

"Try," he said.

"But you must already know something about Morgan's Pickles," I protested. "After all, you grew up in this area." Well, not exactly. He grew up in Seguin, which is far enough away so that he might not know much about the Pecan Springs locals. And his work at the university wouldn't have introduced him to—

"Pretend I never heard of it," he said. Another look at his watch. "You've got five minutes. Starting now."

I shrugged and began. "The Morgans," I told him, "were the crème de la crème of the Adams County aristocracy, local folk who had made good, hoisting themselves out of poverty by an impressive combination of sense, skills, and luck. In the early years of the Great Depression, Mick and Polly Morgan lived five or six miles out of town, on a piece of land that was too small to run cows and too rocky to farm. They were scraping together a bare living raising chickens when a big wind tore the chicken coops apart and scattered feathers across the county. All that Mick and Polly had left was their son, Randolph, their old house, and a half-acre plot of dead-ripe cucumbers that Polly had planted in the sandy bottomland along the creek.

"Polly, however, was not intimidated by a mere windstorm. She tied on her apron and sent Randolph out to pick cucumbers, while she got out the canning kettle and her mother's secret recipe for dill pickles. When the first batch was ready, Mick loaded up the Model T and peddled Polly's pickles in Pecan Springs and nearby New Braunfels, where they went over big with the German families. Before long, there was enough demand for Polly's pickles to justify moving the operation into the new barn Mick had built. The next day, Mick hired a sign painter to paint MORGAN'S PREMIER PICKLES in big red letters on the east side of the barn, where you could see it when you drove along the county road. By the end of the year, barns all across Texas and even into Oklahoma and Arkansas sported the big red words MORGAN'S PREMIER PICKLES, their owners seduced by the promise of a free paint job on the barn, ten dollars in their overall pockets, and a case of Polly's pickles. In another couple of years, you could see MORGAN'S PREMIER PICKLES on barns in Mississippi, Georgia, and the Carolinas. People around Pecan Springs used to joke that the only thing that kept Mick from painting the name of his pickle business on the barns on the other side of the Mason-Dixon Line was the unfortunate fact that the farmers had already sold out to SEE ROCK CITY.

"And that was the start of Morgan's Premier Pickles, which by the end of the decade was the biggest little pickle business in Texas. Things went along very well, in fact— but only as long as Polly and Mick were alive. When they cashed in their dill chips and went to wander in Elysian cucumber fields, the management of Morgan's Premier Pickles fell to Randolph, who was neither as inspired as his mother nor as hardworking as his father. In fact, he didn't seem to have a brain in his head, at least as far as the family enterprise was concerned. Not to make a pun of it, things swiftly went sour in the pickle business, and for the next decade or so, Morgan's did not flourish.

"The situation changed, however, when Randolph, his wife, and their son died in a plane crash. Their daughter, Phoebe Morgan Knight, recently married and about to be a mother, was the only Morgan left, and folks around here didn't expect much from her. After all, she'd only been out of college for a couple of years. If the guys at Ben's Barber Shop had been placing bets, they would have bet that Morgan's Pickles would be down the drain by Christmas, and Phoebe would be back making babies with her husband, Ed, who had been a fullback on the CTSU football team and was widely admired by the Good Old Boys.

"Phoebe, however, had other ideas. Her first stop was the delivery room, where she spent the morning giving birth to a son, Brad. Two days later, she was sitting in the office of the president of Ranchers State Bank, mortgaging the Morgan property to buy new equipment and build an addition to the plant. Before the baby's first birthday, she'd ditched her grandparents' line of low-profit retail products and reorganized the plant to produce whole pickles, sliced pickles, and relish for the institutional market—all with new and highly automated equipment. This allowed her to consolidate her marketing efforts, increase productivity and efficiency, and reduce her payroll by nearly ninety percent—which did not endear her to the locals, of course. By the time Brad went off to nursery school, Morgan's was supplying pickles in two-gallon jars, five-gallon pails, and forty-gallon kegs to prisons, potato salad and pickle loaf manufacturers, and school lunchrooms from Texas to Florida. Mick and Polly would have been proud.

"But Phoebe was not the easiest woman in the world to work with, and over the twenty-five years she'd been making Morgan's more profitable, she'd gotten a reputation as an ambitious, aggressive woman who knew exactly what she wanted and didn't let anybody—and that means *any-body*—get in her way. Folks around here can't forget that nearly 150 people used to work for Morgan's, while now the year-round staff is down to about fifteen. They don't like her, in spite of the fact that she has become a commu-nity activist, volunteering for every board in town. They call her the Pickle Queen, along with other less-flattering names, some of them rather vulgar. They—"

"Very interesting," McQuaid interrupted. "You tell a good story, China. You'll have to finish later, though. I've got to get going."

"What do you think she wants?" I asked curiously. "Se-curity for the plant, maybe?"

"I have no idea. She didn't give me any details over the phone. But I don't plan to take any security jobs, so if that's what she's after, she's out of luck." He drained his coffee cup. "Anyway, whatever the lady has on her mind, it's confidential. Which means I won't be able to tell you about it."

"A confidential tête-à-tête with the Pickle Queen?" I snickered. "Sounds like a real sweet dill to me."

McQuaid put down his cup with a loud groan.

I leaned forward. "What's green and swims in the sea?"

"Excuse me," McQuaid said, standing hastily. "I've got to get ready to see Ms. Morgan."

"Moby Pickle." I chortled. "My roommate Allie and I used to trade pickle jokes while we were studying for ex-ams. It kept us sane. What do you get when you cross an al-ligator with a pickle?"

McQuaid went to the kitchen door. "I'm not biting," he said firmly. "I have more to do than sit around trading stupid pickle jokes."

"A croco-dill!" I crowed. I got up and followed him into the hall. "What business does a smart pickle go into?"

The only answer I got was the sound of McQuaid's office door closing firmly. "A dilly-catessen," I said to myself, chuckling.

And then I thought about McQuaid's announcement and sobered. This would be his third career. Would the change make him happy, at last? Could he really manage to choose the cases he wanted—and stay out of trouble?

And would a smart pickle really go into the PI business?

Chapter Two

In many cultures, dill has enjoyed a reputation as a potent aphrodisiac. In northern Europe, a strong dill tea added to bathwater was supposed to make the bather irresistible. In Romany lore, dill seeds in wine were thought to increase sexual desire, and in China dill leaves were chopped into food for a love feast.

I was still mulling over my questions when Howard Cosell lifted his head and bayed apprehensively, announcing the trespass of an unfamiliar vehicle upon his private territory. Howard is a philosophical sort of dog and given to worrying, especially when some new event or person appears on his horizon.

"Hush, Howard," I said. "It's only a client. If you keep on making that noise, you'll scare it away. Which might mean no money for puppy biscuits next month."

Knowing his priorities, Howard stopped baying, got up, and went to cool the tips of his long ears in his water bowl. But I was wrong. It wasn't McQuaid's client he was announcing—a client would certainly have presented herself at the front door. I heard the squeak of the back porch step, then a hesitant knock at the kitchen door. It was Amy Roth. She was wearing a pair of skin-tight black jeans, red platform heels, and a stretchy red strapless tube top that left her midriff bare.

I suppressed an interior uh-oh. Amy is Ruby Wilcox's wild child. Like her mother, she's impulsive and full of good (if sometimes misguided) intentions, which often cloud her judgment. Like Ruby, when Amy sets her mind to something, there's no moving her, but unlike her mother, she doesn't yet have the benefit of experience. She is even more of a flake than Ruby, and since she's a great deal younger, her flakiness is a great deal more, well, conspicuous. Amy had been living in an apartment over a garage in a quiet Pecan Springs residential neighborhood, but the owner's brother claimed the apartment, and Amy has been staying with Ruby until she can find something she likes and can afford. I'm not sure how well it's working out, though. Ruby loves her daughter, of course, but loving Amy is a lot like hugging a porcupine. A prickly bit of business.

I pasted on a smile and opened the door wider. "Hey, Amy, come in out of the wet."

"You're sure I'm not interrupting anything?" she asked uncertainly.

"McQuaid's expecting somebody, but I'm just being lazy," I said, deciding not to mention McQuaid's New Career Plan. Amy might tell her mother, and Ruby would immediately volunteer her services as an assistant investigator. If you've met Ruby, you know that she'd like nothing better than to be Kinsey Millhone or V. I. Warshawski when she grows up. Given half a chance, she'll make a mystery out of a molehill—although I have learned that her intuitive, right-brain wisdom is every bit as good at solving puzzles, and perhaps better, than my linear left-brain logic. Still,

McQuaid would not be likely to employ her talents, so I only said, "What's going on with you these days, Amy? I haven't seen you for quite a while."

Amy sat down at the kitchen table and bent over to fondle Howard's ears. She looks a lot like her mom: not quite so tall but even more slender—skinny, really—with a smattering of freckles on her delicate, triangular face, and a thick mane of naturally curly red hair that corkscrews all over the place. At some point in the recent past, however, she's dyed her hair different colors, and the purple, pink, and black has not yet grown out. In a dim light, she might pass for a rainbow. Add the flash of rings on her fingers, the glitter of gold in her pierced ears, nostril, eyebrow, and belly button (to name just the visible piercings), and enough turquoise and black eye makeup to gratify Cleopatra, and—well, you get the picture. In flash and flamboyance, Amy is her mother's daughter.

In ways that count, though, Amy isn't at all like her mother. Ruby has the wisdom and self-confidence of a few decades of life experience under her belt, while Amy hasn't yet discovered True North, and if she's gained any wisdom, she doesn't bother to display it very regularly. Like a great many young people, she flounders all over the map in pursuit of her passions, which mostly seem to involve what Ruby calls Amy's Lost Causes, animals and people she attempts to rescue and rehabilitate. She may be twenty-five, but there's a childlike fragility about her that makes her seem younger and more vulnerable than she is—sixteen, sometimes, going on fourteen or even twelve.

"What's going on these days?" Amy repeated my question, her sharp-featured face pale and set. "Well, for starters, I'm pregnant."

I said the only thing I could think of. "Let's have a cup of tea."

"Sure," Amy said, without enthusiasm. She straightened up, and Howard stretched his length across her feet, licking her bare toes with affectionate relish. Amy has a way with animals, and when Howard finds a new friend, it doesn't matter to him that she looks like a Spice Girl. "Tea would be fine."

I went to the cupboard and reached for a jar of dried chamomile, which has been used for centuries to smooth the bumps in life's rocky road. The kettle was already steaming, and as I poured it over the loose tea in the pot, I said, "I guess you want to talk about it, or you wouldn't have brought it up."

Amy nodded bleakly. "I've been trying to talk to Mom, but she's only got one idea in her head, and we can't seem to get past it." A little-girl quaver came into her voice, and Howard sat up, regarding her with a worried frown. "She says I should get an abortion."

"Well, I can see why she might say that." I put the lid on the teapot and put it on the table. "You're her daughter and she's worried about you. She's thinking of your welfare."

"My welfare?" Amy stared at me, her hazel eyes darkening. "*My* welfare? I couldn't live with myself if I killed my baby. And I'm not giving it up for adoption, either," she added bitterly, "the way *she* did." Howard, who feels great empathy toward other suffering beings, moaned low in his throat, commiserating. He had known Amy for all of five minutes, but he had found a soul mate.

My own relationship with Amy, however, was not a love-at-first-sight affair. She appeared out of the blue at the shop one day a couple of years ago, announced that she was looking for her mother, and that I was it. After I managed to convince her that this was a serious case of mistaken identity, we figured out that she was looking for Ruby, not for me. And when the whole messy story finally unfurled, it turned out that she was an out-of-wedlock baby, whom Ruby bore in a home for unwed mothers and had immediately given up for adoption. Amy's adoptive parents didn't tell her the truth about her birth until she turned twenty-one, and she immediately began moving heaven and earth, searching for her birth mother. This became the biggest, most significant thing in her life, and she ate, slept, and breathed the search.

But the mother-daughter reunion did not guarantee that the two of them would live happily ever after. Behind Amy's rosily idealistic dream of being reunited with her birth mother lay the dark, dangerous shadow of resentment for having been abandoned, and a smoldering jealousy toward Shannon, Ruby's other daughter. Ruby was burdened by a matching guilt, and the two of them haven't been able to find a comfortable way to talk or listen to one another. From the word go, their relationship has been a tug of war, a sizzling love-hate relationship with neither of them willing to let go and neither able to give in. And Amy's life was turned upside down again last year when her adoptive parents were killed in a multicar pileup on a rain-slicked Dallas freeway—a loss that threw her into a serious tailspin. Ruby and Shannon have done their best to be a family for her, but it's a difficult and complicated situation—made even more awkward by Ruby's mother and grandmother, who have taken it on themselves to fret and stew about Amy's welfare. Not long ago, the two of them moved to a retirement community near Fredericksburg, which is only an hour's drive to the west, well within interfering distance. Amy resents their intrusive fussing and she's made no secret of it.

Amy and I have had a rather better relationship, however. She has been a radical animal-rights activist since she was a teen; in fact, at the time I first met her, she was involved in a protest against animal experiments at CTSU. The researcher wound up dead and she and a couple of other protesters found themselves in a truckload of trouble. After I helped her clean up that mess, she entered grad school at Texas A&M to work toward a degree in veterinary medicine. She doesn't have a lot of staying power, though, and she didn't make it through the program. She's been back in Pecan Springs for the past few months, working for Jon Green at the Hill Country Animal Clinic, a job I helped her to get. Her love for animals makes this a natural, and everybody at the clinic seems to like her.

"Your mom is probably wondering," I said mildly, "how you'll manage to earn a living and handle a baby at the same time." I put some cookies on a plate and set it beside the teapot. "What about the baby's father? Is he in the picture?"

Amy shook her head, her mouth set in a stubborn line. "I'm not going to marry him, if that's what you mean."

"Actually, my question was simpler than that. I was wondering if he's around, and if you're in touch with him."

"Sort of," Amy replied evasively. "That's another thing Mom's mad at me about. I won't tell her who he is. At least, not right now. I have some very good reasons for keeping it to myself. For one thing, I don't want Gram and Grammy to know. It's hard enough to handle their interference as it is." As I poured the tea, she gave me a dark look. "I won't tell you, either, China. So don't bother asking."

"Far be it from me," I said, being agreeable. I've tried to be a friend to Amy, which means that I give her advice, she listens more or less politely, and then she does what she damn well pleases. I could see that today wasn't going to be any different, so I didn't think I'd bother to try. After a rather long silence, I said, "You're going to be a single mom, then? On your own and all that?"

"There are a lot of us around." She squinted at me, defiant. "Anything wrong with the idea?"

I set a strainer in the cup and poured tea. "Personally, I think it's a difficult job. But you're a capable and determined young woman." *Determined, hell!* I could hear Ruby exploding. *We're talking obstinate and intransigent here, not to mention foolish, impulsive, and immature. She's barely able to take care of herself. She's got no business with a baby.* I might not put it in just those terms, but I had to agree that Ruby had a point.

Amy didn't want to hear that, though. "I'm sure you'll manage just fine," I went on, with greater assurance than I felt. "You can put the baby in day care. You've got a good job, and health insurance. You're better off than a lot of single moms."

Amy's manner changed subtly. "Yeah," she said, straightening her shoulders, "I've got a good job. And I'm sure I'll be able to work right up to the last minute." She managed a small smile. "I might not be able to wrestle horses and alligators in the last few months, but there are plenty of ferrets and parrots and rabbits to take care of." At the word *rabbits,* Howard Cosell looked around hopefully.

"When exactly is 'the last minute'?" I asked, measuring her slender waist with my glance. "I must say that you still look every inch the virgin—as slim and svelte as ever."

That brought a grin, and a flash of the Amy I enjoyed. "I'm just twelve weeks. December, the doctor says. He'll be a Christmas baby. Or she. I don't know yet whether it's a boy or a girl."

"Deck the halls," I said in a celebratory tone, and passed her the plate of cookies. "Take two. You guys need to keep up your strength."

Amy complied. "Mmmm," she said, munching appreciatively. "What kind of cookie is this? It's not like anything I've ever tasted."

"It's a Norwegian pepper cookie," I said. "Made with black pepper and cardamom. Designed to wake up your taste buds and make them flex their muscles."

"Yummy," Amy said. She sighed, going back to the subject. "Why can't my mother be more like you?" she asked rhetorically. Howard, having given up on rabbits, was now sitting on his haunches, alert for possible cookies.

"Because she's your *mother*," I said. "And because you're *not* my daughter. If you were, I'd give you the same advice she's giving you. You're in for a lot of work, Amy, and it's not all going to be laughter and lollipops."

"Mom doesn't treat me like an adult." Amy broke off a small piece of cookie and gave it to Howard. "You do."

"Give her time," I said. "Your announcement probably took her by surprise. I don't think she even knew you were involved with anybody. If she did, she didn't mention it to me."

Howard, finding pepper cookies to his liking, asked for more.

"Mom didn't know," Amy said shortly, giving Howard another bit of cookie. "She doesn't tell me all her secrets, and I don't tell her mine." She looked up, her eyes intent. "I need to ask you a favor, China."

"Yeah? What?" I was glad that she'd already said that adoption wasn't in her plans. From the look on her face, she might have been about to ask if McQuaid and I would be willing to take the baby, which was of course out of the question. *Definitely* out of the question.

"Would you be willing—" She paused, swallowed, then tried again. "Do you think you could . . . well, could I maybe stay here for a month or so, until I can find another place? It's just one bad scene after another at Mom's house." She wrinkled her nose. "It seems like we can't get along, no matter how hard we try."

I had my doubts about how hard Amy had tried to get along with her mother, and I could think of several reasons why staying here was not a good idea. On the other hand, I was relieved that I was only being asked to play landlord, not mom. Well, most of me was relieved. There was a teensy little part, the same treacherous part that had been envious of Jill, which was voicing disappointment. But the voice was just a whisper, so low that I could safely ignore it.

Seeing my hesitation and not quite reading it right, Amy added, "I can get my meals out, if that's a problem. And of course I'd be glad to pay rent."

"Don't talk nonsense," I said warmly. "Sure, you can stay for as long as you'd like. There's just one rule, though." I gave her a long, steady look. "No drugs. Absolutely none. And that includes grass." I wasn't just sending up smoke signals. A year or so ago, Ruby told me that Amy was doing drugs—how much and how often, I didn't know, and I had no idea whether she was still using. I didn't want to turn the girl away, but I was not going to have drugs in the house, and that was that. Period. Paragraph. End of story.

Amy colored. "I didn't know you knew. Last year, I kind of had a meltdown, but I'm finished with it now. Really." She took a deep breath. "And anyway, I'm pregnant. I know better than to take any risks with my baby's health. I'm determined to be a good mom, China. There won't be any drugs."

"No drugs, no problem," I said cheerfully. "You can sleep in the guest room. You'll have to share Brian's bathroom, though."

"Super!" Amy yelped, like a delighted twelve-year-old. "Oh, thank you, China! You're a peach!" Howard ducked his head as she jumped up and hugged me.

"You won't be so enthusiastic when you find a lizard lounging in the clothes hamper," I cautioned.

"I can live with Brian's lizards," Amy said, "if you can live with me. And I want to do my share of the chores—cooking, dishes, housework, yard work." She put her hand on mine. "Thanks, China, I really mean it."

"You're welcome," I said, and added, "Your whereabouts aren't a deep, dark secret, I hope. I mean, I wouldn't feel comfortable lying to your mother."

She shook her head. "I told her I was coming over here." She flashed an elfin grin. "For what it's worth, she said she'd rather have me staying with you than hanging out with some sleazy guy she didn't know."

"Gee, thanks," I said dryly. Howard lifted his head again and began to bay, and Amy turned at the sound of a car in the drive. "It's probably just the Pickle Queen," I added. "McQuaid is expecting her."

Amy frowned. "Phoebe Morgan? She's . . . coming here?"

"She has business with McQuaid. She won't bother us." I stood. "Did you bring your things? If you did, we can go upstairs and get you settled." From the front of the house, I heard McQuaid's voice, then an indistinguishable female murmur, and then the closing of his office door. McQuaid was about to interview his first client. I could only wish him luck.

Amy sat back down. "Let's wait a bit before we go upstairs," she said guardedly, "if you don't mind."

If I had known that there was a connection between Amy and the Pickle Queen, I might have probed deeper, asked more questions. But I was more interested in putting Amy at her ease than in finding out what was behind her concern about being seen by Phoebe Morgan. And I'm not sure that anything could have halted the momentum of what was about to happen. The present has its roots in the past, and while we have the ability to change some things, others—like a runaway car going over the edge of a cliff— are beyond our control.

So I poured another cup of tea and changed the subject, and we chatted more or less comfortably until the front door closed and Phoebe Morgan drove away. Then Amy and I went upstairs and I played the gracious hostess, showing her the guest room, the closet, and (horrors!) Brian's bathroom, which was littered with wet towels and dirty clothes.

"The fact that you can't see a snake doesn't mean

they're not here," I said matter-of-factly, picking up a dripping washcloth and tossing it into the sink. "He's supposed to keep his creatures in their cages, but they have a way of oozing out. His lizards even got into the washing machine once."

"I'll keep my eyes peeled," Amy said. "Don't forget, I enjoy working with animals. I'm not likely to be fazed by a few spiders and snakes." Impulsively, she gave me a hug. "And thanks again, China. This means more to me than I can say."

"Just remember that," I said, returning her embrace, "when you're sitting on the potty and Brian's tarantula crawls across your bare foot."

With some of the makeup washed off and wearing a less revealing top, Amy joined the three of us for sandwiches and soup that evening, and afterward we watched the first Harry Potter movie again, for the umpteenth time. McQuaid and I didn't get a chance to talk privately until nearly ten, when we were getting ready for bed. At supper, I announced that I had invited Amy to be our guest for a few weeks, until she got a new place. Now, slipping into my sleep shirt, I told him why.

"I hope it was okay," I added. "I thought it would be better for her to be here, where she has some connection to her mother."

"I can't say that I blame Ruby for suggesting the abortion." McQuaid pulled his T-shirt over his head, dropped it on the floor, and made for the bathroom in his undershorts. "From what you've told me, Amy's got a lot of growing up to do. I don't mind the tattoo but I *hate* all that body piercing."

"She's had her problems," I acknowledged. I watched him go, walking with only a slight limp, and was swept, as I often am, by a wave of gratitude for what seems like a miracle. When he was shot doing the undercover work for the Rangers a couple of years ago, the doctors said he'd probably never walk again. But they had no idea how strong-willed he is, and how determined he was to prove them wrong. He can do everything he did before the accident—maybe a little slower, but some things are better done slow than fast, in my experience.

McQuaid came out of the bathroom, his toothbrush in his mouth. Around it, he said in a muffled voice, "If Amy were my daughter, I think I'd give her a spanking."

"Sadist," I said, picking up my hairbrush. "It's a good thing she's not your daughter. Anyway, who knows—maybe a baby in her life will help her grow up."

"Yeah? I thought it was supposed to work the other way around. The parents helped the kid to grow up." He went back into the bathroom and I began the daily fifty licks. Of course, brushing doesn't do anything to change the wide streak of gray in my brown hair, or erase the parentheses on either side of my mouth and the lines at the corners of my eyes. I tell myself that the wrinkles are the work of the Texas sun and wind, sculpting my skin—and that's true in part. Anybody who spends as much time out of doors as I do is bound to show it. But whatever the cause, it's disconcerting to look in the mirror, so I put down my brush and reached for some herbal skin cream I had made as a gift for myself and Ruby, with comfrey, calendula, and aloe in an almond oil, cocoa butter, and beeswax base, with a few drops of rose oil for scent.

"How'd you like your new client?" I asked after a moment, raising my voice over the rush of running water. "Did she offer you a free keg of dills?" If I knew Phoebe, though, she wouldn't offer anything free. With her, everything comes with strings attached.

"Doesn't matter whether I like her or not," McQuaid said, coming out of the bathroom. "It's going to be an interesting investigation. That's all I care about. That, and whether she pays the invoice on time."

"I'll bet she wants you to dig up dirt on somebody," I said, putting the lid on the skin cream. "That's Phoebe for you. She needs to know what people are up to." I got into bed and stretched out. The clean sheets smelled deliciously of lavender. "Something to do with the pickle plant, or is it personal?"

"It's no use trying to get me to talk," McQuaid said, in a mock-gangster tone. "I ain't sayin' a word." He stepped out of his shorts and they joined his T-shirt on the floor. Brian gets his littering habit from his father, and if there's a socially acceptable way to break either of them, I haven't found it yet.

I raised myself up on my elbows. "Oh, for heaven's sake, McQuaid," I said, teasing. "What will be the fun of your being a detective if you're going to keep everything to yourself?"

There was more to it than that, of course. When McQuaid was doing the job that led to his being shot, he kept the assignment a secret. This led to some serious misunderstandings between us, and I don't want that to happen again. I want to be involved, at least as a spectator, with the things my husband does—not in a possessive way, but because I love him. Because I want to be a part of his life, a partner. And I want him to be a part of mine.

But McQuaid knows all this, so I didn't repeat it. Instead, I made my voice light. "Honest, McQuaid, I swear to keep my mouth shut. I won't say a word. Scout's honor."

"You aren't a Scout." He got into bed beside me, lifted the sheet, and looked down the length of my body. "I am delighted to report that you do not even remotely resemble a Scout."

"I used to be. Scouts are like cops. Once you're a Scout, you're a Scout forever. Come on," I wheedled, trailing my finger down his cheek. "I promise to keep it to myself."

"What'll you give me?"

I made a seductive noise deep in my throat. "Me. I'm all yours."

"An offer I can't refuse," he replied with a chuckle. He leaned on his elbow, his free hand smoothing my skin. "According to Phoebe, her plant manager—a guy named Vince Walton—is embezzling. She's working from the inside to get the evidence, but she wants me to follow the money. To take a look at his lifestyle and see what he's spending it on. She needs to get the goods on him, but she doesn't want the sheriff's office involved. No cops, no publicity."

"Of course not," I said. "Phoebe is very image-conscious, which is the reason she volunteers for all those community boards. She hates anything that makes her look bad, and she *especially* wouldn't want anybody knowing that she's been taken advantage of."

"I got that impression," McQuaid said. "She'll make a private visit to the DA when she's got all the evidence. She can keep it quiet until the case goes to the grand jury, at least." He rolled over and reached out to turn off the bedside lamp. "Not a bad job for a first one, I guess, although I doubt whether it'll take more than a couple of days. Charlie said he might have another client or two for me. I told him I wasn't eager to take divorce work, but maybe I will, just to get started."

"Sounds great," I said. Charlie Lipman is a friend, a lawyer—a good source of clients, over the long run. I could also let Justine Wyzinski—my friend, the Whiz— know about McQuaid's new business. As McQuaid turned back, I snuggled against the curve of his body. The rain had gone, the sky had cleared, and the full moon snared in the trees cast pale shadows on the ceiling, like light reflected from a shimmering pool. "But please don't take on any jobs you don't want," I added. "Something else will come up, and you'll be—"

"Something else has already come up," McQuaid growled, in his most lecherous tone. "Give me your hand and I'll show you, wife."

He showed me, and he was right. We were happily occupied for the next little while, and when that was over and we were lying quietly in each other's arms, I said again, "I'm glad you've decided to make a change, McQuaid. I think you'll be happier." And as much as I hate to admit it, his happiness has a great impact on mine. Being married to somebody who's depressed is almost as painful as being depressed yourself.

"Make a change?" he asked sleepily. His hair was damp and curly, and he smelled of toothpaste. "What change did I make? It felt the same as it always feels. Like a ten."

I laughed. "Did you know that dill is an aphrodisiac?

People used to put dill seeds in wine and drink it. Or they'd put dill in the bathwater. It made them irresistible."

"No kidding." He turned on his side, away from me, and punched up his pillow, ready for sleep. "Sounds pretty resistible to me. Anyway, I don't think we need an aphrodisiac. Do you?"

"Probably not," I said. I might have a gray streak and a few wrinkles, but lustful feelings don't go away just because you've gotten a year or two older. I agreed with McQuaid. A ten—at least. And certainly much, much more satisfying than those high-voltage, low-wattage explorations of my youth.

"So the Pickle Queen is being embezzled," I murmured. "Boy, somebody's got a lot of nerve, snatching money right out from under her nose. I'd be afraid she'd bite. Hard."

McQuaid rolled over to face me. "Remember," he said. "No talking about this." He paused. "You're not going to be seeing this woman any time soon, are you?"

"Wednesday," I said. "Ruby and I are on the planning committee for PickleFest—again. It's my civic duty, and it's good for business." That's how I happen to know the Pickle Queen. She's all but taken over the management of the planning committee.

"Just remember your promise, China," McQuaid said in a warning tone. "You're not to say a word about what I told you, to anyone. If you do, I'll never be able to share another case with you. Understand?"

"It's a dill," I said agreeably.

McQuaid groaned and pulled the sheet over his head.

Chapter Three

JANET'S LAVENDER SCONES

2 cups flour
⅓ cup plus 2 Tbsp. sugar, separated
2 tsp. baking powder
¼ tsp. salt
6 Tbsp. unsalted butter, chilled and cut into small
*   pieces*
3 tsp. lavender flower buds, fresh, or 2 tsp. dried
1 large egg
½ tsp. vanilla
½ cup milk or half-and-half
egg wash: 1 beaten egg plus 1 Tbsp. water and
*   pinch of salt*

Preheat oven to 375°. Whisk together the flour, ⅓ cup sugar, baking powder, and salt. Cut in the butter with a pastry blender until the mixture looks like coarse bread crumbs. Stir in the lavender flowers. In a small bowl, combine the egg, vanilla, and milk. Add to the flour mixture and stir to blend into a soft, sticky dough. Turn it out onto a well-floured board, cover, and let rest for 15 minutes. Knead gently, adding just enough flour so that the dough doesn't stick to your fingers. Pat it out to about an inch thick. Using a biscuit cutter that has been dipped in regular sugar, cut into rounds. Brush off excess flour with a pastry brush and place on un-

greased baking sheet. Brush each round with egg wash
and sprinkle with the reserved sugar. Bake until light
golden brown (12–16 minutes). Remove immediately
from baking sheet to wire rack to cool.

The shops are closed on Mondays, but that doesn't
mean that Ruby and I can take the day off. Owning a
small business is like living with a Great Dane. You're not
always as much in control of the situation as you'd like,
and you spend a lot of time cleaning up very large messes.

But today, my messes promised to be green and sweet-
smelling. I was planning to work in the herb gardens
around the shop, pulling weeds, trimming exuberant
plants, and staking the hollyhocks at the back of the border. It was a good morning for this kind of work, with the
soil still damp from yesterday's rain and the air relatively
cool, with a soft breeze. But by ten o'clock it was plenty
humid, and with the thermometer on the high side of
eighty, my T-shirt was plastered to me, front and back. I
tugged off my red bandana sweatband, brushed the dirt off
my shorts, and adjourned to the cooler comforts of Thyme
for Tea. I headed straight for the refrigerator, where I
hoped Janet might have stashed a pitcher of iced tea.

Janet Chapman is our cook in the tearoom, and a good
one, too. Her lavender scones are the hottest item on our
afternoon tea menu, and her herb quiche is so popular that
people make reservations for the day she plans to serve it.
While I was looking for the iced tea, I happened to notice a
couple of slices of leftover quiche, lonely and abandoned

on a plate, and helped myself to both of them. Janet's quiche is almost as good cold as it is warm and just-baked, and if I'd taken only one, the one that was left behind would have been lonely.

As I shut the refrigerator door, I was joined by Khat, the self-confident Siamese who is Top Cat and Chief of Security at the shops. His previous person had named him Pudding, which neither he nor I considered even remotely suitable. When she died and he moved in with me, Pudding became Cat, but Ruby pointed out that such a large and imperial animal (he weighs seventeen pounds) ought to have a more elegant name. We compromised on Khat, which Ruby amended to Khat K'o Kung, after Koko, the talented Siamese in the Cat Who mysteries. Khat enjoys a bit of chopped, barely decent liver, so I found some that Janet had cooked especially for him and put it in his dish in his special corner, where he settled down to his snack. I settled down to mine, and for a companionable few minutes, nothing could be heard but the click of my fork and Khat's throaty purr.

If you've visited our shops and know your way around Pecan Springs, you can get on with the story, but for those of you who are new to the neighborhood, I'll describe the lay of the land. Ruby and I do business at 304 Crockett, a couple of blocks east of Courthouse Square. We're located between the old Victorian mansion that houses Constance Letterman's Craft Emporium on the west and the children's bookstore Hobbit House, which Molly McGregor recently opened in the house on the east. It's a quiet neighborhood on its way from run-down residential to trendy commercial, but the businesses are pleasant and neighborly—the sort you don't mind having next door.

Thyme and Seasons and the Crystal Cave are situated side by side in the front half of a century-old two-story building, built of Texas limestone by a skilled German stonecutter, one of the many German immigrants who settled in Pecan Springs, New Braunfels, and Fredericksburg in the 1840s. The tearoom is located in the back half of the building, in the space where I lived before McQuaid and I moved out to the house on Limekiln Road. At the rear of the large lot, next to the alley, is an old stone stable, remodeled before I bought the place into a three-room apartment. Sometimes it serves as a bed-and-breakfast and sometimes (when we don't have a guest in residence) as a classroom, where I teach herb crafts and gardening, Janet holds her classes in herb cookery, and Ruby offers tarot and meditation (which McQuaid calls, rather scornfully, "mystical claptrap").

And spread like a Jacob's coat of color around these two buildings, from the street in front to the alley in back, and connecting with the Hobbit House garden to the east and the Craft Emporium garden to the west, are my herb gardens. This time of year, the Butterfly Garden is a riot of color, the bright blossoms of Joe-Pye weed and coreopsis and salvia playing host to flocks of bright butterflies and ruby-throated hummingbirds. The Moon Garden is a study in cool contrast, with its silvery artemisia, soft white roses, and pale moonflower vine. Even the Apothecary Garden, where the plants are grown for their medicinal value rather than their beauty, is pretty: the stalks of fuzzy-leafed mullein, glowing like yellow tapers; the striking blossoms of echinacea, with their drooping purple petals and bright orange centers; and the passionflower, so useful in treating menstrual disorders, clambering happily up its trellis. Before the frost knocks it down, this enthusiastic vine will grow to thirty feet, and it will show up next year to make another grand show. If you come by the shop, be sure to pick up a packet of passionflower seeds, and try them in your garden.

Having taken the edge off my hunger and thirst, I put down my fork and looked around the tearoom, liking what I saw inside, as well as out. Thyme for Tea, with its green-painted wainscoting, chintz chair seats and place mats, and pots of ivy and bundles of dried herbs hanging from the ceiling, is a collaborative enterprise. Ruby put up the capital to get things started (believe it or not, she won it in the lottery!). I provided the space at the back of the shops. And both of us have contributed ideas and labor. The project was a study in hard work and frustration, especially when it came to setting up the kitchen and getting it certified by the state health department, but as a business, Thyme for Tea has surpassed even our most optimistic projections. This is partly because Janet has developed her own loyal following, and partly because the tearoom is a lovely, quiet retreat where you can meet friends for lunch or afternoon tea, a very different environment from the local diners, cafes, and barbecue joints. Recently, we've also been taking a few catering jobs—a luncheon at the Pecan Springs Women's Club, for instance, and several fancy dinner parties. I don't get involved with that end of the business—Janet and Ruby enjoy catering a lot more than I do—but it's nice to see our homegrown enterprise growing in several directions at once.

I was just beginning to relax and get cooled off when Ruby shouldered the back door open and came in, her arms full of groceries. Janet leaves a list when she finishes up on

Saturday, and Ruby does the week's shopping on Monday morning. I jumped up from the table and went out to the van to help unload, and by the time we'd carried everything inside, I was sweaty again and Ruby was wilting. I poured a glass of tea for Ruby and moved the second piece of leftover quiche from my plate to hers, and we sat down together at the table.

"Whew," Ruby said, leaning back in her chair and stretching out her legs. She is over six feet tall, so there's a lot of leg to stretch. Attention-getting legs, too, especially when she's wearing lipstick-red shorts and sandals, with her toenails painted to match. She chugalugged her tea and poured some more, then gave me a questioning look. "I hope Amy showed up at your place yesterday."

"Yep. She's installed in the guest room. You're okay about it?"

"I'm okay with her staying with you," Ruby said with a sigh. "It's better than camping out in a cheap motel, or moving in with some guy. But I am definitely *not* okay with her being pregnant. She's too wild and irresponsible to have a baby. Why won't she listen to me and get that abortion?"

"Because you're not telling her what she wants to hear. If you say she'll be a wonderful mom and you're overjoyed at the idea of being a grandmother, she'll listen to you."

Ruby's eyes—today's contacts were blue, chosen to complement today's colors—widened in alarm. "A grandmother!" she wailed despairingly. "I'm too *young* to be a grandmother, China!"

"Well, no," I said. "Biologically speaking, you're just about the right—"

"No, I'm not!" Ruby ran her hands down her firm,

tanned thighs. "Look at me. Are these the thighs of a grandmother? Is this the body of a grandmother?"

Without giving me time to answer, she jumped up and turned around so I could admire her tight-fitting top, a red and blue and green Hawaiian print that made her look like a long-legged bird of paradise. If you didn't know, you'd never guess that she'd lost a breast to cancer a while back.

She raised both arms to her floppy red corkscrew curls. "Is this the hair of a—"

"You're over the top on this, Ruby," I interrupted. "Amy isn't the first young woman to get pregnant outside of marriage, and she darn sure won't be the last. Maybe having a baby will be a good thing for her. Maybe it'll teach her some responsibility."

Ruby sat down and picked up her fork. "And to make matters worse," she went on, as if I hadn't spoken, "she's moved out the week before Grammy's birthday party."

"Yikes!" I said. "I forgot about the party." Ruby had invited her mother and grandmother, her sister Ramona, and her other daughter, Shannon, to come for PickleFest on Saturday and stay over for a big dinner party on Sunday, to celebrate her grandmother's eighty-third birthday. Ruby had been planning it for weeks and had enlisted my help.

"Well, I haven't forgotten," Ruby replied darkly. "You tell Amy that she'd better not skip out. If she doesn't come to the birthday dinner on Sunday, they'll start asking questions. And what am I going to tell them?"

"Don't tell them *anything*," I said. "You know how they are. They already meddle too much in Amy's life. Once they find out she's pregnant, they won't give her a moment's peace."

"Don't tell them anything?" Ruby shook her head despairingly. "It doesn't work that way, China. Not in *my* family. You know Grammy, and my mother is every bit as bad, if not worse. If you don't answer their questions, they keep after you until you do. It's like the Spanish Inquisition and Chinese water torture, rolled into one."

"That's true," I agreed. "You've definitely got a problem. Maybe you should cancel the party and reschedule for next year. Amy can bring her baby and they'll be so crazy about it that they'll forget everything else."

"Reschedule for next year? Out of the question. Grammy is eighty-three. There might not *be* a next year." Ruby gave a low moan. "And what am I going to say when they ask me who the father is? Amy won't even tell *me!*" She gave me a sideways glance. "I don't suppose she told you."

"No, she didn't. But I understood her to say that she's only keeping it secret for a while, for very good reasons. Maybe she hasn't told him yet."

"Maybe she doesn't plan to tell him at all."

I frowned. "Now, that would be a problem."

"You're darn tootin' it'd be a problem. If she's going to do the work of raising the baby, *he's* going to pay child support—if I've got anything to say about it, that is." She made a face. "Which I probably won't. She doesn't listen to me about *anything.*"

I shook my head. "Child support is part of it. But even if the child's parents aren't married, there's more to fatherhood than shelling out money."

"Of course. But if Amy doesn't tell him he's the father, how can he be expected to do the right thing?" Ruby shook her head. "*Why* won't she say who he is, China?"

"If he's not the kind of man she wants to marry, he's

probably not the kind of man she wants in her baby's life," I suggested. "Maybe it was one of the guys she hung out with last year, when she was doing drugs. Or maybe it was just a one-night stand, and she realizes it was a big mistake." If love can make you blind, lust can turn your world upside down, make you think that wrong is right and day is night. Lots of smart women have done very dumb things under the influence of lust, including me. I've put some special effort into erasing those memories, though. They're ugly and painful, even after a dozen years. Worse, the pain wasn't just mine. Other people were involved, and there was more than enough hurt to go around. But that was all part of my old life, the life of the person I used to be. I had pushed all that down and out of my consciousness, so deep that I scarcely thought about it any longer.

"Or maybe it was a one-night stand with a married man." Ruby's eyes widened in a look of sudden comprehension. "That could be it, China! Amy's had an affair with a married man, and he refuses to acknowledge her. She's confused and ashamed and doesn't know where to turn. She—"

"Oh, stop it, Ruby. This isn't a soap opera. Amy may be a little impulsive, but she shows absolutely no signs of being confused and ashamed. Quite the contrary, as a matter of fact. And you don't have any evidence that—"

But Ruby's mouth was set in a firm line. "You don't have to be psychic to figure out who the father of this baby is, China. Who has Amy been spending most of her time with for the past few months? Ten, sometimes twelve hours a day?"

I frowned. "Amy doesn't have ten hours a day to spend with anybody, Ruby. She's at the clinic all day." And then I saw what she was driving at. "Oh, come on," I said. "You can't be serious. Why, he's—"

"Of course I'm serious. It's Jonathan Green, that's who it is! Why didn't I think of that? Amy has been crazy about him ever since the day she met him."

Jonathan Green opened the Hill Country Animal Clinic six or seven years ago, and since McQuaid and I have our fair share of animals, I've had frequent opportunities to get to know and like him. A couple of years ago, he married Brian's middle school teacher, Rebecca, a really sweet young woman who helped inspire Brian's passion for lizards. Jon is personable and engaging and obviously enjoys a little harmless flirtation, but I couldn't imagine that he would get romantically involved with anybody but Rebecca.

"I know what you're thinking," Ruby said. "He's happily married. Right?"

"Right," I said firmly. "He and Rebecca are a perfect couple. Jon would never—"

"China, you are *so* wrong." Ruby shook her head. "They've been having trouble ever since they got married. In fact, Rebecca moved in with her sister around Valentine's Day, and they've been separated ever since. I know, because her sister Kelly is in my tarot class, and she told me."

I gaped at her. "Rebecca and Jon are separated?"

"For almost six months. I didn't think anything of it when Kelly told me—except to feel sorry for them, of course. It's always sad when a marriage goes sour. But now I see that it's all connected. Even the dates make sense."

"Dates? What dates? What are you—"

"Don't you remember?" Ruby asked patiently. "The clinic installed a new computer bookkeeping system in

April. Amy and Jon worked late every night for a couple of weeks, getting things set up." She counted on her fingers. "April, May, June—that's just about right."

"You can't go jumping to conclusions like this, Ruby. It's not fair to Jon and Rebecca, and it certainly isn't fair to Amy. She—"

But Ruby wasn't listening. "Poor thing," she said sadly. "I don't know how she can work with him every day, knowing that she's carrying his baby. She must be planning to quit before he notices that she's pregnant." She scowled. "It's not fair for her to carry this burden alone. I've a good mind to talk to him myself and—"

"Lighten up, Ruby." I stood up and picked up my plate and glass. "It's one thing to sit around and speculate, but meddling is something else altogether. She's got enough of that from her grandmother and great-grandmother. You stay out of Amy's affairs."

"But she's my daughter!" Ruby cried. "It's my responsibility to—"

I bent over and looked her straight in the eye. "She was your daughter when you gave birth to her. For twenty-some years she was somebody else's daughter, and now she's her own person. Be glad that she's included you in her life and that she comes to you for advice, but don't be upset if she doesn't take it." I straightened up. "And don't try to get involved, or you'll drive her away. And drive yourself crazy, to boot."

Ruby's face darkened. "Who are you to tell me how to deal with my daughter, China Bayles? You've never had a child. You've never even *wanted* a child—it might have gotten in the way of all the other wonderful things you wanted to do." She took a deep breath and narrowed her eyes. "So what makes you such an expert?"

"I'm not an expert." I felt as if I'd just been slapped. In all the years that we've been friends, Ruby had never spoken to me in that tone. I felt the anger mounting inside, and I could hear it, sharp and ragged, in my voice. "I'm just trying to tell you to leave her alone and let her make her own—"

"Her own mistakes?" Ruby broke in icily. "Well, that's good enough for you, China Bayles. You can be her soul sister, but I'm her mother, and I have the responsibility of telling her what I think she should do."

She began to cry, and I immediately felt ashamed of myself. Here I was, telling Ruby to stay out of Amy's life, when I was interfering in hers. Ruby had every right to her feelings, and even if I thought she was wrong, her relationship with Amy was none of my business.

I leaned over the back of her chair and put my arms around her. "Let's not fight, Ruby," I said, against her hair. "Things are tough enough, without having trouble between the two of us."

Crying harder, Ruby turned toward me, and we hung on to one another for a little while. Nothing had been solved, obviously, but I certainly felt better and I thought Ruby did, too.

After a moment, she pulled away. "I still think it's Jon," she said in a low voice, wiping her eyes with the back of her hand and smearing her mascara. "She may have run around with a few other guys last year, when she was in her wild phase. But she hasn't been serious about anybody."

"Anybody that you know of," I said lightly, at the risk of

setting her off again. "Does she give you a list of every-body she goes out with? And maybe it was only once." I gave her a wry grin. "Once is enough, sometimes. Not that I have any personal experience in getting pregnant," I added hastily. I had thought I was pregnant once, a long time ago. I still remember how frightened I was, though, and how relieved and grateful I'd been when my period finally showed up. A pregnancy would wreck everything, I had thought then. After that, I had popped the Pill much more faithfully.

"Yeah, once is enough." A smile ghosted across Ruby's face. "It was for me, anyway, when I got pregnant with Amy. Her father and I were together one night, in the back of his dad's old Buick. The next morning he was off to Vietnam. By the time I found out I was pregnant, his parents had gotten a telegram saying that he'd been killed." She shook her head, remembering. "Mother was furious when I told her. I knew where to get an abortion, and that's what I wanted to do. But Mother and Grammy thought they had a better idea. The two of them packed me off to Dallas, to the Sunnyside Home for Unwed Mothers."

"Uh-*huh*," I said, and waited for her to get it.

There was a moment's silence, then she said, in a small voice, "Omigosh. Is that why I'm being so hard on Amy, China? Because Mother and Grammy were so hard on me?"

"Sounds reasonable," I said. "What goes around comes around." Probably most of our difficulties with our lives come down to that, when you really think about it—to the past reasserting itself in the present. It was entirely possible that my reluctance to have a child was a product of my mother's inability to mother me, which was partially born

out of the alcohol addiction that she inherited from her father, who—

"Maybe it is the past repeating itself," Ruby said, interrupting my thoughts, "but with a twist. Amy says she wants
her baby. I didn't want mine because I knew I wasn't mature enough to deal with a child." Ruby's freckles stood out
on her pale face but her voice was steady. "But when Amy
came back into my life a couple of years ago, I realized
that it had been a terrible mistake to give her up—and that
it would have been an even worse mistake to have gotten
an abortion." She swallowed. "What was I thinking,
China? Why did I tell Amy to—"

"Because you'd rather that she waited to bring children
into a loving and supportive marriage," I said gently.
"There's no harm in wanting that for your daughter."

Ruby cast me a grateful look. "I hope that's what I
wanted. I hope I didn't want to force her to do what *I*
wanted to do, once upon a time."

I shrugged. "If you did, it's no big deal. Just tell her that
you'll be there for her, no matter what she decides to do.
That's all she wants to hear."

"I'll do it," Ruby said in a decided tone, pushing her
chair back. "I'll drive to the clinic right now and ask her to
move back home with me. It doesn't make sense for her to
impose on you when I've got plenty of room. And while
I'm at the clinic, I'll talk to Jon."

"You'll do no such thing," I said emphatically. Where
affairs of the heart are concerned, Ruby's only speed is all
ahead full, and damn the torpedoes. "Instead of going to
the clinic and interrupting Amy's work, you can come out
to the house tonight and have dinner with us and a talk with

her. And you can leave Jon alone. Proximity doesn't always spell pregnancy, you know."

Ruby bit her lip, looking chagrined. "I'm doing it again, aren't I? Interfering, I mean. I'm as bad as my mother and Grammy."

"And so am I," I said cheerfully. "Telling you what to do, that is." I grinned and picked up our plates. "We're incorrigible, Ruby. We are who we are and we might as well get used to it."

She nodded. "But you're right. I'll accept your dinner invitation, and I'll keep my mouth shut about Jon—although I'm still convinced that he's the father." She glanced down at her watch. "Anyway, I don't have time to go out to the clinic just now. I have to finish some ordering, and then I need to drive over to Marge's house and pick up the new PickleFest posters. They had to be redrawn."

"Redrawn? Why? Is that how come they're not up yet? What was wrong with them?" The posters were supposed to be plastered around town to advertise PickleFest. They should have been up a week ago, and I was wondering what had happened to them.

"Nothing was wrong with the posters," Ruby said. "In fact, Pauline and I thought they were just fine. Phoebe Morgan, on the other hand, said the pickles looked like green you-know-whats. With warts." She grinned. "Anyway, she told Pauline to tell Marge to put on some leaves and vines and stuff, so they'd look a little less phallic. Pauline hates taking orders from Phoebe. She was really PO'd."

I'll bet. Pauline Perkins is Pecan Springs's ex-mayor, drummed out of office during her fourth term because of a scandal involving a local developer who had turned up dead after he had tried to blackmail Pauline and several other members of the city council, as well. It had been an unsavory episode, and at the end of it, Pauline's political career looked as if it had come off the rails.

But Pauline has a way of landing on her feet, waving the flag and ready to renew the charge. After a vacation from community affairs, she was back like gangbusters, managing this year's PickleFest as if it were her next mayoral campaign—which maybe it is, come to think of it. She could be hankering after another term on the city council, and this is her warm-up.

Far be it from me to complain, however. I chaired the PickleFest committee a few years ago and I wasn't anxious to go another round. Doing PickleFest means working closely with Phoebe Morgan, which is not my idea of fun. Even Pauline, who is the dictatorial type, has to admit that she's up against a bigger and better dictator.

Ruby went off to redeem her newly nonphallic pickle posters, I went back to my steamy weeding, and all went well for the rest of the day. For the next couple of days, actually. Ruby's Monday evening talk with Amy seemed to restore some harmony and equilibrium to their relationship, although Amy, still keeping her distance from her mother, decided to stay where she was. Ruby didn't confront Jonathan Green—or if she did, she didn't mention it to me, and I didn't ask, for a very good reason.

The less I knew, the less likely I was to stick my nose into something that was definitely none of my business.

As everybody knows, a smart pickle is a dumb pickle.

Chapter Four

pickle. *fig.* a. A condition or situation, usually disagreeable; a sorry plight or predicament. Now *colloq.* 1741 Richardson *Pamela* (1824) I. 77, I warrant, added she, he was in a sweet pickle! 1893 Stevenson *Catriona* 291, I could see no way out of the pickle I was in. 1960 M. Spark *Bachelors* ii. 19 You're going to leave Alice in a nice pickle if the case goes against you.

Oxford English Dictionary

Things stopped going well, however, on Wednesday. For one thing, the weather for PickleFest weekend was looking iffy, and the forecast for Saturday included a 50 percent chance of thunderstorms, with a no-name tropical disturbance that looked like it might blow into South Texas and mosey on up I-35. For another thing, the final, all-important wrap-up meeting of the Pretty Pickle Planners (our tongue-in-cheek name for our planning committee) didn't happen the way it was supposed to, which caused a great deal of anxiety for those of us who had already invested more hours than we cared to count in this annual project.

All six of the Pretty Pickle Planners—Pauline, Erin Talbert, Cassie Michaels, Caroline Murray, Ruby, and I—

drove out to Phoebe Morgan's palatial home in the River Road development, where the meeting was supposed to take place. All of the land in the upscale development was once Morgan land, sold and subdivided into large estates a couple of decades before, the Morgans themselves keeping the choicest twenty acres for their house, and another patch for the pickle plant, which is three or four miles up the road, at the site of the old Morgan homestead. Phoebe has her fingers in a great many different enterprises that have nothing at all to do with the pickle business—real estate, land development, private philanthropies, and investments, not to mention all those boards she serves on—so she has a personal office at home. In fact, one entire wing of her house is dedicated to her office, which is staffed with a full-time administrative assistant and a secretary. We were expecting to meet in Phoebe's conference room, where we'd met several times before.

But when we arrived, a few minutes before seven, Phoebe's assistant, Marsha Miller, met us at the door. She was thin and angular, her brown hair straight, with a slick, almost greasy look to it, tucked unflatteringly behind her ears. She wore large, owlish glasses and a black sleeveless top that revealed toothpick-thin arms. She seemed skinnier than the last time I'd seen her. The first thought that came to my mind was *eating disorder*.

"I'm sorry," she said in a taut, wire-strung voice. "Ms. Morgan has been detained at a previous engagement. She won't be available to meet with you this evening."

Pauline became huffy. "Well, when *will* she be available? The festival is this weekend." Her voice rose. "We have just two days to get all the kinks straightened out. That's only forty-eight hours. Forty-eight hours!"

I'm acquainted with Marsha, who worked in the County Clerk's office before she went to work for Phoebe a couple of years ago. Her eyes slid to me, and she bit her lip. I gave her a nod, and she managed a small smile. To Pauline, she said, a little more calmly, "I'm really sorry, Ms. Perkins. I'm sure that Ms. Morgan didn't intend to miss this meeting. She knows how important it is. I'll give you a call when she's ready to reschedule—tomorrow, I hope."

And with that, she closed the door, leaving the six of us staring blankly at each other and wondering what to do next.

"You'd think Marsha would have the courtesy to call and tell us not to come before we drove all the way out here," Pauline growled, irritation oozing from every pore. Pauline is a substantial woman, with at least one extra chin and a pair of extraordinarily powerful shoulders, and she has a great many pores. But despite her size (or perhaps because of it), she usually brims with authority and brisk confidence. Right now, she was brimming with indignant frustration.

"I wonder what's happened to keep Phoebe away," Cassie Michaels remarked curiously. "It's not like the Pickle Queen to miss an important meeting." She wrinkled her nose. "If for no other reason than to make sure her Pickle Planners are doing things the right way—*her* way."

"Yeah," Ruby agreed, as we trailed down the path to our cars, which were parked along the road. "Talk about your control freaks." Ruby had gone to high school with Phoebe, and knew her somewhat better than the rest of us. "What happens if she doesn't show up tomorrow—or Friday? Or even Saturday?"

"Oh, she'll show up," Cassie replied. "That woman never misses a chance to strut her stuff, and PickleFest is definitely her thing."

Erin turned to cast an apprehensive glance over her shoulder, and I remembered that, at the last meeting, Phoebe had shredded her ideas for the pickled foods competition. I wouldn't blame Erin for not looking forward to this session. "I'll bet she's there," she muttered, "but she just doesn't want to meet with us."

I followed Erin's glance. The Morgan mansion is built on a bluff above the Pecan River, which wanders scenically through the Hill Country before looping through Pecan Springs and on to the south, joining the Guadalupe somewhere east of New Braunfels. The house—which Phoebe and her husband, Ed Knight, built just before he died—is one of those large, boldly futuristic residences designed to display the owner's artistic taste and affluence, not necessarily in that order. The front is mostly glass, and you can see into softly illuminated rooms that are exquisitely decorated in glowing pastel colors, designed to showcase Phoebe's unique collection of Southwestern paintings, textiles, and sculpture. Unfortunately (or maybe it was the architect's own private joke), there is a two-story glass tower at the front of the house, tinted green and with a copper roof, which looks very much like a large pickle bottle. The local residents, not failing to notice this amusing similarity, call the place the Pickle Palace.

"Speaking personally," Pauline said with a frustrated snort, "I could care less where Phoebe has gone or how long she plans to stay away. Forever wouldn't be a bit too long. But it is monstrously rude of her to leave us in the lurch like this, especially since she insists on running this affair herself. I hate to say it, ladies, but we are in trouble. Big time."

With her usual mayoral flair, Pauline had summarized the problem rather neatly. If this had been an ordinary Pecan Springs event, nobody would give a hoot if one of the planning committee members dashed off to New Orleans or Cozumel for a few days—the rest could take up the slack. But in the past several years, Phoebe Morgan had assumed control of PickleFest, and nothing happened that she hadn't personally approved, from the music that was played over the PA system to the strategic placement of the Porta-Potties.

"Where can we go for our meeting now that she's stood us up?" Cassie asked, as we reached our cars. Cassie, who was in charge of the children's activities at PickleFest, is short and as round as a tumbleweed, and she was comically dwarfed by Pauline's soldierly sturdiness. But she certainly had a point. It was growing dark, and we weren't going to get anything done standing beside our cars.

"We can drive over to my place," I suggested. "It's not very far."

"That would be quicker than driving all the way back to town," Ruby agreed.

"You ladies lost?" a male voice asked.

We all turned to see a jogger with a dog on a leather leash. The dog was a fierce-looking Rottweiler with one of those prong-toothed collars that suggest that the animal can't be reined in by ordinary measures. The jogger, shirtless and in shorts, was tall, lean, sun-bronzed, and flat-bellied, with rippling muscles and a chest mat of dark male fur. He'd tied a sweaty red bandana around his tousled brown hair, and he carried a half-full bottle of water. He stopped in front of us, jogging in place. The dog kept on going until the man jerked at the leash.

"Sit, Sampson," he commanded. Sampson sat, giving us a red-eyed glare.

"Art Simon!" Pauline said, in the flirtatious voice she reserves for attractive men. She tilted her chin at her best angle. "How long has it been? Three years? Four?"

"If it's been that long, it's been too long, Pauline," Simon said, with careless gallantry. He swigged at his water bottle and glanced up at the Pickle Palace, an unmistakable look of distaste crossing his face. "You looking for the Pickle Queen?"

Pauline assumed her mayoral posture. "We were expecting to meet with her this evening on an important matter," she replied. "But it appears that she's not available."

Simon snorted. "Figures," he said. "Now, if you had a couple of media people with you, you could be damn sure she'd be here." He lifted his hand. "Evenin', ladies. Pauline, I'll give you a call."

"Do that," Pauline said. She turned back to us, trying not to show how pleased she was at the tantalizing idea of having lunch with this virile, attractive man. "Now, where were we?"

"Lusting after Art Simon," Ruby said, turning to watch as he and the Rottweiler jogged off down the road. "I went to high school with him. He was a stud muffin then, and he's still a stud muffin." She made a little face. "He didn't recognize me, though."

"We were talking about going to China's place," Erin said in a prissy tone.

"Oh, right," Pauline said briskly. "All in favor say aye."

There was a loud chorus, and within fifteen minutes, the six Pickle Planners were seated in my living room, with the PickleFest schedule and Pauline's multitudinous to-do lists spread out on the old pine carpenter's chest that serves as our coffee table. I brought in a pitcher of rosemary lemonade, a basket of chips and raw veggies, and a bowl of yogurt-and-dill dip, and after a couple of hours of checking lists, shuffling papers, and making phone calls, we could see exactly what kind of a hole we were in. A *big* hole, very large and very deep.

"What a mess," Pauline said, scowling.

"That's putting it mildly," Erin replied. Erin is very well organized and doesn't like it when things are out of kilter. "I must say I'm relieved not to have to deal with Phoebe tonight, after the way she behaved last time. But if she doesn't show up by tomorrow, we are in a pickle, big time."

Those of you who have attended PickleFest in the last few years probably have a pretty good idea of why the six of us were so upset by Phoebe's absence. But for the rest, a little bit of history may help you understand our dilemma.

This was the tenth anniversary of PickleFest, so it was a rather special occasion. For the first half dozen years, the festival stayed small—just a couple of hundred townsfolk, gathered in Pecan Springs Park to enjoy a little community silliness and celebrate the county's largest employer.

Maybe it's the sound of the word—say *pickle* and you'll find yourself smiling—or the shape of the thing, with warts yet. Whatever, pickles are undeniably funny, and PickleFest was created so the local folk could amuse themselves on a hot July Saturday. There was a Pickle Parade, with prizes for the best pickle float; a pickled foods contest, where people submitted every pickled thing you can imagine (and some you can't); and a Pickled People booth where the kids could turn pickles into—well, you get the idea. And of course, there was the Pickle Plaza, where vendors sold goofy pickled stuff: Fried Dill Pickles, Pickle Pizza Pizzazz, Sweet Pickle Popovers, Pickled Potato Chips, and on and on. And where else under the sun could you get your picture taken with a seven-foot pickle wearing an Aggie football jersey and a Texas Rangers baseball cap? (I am not making this up.)

All this was glorious, homegrown fun, and PickleFest bumped along, enjoying a local but expanding popularity. It always got plenty of coverage in the Austin and San Antonio papers, and the attendance climbed from a couple of hundred to nearly a thousand—bigger than the Fourth of July celebration and the annual Chili Cookoff, although not quite as large as the Adams County Fair.

That's when Phoebe Morgan, seeing the event's promotional possibilities, announced that she was taking charge of PickleFest. She had a right to do this, most people agreed, since Pecan Springs probably wouldn't even have a PickleFest if it weren't for Morgan's Pickles. And if there were any naysayers, they hushed up in a hurry. Once Phoebe got rolling, it was clear that she intended to turn our little homegrown festival into a grand pickle extravaganza the likes of which the world had never seen. The Chamber of Commerce waxed ecstatic at this opportunity to put Pecan Springs on the map, while the city council started counting its lucky stars, each one of them engraved with Phoebe's name.

When Phoebe gets an idea, she is driven, and under her management, PickleFest shifted from high gear into warp drive. She moved the festival out to the Morgan Pickle grounds, added guided tours of the pickle plant, and came up with the idea for a children's beauty contest where the winner was named Little Miss Sweet Pickle. She also invited a number of notable country music singers who entertained the crowds in fine country style; a clutch of stand-up comics who told pickle jokes, some good, some better; the governor, who was photographed, looking foolish, with the seven-foot pickle; and the Grand Champion 4-H Steer who looked a lot more impressive than the governor.

While Phoebe managed these important matters, the Pretty Pickle Planners handled activities like the scavanger hunt, the kids' booths, and the pickled foods competition—all with Phoebe's approval, of course. Which was okay with us, actually, since we're just little pickles (except for our ex-mayor, of course, who still dreams of being a Big Pickle), and we don't need the grief of dealing with prime-time celebs.

Now, Pauline shuffled her to-do lists into order, frowning. "I suppose we've done about all we can do tonight," she said. "The activities we're responsible for seem to be in pretty good shape—although we still don't have the names of the special guests, and we have no idea who Phoebe asked to judge the beauty contest, and—"

"Marsha must know some of those details," I said. "We should have thought of asking her to meet with us."

"Are you kidding?" Ruby gave a sarcastic laugh. "Phoebe would fire anybody who presumed to take her place, emergency or not. Even when we were in high school, Phoebe was always jealous of her prerogatives. What was hers was *hers,* and that was that."

Pauline started to say something, then thought better of it. She bent her head and picked up her notes.

Cassie made a face. "Well, Phoebe certainly played fast and loose when she was married to Ed Knight," she remarked. "I haven't thought about this for years, but there used to be plenty of rumors about her affairs. She was always on the prowl."

Pauline looked up. "Oh, really?" she asked with interest. "Anybody in particular?" I was surprised at Pauline's question, since she usually holds herself aloof from gossip, or at least pretends to.

"Well, to tell the truth, there were a lot of rumors about her and some guy," Cassie said. "But for the real scoop, you ought to talk to Constance Letterman. I don't remember the details, but I think she was involved somehow." If you want the real scoop on anything in Pecan Springs, you need to talk to Constance, who used to write the "Dilly Dally" column for the *Enterprise*.

"You can always count on Constance to know three or four stories about everybody," Caroline Murray said with a giggle, "and at least one of them is bound to be true. The problem is in knowing which one."

"My, my, ladies," Ruby said mildly, "we are so *tacky* tonight."

"Tacky doesn't apply when you're talking about Phoebe," Cassie said.

Erin looked at her watch. "Sorry to break this up, but I need to get home before my husband sends out a search party."

"Me too," Caroline agreed, standing up. "Who's riding with me?"

Ruby stood. "I'd like to say hi to Amy before I go home," she said quietly to me. "There's something I need to talk to her about."

"Be my guest," I said, putting the empty glasses on the tray. The dip bowl was completely empty, a sign that everybody had enjoyed it. Howard would be disappointed, though. Licking bowls is his job. "She's upstairs," I added. "Second door on the right."

Whatever Ruby and Amy talked about, it didn't take long. Ten minutes later, I heard Ruby come down the stairs and go out the front door. A few minutes after that, while I was unloading the dishwasher and putting the kitchen to rights, Amy came down to the kitchen. She was wearing wrinkled gray sweats and ratty pink house slippers, and her hair was even more disheveled than usual. Without her makeup and face jewelry, she looked almost naked, and very young. Her face was troubled.

"You feeling okay these days, babe?" I asked over my shoulder.

"Sort of," Amy replied. She grinned crookedly. "Except for mornings. Mornings, I feel rotten. I hope it doesn't bother you too much to hear somebody barfing in the bathroom."

"If I had to share a bathroom with Brian's lizards, I'd barf too," I said. "Hungry?"

"Yeah. I'm always hungry, even when I'm barfing." Amy sat at the table and put her chin in her hands. "I guess it goes with the territory, huh?"

"I wouldn't know," I said, taking out a serrated knife and the loaf of bread I'd baked the night before. "I thought I was pregnant once, but I managed to dodge the bullet."

"So you've never wanted to have children?"

"The Pill was made for women like me." I opened the refrigerator to make sure that the corned beef and sauerkraut were still there. With two guys in the house, you can never be sure that what you put in the fridge will stay in the fridge. But there it was, waiting to meet its manifest destiny, and right next to it sat a pot of my favorite homemade German mustard. I glanced at Amy. "In the mood for a Reuben?"

"Wonderful!" Amy's grin was elfish. "I came to the right place, didn't I? A bed, a bath, meals, and late-night snacks. You've been a fairy godmother, China. What more could I ask?" She sobered. "Well, maybe one or two other things. But I guess there are no guarantees that life is going to hand you your heart's desires." She hesitated and said slowly, "I just wish that Mom wouldn't . . ." Her voice trailed off.

"It's hard on her, too," I said. I popped the sliced corned beef and sauerkraut into the microwave to warm them up, then began heating a nonstick skillet on the stove. "I get the idea that becoming a grandmother wasn't high on her agenda," I added. "Give her a break, why don't you? She's having a hard time adjusting."

"Like I said," Amy muttered, "we don't always get our heart's desires." Her voice took on an edge. "Now she's got it into her head that Jon is the father. Can you imagine that?"

I finished slicing the bread, buttered one side, and put two slices in the skillet. "I can imagine why she imagines that," I said. "Jonathan Green is attractive, sexy, sweet—"

"And married."

"I understand that he and his wife are separated."

"That's got nothing to do with me." Amy had put on her

wild-child face, sullen eyes, pouty mouth. "Now, can we just drop the subject, please?"

I refrained from pointing out that she was the one who had brought it up in the first place. I silently layered corned beef, sauerkraut, and Swiss cheese on the two slices in the skillet, and topped each one with another slice of buttered bread. I had heard the unhappiness threading through Amy's voice. Maybe Ruby's guess was on the mark, and Jonathan was the father of her baby. If so, I felt sorry for the unhappiness that lay ahead for all three of them—Amy, Jon, her baby—and Jon's wife, too. But I felt sorriest of all for Amy. Pregnancy—especially the first—ought to be a happy time in a woman's life. As it was for Jill, who was bringing a much-longed-for son into a family that would welcome him with cries of pure joy.

When the bottom slices were brown and the cheese was beginning to soften, I flipped the sandwiches, got out the mustard, and sliced the onion. If Amy didn't want to talk about Jon, there were other subjects. I searched my memory and came up with one I thought would be more acceptable.

"Have you seen Kate Rodriguez lately?" I set two glasses on the table. "How's she doing?"

Amy brightened. "Really well," she said. "Kate is such a good friend." She smiled a little, regretfully. "I was going to ask her if I could stay with her, but her house is pretty small. There's barely room for her, let alone a guest."

Amy's best friend, Kate Rodriguez had been one of my favorite tellers at Ranchers State Bank until she'd quit to finish her accounting degree and open her own bookkeeping business. Her little one-woman company seems to have flourished. I saw her last at the vet clinic, where she was helping set up the books on the new computer system.

"Your mother and I have been thinking of asking Kate to manage the accounts for our three businesses—mine, hers, and ours," I said. "It would cost us, but we'd free up some time to spend on other things we'd rather be doing." I took the sandwiches out of the skillet, sliced them diagonally, and put them on plates, along with a couple of slices of fresh tomato, red onion, and a fat, juicy dill pickle. I added a handful of potato chips, poured milk, and we were all set.

"I'm not sure Kate's taking on new clients right now," Amy said, looking admiringly at the plate I set down in front of her. "Wow, China—it looks just like the Reuben at Krautzenheimer's."

"It'll taste even better," I replied immodestly, sitting down. I raised my glass of milk in a toast. "Here's to us. All three of us. Me, you, and the babe under your belt."

"To us," Amy added, a little self-consciously. She put down her glass and bit into her sandwich. "Wonderful," she murmured. "Is this sourdough bread? What kind of herbs did you put in it?"

"It's beer bread," I said, "but it tastes like sourdough, doesn't it? The herbs are dill, mostly, with some garlic and onion salt. Remind me, and I'll write out the recipe for you." We were silent for a moment, enjoying our sandwiches.

"So how come Kate's too busy to take on a new client?" I asked finally. "Got her hands full at the clinic?"

Amy shook her head. "She's only working for us one day a week now, and the rest of the time at Morgan's Pickles. It's a temporary situation, though. The company's going to be sold in another few weeks, and she—" She stopped. "Uh-oh," she said. "That's not official yet."

"Mmm," I said, wondering whether McQuaid had neglected to tell me this important detail, or whether Phoebe had neglected to tell him. Either way, it was interesting.

We ate companionably for another few moments, and then Amy went on, in an explanatory tone, "I don't know that it's a big secret or anything like that. The company being sold to Parade, I mean." I raised my eyebrows at this. Parade Products is one of the largest condiment producers in the country. "But Morgan's is such a local fixture," Amy added, "the sale is bound to have some sort of impact. I guess that's why the employees were told not to talk about it."

"I can certainly understand that," I said. After Phoebe finished automating the plant and getting rid of her surplus employees, Morgan's probably employed a tenth of its original labor force, which made it a fairly small player in the current local economy. Still, the plant has been in operation for nearly seventy years, and the Chamber of Commerce brags that it is one of our oldest local enterprises. And there's PickleFest, too, which brings in a substantial amount of tourist revenue and which Parade might not be willing to continue. No wonder the sale wasn't being publicized. But I knew that the deal couldn't be kept under wraps, especially in a town like Pecan Springs, where gossip travels at the speed of sound and everybody is hardwired into the grapevine.

Amy chewed reflectively. "What do you know about the Morgans?" she asked after a minute.

I shrugged. "What everybody else knows, I guess. The plant was started in the thirties, when Mick and Polly—"

"No, not those Morgans." Amy licked mustard off her fingers. "The current Morgans. Phoebe and her son."

I looked up sharply. There was an odd, jarring note in

Amy's voice. "The Pickle Queen? Haven't you heard enough of those stories?" I thought for a moment, then said, "Oh, but you didn't grow up around here, so maybe you haven't." Amy was raised in Dallas, where her adoptive parents lived.

"All I know is that people don't like Ms. Morgan very much," she said slowly, "and I think I can see why. But I just thought you might know something more . . . well, definite."

"You've met her, then? At the vet clinic, I suppose." Phoebe had a yappy little Chihuahua named Chico to which she was deeply attached. I didn't think she would take Chico to the vet, however. That was a menial task, and more likely she delegated it to Marsha.

"No, not at the clinic," Amy said vaguely. "Just . . . around. No place special." She paused. "Why don't people like her?"

"For the same reasons some people don't like Martha Stewart, I guess," I replied, wondering at Amy's evasiveness. "She's an extraordinarily successful woman, for one thing. Morgan's was on the skids when she took it over from her father. She's brought it around, mostly by making hard choices—turning the plant into a moneymaker by getting rid of products that had the family name on them. Some people would have been too sentimental for that kind of drastic pruning, but Phoebe is smart and aggressive. She knows what she wants and she goes for it, which is positive, in my book." I drained the last of my milk. "I respect her business sense, but to tell the truth, I wouldn't want her as a friend."

"Oh?" Amy cleared her throat. "Why?"

"It's the way she treats people," I said. "When I moved

here from Houston, I intended to leave the sharks behind. Phoebe Morgan is a female shark. She hides her teeth, but they're there, and very sharp. My only connection with her is PickleFest, and after this one is over, I think I'll just say no."

"I . . . see," Amy said quietly, as though what I had told her confirmed something she'd already thought. "And her husband?" She frowned. "She didn't take his name, I guess, since everybody calls her Ms. Morgan. When they're not calling her something else."

"He's been dead for ten or twelve years," I said, and told her the story as somebody—Ruby, I think—had told it to me. One night after boozing it up with his buddies at the Ten-Dollar Saloon, Ed Knight drove his pickup truck off a sixty-foot bluff and into the Pecan River. An accident, according to the investigators, but that didn't stop the guys at Ben's Barber Shop, several of whom had been drinking with Ed on the fatal night, from declaring his death a suicide. Ed was a good-looking, easygoing guy who drank more than was good for him and gambled more than was good for Morgan's. He was in charge of production at the plant, and his wife, who ran the operation herself back then, was his boss. He'd make mistakes and she'd ride him, or she'd demand that he cut another employee or two and stretch the rest. It got to the point where he couldn't take it any longer and killed himself—at least according to the boys at the barber shop, who thought they knew him pretty well.

"I can't vouch for any of this," I added. "You know how people talk. Anyway, nobody can tell from the outside what's going on in a relationship. Maybe Phoebe was wild about him, and he just couldn't handle his booze. She's never married again, although she's a very attractive woman. I imagine she's had plenty of opportunities." I paused. "Your mother knows Phoebe—they went to high school together. If you want more details, you could ask her."

Amy finished the last of her sandwich. "And her son? Brad, his name is."

"Brad? I've seen him around, but I don't really know much about him." What I had seen I hadn't liked very much. Weird hair, sloppy pants, piercings in unusual places—unusual for Pecan Springs, that is. "For a while, he went to Tulane University over in New Orleans, but I heard that he got suspended for hazing, and there was some other kind of trouble—I don't know what. He works at the plant, which I suppose he will someday inherit, unless his mother sells it." I paused and gave her a curious glance. "Do you know him?" Brad and Amy had a similar look, somehow. Maybe it was the weird hair and the multiple piercings. They seemed to have a similar taste in hairstyles and body adornment.

"I saw him a few times last year," Amy said, pushing back her chair. "And he brings his mother's dog to the clinic." Her answer was complete enough but her tone was evasive, as if there was something more that she didn't want to mention, something hidden.

"So what do you think of him?" I asked casually. "I've heard people say he's a spoiled rich kid. True?"

There was a flicker of something in Amy's eyes— alarm, maybe? apprehension—and then her face closed down. "You're not going to give me the third degree, are you, China? I thought that was Mom's special trick."

I shrugged. "I wouldn't dream of it," I said. But Amy

was still young, and not as practiced at hiding her feelings as she would be in a dozen years or so. I'd bet there was— or had been—something between her and Brad. If I were making a list of paternity candidates, I'd have to add his name.

Amy summoned a crooked smile. "Hey," she said. "I'm sorry. I guess I'm so used to snapping back at Mom that I just forgot. Authority complex, you know? I apologize for jumping down your throat, China."

"Apology accepted," I said, and changed the subject. We chatted a while longer, rinsed off our dishes, then turned out the lights and went upstairs. At the door to her room, Amy paused.

"Thanks for the sandwich, China." She leaned forward and kissed my cheek. "And thanks for being around when I need you. As authority figures go, you're tops."

"Well, hey," I said, touched, and kissed her back.

McQuaid was in bed with one of Tom Clancy's thrillers. He looked over the top of his reading glasses. "What are you shaking your head about?"

"Just wondering how it would be to have a daughter like Amy." Underneath all that wild hair and elaborate makeup and piercings, there was the soul of a sweet, loving girl. Mixed up, maybe, but loving.

McQuaid made a face. "If we had a daughter like Amy, we'd be about to become grandparents. How would you like them apples?"

"Point well taken. I'm glad that Brian is only four-teen—we can put that off for a few years." I shivered. "Poor Ruby. She can't quite get used to it."

"Can't say I blame her," McQuaid replied, grinning, and went back to his reading.

I started stripping. "Have you heard about the Morgan sale?"

He looked up, immediately interested. "The Morgan sale? What sale?"

"The plant is for sale, and Parade Products is interested." I gave him a knowing look. "It hasn't showed up on your radar, huh?"

"Not a blip." He put down his book. "Parade Products, huh? That sounds like a big deal. How'd you find out?"

"Amy told me. The employees know about it—some of them, anyway." I paused. "I wonder if there's any connection to the situation you're investigating."

"Just might be," McQuaid said. He eyed me. "Of course, you didn't say anything to Amy about—"

"Of *course* not!" I protested indignantly, getting into bed. "I promised, didn't I?"

"Yes, but . . ." He looked thoughtful. "Maybe we'd better renew that agreement we made last night, just so that we both remember it. Let's see. What were the terms? One naked wife, in return for—" He kissed me.

It was a very fair agreement, I felt. Entirely satisfying.

Chapter Five

"Fit Only for Cows"
A Brief History of the Cucumber

Cousin to the Persian melon, the cucumber has been around for at least three thousand years. The plant originated in India, migrated both east to China and west to the Mediterranean and Europe, and then discovered America with Columbus, who carried seeds to Haiti in 1494. The Pilgrims planted cukes in their gardens, and the plant was off to a promising new career in North America.

By the late 1600s, though, some began to worry that eating raw vegetables and fruits might lead to illness, and the uncooked cucumber (often spelled *coucumber*) fell from grace. "This day Sir W. Batten tells me that Mr. Newhouse is dead of eating cowcumbers," lamented Samuel Pepys in his famous diary. "Fit only for cows," sniffed another writer. Pickled cucumbers, however, were quite another matter, for the pickling process was judged to be enough like cooking to redeem the cucumber from its sins. Pickles became the fad food of the eighteenth century.

But while raw cucumbers might be thought unhealthy as food, they were in great demand at the local apothecary shop. Cucumber seeds were employed to treat inflammations of the bowel and urinary passages and to expel tapeworms, and the pulp and juice were used to ease skin inflammations and treat sunburns. Even today, beauty consultants often recommend placing cooling, soothing slices of cucumber over tired and inflamed eyes.

China Bayles
Home and Garden section
Pecan Springs *Enterprise*

For the last couple of years, I've been editing the Thursday Home and Garden section for the *Enterprise*. Mostly, my page consists of gardening tips; Fannie Couch's "Kitchen Korner" recipe column; reports of the doings of the Pecan Springs Garden Club and the Myra Merryweather Herb Guild; and the occasional food feature. The week before PickleFest, Fannie usually runs a dozen pickling recipes. And this time, just for fun, I wrote a brief history of the cucumber, which found its true calling when it was soaked in salt, vinegar, and water, and turned into a pickle.

The *Enterprise* usually hits the street about noon, so I stopped by the office on my way to lunch, to pick up a copy and see how the page turned out.

"Looks okay to me," I said to Harkness Hibler, the editor. "You did a nice job with the layout."

Hark was standing behind the counter, his sleeves rolled up, his collar open, wearing the cynical look of somebody who knows that today's newspaper will be in the landfill tomorrow. He became editor a few years ago, back when Arnold Seidensticker published the *Enterprise* as a weekly. Then Arnold's daughter Arlene took over from her dad and decided that Pecan Springs deserved a daily. Hark says he liked it better before, when he didn't have to scramble to find a juicy front-page news story every day, but I don't really believe him. Hark is a true-blue newspaperman, and he can make a story out of almost anything—when he's sober.

Anyway, while Pecan Springs is a small town, there's always plenty to write about. If nothing is happening at CTSU or the city council or the school board, there's still the zoning commission, the hospital board, and the county commissioners. Somewhere, somehow, some controversy will generate a headline: COMMISSIONERS BICKER OVER BAD-NEWS BUDGET or SCHOOL BOARD LECTURES UNRULY PRINCIPAL. And of course, we have our share of crime: domestic violence, the occasional drug bust, goat theft and horse rustling, and lately, a series of burglaries. Just last week, old Mrs. Holeyfield died of a heart attack when burglars tied her up while they were robbing her house.

Of course, things like this have always gone on, but in the past, the facts were scrubbed and sanitized before they put in an appearance in the *Enterprise*. Arlene's father had insisted that any bit of bad news be washed off and spruced up before it was printed, which gave the impression that Pecan Springs was a perfect little town where peace and harmony ruled and nobody ever stepped out of line. Today's news may be bitter, hard to swallow, and even harder to digest, but it's better than the sugarcoated pill the old weekly offered its readers. Now, at least, we're fully informed, although Hark and his team of apprentice reporters, on loan from the journalism department at CTSU, are often stretched to the limit. I guess Hark can be forgiven for occasionally hitting the bottle.

"Pretty nice," Hark agreed, looking over my shoulder at the garden section. "I didn't know that stuff about cucumbers expelling tapeworms." He frowned. "Hey, speaking of pickles, what's this I hear about Phoebe Morgan?"

"I don't know," I said, folding the newspaper and wondering whether news of the sale had reached Hark's ears. "What did you hear?"

"That she hasn't been around for the past few days."

"I don't know anything about that," I said cautiously. "I do know, though, that she didn't show up to meet with the Pretty Pickle Planners last night, which is causing Pauline Perkins a great deal of heartburn."

Hark squinted at me. "The Pretty . . . who?"

"You know. Peter Piper picked a peck of pretty pickled planners." I grinned at the confusion on his face. "Officially, we're the PickleFest planning committee. Actually, we're Phoebe Morgan's flunkies." I regarded him curiously. "How do you know she hasn't been around?"

"Because I was hanging out at the sheriff's office, catching up on the news, when Phoebe's assistant came in and asked Jennie—in a roundabout way—whether there'd been any accidents reported in the last couple of days."

Jennie sits at the front desk in the sheriff's office, doing paperwork and dealing with the public. "Her assistant," I said. "That would be Marsha Miller. Right?"

Hark pulled a tattered notebook out of his shirt pocket. For a newspaperman, he has a notoriously bad memory. If he doesn't put something on his tape recorder or write it down, it's gone forever. He flipped a couple of pages, pursed his lips, and nodded. "Yeah, that's right. Miller. Said she hasn't heard from Ms. Morgan since Monday."

Monday! I whistled between my teeth. So Marsha hadn't been telling us the whole truth the night before. She'd given us the impression that Phoebe had been temporarily detained somewhere, not that she had taken a powder. I couldn't blame Marsha, though. With Phoebe off somewhere and Pauline scowling at her, she had been stuck between a rock and a hard place. "And on the eve of Pickle-Fest," I muttered. "Marsha must be beside herself." But nothing like Pauline, I'd bet, when she heard the news.

"Well, the young lady did seem a tad upset." Hark re-pocketed the notebook. "Didn't want to talk to me about it, though. Said the family didn't want any publicity. So you're sayin' this is something serious, huh? I thought maybe—" He shrugged. "You know. Somebody who's got as much money as Phoebe Morgan can afford to kick up her heels now and then. London for breakfast, Paris for shopping, the Riviera for dinner and drinks."

"Possibly." I eyed him. "But that doesn't seem like Phoebe's style. How well do you know her?"

"I've done a couple of stories on the pickle factory, and I've seen her at some of the local events. Good-lookin' lady, stylish, sharp clothes, very intelligent. I like my women a little softer, though." Hark gave me his lecher's grin. Since the *Enterprise* became a daily, he's lost forty pounds and has become quite the bachelor-about-town. "Ms. Morgan looks like she could chew horseshoes and spit nails." He pursed his lips. "So what happens if Phoebe fails to show up for PickleFest?"

"Pauline Perkins will have a nervous breakdown," I

said, thinking I'd better call her right away. I glanced at my watch. "I'm meeting Sheila and Ruby for lunch at Krautz's. Want to join us?"

Hark shook his head regretfully. "We're shorthanded today. Lois is out sick, and the only kid reporter I've got has classes until two. I'd better hang out here and mind the store." As I headed for the door, he added, "Your buddy Sheila might know something more about this Morgan business. She was in the sheriff's office when the assistant came in. Ask her."

"I will," I said. It was no surprise that Sheila Dawson, Pecan Springs's chief of police, was in the sheriff's office. She and the sheriff, Blackie Blackwell, were probably discussing their wedding arrangements. They're due to get married in a few months—or at least, that's the current plan. They've put it off twice already, so the date is anybody's guess.

As I turned toward the door, Hark said, "And if you hear anything about the Pickle Queen, you let me know, d'ya hear? Sorta smells like a story."

I was opening the door when he thought of something else. "Stop me if you've heard this one," he said, "but who was the number one pickle hunter of the Wild West?"

I turned and stared at him. "I don't know," I said humbly. "I'm ashamed to admit it, but I don't know."

"Why, it was Wild Pill Dickle, of course!" he said, and began to laugh. "Wild Pill Dickle," he repeated, laughing so hard he could hardly speak. "Old Wild Pill Dickle, with his Wild Pill Dickle pistol!"

"Amazing," I said. It was, truly. A pickle joke I hadn't heard before.

* * *

If you find yourself anywhere near Courthouse Square when the Pecan Springs Fire Department blows the noon whistle (which is also a test of the fire siren and the tornado alert system), you have several options for lunch. If it's a Tuesday, Wednesday, Friday, or Saturday, you can join us at Thyme for Tea. On Mondays and Thursdays, you should check out the special at Lila's Diner, kitty-cornered from the bank. If it's meatloaf, you're in for a real down-home taste treat. If it's not, cut across the square to Krautzen-heimer's German Restaurant, in the narrow stone building wedged between the Ben Franklin Store and the Sophie Briggs Historical Museum. Today was Thursday, and I was headed for Krautz's, to meet Sheila and Ruby.

I didn't have to look for Ruby when I got to the restaurant, because she stood up and waved, her scarves flying like kites in a high wind. She and Sheila were seated at a front-window table where they could watch the action on the square. Ruby sits there because she likes it when people notice her. She was definitely noticeable today, in a blue tie-dyed tunic over darker blue patio pants, with a filmy blue scarf tied around her red hair and another looped around her neck, and turquoise earrings shaped like crescent moons dangling from her earlobes. Sheila, on the other hand, sits there because she likes to notice people. She's been the Pecan Springs police chief for something over a year, and noticing is part of her job description.

"Hey, China." Sheila raised her hand in a salute.

"Hey, Chief." I grinned. "You're looking *très* chic to-day." She was dressed in a navy skirt, blue-and-brown-checked blouse, and smart khaki blazer, her badge displayed prominently on her lapel.

Sheila Dawson, known to her friends as Smart Cookie, is not your average, garden-variety police chief. When I first met her, I had to swallow down my envy, and the feeling hasn't worn off. In her late thirties, she is slender and willowy, her blond hair sleek and shining, her skin like Devon cream, her nails beautifully manicured—in fact, she's so blond and beautiful that some people are not inclined to take her seriously. But don't be deceived. Sheila has fifteen-plus years of law enforcement experience under her belt—that's a black belt in karate, if you please—and I've seen her outshoot the entire PSPD, much to the chagrin of the macho males on the force. If you're on her hit list, it's time to duck.

Sheila smiled and pushed out the empty chair with her foot. "You look hassled, China. Sit down and let Ruby tell your fortune." She signaled to one of the numerous Krautzenheimer granddaughters to fill my glass with iced tea. The senior Krautzenheimers keep the junior K's in line by employing them all in the restaurant.

"My fortune?" I sat down. "If Ruby's peering into crystal balls, I've got a more pressing question."

"Ask away," Ruby said. She put both hands on her iced tea glass, and I noticed that her long nails were painted blue, to match her costume. Her contacts were blue, too. When Ruby chooses a color, she goes all out. She peered into the glass and said, in a husky voice with a fake Hungarian accent, "Madame Ruby, she has ze power of ze second sight. She will show you all zat is hidden in ze mists of ze future."

"I'd settle for what's hidden in the mists of the early part of this week," I said. "How about Monday? And instead of looking me up, try doing a search on the Pickle Queen, why don't you?"

Ruby looked up, her eyes widening. "Phoebe Morgan?" she asked, startled into her ordinary voice. "How come?"

"Because it seems she has become a missing person," I said. "If you can locate her, you'll save the sheriff a whole lot of trouble."

"She is not a missing person," Sheila objected. "Nobody's filed a report, to my knowledge."

"That doesn't alter the fact that this person is missing," I replied firmly. "Since Monday."

"Sunday," Sheila amended. "Marsha Miller last saw her on Sunday afternoon, about three o'clock. She was headed out to the plant to do some book work in the office. After that, she had a date to see somebody, Marsha didn't know who. I heard her telling Jennie," she added. "In the sheriff's office. She never got around to talking to Blackie."

A date? That must have been Phoebe's appointment with McQuaid. I opened my mouth to mention this, then thought better of it. After all, I'd promised.

In a meaningful tone, Sheila added, "Turns out that her live-in boyfriend hasn't been seen in the past week. Marsha mentioned that, too."

"Live-in boyfriend?" Ruby asked, arching her eyebrows. "That's the young artist who's been staying in her guest house. Phoebe's bought a lot of his paintings, and she's persuaded the bank to hang some in the lobby." She frowned. "I knew his name, but I've forgotten it."

"How'd you find all that out?" I asked curiously. Ruby's

ability to dig up odd, inconsequential facts continually amazes me.

"Janet's aunt Lunelle is Phoebe's housekeeper." Ruby sipped her iced tea. "Of course, Lunelle isn't supposed to talk about what's going on with her employer, but she doesn't think this applies to Janet."

That's the thing about small towns. Everybody knows somebody who knows all there is to know about somebody else, and prohibitions against talking only encourage people to spread the word more widely.

"A boyfriend," I said thoughtfully. "The thick plottens, doesn't it?"

The Krautzenheimer granddaughter arrived to pour iced tea and recite the day's soup and salad special, which turned out to be our favorite combination: *Lauchsamt-suppe*—cream of leek and potato soup—and German cucumber salad: cucumbers, green onions, and sliced tomatoes in a sour cream and mustard dressing, heavy on the dill. All three of us ordered it, simplifying matters for Mother Krautzenheimer, who oversees the three or four grandchildren working in the kitchen, probably in violation of child labor laws.

When the girl was gone, Sheila folded her hands and looked at me. "Where were we?"

"Boyfriend," I said. "As in running away with."

"I don't know," Ruby said thoughtfully. "Phoebe isn't the type to get carried away by passion. She's too calculating. She probably made him go off with her. Maybe she decided to marry him after all."

"After all what?" I asked.

"After turning him down several times. At least, that's

what Lunelle told Janet." Her eyes widened. "Omigosh, China! What'll we do if she doesn't come back in time for PickleFest?"

"Run and hide," I said. I looked at Sheila. "So what else did Marsha Miller say?"

"Nothing." Sheila looked uncomfortable. "I really shouldn't be talking about this, China. Blackie wouldn't—"

"If Phoebe isn't an official missing person," Ruby said reasonably, "it's not a police matter."

"And since Marsha asked her questions in the presence of the local newspaper editor," I said, "she can hardly have any expectation of privacy."

"Anyway," Ruby went on, "China and I are the Pretty Pickle Planners. If Phoebe doesn't come back, we're the ones who'll have to deal with the fallout on this."

"Pretty Pickle Planners?" Sheila gave me a helpless look. "What's she talking about, China?"

"Ruby and I are on the PickleFest planning committee," I explained. "It's chaired by Pauline Perkins, but Phoebe runs the show. If she's not around to make things happen, the festival is going to be a disaster."

"A calamity," Ruby said fervently. "Of catastrophic proportions." She reached into her purse and pulled out her cell phone. "I guess we'd better call Pauline and let her know, huh?"

"Let's wait until after lunch." I made a wry face. "I'd like to enjoy my soup and salad." Turning to Sheila, I changed the subject. "How are the wedding plans shaping up, Smart Cookie? We probably need to put our heads together about details." Sheila and Blackie are planning to be married in the garden at Thyme and Seasons.

Sheila's mouth turned down at the corners. "The wedding is taking a backseat to police work just now, China. I've got a murder to solve."

Ruby put away her cell phone. "That was too bad about Mrs. Holeyfield," she said, very seriously. "She was a sweet old lady."

I agreed. Mrs. Holeyfield, who supported the local Humane Society practically single-handed, was one of the best-loved citizens of Pecan Springs. "You haven't turned up any clues?" I asked.

Sheila shook her head ruefully. "No clues, no suspects, nothing. *Nada.* I'm beginning to think that the investigation is jinxed."

"Sounds serious," I said. For the past six or eight months, Pecan Springs had been plagued by a series of burglaries—and not just any old burglaries, either. It was the members of the Pecan Springs aristocracy who were targeted, the ones who live in the elite neighborhood between Guadalupe Street and the Pecan River. And while the burglar had been taking only small, distinctive works of art—a set of miniature jade chess pieces, a filigree gold bracelet, several ivory *netsuke* figures—he'd also committed some fairly extensive vandalism—paintings and photographs destroyed, graffiti sprayed on walls, furniture knifed, crystal smashed.

By themselves, these unsolved burglaries were bad enough. But in a small town, repeated crimes have a tendency to make people feel unsettled, frightened, and anxious. After each new incident, Smart Cookie took a little more heat from her bosses on the city council, some of whose families had been hit. As a result of the burglaries, the council began to demand nightly police patrols and a more extensive investigation, to which Sheila repeatedly replied that she simply couldn't stretch the department's thin resources any further. They'd do the best they could, she added deferentially, but if the neighborhood wanted additional patrols, perhaps people should hire security guards.

But then things got worse. Wilhelmina Holeyfield came home from a gala dinner party celebrating her eightieth birthday and apparently surprised the burglar. She was bound, gagged, and blindfolded, and at some point during this tragic indignity, suffered a heart attack and died. At the city council meeting the next night, Judy Cramer—Mrs. Holeyfield's niece—angrily demanded that the Texas Rangers be called in to handle the investigation, since the local cops were clearly incompetent. It was time to start looking around for a new police chief, she added, some-body who might be a little less decorative but a lot more capable.

"It is *definitely* serious," Sheila said grimly. "I'm think-ing about looking for another job." She managed a small, sour smile. "Which might please Blackie. You know how he feels about a two-cop family. Particularly *this* two-cop family."

Blackie Blackwell, a close friend and fishing buddy of McQuaid's, has been the Adams County sheriff for seven years or so, but he's still a very nice guy, as Texas sheriffs go. He gets gold stars for being intelligent, careful, and (mostly) compassionate. His father, Corky Blackwell, was sheriff before him, and Reba, his mother, cooked for pris-oners in the county jail. As a boy, Blackie carried tin plates, scrubbed out the cells, and grew up wanting to be a lawman.

But Texas has changed since the old days. Adams

County may be mostly rural, but Blackie has his share of dope dealers, stolen autos, illegal aliens, and the occasional killing. He and Smart Cookie have been going together for several years, but just about the time he got up the nerve to propose, she moved from her post as security chief at CTSU to police chief for Pecan Springs, which complicated the situation considerably. He says he supports Sheila's career in law enforcement, but even a casual observer (and I'm not very casual, where Sheila and Blackie are concerned) can see the stresses and strains. Blackie will be up for reelection next year, and his major challenger is a popular militia type who would like to see armed citizens riding around the county in unmarked cars to defend us against lurking terrorists. There's a great deal of animosity toward Sheila, too, some of it underground, some out in the open. The departmental reorganization she carried out in the first few months of her tenure may have been necessary, but it certainly didn't earn her many friends among the Old Guard on the force. And now these burglaries.

"It's hard to believe that forensics hasn't turned up *any* leads," I said. "As many times as this burglar has done this, you'd think he'd get careless."

"You'd think," Sheila agreed glumly. "We're obviously dealing with a very smart thief—or thieves, as the case may be. We're not even sure if it's singular or plural."

"Since he's obviously overlooking some really valuable items," Ruby remarked, "you could argue that he's very dumb."

"If this were happening on the east side of town," I said dryly, "the council would never notice. What's the average take on these burglaries?"

"Oh, maybe a thousand dollars," Sheila replied, "usually something unique and hard to fence. A piece of art or jewelry, almost like a souvenir. The price tag on the vandalism is higher, of course. Whoever is doing this seems to get off on smashing the family crystal and slashing the family paintings—portraits of the ancestors, usually. Until Mrs. Holeyfield was killed, the burglaries were more like insults than crimes. Especially since the thief has been taking"— she leaned forward and lowered her voice—"panties."

"Panties!" Ruby exclaimed. "But that's crazy!"

"Not so loud," Sheila said. "We've managed to keep that little detail out of the *Enterprise*." She made a face. "It's the sort of news Hark would love to turn into a banner headline: PANTIES PURLOINED or LADIES LOSE THEIR UNDIES or something equally awful."

"He wouldn't dare," Ruby said.

"Don't bet on it," Sheila replied darkly.

I frowned. "Mrs. Holeyfield wasn't sexually molested, I hope."

"No," Sheila said. "She's just dead, that's all."

"But even that doesn't seem deliberate," Ruby said. "They couldn't have known she would have a heart attack."

"Maybe," I said, "but it's still murder. The DA will love this one. In the process of committing a felony—one of a string of felonies—the thief trussed up a fragile old lady and frightened her to death. Life without parole."

"I can understand about tying and gagging," Ruby said with a frown, "but why do you suppose she was blindfolded?"

"Maybe he was afraid she'd recognize him," I said.

Ruby played with her fork. "It sounds to me like somebody with a grudge. A kid from the wrong side of town who has it in for the rich folk."

"But if he's from the wrong side of town," I objected, "he wouldn't risk going to jail for a thousand dollars or so per job. He'd clean the place out. Stereos, jewelry, silver, anything he could convert to cash." I gave Sheila a narrow look. "Could it be a grudge of a different sort? Against you, maybe? Those panties could be a red herring—or even a deliberate clue of some demented sort."

Sheila looked at me, her gray eyes steady and serious. "A cop crime, you mean, designed to make the female police chief look incompetent? Yes, the possibility has occurred to me. I've even run my finger down the duty roster, to see who might have been off-duty when the crimes took place. But somehow I just can't believe that—"

"Why not?" I asked bluntly. "Those guys who hated your guts last January probably still feel pretty much the same way today, especially the two you pushed to take early retirement. And their friends, of course. I'm sure they have plenty of friends. Some of whom Mrs. Holeyfield might recognize."

Under Bubba Harris, Smart Cookie's predecessor, a certain number of the senior members of the Pecan Springs PD had gotten lazy and self-assured, and when Sheila had placed several women and minorities in responsible positions in the department, they voiced their feelings. There were fewer open complaints after the first couple of early retirements, but sentiment still ran high. I'd heard this from McQuaid, who'd heard it from Bubba, with whom he occasionally plays poker. Even Bubba carries a chip on his shoulder about the situation, and is pretty free with his criticism. After all, Sheila was hired to replace him, and if she looks bad, he'll look better. He might be angling to get his old job back, especially if the liberals who were responsible for his demise get the boot in the next city council election.

"I don't think this has to do with me," Sheila said, shaking her head. "These unsolved cases make the whole force appear incompetent. If a cop or a former cop wanted to get me, he'd surely find a way to do it without harming the department."

"That's assuming the cop is smart," I said. "I've seen cops pull some pretty stupid tricks. Tampering with evidence, filing false reports, kicking and beating a guy when—"

"I know, I know," Sheila said testily. "You lawyers are always pointing out our shortcomings. But cops are no different from anybody else. We make mistakes, occasionally cut a few corners—"

"And sometimes," I said, "a cop tries to cut the ground out from under his commanding officer. It's been done, Smart Cookie," I added. "Don't say it hasn't. I once knew a cop who hated his sergeant so much that he set him up to take a fall on—"

"Hey," Ruby said. "Here's lunch."

We suspended conversation while we attacked our lunches, and when we started talking again, our fervor had died down. Sheila conceded that it was possible that these burglaries were designed to make her life difficult, if not to get her fired; I conceded that there might be an entirely different explanation; and we both agreed that the crimes had to be solved, today, if not yesterday.

We were just exchanging apologies when Pauline came

in, saw us, and came to the table. She was wearing one of her mayoral power suits—tailored gray jacket and skirt, blue jewel-necked blouse, and modest pearls—with a saucer-sized campaign button pinned to her bosom, blazoned with PERKINS FOR MAYOR. The election is months away, but Pauline was obviously off and running.

"Hello, China, Ruby," she said energetically, putting a broad hand on my shoulder. With less enthusiasm, she nodded at Sheila. "Good to see you, Chief Dawson." Her voice became barbed. "Any new leads in Mrs. Holeyfield's death?"

"Not at the moment," Sheila said with the practiced cheeriness of someone who is used to working for the public, "but it's our highest priority."

Ruby and I exchanged glances. "Speaking of priorities," Ruby said, putting her hand on the cell phone lying on the table, "China and I were planning to call you. We have some news about Phoebe."

"Oh, good!" Pauline exclaimed happily. "Has she set up a meeting for tonight? We simply *must* get together with her."

"It turns out," I said, "that Marsha wasn't telling us the whole truth last night. Phoebe didn't just miss our committee meeting. She's been gone all week. The last time Marsha saw her was three o'clock on Sunday afternoon." Of course, I thought, McQuaid saw her after that, but I couldn't mention it.

Pauline went white. "Good Lord!" she gasped. "She's . . . gone?"

"She probably went off with her boyfriend," Ruby said, as if that made it easier to understand.

"I don't give a flying flip who she went off with,"

Pauline retorted heatedly, the white turning to mottled red. "The point is that she's not here, and without her, Pickle-Fest will be a disaster. So what are we going to do?"

I looked at my watch. "If Ruby will mind the shop for a couple of hours, you and I can drive out to the Morgan house and talk to Marsha. She's bound to be able to help us. I have to get back early, though." Thyme for Tea doesn't do lunch on Thursdays because that's the day we do High Tea, usually for a local organization. Today, we were hosting the Myra Merryweather Herb Guild.

"No problem," Ruby said generously. "Go right ahead." She leaned over and whispered in my ear, "Todd. His name is Todd."

I frowned. "Whose name is Todd?"

"Phoebe's artist. Her boyfriend. I just remembered."

"Thanks," I said, and stood up. "Let's go, Pauline." To Ruby, I said, "I'll be back in time to deal with the Merry-weathers. Anyway, they're an easy bunch to please."

"But I haven't had lunch yet," Pauline protested.

"Do you want to have lunch, or do you want to save the PickleFest from utter chaos?" I asked.

Pauline considered her options. "Let's go," she said, with stoic resignation. "We can stop at McDonald's on the way out of town and get some chicken McNuggets."

"Attagirl." Ruby waved her scarf. "Go get 'em, Pauline."

Chapter Six

In Colonial America, mothers brought little muslin bags of dill, fennel, and caraway seeds for their fidgety children to chew during long sermons. These became known as "Meetin' Seeds."

"I have never understood," Pauline said as we rang the bell, "why Ed and Phoebe wanted to build a house like this." She looked up at the green glass pickle bottle towering over us. "It is so out of place here."

"The exterior might not fit into the landscape," I agreed. "But you've got to admit that the interiors are stunning."

"I suppose," Pauline said with a shrug. "But the house certainly didn't fit Ed, inside or out. He was the six-pack and pickup type. He'd have been happier in a converted barn."

"You knew him?"

She hesitated. "We . . . went to the senior prom together."

"Oh," I said, wondering if Pecan Springs was the kind of high school where going to the senior prom with somebody was like announcing your engagement.

Pauline nodded, matter-of-fact. "Even after he married Phoebe and I married Darryl, we stayed friends. He used to come over to my house and sit at my kitchen table and tell me all the awful things she made him—"

Marsha Miller opened the door. I wouldn't get to hear what Ed had confided to Pauline.

Marsha wasn't delighted to see us, but she clearly felt obligated to make up for the problems caused by her employer's unexpected absence. So she showed us into the conference room and retrieved a scrambled stack of folders and notes from Phoebe's office down the hall. The three of us sat down at the table and Marsha did her nervous best to answer our questions. If anything, she seemed more taut and fidgety than she had the evening before.

While we worked, my eyes kept going to the window. The view from the conference room is so spectacular that it's a wonder Phoebe gets anything done there. From where I sat in a plush swivel chair, I could see a wide sweep of Texas Hill Country, reaching south toward Kerrville, west toward Fredericksburg. At the foot of the bluff below was the Pecan River, clear and shallow. Beyond, to the western and southern horizons, the rolling hills were cloaked in dark green junipers—cedars, we call them here—broken occasionally by a massive outcrop of Cretaceous limestone. This part of Texas was once covered by a warm, shallow sea, until, some hundred million years ago, the land was gently lifted up, breaking along the escarpment on the eastern rim of the Edwards Plateau. Over the eons since, streams have etched the thick limestone layers into shallow valleys and deeper canyons, the cedars and oaks covering the hillsides, the mesquite settling into the open meadows. If you listen hard, and use a little imagination, you might hear the calls of Tonkawa Indian children, foraging for wild onions and prickly pear fruit and agarita berries in the creek bottoms. Or you might see the ghosts of the aggressive Comanches—the name means "anyone who wants to fight me all the time"—astride their fierce Spanish horses, pushing the peaceful, compliant Tonkawa eastward to the Gulf.

"What do you think, China?" Pauline's impatient tone suggested that this wasn't the first time she'd asked.

"I'm sorry," I said guiltily, pulling my attention back to the papers that Pauline and Marsha had spread out on the table. "I'm afraid I wasn't listening."

"It's the view," Marsha said, with a nervous, tittery laugh. "It's terribly distracting." She glanced out the window. "I've seen as many as a hundred vultures in the sky at once, circling in a thermal. And migrating sandhill cranes, and hawks, and even once a bald eagle. It's one of the perks of working here."

Pauline gave up. "As long as you two are taking a break, I might as well make a trip to the little girls' room."

When Pauline had gone, I smiled at Marsha. Never very pretty, she looked even less attractive than usual. Her dark hair was pulled into a straggling ponytail at the back of her neck, giving her a strained, severe look, and behind her owlish glasses her brown eyes were puffy, as if she hadn't been getting enough sleep. She had traded the black sleeveless top she'd worn the day before for a pink skirt-and-blouse combination. The silky blouse had a frilly lace jabot that gave her a kittenish, fake-feminine look, and she had drawn lip-liner on the outside of her thin lips, trying to make them look more plump. I wondered who she was making herself pretty for.

"I'm sure there must be a great many perks connected with working here," I said. "It's a lot better than the County

Clerk's office, huh? Especially since you don't have to deal with irate property tax payers, or work in that un-air-conditioned filing room."

"Yes." Marsha seemed to relax a little. "I certainly don't miss that part of it, China. And I live here, you know, which has also been wonderful. I have a little apartment over the garage, with its own kitchen and a lovely view of the garden. And there's the pool, of course. I swim every day. But—" She stopped.

"But it must be kind of difficult, working with Phoebe," I said in an offhand tone. "I'm not sure I could handle her demands." I grinned. "Having her out of your hair for a few days must be like a vacation for you."

"Oh, yes," Marsha said eagerly, "if it weren't for not knowing—" She broke off, biting her lip.

"Where she is?" At her frown, I added, "A friend of mine happened to be in the sheriff's office when you were asking about accidents. He thought you looked worried."

Absently, she took off her glasses and began to polish them on the front of her blouse. Without them, her eyes looked blurry and out of focus. "Well, I suppose I am, a little," she said in a studiedly diffident tone. "Of course, Todd is gone too, and his car. Since her car is here, I'm sure they must have gone off together." She hesitated, then added, "Phoebe gave him a new car, you see, and they were planning to drive to Santa Fe next week, after PickleFest is over. She's arranged for Todd to hang some of his paintings in a prestigious gallery there."

"That's Todd's work?" I asked, gesturing toward a series of large oil paintings displayed in elaborate frames on the end walls of the room. Desert scenes, mostly, in strong Southwest colors. Lots of color.

Marsha's eyes went to the paintings and she nodded. "Todd Kellerman," she said.

"These are quite good, don't you think?" I asked. I got up and went to look at the nearest one, a desert scene with a range of blue mountains in the background, the foreground populated by large saguaro cactuses. "Quite good," I repeated, as if I knew something about it. Actually, it looked to me like the work of a dozen other Southwestern artists, with nothing particular to distinguish it. But what the heck do I know? Todd Kellerman might be an undiscovered talent, poised on the threshold of fame. "The, ah, brushwork is quite distinctive," I added, trying to sound authoritative. "And the colors are, er . . . remarkable."

"I'm glad you like it," Marsha said eagerly, and with a disturbing transparency. "Todd is so extraordinarily talented, and such a nice person, too. Always cheerful, always ready to—" She flushed, suddenly aware of the tone of her voice, and put her glasses back on. "Phoebe says it gives her a great deal of pleasure to foster such a talent," she added painfully.

"Todd is from around here?"

Marsha shook her head. "Albuquerque. He's a friend of Brad—Phoebe's son." At the mention of Brad, her mouth tightened almost imperceptibly.

As I came back to the table, I paused to look at the silver-framed photographs of Phoebe displayed on the long wall. Phoebe in front of Morgan's Premier Pickles. Phoebe trading smiles with a former governor and future president, in front of the Texas state capitol in Austin. Phoebe in a swimsuit, sunning herself on the teak deck of a classy yacht. Phoebe in a designer ball gown with a glass of champagne, on the arm of . . . was that really Warren

Beatty? Phoebe in a silk Western shirt and a white cowboy hat, on a handsome horse with a handsome silver-inlaid saddle and bridle. The pieces of her face might not quite go together: her mouth was too wide, her eyes set too closely together, her chin too pointed. But what did that matter? In every photo, she radiated confidence and self-assurance, her blond hair sleek and shining, the picture of success and achievement. I smiled at the thought that all this social and financial success had sprouted in a cucumber patch—although of course everybody's got to start somewhere, and making a fortune from a patch of cucumbers is a lot less problematic than making a fortune from a patch of opium poppies.

"Todd's lucky to have found a generous supporter," I said, sitting down. "He lives here too, I understand?"

"In the guest house, on the other side of the pool. It's a . . . a very nice place. Very cozy." Marsha dropped her eyes and turned her pencil in her fingers, her mouth softening, a half-pretty flush staining her cheeks. In my former life, I'd trained myself to read people's guilty knowledge from what they said and how they looked, but this one was no great challenge. Marsha's secret sang out in her voice and was sketched all over her face: that she had been in the guest house with Todd, and that the two of them had made love.

Only once? I wondered. Or more often than that? From the look on Marsha's face, it wasn't a casual affair, at least for her. It wasn't the kind of thing Phoebe would tolerate, either. I didn't blame Marsha for keeping the relationship a deep, dark secret. If her employer found out, she'd be out of a job and a place to live in a New York minute.

Tactfully, I changed the subject. "Do you have much to

do with the pickle plant, Marsha? I've always thought that would be an interesting line of work."

"Making pickles, interesting?" Marsha shook her head as if to say that would be an incredibly boring job. "No, Vince takes care of the day-to-day running of the plant. Of course, I'm involved with other plant-related things. Permits, the purchase of major equipment, new construction, that sort of thing."

Vince Walton, the man Phoebe suspected of embezzlement. The man McQuaid was supposed to be investigating. "Walton has been with Morgan's for a long time?"

"He came about the time I did," Marsha replied, turning her pencil over in her fingers. "Three years ago. Phoebe hired him when she decided to step out of the operation of the plant and get more involved in some of her other interests. Unfortunately, he didn't have quite as much experience as she thought, especially with computers. But they've managed to get along, more or less." There was an undertone of something in her voice—sarcasm, maybe. I had the feeling that there was no love lost between Marsha and Vince.

"Phoebe seems to have her finger in a great many pies," I said. "You must have to work with a great many different projects."

Marsha rolled her eyes. "You have no idea. Just this morning, I met with Vince about production schedules, then with our accountant about the taxes, and finally with a neighbor who's angry about effluent."

"Effluent!" I laughed. "You mean, as in—"

"That's what I mean," Marsha said. "The liquid waste from the pickle plant is highly acidic, and can't be discharged until it's impounded and treated." She made a face. "The plant's been inspected and permitted and everything's just fine—but not according to Art Simon, who has a place on the river just below the plant."

I raised my eyebrows. "Art Simon? We met him last night, as we left. He was out jogging, with his dog."

She nodded. "He's pretty upset, but I think I handled his concerns. He—"

"Well, if we've finished with our little break," Pauline said briskly, coming into the room, "shall we see what's left to be done? Marsha, would you look over this list and tell me how to reach these people?"

It went on like that for another half hour, Marsha answering questions, making phone calls, and scurrying off to look for notes and papers, while Pauline ticked off the items on her list, one by one. At last she was satisfied. Marsha promised to meet her early the next morning at the Morgan plant, where several Morgan employees were supposed to be setting things up. And then we were finished. It was not quite two-thirty. I'd be back at the shop in plenty of time to meet the Merryweathers and help Ruby with High Tea.

Marsha was letting us out the front door when a sleek red sports car slewed around the circle drive, fast, scattering gravel. "That's Brad," Marsha said with a look of distaste. "Vince sent him out to West Texas last week to scout out some potential new cucumber growers."

A slim-hipped, deeply bronzed young man got out of the car and opened the trunk to take out a duffle bag. He sauntered toward us, moving with an almost feline grace. This was not the Brad I had seen around town in previous years, with weird hair, multiple piercings, and ragged baggies hanging down around his crotch. This was a reformed

Brad, in khakis, blue chambray shirt, and loafers. His fea-
tures were regular, almost pretty, and he wore his blond
hair brushed back in designer waves. In terms of appearance, anyway, it was a distinct improvement.

He lifted a hand to us, and Marsha introduced us. He
smiled pleasantly, but when he turned back to Marsha,
there was a frown on his forehead and concern in his eyes.
"Phoebe get home yet?"

Marsha shook her head.

"She's been gone since the first of the week and hasn't
let you know where she is?" He sounded almost accusing,
as if it were somehow Marsha's fault that his mother
wasn't keeping in touch. "That's not like her. At the very
least, she picks up her messages."

"Your mother is over twenty-one," Marsha retorted de-
fensively. "There's no law that says she has to check in
every day. Or tell you where she's going," she added, "especially when you haven't been home for a week yourself."

If Brad was stung by Marsha's remark, he didn't show
it. "I suppose Todd finally talked her into going off with
him," he muttered. "The Golden Boy. I was a damned fool
to bring him here, where he could worm his way into her
affections. Phoebe doesn't know him the way I do. She
didn't realize what she was letting herself in for. He—"

"That's enough, Brad." Marsha cut him off sharply. She
cast an oblique glance at Pauline and me. "We don't need
to talk about this now." In front of strangers, she meant.

"But I'm worried!" Brad's face was dark. "And you're
protecting him, Marsh. You're just like Phoebe. You're
covering for Todd because you've got some screwy idea
that—"

"I said stop it!" Marsha's face was pink, her eyes bright

with anger. She turned to Pauline and me, obviously struggling to keep control. "Thanks for coming. I'll see you at nine, at the plant."

"Not me," I said, holding up my hands. "I've got a shop to tend."

"But I need you," Pauline protested, "and Ruby, too. I'll ask a couple of the other women to help out tomorrow afternoon, so you can go back to work."

"I'll have to check with Ruby," I said. "But I suppose we can manage, as long as we're back in time to handle the lunch bunch." I turned to Brad. "If you're concerned about your mother's whereabouts," I said pleasantly, "you can file a report at the sheriff's office. I'm sure Sheriff Blackwell would be glad to—"

"Now that I'm home, I plan to do just that," Brad replied, "if I haven't heard from her by the weekend." He narrowed his eyes at Marsha. "And you're not going to stop me, either."

"You *can't* do that, Brad." Marsha sounded almost frantic. "What if there's bad publicity? What if she has to come home to—?"

"What if it wasn't her idea to go off with the bastard in the first place?" Brad demanded impatiently. "What if he forced her into it? Use your common sense, Marsha."

Marsha put her hands over her ears, ran into the house, and slammed the door. Brad stood there a minute, staring at the door, shaking his head. "Stupid little fool," he growled. "Just like my mother. Neither of them can see what he's really like." Then, still muttering to himself, he stalked off around the house.

Pauline shook herself. "My goodness, what a soap

opera. If I didn't know better, I'd think we were watching a scene from *All My Children*."

I agreed. But Brad's relationship with Marsha or his mother or his mother's lover was none of my business. "Come on," I said. "There's nothing more we can do here, and I've got to get back to the shop."

"Right," Pauline said, going ahead of me down the walk. At the car, she stopped and looked up at the house. "And to think I used to envy her," she said, half to herself.

"Envy her?" I asked, opening the passenger door of Pauline's Mercedes and climbing in. Pauline's husband, Darryl, owns Do-Right Used Cars and makes sure that Pauline always has something mayoral to drive, even if it is four or five years old. "Envy Phoebe, you mean?"

"Yes, Phoebe." She put the key into the ignition. "After all, she has a great deal of money." After a moment, she added reflectively, "She had Ed, too, at one time."

"Ah." Pauline's date to the senior prom. "He was a football player, Ruby told me."

Pauline gave a little sigh. "Ed Knight was my first love, and in some ways, I suppose I've never quite gotten over him. We were just about ready to announce our engagement when—" She broke off, shifted into gear, and pulled out of the drive.

"That's when he got together with Phoebe, I take it," I said sympathetically. I'd never gotten a glimpse into Pauline's pre-mayoral past, and it was fascinating. "It happened when you were away at college?"

"Not exactly." Pauline was trying to keep her voice even. "Ed and I couldn't afford to go away to college. We had to live at home to keep expenses down. Anyway, we'd both gotten scholarships at CTSU, so there was never any question of going anywhere else. Phoebe's father sent her to Newcomb College in New Orleans, where she could learn the social graces as well as get a degree in art. And of course, there was Europe in the summers."

"Ah," I said. I knew about Newcomb; my mother had gone to school there a generation before Phoebe, when it was still a women's college. By the late seventies, when Phoebe would have attended, it had already been integrated into Tulane University. But in many ways it was still very much a Southern women's college.

"But then she ran into Ed at the plant," Pauline went on. "He worked there during green season, when the cucumbers came in."

"And she decided she wanted him?"

"Exactly." Pauline's voice took on a sour edge. "She was beautiful, rich—she could have had anybody. But she wanted *him* because he was mine, and because her parents opposed it. . . ." She was silent for a moment, the muscles in her jaw working. "The next thing I knew, she was wearing his letter sweater, and a few weeks later, a ring as big as a house. He must have mortgaged his soul to pay for that diamond. Ed was really excited about becoming a teacher and a high school coach. Instead, he married Phoebe and wound up pushing pickles."

"It must have been difficult for you," I murmured, wondering if Pauline had married Darryl on the rebound.

"It was *hell*," Pauline said fervently. "I knew she'd make him unhappy. He was a very sweet guy, but not very—" She shrugged. "You know. Not very aggressive. He'd go along once you got him headed in the right direction, but Phoebe had to have made the moves."

There was silence for a moment, as Pauline negotiated the first of a trio of hairpin turns and I thought about the irony of all this. Pauline might have been different when she was younger, but I somehow doubted it, and in her own way, she was as manipulative and in-your-face as Phoebe. If Ed and Pauline were dating, he was probably already sizzling in Pauline's frying pan before he jumped into Phoebe's fire.

I broke the silence, going back to something she'd said earlier. "Ed came to talk to you, though. When he and Phoebe were having difficulty, I mean."

"Yes." The word was colored with remembered pleasure. "He would sit in my kitchen and drink a beer and tell me how unhappy he was. Of course, this was later, after Darryl and I were married. After Phoebe's family were all dead, and she was running the plant." She turned the wheel, going into the second curve. "She was his boss, and she never let him forget it."

Another silence. "I heard that he drove off a road somewhere," I said.

Suddenly, without warning, Pauline swung the wheel toward the outside of the road, and I grabbed for the armrest, panicked. She braked hard, pulling into a graveled overlook, within inches of a metal guardrail.

"Here," she said. "Here's where it happened." She put both elbows on the wheel and covered her face with her hands. "The road was narrower then, and they hadn't yet put up the guardrail. There were no skid marks, no evidence that he'd tried to brake, nothing. He just sailed right off the road and into the river."

I sucked in my breath and looked down, feeling cold at the pit of my stomach. The limestone cliff fell steeply to the river below, lined with cottonwoods and sycamores. It was a long way to the bottom.

Pauline dropped her hands. "The sheriff said it was an accident. Drunk driving. I don't doubt that he'd been drinking—toward the end, he was always half drunk. But it wasn't an accident."

I turned to face her. "You think he drove off this cliff intentionally?"

"I think he felt he didn't have any other choice," Pauline replied stoically. "She had completely destroyed him. There was nothing left of the man he'd been."

"How old was Brad when this happened?"

"Twelve. Old enough to know what was going on between his parents. He must have realized the truth. I'm sure that's why he's been so aimless and unmotivated in the past few years."

We sat for a moment in silence, Pauline staring through the windshield as if she were looking into the long-ago past of her relationship with Ed Knight. I was silent too, thinking quizzically about Brad's mother going off with her young lover on the eve of PickleFest, leaving the rest of us to guess where she was and when she'd be back. It was the ultimate kind of manipulation and control, designed to keep everybody in the dark while Phoebe went out and enjoyed herself. But there were other puzzles as well: the relationship between her and her son, that business with McQuaid about a suspected embezzlement, the rumor that Morgan's was for sale. There was an intricate web of complexities here, and Phoebe was like a spider, crouching in the center of it all. A black widow spider, if I wanted to carry the metaphor a little further.

Pauline broke her reverie with a shiver. She shifted into first gear, spun the wheels, and we lurched back onto the asphalt, heading downhill, gathering speed. I'd be back at the shop by three.

Chapter Seven

Echinacea (*Echinacea purpurea*), also called purple coneflower, is a perennial herb native to North America. It has a daisy-like blossom, with purple petals that droop around an orange center. The plant was called "snake root" by the Plains Indians, because they dug the roots and used them to make a poultice to treat snake and spider bites.

Thursday night is McQuaid's night to cook, and I got home to find a Tex-Mex casserole on the table and everybody ready to eat. We all sat down without any preliminaries and polished off the casserole and salad with gusto. I usually do the cleanup when McQuaid cooks (and vice versa), but Amy had volunteered for that assignment while she was staying with us. McQuaid and I left her and Brian to deal with the kitchen and went for a walk through the garden and down by the creek.

There's nothing spectacular about our small slice of the Hill Country, but it does have its own unique beauty. The weekend rain had given the early summer wildflowers a new lease on life, and the purple-and-orange echinacea, lavender horsemint, black-eyed Susans, bright yellow Mexican hat, and red-and-yellow firewheel splashed the garden and meadow with color so bright it looked as if paint had been spilled over the landscape. As we left the backyard and took the narrow, winding path down to the creek, I saw that the plump reddish pods of the antelope-horn milkweed were splitting open, spilling a creamy fluff. I paused to pick one, opening it wider and pulling out a pinch of the soft white silk. In pioneer times, milkweed down was used to make a candlewick that was said to burn cleaner than cotton. I prefer to leave the milkweed to the finches, which carry off the down to line their nests, and to the Monarch caterpillars, which feed solely on this bitter-tasting plant (which in turn, is said to give them a thoroughly disagreeable taste, so the birds won't eat them). Without milkweed, there wouldn't be any Monarchs.

I dropped the pod and hurried to catch up to McQuaid. We hadn't had a chance to talk privately yet, and I was eager to let him know what I'd learned that day and find out if he'd discovered anything interesting.

"Have you heard from Phoebe Morgan since you began that investigation for her?" I asked.

McQuaid shook his head. "I told her I'd contact her when I was ready to make an interim report. That won't be until Monday, probably. Why?"

"Because," I said, "she seems to have gone off somewhere."

"Gone off?" McQuaid gave me a puzzled look. "I know she missed a meeting with your committee last night, but— gone off? What's that supposed to mean?"

"Phoebe's assistant, Marsha, last saw Phoebe on Sunday afternoon. Phoebe told Marsha she was going to the plant to do some work on the books, and then she had an appointment—with you, I presume, although Marsha doesn't seem to know that. Anyway, that's the last anybody's seen of her." I paused. "What did she tell you about her plans for the week? Did she say that she was going anywhere? Santa Fe, maybe?"

McQuaid's puzzled look changed to a frown. "She didn't say a word about traveling, and she certainly gave the impression that she'd be around if I wanted to get in touch with her. What makes you think she might have gone to Santa Fe?"

"Because Todd, her live-in boyfriend, is gone, as well, along with the new car Phoebe gave him. Marsha says they may have driven to Santa Fe, where Phoebe's arranged for a showing of Todd's paintings. I'm not sure Marsha actually believes it, though," I added. "Phoebe's son Brad is worried. He said he was sorry he brought Todd into the household. He thinks Todd is out to take advantage of his mother and—"

"Take advantage of Phoebe Morgan?" McQuaid laughed shortly. "In a pig's eye. The way I read the lady, it'll turn out to be the other way around. *She's* taking advantage of him."

"Could be," I said. I bent over to admire a clump of fragile-looking mountain pinks, or quinine weed, thrusting like a small bouquet out of the gravel-strewn limestone soil. Years ago, the plant was dried and brewed as a tea to reduce fevers. I'm always amazed at the great variety of plants that have appeared in somebody's medicine chest. I straightened up. "How's your investigation going? Have you learned anything about Vince Walton?"

"Plenty," McQuaid said. "It looks as if Phoebe was right in her suspicions. He hasn't been very clever about it, either." He made a face. "The investigation was almost too easy. Personally, I prefer a bit more challenge."

"Too easy, huh? What's he been buying? Cars? Real estate?"

"Both of the above, and more." The corner of his mouth quirked. "Several hundred acres in Arkansas, a four-wheel-drive off-road vehicle, a muscle boat. And a couple of bank accounts, totaling about a hundred thousand dollars."

I nodded thoughtfully. "Not the kind of thing he could finance on what he's making as plant manager. Which is what? Sixty thou?"

"Fifty. Phoebe doesn't believe in pampering the hired help. That's probably why he decided to skim. And he's not financing any of his purchases. He's using cash, and investing in the market, to boot." He grinned. "Not the smartest place to put the money, maybe."

I raised my eyebrows. And he didn't consider this investigation challenging? "How'd you get all that information—and so quickly, too?"

"Hey," McQuaid said in an injured tone, "are you asking me to share my trade secrets?"

"I was just wondering what happened to personal privacy," I said in a teasing tone. "So how *did* you get all that information?"

"I'm a devious son of a gun," McQuaid said lightly. He hooked his arm over my shoulder. "I lie a lot—except to my nearest and dearest, of course. I always tell her the truth, the whole truth, and nothing but the truth, so help me God." He leaned over and kissed the top of my ear.

"Did Phoebe give you any hints about how Walton has managed to get that kind of money out of the business?" I persisted.

"Boy, when you start in on a guy, you don't quit," McQuaid said, smiling crookedly. "She told me that she was handling the inside investigation herself. I got the impression that she's brought somebody in to go over the books. It's not a formal audit, though. She didn't want to raise any suspicions at this point. I gather that she'd like to catch her embezzler red-handed." He grinned. "Maybe she's planning on having him drawn and quartered, instead of letting the DA have all the fun."

"Kate Rodriguez," I said thoughtfully. "I'll bet that's who."

"Who what?"

"The person Phoebe brought in to go over the books. Kate helped Jon and Amy set up the new computer system at the vet clinic, and Ruby and I were thinking of hiring her to help with our bookkeeping. Amy told me that she's working at Morgan's three or four days a week. She's a good choice. Very thorough and meticulous, but sweet and innocent-looking. She's thirty, probably, but looks twenty. Totally nonthreatening."

McQuaid was silent for a moment. "I wonder what Kate Rodriguez has dug up so far," he said in a speculative tone. "And I wonder how much Phoebe told her about the situation."

I had to smile. "Kind of hard, not being able to see the whole pickle, huh?" In the old days, when he was on the police force, McQuaid would have been in charge of the entire investigation, rather than just a piece of it.

"Maybe." McQuaid shrugged. "But as long as I've got a paying client, I'll settle for half a look." He pursed his lips. "Assuming that she *is* a paying client, and not a flight risk. Run that by me again, China. Santa Fe, was it?"

"That's what Marsha says." I frowned. "But I wonder.

Why would she just up and leave, the week before Pickle-Fest? And why hasn't she checked in?"

"Hell, I don't know," McQuaid said. "A sudden, virulent attack of passion? Or maybe she heard that Vince Walton is squirreling away a stash in Santa Fe, and she went out to take a look. I'm not going to worry about it. Chances are she'll be back tomorrow, ready to roll up her sleeves and take over again." His eyes glinted mischievously. "That'll make you happy, huh?"

I shuddered. "I don't think so. We got more done in ninety minutes with Marsha than we do in three or four hours with Phoebe, who always has to pick over every detail, like a chicken with a bit of moldy corn. As far as I'm concerned, she can come back after PickleFest is over. Then she's your problem. Yours and Vince Walton's."

"Thanks, China," McQuaid said dryly. "You're sweet. The joy of my life."

"I know. I love you too." I gave him a wicked grin. "What did the girl pickle say to the boy pickle on Valentine's Day?" When he didn't answer immediately, I said, " 'You mean a great dill to me.' "

"Grrr," McQuaid said, snatching at me.

I ducked under his arm and danced just out of reach. "What's green and flies through the air?"

"Super Pickle, of course." McQuaid scowled. "How long are you going to keep on digging up these stupid pickle jokes?"

"Until I can't remember any more," I replied. "What do you call a pickle who is a poor loser?" I couldn't wait for him to guess, so I yelled, triumphantly, "A sour pickle!"

I had to run fast to get away from him.

* * *

I was in the room I use as an office, finishing up a new
menu on the computer, when Amy came in, barefoot and
wearing a ragged green T-shirt and frayed cutoffs. Her face
was clean, and she had taken out all but three or four earrings. She sat down on the sofa and pulled her knees up
under her chin, looking sad, vulnerable, and not much
older than Brian.

"A long day at the clinic?" I asked. I moved a graphic
from one side of the page to the other and sat back to admire the effect.

"Sort of." She cleared her throat. "Actually, I was hoping that you could give me some information."

"If it's about having babies," I said, "I'm not the person
to ask. Haven't been there, haven't done that."

"Yet," Amy said with a small smile. "There's a first time
for everything." She hesitated. "Actually, my question has
to do with Texas law."

"Oh, that," I said. I made another small adjustment on
the page and nodded, satisfied. Funny how an eighth of an
inch can make such a big difference. "Yeah, I might be able
to help. What's your question?"

"It's about parental rights. I'm not going to marry the
baby's father, but I need to know what rights he has, and
how this might affect me and the baby."

"Very good," I said approvingly. "You're headed in the
right direction."

She raised her eyebrows. "Why do you say that?"

"Because fathers *do* have rights, and mothers don't always take them into consideration." I pushed the print button and watched tomorrow's menu inching out of the

printer, looking as if a professional designer had created it. Janet would be thrilled.

"And babies have rights, too," I added. "Quite apart from anything else, there are a lot of diseases with genetic roots." I thought of Huntington's disease, the awful genetic illness that had cropped up in my mother's family, where the relationships were obscured and confused, both by adultery and by adoption. "If nothing else, children ought to be able to identify their biological parents." It was something that Amy knew from her own experience, having had to search for her birth mother.

"That's true, of course, but it's not exactly what I'm thinking of." Amy's triangular face looked pinched, and there were dark shadows under her eyes. "Once I've told the father that I'm pregnant, what can he do?"

"Well, I'm not a family law specialist," I said, "but there are some pretty basic things here. First off, it doesn't matter who you *say* the baby's father is. You can name anybody, but he's not considered the father, judicially speaking, until he either voluntarily acknowledges paternity or his paternity has been established through DNA testing. And even if he acknowledges it, he ought to insist on testing, to make sure there's no fraud."

"Fraud?" Amy looked puzzled.

"Well, I know *you* wouldn't stoop to naming the wrong man, but some women do." The printer was on its sixth copy and everything looked good. "In fact, almost a third of the men who are tested for paternity turn out *not* to be the biological fathers. There are plenty of cases of paternity fraud around, and too many guys have let themselves be deceived or bullied into paying the bills for some other man's kid." I grinned. "Excuse me for lecturing. I used to be a defense attorney, remember? My sympathies are naturally with the underdog."

"So how does the guy get tested?"

I countered with another, more specific question. "Is the father likely to acknowledge paternity?" I thought fleetingly of Brad. I had no idea how he would respond if Amy were to name him, but I could predict what Phoebe would do. Her first instinct would be to deny the allegation. But if the test proved that Brad was the father, it would be like Phoebe to try to step in and get custody of her grandchild. Was that why Amy was so reluctant to identify the baby's father?

"Would he acknowledge paternity?" Amy repeated thoughtfully. "I doubt it. He probably wants to keep it a secret even more than I do." She shook her head with an ironic half-smile. "But I'm afraid I don't know him well enough to guess. Doesn't say much for my judgment, does it?"

If Ruby were here, I might point out that this remark seemed to let Jon out as a possible paternity candidate, since Amy must know Jon fairly well. But she would probably just shake her head and say something like, "Since when does a woman know a man well enough to guess what he'd do in a situation like this?" And she'd be right, I suppose.

"If the man voluntarily acknowledges paternity," I said, "there's a Texas Administrative Code form that both of you can sign. Once it's filed with the Bureau of Vital Statistics, it's official."

She raised her eyes. "And if he doesn't want to sign the form?"

"If you want him to accept his parental rights and obligations, you get a lawyer and file suit. The court will order the testing and rule on the results." The printer stopped and I gathered up the copies and put them into an envelope. Tomorrow, I would insert them into the menu folders. "Once paternity has been established, the court rules on custody, the amount of support, and the noncustodial parent's visitation."

"And if I don't want this guy involved in my baby's life? If I'm willing to forgo child support?" Amy's voice became brittle, urgent. "Is there a law that says I have to do any of this, China?"

I began to shut down the computer. "Only if you're seeking state support for the child. As long as you can support your child yourself, you can go it alone." At the look of relief that crossed her face, I added a caveat. "But concealing paternity may not be a good idea in the long run, Amy. As I said, children ought to be able to identify their biological parents. And what if something should happen to you? Who will take care of your child?"

"Take care of—" She frowned at this new idea. "My mother, I guess. She's my only relative. She and Shannon."

"Your mother has had breast cancer," I said bluntly. "And your sister is busy with her own life. What if neither of them can do it? Or what if they don't want to? After all, taking on somebody else's child might not be on their agenda."

She bit her lip and looked away again.

"It's something to consider," I said, putting the envelope out where I'd be sure to see it in the morning. "If a mom gets sick and can't work, somebody has to help pay the bills. And if the mom dies—" At the look on her face, I stopped.

She sighed. "Well, if you want to know the truth, I wrote to him last week." She added hastily, "I thought he had a right to know, that's all. I don't want anything from him, but I thought he should decide how he wants to be involved."

"Has he written back, or called?" I was guessing that he hadn't, or she would have been asking different questions.

She shook her head mutely.

"Well, your questions show that you're thinking about what's best for everybody concerned," I said. "And I'm glad you've let him know, Amy. The baby is his, too."

"But if he were involved, he'd probably just mess things up." With a wry irony, she added, "I know I don't always act responsibly, but he's even less responsible than I am."

I nodded, thinking that her description certainly fitted what I had known of Brad, although I had been rather favorably impressed earlier that day. And for what it was worth, it didn't fit Jon Green—at least, the Jon Green I thought I knew. But then, I didn't know much about him, did I? I hadn't even known that he and his wife were separated.

"It's hard to decide what to do," I said sympathetically.

She nodded and the tears started to come. "Everything just seems so damn complicated, China," she said in a little-girl voice. "Maybe Mom is right. Maybe I should just have an abortion and be done with it."

"Don't make that decision when you're feeling down," I said. I went over to the sofa and sat down beside her, gathering her against me. "Anyway, you don't have to do anything right away. Can you take a few days off work to get some rest and think about what you want to do?"

She leaned her head against my shoulder. "I think I'd rather be at work," she said in a muffled voice. "Jon depends on me, and I hate to let him down. And when I'm busy, I don't have time to keep going over things in my mind." She paused, and added more firmly, "But I know what I *don't* want to do. I don't want to go to that birthday party Mom's giving on Sunday."

"I can't blame you for that," I said. "But sometimes we just have to do things, even when we don't want to."

"Why?" she asked, pushing out her lower lip. "Grandma will ask me all sorts of questions, and Grammy will make nasty cracks about my hair and my—"

"Hey," Brian said, coming into the room, "you guys want some popcorn? Dad and me are makin' it." His pet tarantula, Ivan the Hairible, crawled around his neck and perched on his shoulder. Ivan is about the size of a saucer, and quite impressive. He impresses me, anyway. Brian has never been bitten, but I keep thinking that it's bound to happen. I've been assured that tarantula bites are no worse than a bee sting, but you can't prove it by me.

Beside me, Amy sat up straight. "You know, Brian, if Ivan falls off your shoulder, she could be badly injured. It's really not a good idea to carry her around."

Brian frowned at her. "Ivan's a boy, not a girl. Anyway, he can jump. He won't fall."

"If she's startled, she can easily lose her grip," Amy replied. "And tarantulas are more fragile than they look." She flashed a smile. "And she *is* a female, honest. For one thing, she's big. Male tarantulas are pretty small. For another—" She got up from the sofa, gently took Ivan from Brian's shoulder, and turned her over. "See that little ridge at the bottom of her abdomen? Only females have it. And she doesn't have tibula spurs on her front walking legs, either. A male needs them, in order to lock the female's fangs open while he's mating with her."

"So she can't eat him, huh?" I shook my head. "Females are *so* predatory."

"Bummer," Brian said, chagrined. "I can't believe I made a mistake like that. Except that the guy I bought him—her—from said she was a he. She was a lot littler then."

Amy put the spider in Brian's hand. "It's an easy mistake to make. Anyway, females are more interesting—and they live longer. Are you going to change her name?"

"I'll have to think about it." He stared down at his spider, then looked up at Amy. "Will she have babies?"

"She might. When did she molt last?"

"About three months ago. I've got it written down in my notebook upstairs. I took some pictures, too." He eyed her eagerly. "Want to see them?"

I shuddered. Spiders are one thing—I've learned to live with them. A molting spider is something else altogether, and Brian's pictures are what Ruby would call gross. But the idea did not faze Amy.

"Sure I'd like to see them. Three months means that she's not too far into her molt cycle to mate and produce an egg sac. Do you know what species she is?"

"A Costa Rican zebra," Brian said authoritatively. *"Aphonopelma seemanni."*

She nodded. "I'll ask Jon to check with some of the local arachnid folks. Maybe somebody has a male zebra you can borrow. You'll have to watch pretty closely, though. Female tarantulas can be fierce. Given half a chance, she'll eat him."

I stood up. "All this talk about mating rituals is making me hungry. Did somebody mention popcorn?"

"Dad's making it in the kitchen," Brian said. He stopped. "Hey, thanks, Amy. You're pretty neat." He blushed furiously, not looking at her. "Really. I'm not just saying that," he muttered. "I don't know any girls who can tell the difference between a male *Aphonopelma seemanni* and a female."

"You're pretty cool too," she said, ruffling his hair. "I'm crazy about guys who are crazy about spiders."

I smiled, thinking that if Brian had to fall in love with an older woman, Amy wouldn't be a bad choice. She might be a little on the wild side, but she was a whiz when it came to spiders. I could stop worrying about a close encounter between her and Ivan in the bathroom.

"Let's go," I said, "before your father eats all the popcorn." And with that, our mutual admiration society headed for the kitchen.

Chapter Eight

PICKLING SPICE BLEND

Many people who make pickles create their own secret
blend of herbs and spices. Here is a standard recipe
that you can vary by adding hot peppers, coriander,
nutmeg, mace, allspice, or anything else you prefer. If
you want a stronger taste of dill, tuck several sprigs of
fresh dill weed into the jar as you pack your pickles.

>   2 Tbsp. mustard seed
>   2 Tbsp. dill seed
>   2 tsp. black peppercorns
>   2 tsp. whole cloves
>   1 tsp. ground ginger
>   2–3 small bay leaves, broken
>   2-inch cinnamon stick, broken
>   1 tsp. cardamom

Mix and store in a tightly covered jar.

I got to the shop early the next morning, because I
had several things to do before Ruby and I could
meet Pauline at Morgan's Pickles. I always enjoy unlock-
ing the door and stepping into Thyme and Seasons, partic-

ularly on a sunny morning, when the light cascades through the east window and puddles on the floor, brightening the room with its golden reflection. The shop isn't large, but it's crammed to overflowing with beautiful things, fragrant things, things I love to look at and smell and touch.

Ceiling-high shelves along the back wall display dozens of gleaming jars and bottles of dried herbs, salves, and tinctures. A corner rack holds colorful herb, gardening, and cookery books, and on a wooden table, I've arranged essential oils, a display of pretty bottles, and aromatherapy supplies—everything you need to enjoy herbal fragrances. Along another wall are the herbal products made by local crafters: herbal jellies, like jars full of jewels; vinegars with interesting labels; all sorts of seasoning blends; and soaps and lotions and body balms. Baskets of dried herbs are arranged in the corners, bundles of dried plants are tucked into jars and hung from the overhead beams, and braids of bright red peppers and garlic, tied with raffia, are displayed on the stone walls. And the whole place is filled with the sweet, earthy aromas of potpourri: patchouli, roses, violets, cinnamon, sandalwood. People sometimes ask if I miss my work in the city, or the city's excitement and entertainment. I don't have to even think about the answer. I *love* it here. I'm doing what feels right and healthy, what's good for me and good for the planet, as Ruby would say. I don't intend to quit doing it anytime soon.

I had already opened up, swept out, and dug the cash drawer out from under the dust rags and stuck it into the register. I was inserting the new menus into the menu folders when Laurel Wiley came in with her usual shy smile and cheerful greeting. Laurel works half-days three or four days a week in either my shop or Ruby's. This gives Ruby time to do her thing, and allows me to get into the garden—usually in the morning, when it's cool. In the afternoon, when the garden turns into a sauna, I prefer to be in the shop, which is air-conditioned.

Ruby was already in the tearoom, setting up the tables for lunch. She had asked Lisa Conrad—a young woman who helps with the catering—to come in at eleven and manage things. Janet was serving her famous herb quiche today, along with an impressive-looking but easy-to-make herbal salad and an equally easy orange-and-melon dessert flavored with lavender syrup. She had made the syrup the afternoon before, and she was already in the kitchen, setting up the dessert.

"Pauline promised we'd be back by lunchtime," I told Ruby, who was putting a vase of garden lilies on the green-painted table by the door, where we greet tearoom guests. I gave her a once-over, blinking a little at her getup: bright white bib overalls, a lime-green long-sleeved tee, lime-green sneakers, and a lime-green ribbon tying back her frizzed red hair. "Looks like you're dressed for some heavy lifting at the pickle factory," I said.

"I'll change when I come back," she replied with a grin. "I like to be a little dressier for our lunch bunch."

We said good-bye to Janet and went out to our red van, which we affectionately call Big Red Mama. Mama's former owner had painted an imaginative design of blue, green, and yellow lines and shapes on her sides, so she looks something like a Crayola box scuttling down the road. Everybody in the neighborhood is jealous because their vehicles are less entertaining, but who cares? Big Red Mama willingly hauls Janet's catering stuff and the inventory and equipment Ruby and I need to set up our booth at herb and garden shows. She was secondhand and she's got a lot of miles on her, but then so do I. Anyway, she hasn't let us down yet.

"I'm just glad that we don't have to manage a booth at PickleFest this weekend," Ruby said as we climbed into Big Mama. "Although I think we'd make money. There'll be a big crowd."

"You're optimistic," I replied, eyeing the sky. The sun had gone pale at the sight of a line of menacing thunderheads rising in the southwest. "This morning's forecast was a little ominous." No, not a little, a whole *lot*. The KVUE-TV meteorologist had pushed up the rain chances for today to seventy percent and ninety percent tomorrow, which was his way of saying that rain was a dead certainty. And even a little rain cuts into the crowd.

Ruby slammed the door as I coaxed Big Mama to start. She's not crazy about humid days. "It wouldn't dare rain on Phoebe's parade," Ruby said.

"Yeah, well, maybe Phoebe had better get her butt back here and tell that to those clouds," I said, as Mama choked and sputtered into life. I put her in gear and pulled into the alley.

"Speaking of parades, have you heard the latest?" Without waiting for me to answer, Ruby went on. "Phoebe is going to sell Morgan's to a huge pickle conglomerate in St. Louis. Parade Products."

"Where did you hear that?" I asked. I braked to let an orange tabby cross in front of us. We pause for paws. I pulled onto the street and turned left.

"One of the women in last night's astrology class works at Morgan's," she replied. "Mona—that's her name—said

the employees already know all about it, so I don't see that
it's any huge secret."

"Bet there's a lot of sour pickles out there at the plant,"
I said. Constance Letterman was sweeping her front steps
as we drove up to the corner and made a right turn. I
waved, but she didn't look up. "If I were Phoebe, I'd leave
town too."

"Folks aren't very happy, Mona says. They're afraid
that Parade will bring in their own people, and they'll lose
their jobs." Ruby looked at me. "If it was supposed to be a
secret, how did *you* find out?"

"Amy told me. Her friend Kate is working part-time on
Morgan's books."

At the mention of Amy, Ruby's face clouded. "I saw
Jonathan Green yesterday afternoon. I took my cat to the
clinic and—"

"Cat? What cat? You don't have a cat."

"I borrowed my next-door neighbor's Manx." Ruby's
tone was defensive. "The cat needed shots, so I was doing
my neighbor a big favor." She gave me an innocent look.
"Well, I had to find out, didn't I? I didn't actually come
right out and ask Jon if he was the father of Amy's—"

"I certainly hope not!" I exclaimed, horrified.

"All I asked," Ruby said patiently, "was whether he enjoyed working with Amy. After all, it's a natural question.
I'm her mother."

"And what did he say?"

"He said that Amy was indispensable." Ruby gave me
an I-told-you-so look. "He said he couldn't get along without her, and he'd be utterly lost if she went somewhere
else. Those were his exact words, China—'I'd be utterly

lost if she went somewhere else.' You see?" she added triumphantly. "I was *right*."

"See what?" I asked. "The guy sounds like a satisfied employer. Everybody should be so lucky." We were driving past the courthouse, and I saw that MaeBelle Battersby, Pecan Springs's peerless meter maid and traffic officer, was already at work. She was happily putting a ticket under the windshield wiper on Mildred Goddard's old green Buick, double-parked in front of Pratt's Drugs, where Mildred had probably gone to pick up some antacid tablets. Everybody agrees that Mildred is Pecan Springs's biggest sourpuss. She was in the shop the other day, asking about herbs for chronic indigestion. I suggested that she might try peppermint or ginger tea, or chew a few fennel seeds— and that while she was at it, she might take a close look at her diet, to see if the problem might be something she was eating. She asked me how much ginger tea she should drink, but when I told her she'd have to experiment and see what worked for her, she scowled and shook her head. She said she didn't want to have to think about it, just *take* it, so she'd go to the drugstore and get an over-the-counter remedy.

I rolled down Big Mama's window as we drove past Mildred's Buick. "Go get 'em, MaeBelle," I said, and Mae-Belle gave me a gleeful grin and a big thumbs-up. Mae-Belle puts her whole heart and soul into her work.

"Jon didn't sound like a satisfied employer to me," Ruby said darkly, when I had rolled the window back up and turned the corner onto Arroyo Street. "He sounded like a lover with a guilty conscience. And that's exactly what he looked like, too. He was blushing beet red, the whole time we were talking. He couldn't look me straight in the eye. He kept looking at the cat."

"Well, he's a vet," I said. "He's supposed to look at the cat. How else is he going to treat it? Anyway, he was probably very embarrassed. I'm sure he thought you were sticking your long nose in where it didn't belong, and he didn't know how to tell you that without hurting your feelings."

"I notice you don't have that problem," Ruby said in an injured tone. She touched the tip of her nose as if she were feeling how long it was.

"I'm just calling them the way I see them." I shook my head. "Really, Ruby, you've got some nerve. No wonder Amy gets upset at you."

At Amy's name, Ruby's tone softened. "How is she?" she asked. "I miss her, China. And I worry about her. Is she feeling okay? Does she have morning sickness?"

"Well, maybe a little," I said. "Nothing she won't get over."

"I hope she's not giving you any trouble," Ruby went on anxiously. "Not staying out too late or anything like that." She sighed. "When she was at my house, she was out every night. She almost never came home before midnight."

"She's been sticking around pretty close," I said, wondering whether Amy had changed her behavior because she was pregnant, or because she didn't have to act out for her mother. I grinned. "Last night she informed Brian that Ivan is really a girl tarantula and promised to locate a boy tarantula so the two can make tarantula whoopee. She's a girl after Brian's own heart. He is totally smitten." Then, not wanting to betray any of Amy's confidences of the night before, I changed the subject. "I was concerned about

Sheila yesterday, though. She seemed . . . well, pretty dejected. Do you really think she's looking for another job?"

"I don't know," Ruby replied, not very happily. "But if she doesn't find Mrs. Holeyfield's killers, she might want to get started. I dropped in at the newspaper yesterday afternoon to leave next week's ads, and Hark showed me the headline for today. It says, COUNCIL PRIMED TO FIRE CHIEF."

"Uh-oh," I said. "That's grim."

"You bet. The article quoted Ben Graves as saying that unless Sheila comes up with the killers by next Tuesday, he's going to make a motion to fire her and start a search for another police chief."

"Graves carries his brains in his back pocket," I said angrily. "And Hark does too, if he prints crap like that. Smart Cookie is twice as competent as anybody else they could find."

Ruby gave me a sideways glance. "Do you think we could . . . well, maybe help her out?"

"I'll do anything I can for Sheila," I said. "But if you're suggesting that the two of us should turn sleuth, you'll have to count me out. I know how much you like to play detective, but this isn't the kind of case a couple of amateurs are going to crack."

"I don't see why," Ruby replied stubbornly. "We've cracked one or two cases before, if you will recall. Tough ones, too."

"Yeah, but we got lucky. Think about it, Ruby. Where would you start your investigation?"

Ruby frowned uncertainly. "Well, I guess I'd have to visit the crime scenes. Do some investigation."

"What kind of investigation? What would you do that the police haven't already done, ten times better?" I shook my head. "Nah. This is a case that's going to be solved with forensic evidence—fingerprints, hair, fiber—or by sheer investigative persistence. Not by accident or intuition. If the city council wants to move the investigation along, they can post a reward that's big enough to tempt an informant. But if Smart Cookie's cops can't latch on to Mrs. Holeyfield's killers, there's nothing *we* can do to help—except maybe nuke Ben Graves the next time he opens his big fat mouth."

"Now there's an idea," Ruby said thoughtfully. "Maybe we can find a way to discredit him."

"No!" I said. "This is Sheila's baby, Ruby. She's the one who has to deal with it."

"Maybe you're right," Ruby conceded reluctantly. After a minute, she added, "If they do fire Sheila, you don't suppose they'll come knocking on McQuaid's door, do you? He was the acting chief after Bubba and before Sheila. Remember?"

"Oh, *rats,*" I said feelingly. "I'd forgotten about that."

Ruby grinned. "Does that make you feel more like giving Sheila a helping hand?"

I shook my head. "If the cops can't solve it, it can't be solved." Anyway, I wasn't too worried about McQuaid. He had an exciting new job to keep him busy. I wasn't going to tell Ruby about it, though. She'd offer to sign on as his Watson, and I didn't think he'd have the stomach for it.

Morgan's Premier Pickles is housed in a large concrete cube planted on a pleasant green knoll, with a parking lot in front and open fields all around. This morning, the fields were busy with a swarm of workers setting up carnival rides, judging tents, vendors' booths, an entertainers' stage, and an orderly rank of pink and blue Porta-Potties, pink for the girls, blue for the boys. Phoebe thinks of everything.

With clipboards under their arms, Marsha and Pauline were standing at the front entrance to the plant, next to a sign that said, TOURS START HERE EVERY HOUR. They were staring up at the looming gray-blue clouds, Marsha anxiously, Pauline with narrow-eyed determination. Pauline was no doubt mentally instructing the Powers That Be to hold off on the rain until the PickleFestivities were concluded.

"Good morning," Ruby said brightly, as we came up. "Looks like showers, doesn't it?"

"That's not funny," Pauline said with a frown. She adjusted the lapels of her blue mayoral blazer, which she wore over black slacks. "We don't joke about rain on Pickle-Fest weekend."

"I'm not joking, Pauline," Ruby protested. "Just look at that sky. Have you heard the weather forecast? It's—"

"Yes, you are joking," Pauline said, with the air of a schoolteacher rebuking a recalcitrant child. "It has *never* rained on a PickleFest, and it's not going to rain on this one." She gestured toward the open door. "We'll start with a quick walk-through of the plant, to check for potential problems with the tour. If this year is anything like last, we'll probably have a couple of hundred people traipsing through here tomorrow, and we don't want any of them to get hurt."

"Hey, we're on *Candid Camera*," Ruby said, pointing

up at a camera positioned to oversee the entrance. "What's that for? Are you trying to keep out rogue pickles?"

Marsha laughed. She was looking a little more relaxed today, in jeans and a yellow shirt, but the color only made her skin look more sallow, and there were dark circles under her eyes. "Actually, it's part of Morgan's antiterrorism response," she said.

"Antiterrorism?" Pauline raised skeptical eyebrows. "Aren't you carrying things a bit too far? I shouldn't think anybody would want to blow up a small pickle plant in the Texas Hill Country."

"I think Marsha's talking food terrorism," I put in tactfully. "I've been reading about this in the organic food magazines. The food industry is worried about potentially lethal pathogens being introduced into the food supply. And even if Morgan's isn't particularly worried about somebody tossing something toxic into a pickle vat, it's just good business. A strong security system is bound to make customers feel more confident."

"That's exactly right," Marsha replied. "There are six cameras working night and day, taking pictures of the entire operation. The pictures are fed into a VCR in the office." She held out her hand and glanced up worriedly at the clouds. "Let's go inside so we don't get wet."

"It's not raining," I said. "Pauline says so."

"Of course it's not raining," Pauline said briskly, opening the door. "Here we go, ladies. Keep your eyes peeled for anything that might be a problem."

"Any word from Phoebe?" I asked Marsha in a low voice as we trailed Pauline and Ruby through the door and down a short hallway.

She shook her head, her lips pressed together.

I hitched my bag higher on my shoulder. "How about Todd? Has he called?"

Another wordless shake.

"Excuse me, ladies," a man said loudly, stepping out of an open office door and blocking our way. "Tour's tomorrow. We're not open to the public today." He smiled, his teeth startlingly white against his olive skin, but his smile didn't reach his shrewd dark eyes. He was in his mid forties, tall and athletic, with a sharply angled face, dark hair, and the look of a B-western heavy.

"Hi, Vince." Marsha stepped forward. "This is Pauline Perkins, the chair of the PickleFest planning committee, and a couple of her committee members. We're just making sure that everything's set for tomorrow's tour." She added, in a conciliatory tone, "We'll stay out of the way."

I eyed the man with considerable interest. So this was the man McQuaid was investigating for embezzlement. If that's what Vince was up to, Central Casting had done a good job. He certainly looked the part.

Vince folded his arms. "Well, okay," he growled, "as long as you don't let these ladies roam around loose. We haven't put the ropes up yet, and I don't want anybody getting hurt." It was clear from his tone that tours of the plant were a damned nuisance, and if one of us fell on her fanny, he wasn't going to be held personally responsible. "Say," he added, "where's the boss lady? She hasn't been around all week, and there's a stack of checks on my desk, waiting for her to sign." He grinned mirthlessly. "The hired hands aren't going to be very happy if their pay is late. Especially under the circumstances."

Under the circumstances? The rumored sale of the plant?

Marsha made an effort to smile. "She's out of town for a few days. I'll let you know when to look for her."

Reasserting her command over the group, Pauline said, "Let's get on with the tour, shall we? We've got other things to see to this morning."

"Hope you brought your umbrellas," Vince said. His eyes rested on Ruby with an openly appreciative glance, and when he turned away, he gave her what could only have been a wink. "Looks like it's starting to come down out there." He went back into his office and shut the door.

"Not a very pleasant fellow," observed Pauline with a dark glance at the closed door. And with that, we were off to see how pickles get pickled.

If you've made your own pickles at home, or watched your grandmother do it, you already have an idea of the basic process. You can do it fast and easy by packing fresh cucumbers and pickling spices into canning jars, covering them with hot salt water and vinegar, and leaving them alone to consider their plight. They will be properly pickled in about six weeks.

Your grandmother, however, most likely made her pickles the old-fashioned way, in a five-gallon pickle crock or stone jar with a layer of pickling spices and dill on the bottom. She'd fill the crock with small, whole cucumbers, then top it off with a mixture of rock salt, vinegar, and water. She'd add another layer of dill and pickling spices, and cover the whole thing with a clean tea towel to keep out the dust and anything else that might fall or jump into it. Every day, she'd take off the tea towel and skim off the powdery film—a yeast that develops during fermentation—to keep the pickles from spoiling, and if one developed white spots or showed a tendency to float, she'd throw it away. In three weeks or so, she'd take the pickled cucumbers out and put them into canning jars, along with fresh dill, more spices, and more brine. The jars went into the canner or the pressure cooker. When they were done, she'd set the prettiest jars aside for the county fair, and line up the rest on the shelves in the cellar.

At Morgan's, they make pickles the way your grandmother did it, except instead of making enough to fill the cellar shelves, they load their finished pickles into a flotilla of eighteen-wheelers and truck them all over the country. Everything starts in the cucumber fields, where mechanized equipment plants, cultivates, irrigates, and eventually harvests the cukes, sorting and packing them into one-ton cardboard boxes that end up at Morgan's back door. A forklift dumps the cukes into ten-thousand-gallon fermentation tanks—huge cement tanks, ten feet high and twelve feet in diameter, a great deal bigger than your grandmother's stone crock. A mix of vinegar and salt water is pumped into the tank and the cucumbers are held until they are pickled—up to six months, sometimes longer. The tanks are only loosely covered with boards (instead of tea towels) and are open to the air. Every day, somebody climbs up to the top of the tank to test the salinity and add salt, if necessary.

When the pickled cukes are ready for processing, a conveyor scoops them out of the vats, they're desalted, washed, and sorted, then sliced, diced (for pickle relish), or left whole. Finally, they're packed in containers and covered with freshly mixed brine; dill oil, which is easier and cleaner to work with than fresh or dried dill; turmeric (for its color, as well as its pungent taste); and Morgan's secret blend of pickling spices. Since these pickles are destined for the institutional market, rather than grocery store shelves, they are custom-packed in two-gallon jars, five-gallon buckets, or fifty-gallon barrels depending on what the customer orders.

During PickleFest tours, the machinery is shut down so that the tour guide is able to talk and people can ask questions. Today, however, production was in full swing, and the place was as noisy as the inside of an airplane factory. We walked quickly through the plant, which smelled deliciously like dill pickle, with Pauline pointing at things and shaking her head and Marsha making notes on her clipboard. Ruby and I (although we'd had the tour before) mostly gawked, amazed all over again at the efficiency of the operation. The workers, who were intent on running the dicing and slicing and filling machines, paid so little attention to us that you'd think we were invisible.

At the back of the pickle-packing area there was a large roll-up door, tall and wide enough to let a tractor-trailer drive in and load up with pickles. We went down a slanting ramp and through the door, standing back out of the way of a forklift truck loaded with a hopper of large, shining pickles on its way up the ramp. Then we were in the tank yard, an area of about an acre that was floored with concrete and filled with rows of pickle tanks, sixty of them, according to Marsha. A noisy pump was running somewhere, but the decibel level had dropped enough to allow us to hear one another.

"Whew," Ruby said, shaking her head energetically as if to unplug her ears. "That was *loud*."

"Look!" Pauline crowed triumphantly. "The rain has stopped." She smiled up at the clouds as if to take credit for this atmospheric acquiescence to her wishes.

And then, with an ironic crack of sulfuric lightning and a bone-jarring clap of thunder, the sky fell.

"Yikes!" Ruby cried, and we dashed up the concrete ramp toward the shelter of the doorway, as the rain came bucketing down. A second bolt of lightning struck a transformer at the back of the yard and produced an impressive cascade of sparks, followed by a colorful mini fireball. The lights went off, the equipment din suddenly ceased, and all I could hear was the pouring, pounding rain. The plant darkened and the production lines shut down by the power failure, employees came to the door to watch.

"Lord love a duck," a woman said reverently. "It's a gol-durned, gosh-amighty, jim-dandy gully washer."

That's what it was, for sure. If you've ever found yourself stuck in a Texas cloudburst, it's not an occasion you're likely to forget, especially if the storm stalls out just as it reaches you and dumps its whole load of rain in your lap. That's what happened to the little town of Thrall, Texas, back in 1921, when a dying tropical depression drifted in off the Gulf and dropped thirty-six inches of rain in eighteen hours—the most that has ever fallen on a U.S. city in that amount of time. If Noah had found himself in Thrall on that fateful day, he would have herded his animals into the ark, battened down the hatches, and waited for the water to rise.

Forty-five minutes later, with the rain still pouring down like Niagara and the electricity still off, that's what it was looking like here—a rainfall for the record books. The roll-up door was run by electricity, so it couldn't be shut, and to stay dry, Pauline, Ruby, Marsha, and I had climbed the stairs to the catwalk, and stood in front of a window overlooking the tank yard. The yard was entirely concrete and was constructed so that it sloped toward a large open drain about the size of a garbage can lid.

"How come everything slopes toward that one drain?" I asked Marsha. "Doesn't seem like the best way to handle runoff."

"It isn't," a man's voice said behind me. I turned to see that Vince Walton had climbed the stairs to join us. "But that's the way the State of Texas says it has to be done," he added with a sarcastic grin. "Smart, those guys in Austin. Very smart."

"It's part of our new effluent treatment system," Marsha explained, ignoring Vince. "The plant produces thousands of gallons a week of highly acidic liquid waste."

"All that vinegar and salt, I suppose," Ruby put in.

"Right. The plant's liquid waste has a pH of less than three, which is highly acidic. It has to be neutralized, so it's drained into a huge underground tank where it's mixed with enough sodium hydroxide to raise the pH to the level of neutral water, which is somewhere around seven."

Sodium hydroxide. Caustic soda. Lye, in other words. I had read that it was commonly used to treat highly acidic wastes so that they could be safely discharged.

"See?" Marsha turned around and pointed. "There are drains all through the plant, not just outside. Every ounce of waste goes into that tank. It cost a fortune to construct."

"And then what?" Ruby asked. "What happens after you've made the waste less acidic?"

"It goes into the river," Vince said, and I remembered the neighbor who was angry about the quality of the effluent. If Morgan's was treating that much waste, maybe they occasionally made a mistake. Maybe there was something to the man's complaints.

"That tank had better be really big," Pauline said pragmatically, looking at the cascading water, "or the water's going to overflow."

"Oh, I don't think there's any danger of that," Marsha replied quickly. "It was sized to handle a much larger quantity of—"

"Oh, yeah?" Vince interrupted. "Think again, Marsh. The tank holds about a hundred thousand gallons max, and it was half full when I checked it this morning. It can take another fifty thousand gallons. But there's better than an acre of concrete out there—call it maybe fifty thousand square feet. And the rain is coming down a couple of inches an hour." He glanced at his watch and seemed to make a quick mental calculation. "An hour's rain will produce over sixty thousand gallons of runoff—and since there's no electricity, the pump has quit."

A fifth-grader could handle that one. "Ten thousand gallons over the max," I said, "and the rain doesn't show any signs of slackening."

"Then the water's going to start coming up," Vince said brusquely. "Looks like that's happening now."

We all craned our necks. He was right. The water was no longer rushing down the drain, but beginning to bubble up out of it, spreading across the concrete. In a few minutes, it was a foot or so deep and still rising. I thought fleetingly of Noah, and wondered how long it took to build that ark.

"My lucky day," Vince growled. "At this rate, it won't be long before it gets high enough to come up inside the plant. Gotta get stuff off the floor." With that, he turned and ran down the stairs, bawling orders.

"Don't you think we'd better get back to Pecan Springs, China?" Ruby asked anxiously. "We can't do what we came for, and I don't want to miss lunch. Janet's serving quiche today, and we'll have a full house."

"I'm not sure Big Red Mama wants to navigate in this downpour," I replied, thinking about the low-water crossing at River Road and Bluebonnet Trail. "She's never learned to swim, and she didn't bring her water wings. Anyway, if this goes on much longer, nobody'll show up for lunch, so you won't have to feel guilty about missing it."

"If this goes on much longer," Pauline said darkly, "we'll have to cancel PickleFest."

"Unthinkable!" Marsha exclaimed, horrified. "Phoebe would never allow that."

"If Phoebe wanted to call the shots, she should be here to do it," Pauline pointed out, in her best I'm-in-charge-here tone. "We have no idea how long it will take Pedernales to replace that transformer, and we can't have PickleFest without power. And even if it stops raining right this minute, which it doesn't show any signs of doing, the overflow parking and the festival grounds will still be impossibly muddy. And there's that dangerous low-water crossing at Bluebonnet Trail, which is probably closed already." She paused for emphasis. "Better to cancel now and reschedule."

"Bummer," Ruby said glumly. "All that work, for nothing. Down the drain, so to speak."

We all stared out the window, watching the pouring rain and thinking about the unthinkable. It shouldn't be too hard to get the word out about the cancellation through KPST, our local radio station. We could call the Austin and San Antonio television stations, too, and put up a big sign on River Road. Pauline would have to notify the entertainers, and somebody would need to call all the vendors, and—

"What's that?" I asked, pointing out the window. "Looks like a bundle of rags. It just popped up out of the drain."

"Came up out of the drain?" Marsha asked. "Why would anybody put rags into the tank? There's not supposed to be anything in there but treated . . ." She frowned. "Actually, it does look like rags, doesn't it?"

Pauline leaned closer to the window, peering out through the rain. "That's not a bundle of rags," she said. "That's a *person!*"

Ruby's hand went to her mouth. "Ohmigod," she whispered. "Somebody must have gotten washed into the tank."

A person? I saw a pale face turned up to the sky and a loose skein of yellow hair, floating. Ophelia, turning and twisting in the water. "It's a woman," I said incredulously.

"Help!" Pauline cried, turning and waving her hands in Vince's direction. "Somebody's drowning out there! Save her!"

There was a clamor of voices and several men dashed through the open door and into the pouring rain, splashing through thigh-deep water out to the place where the body seemed to be buoyed by the water bubbling up out of the underground tank. Then they had her by the wrists and were dragging her roughly through the water, up the ramp and into the plant, as we ran down the stairs to get a look.

Marsha opened her mouth to say something, but nothing came out. Her face had gone completely gray, and I thought for a second that she was going to faint.

"It's . . . it's Phoebe!" Pauline rasped. "Omigod, it's Phoebe!"

"CPR!" Ruby cried frantically. "Does anybody know CPR?"

But as Vince knelt beside the woman stretched out on the wet concrete floor, one look was enough to tell me that no amount of CPR would bring her back to life. Her eyes were wide open, unseeing. One side of her head was slightly concave, and it was grotesquely clear that she hadn't gone into the water in the last hour. Her face, throat, and arms were bleached and puckered, and her jeans and blouse seemed to be shrunken and pasted against her body like a second skin. She'd been in that tank for several days.

I turned away, trying not to gag, and reached into my shoulder bag for my cell phone. We don't have really great coverage around Pecan Springs, and you never know whether you're within range of a tower. But inside a half minute I was talking to the 911 dispatcher, and almost before I could blink, Sheriff Blackie Blackwell himself was on the line.

"You're sure she's dead?" he asked, when I had given him a quick rundown of the situation.

"She's dead," I said grimly, resisting the temptation to say that she was not only totally dead but thoroughly pickled. "You'll probably have to come around the long way, out past the Back Forty and the shooting range. River Road is shorter, but the crossing at Bluebonnet is likely to be under water. And if you need lights, you'll have to bring your own. Lightning wiped out a transformer, and the power's down here."

"Give us thirty minutes," Blackie said. "Meanwhile, don't let anybody leave."

I looked out the door at the rain, which was pounding down as hard as ever. "Are you kidding?" I asked.

Chapter Nine

QUESTION: What is green and carries a gun?
ANSWER: Marshall Dill.

❀ It was more like forty minutes before the sheriff showed up. The rain was slackening somewhat, but the ankle-deep water on the plant floor was still rising. Vince and a couple of guys loaded Phoebe's body on a wooden pallet and used the forklift truck to hoist it waist-high, and hold it there. I wasn't sure exactly why, since the body had obviously spent several days in the water already. Out of respect, maybe—although I have to say that there was a certain macabre comedy about the scene, with the body laid out on the forklift as if it were held in the rigid arms of a giant mechanical monster. Beauty and the beast.

I didn't see much respect written on the faces of the employees, either—fourteen or fifteen male plant workers, mostly Hispanic, plus a pair of women office workers, standing with their arms around each other, shivering. If anything, what I read in the occasional unguarded glance was sheer relief and a few flickers of hope. I could imagine the reasons. With the boss lady dead and out of the picture, Morgan's Pickles might stay in the family and their jobs would be safe—not a very secure hope, I would guess, but when the water's rising, you grasp any straw that floats past, no matter how flimsy.

What Vince might have felt, if anything, was impossible to read on that impassive face. Accepting the inevitable rather quickly, he had given up the fruitless effort to resuscitate Phoebe and had gone back to directing the moving of equipment and pickle products out of reach of the water. I looked around for Brad, but he was nowhere in sight, and when I asked Marsha if she knew where he was, she only shook her head, tight-lipped and white. I got the same wordless response when I asked her if Phoebe had any other relatives—aunts, uncles, cousins—who should be notified of her death. Marsha was standing off to one side, her arms wrapped tightly around herself as if she were cold, or trying to hold in her feelings.

What did we do before cell phones were invented? There was no more debate about whether the PickleFest would or would not be held—Pauline was already calling people to make arrangements to cancel. Ruby phoned the tearoom and learned that, yes, indeed, lunch was a wash-out, big time. Not even Janet's quiche was going to lure people out in this downpour.

I tried calling McQuaid at home, but got no answer. He answered his cell phone, however, in Charlie Lipman's law office, where he had gone to leave his business cards and drum up some new clients.

"I hope you're not driving in this mess," he said. "Wherever you are, stay right there until it stops."

"I don't have much choice," I replied grimly. "I'm stuck at a crime scene. Your client is no longer missing, she's dead. I've already called the sheriff's office. Blackie is on his way."

"My client?" McQuaid asked warily. "Dead? You're telling me that Phoebe Morgan is *dead*?"

"Indubitably," I said. "I hope you got a retainer check from her when she hired you."

In the background, I could hear Charlie Lipman yelp incredulously, "Phoebe? Phoebe's dead? Wot the *hail* did she wanna go and do that for?"

Charlie Lipman grew up in an upper-class Dallas suburb, spent a year at Oxford, and can speak impressively standard English when he needs to. Fishing, hunting, or hanging out with the good old boys at the barber shop, he talks Texan. He also talks Texan during moments of great stress. This was one of those moments.

"Phoebe is Charlie's client, too," McQuaid reminded me. "He represents Morgan's Pickles."

"Well, then, tell Charlie that your client appears to have been murdered," I said. "She might've managed to accidentally bang her head hard enough to cave in her skull, but I doubt that she'd dive into the effluent treatment tank on her own. It's not a place you'd want to go for a swim."

"Effluent tank?" McQuaid asked in a bewildered tone.

I sighed. "It's kind of hard to explain. You'd better come and take a look for yourself. Anyway, you'll want to tell Blackie what you turned up when you went looking into Vince Walton's background."

I could almost see McQuaid narrowing his eyes, assessing the possible reasons why Vince might be at the top of Blackie's suspect list. "You stay there," he said unnecessarily. "I'm on my way."

"Bluebonnet's probably under water," I said, and added, "Would you mind stopping at the Back Forty to pick up some barbecue? I don't know about Ruby and Pauline, but

I'm hungry, and we may be here for a while. I'll call and order chopped beef sandwiches for five if you'll pick them up. You can eat yours on the way."

"Six," McQuaid said. "Get one for Charlie."

The place got very busy when the sheriff and his team arrived, followed shortly by an EMS ambulance, which pulled through the yard, the water up to the top of the tires, then up the ramp and directly into the plant. Then a couple of trucks from the Pedernales Electrical Co-op showed up, one of them with a spare transformer, the other one a cherry picker, to lift the worker up to the top of the pole. Not long after this, McQuaid splashed in with a sack full of chopped beef sandwiches, bags of chips, and (since Coke machines don't work very well when the power is off) the six-pack of cold soft drinks I'd ordered. Charlie Lipman was with him, as well. I left Ruby and Pauline and splashed over to join them.

"Blessings on you," I said gratefully, taking the food. "A girl could starve around here. Hello, Charlie," I added. "Did you come to pay your respects to the deceased?"

"I came to see that nothin' accident'ly on purpose disappears outta the office," Charlie said. He's put on a good twenty-five pounds in the last couple of years, and gravity is doing its thing on his heavy cheeks and jowls. He still carries himself with authority, but there's a sarcastic twist to his mouth. When he occasionally remembers to smile, you can glimpse the man he used to be, before life's disappointments turned him sour. "From what McQuaid tells me," he added darkly, "there's bin some serious monkey bidness goin' on out here. Somebody fiddlin' the books."

The sheriff came over to join us, nodding first to Mc-Quaid, and then to Charlie. The three of them are poker buddies, and they've spent uncounted midnight hours at my kitchen table, growling at each other over a three-dollar pot.

"I figure McQuaid's here to bring lunch," Blackie said, glancing at the bag I was holding. "You here on official business, Charlie?"

"You might say," Charlie agreed. "I'm Phoebe's attorney. Ditto Morgan's. Thought I'd better come and tie things down so they don't float away. Records, ledgers, floppy disks, stuff like that. You never can tell what folks'll do, once the boss ain't around." Charlie regarded the sheriff. "On the other hand, I reckon you'll probably want to take care of some of that, seein' as how it might be evidence."

Blackie thought for a moment. "Reckon you're right," he replied, in his low, slow drawl. "Tell you what, Charlie. Why don't you take Garcia and do an inventory? That way, we'll both know what's what. Garcia's a good man, but he doesn't know a floppy disk from a floppy hat. We'll take custody for now, but you can have all the access you need."

Charlie nodded. He looked past Blackie to where Phoebe lay, stretched out on the pallet on the arms of the forklift. "How long's she been dead?"

"Don't know yet." Blackie pushed his white Stetson to the back of his head. Stetson and cowboy boots: required regalia for Texas sheriffs, on the job and off. "There are abrasions on the wrists and ankles. She might've been tied to something to keep her body from floating to the surface. Looks like there was a hell of a lot of water pouring into that tank," he added. "Could have kicked up enough turbulence to work her free from whatever was weighting her down."

During the nearly fifteen years I was in the legal business, I dealt with a great many law-enforcement types, mostly in antagonistic situations. I didn't much enjoy having them as opponents and there aren't many that I would choose as friends—with the exception of McQuaid and Sheila and Sheriff Blackwell. Blackie looks the way you'd expect an experienced cop to look: big as a truck, square jaw, determined chin, watchful eyes. He's a true straight-arrow, but he often shows more compassion and sensitivity than you'd expect from a cop and when the going gets tough, he just gets quieter, more measured, more deliberate, and slower. I've seen him move fast only once, when he was deep-frying a mess of catfish in a kettle in his backyard and the oil caught fire.

"I saw her come up," I said. "Like a cork." Bodies do that, I remembered with a shudder. The process of decomposition creates intestinal gasses that—I made myself stop. This was not something I wanted to think about with a bag of fragrant Back Forty chopped beef sandwiches in my hand.

Charlie raised his hand. "Guess I better take care of bidness 'fore somebody takes care of it for me," he said, and slouched off in the direction of the office.

Blackie turned to McQuaid. "So how come you're here?"

"Thought I ought to talk to you," McQuaid said. "Phoebe Morgan hired me to take a private look into the finances of the plant manager, Vince Walton. She suspected him of embezzling."

Blackie did not seem surprised by the news that McQuaid was for hire, so I assumed that the PI business was something they had discussed—at length, probably. And probably long before McQuaid let me in on the secret.

"That might narrow the suspect list down some," Blackie allowed. "What did you come up with?"

"More than enough to give you some good leverage. I wrote a draft report this morning, expecting to deliver it to my client next week. Guess I'll give it to you. And to Charlie, if that's okay."

Blackie nodded briefly. "No problem there."

"Right. When I get back home, I'll email the report to your office. You'll probably want to go over it before you question Walton. I don't know if he killed her, but he's damn sure guilty of something."

Blackie seemed relieved. "Yeah, well, maybe we can get this investigation wrapped up in a hurry."

"Don't close it off too fast," I cautioned. "Vince isn't the only suspect."

McQuaid frowned at me. "Oh, yeah? You have another candidate?"

Blackie eyes narrowed imperceptibly. "Are you involved in this, China?"

"Not really involved," I said hastily. "I mean, I know some of the people." I reconsidered. "That is, I don't really *know* them, but I know enough about them to—"

Blackie cleared his throat.

"Right," I said. "You need to see if you can find Todd Kellerman, Phoebe's live-in boyfriend. He's been gone since last Sunday—which, coincidentally, is the last day anybody saw Phoebe. For the details, you should talk to Marsha Miller over there." I gestured. "She's Phoebe's assistant. Was," I corrected myself, thinking that Marsha would definitely have to find a new job. After the past week, she was probably ready to go back to the relative tranquility of the County Clerk's office, where the only people who really give you heartburn are the ones who come in to complain about not receiving their property deeds. Out loud, I said, "Oh, and Marsha will tell you that Phoebe had an appointment with somebody on Sunday afternoon. Just so you know, it was McQuaid."

"That's correct," McQuaid said. "She came over about four-thirty and stayed for about a half hour. I don't know where she was headed when she left, though."

"There's something else you should know," I said. "Phoebe was planning to sell the plant. I can't tell you the status of the deal, but the word was definitely out. The employees knew it, I understand."

Blackie looked toward Ruby and Pauline, then looked back at me with a frown. He knows Pauline well and he's had occasion to deal with Ruby a time or two. I could tell that he wasn't wild about seeing either one of them at his crime scene. "What are they doing here?" he asked, nodding in their direction.

"PickleFest," I said. "It was supposed to be tomorrow, and we came to make sure that the setup was going according to plan. Pauline has canceled, though. First the rain, now this."

He grunted. "Good thing. We couldn't have a bunch of people traipsing around the crime scene. Where's this Marsha person? And the son. Brad Knight. He works here, doesn't he?"

"I haven't seen him—Oh, there he is." I pointed in the direction of the forklift, where Brad, stunned and uncomprehending, was standing beside his mother's body. I looked around. "Marsha might be in the restroom. Want me to find her?"

He nodded. "I'm going to do the first round of questioning in the office back there." To McQuaid, he said, "I'll hold off on Walton until I see your report."

"I'll get right on it," McQuaid said. He bent over to peck my cheek. "You and Ruby stay out of the sheriff's hair," he said, and left.

Blackie was turning in the direction of Brad, but I put a hand on his arm. "At the risk of getting in your hair, I need to tell you something else. The plant is protected by security cameras, six of them." I pointed up at one tucked into a high corner. "Marsha says they're on all day and night, and that the pictures are recorded onto a VCR in the office. I don't know if there's one positioned to spy on the effluent tank, but if so, you might have a shot of the killer doing his dirty work."

"Oh, yeah?" Blackie asked. A grin creased his face. "You're a fountain of knowledge, China."

"We do our best," I said modestly. I took the lunch to Ruby and Pauline, who was still on her cell phone, making cancellation arrangements, and went in search of Marsha. I found her in the darkened restroom, pale and red-eyed, throwing up into one of the toilets. When she was finished and had washed her face, I told her that the sheriff wanted to talk to her.

She grew even more pale. "I don't . . . I can't possibly—" She swallowed.

"Sure you can," I said encouragingly. "Nothing to it. Just tell him what happened. This doesn't have anything to do with you. Not personally, I mean."

"But Todd—" She stopped again, biting her lip.

So it did have something to do with her personally—with her feelings about Todd, that is. She knew he was bound to be a suspect, and she didn't want to be the one to incriminate him. Maybe she knew more about his absence than she had been letting on. She might even know something about Phoebe's murder, as well, and she had been hiding her knowledge all week.

"Look, Marsha," I said, in a lawyerly tone. "If you have information that might help the sheriff find out who killed Phoebe, you need to tell him." I took her hand. "So be a good girl. Go talk to him."

She pulled away from me, standing her ground. Her lips were trembling and she made an effort to tighten them. "Only if you come, too."

I shook my head. "He doesn't want to talk to me, he wants to talk to you. You're Phoebe's assistant. You know more about her business than anybody."

"But I'm entitled to a lawyer, aren't I? Isn't that what the law says?" Her mouth set stubbornly. "You're a lawyer. Come with me."

I frowned. "You're not under arrest, Marsha. Which means that you're free to get up and leave anytime you want to. You can even refuse to answer questions. You don't need a lawyer unless you're afraid of saying something that might lead to your being charged with a crime." I looked at her more closely. What was she hiding? "Are you?"

Her eyes slid away. "Not . . . exactly."

"Not exactly? What does that mean?"

She pressed her lips together and took a deep breath. "It's my constitutional right. If you don't come with me, I won't talk to him until I can find another lawyer, and that will just slow down the investigation. I'm sure the sheriff won't like that."

This was complicated. Prudently, I've kept my membership in the State Bar of Texas, paying my dues and taking the required hours of continuing education. I haven't taken a case in years, however, and I don't plan to take one anytime soon. On the other hand, back in law school, our professors drummed it into us wannabe lawyers that the right to an attorney is as fundamental as the right to free speech. If it was okay with Blackie, I was willing to sit in on the interview, and besides, I was infernally curious. What did Marsha know that made her so wary? What *was* she hiding?

"I'll come with you," I said, "as long as it's very clear that I am not your attorney. If I spot any difficulties, I'll tell you, and if you feel you need legal representation, there's always Charlie Lipman. But I am *not* your lawyer. Understood?"

She nodded mutely, straightened her blouse, and we headed for Vince Walton's office. In the hall, we met Charlie and a uniformed deputy—Garcia, I guessed—carrying stacks of bound ledgers and a file box of floppy disks.

"Speak of the devil," I said pleasantly. To Marsha, I added, "Want to trade horses? You haven't got to the middle of the stream yet."

Marsha shook her head stubbornly.

Charlie frowned. "Don't bother clueing me in," he said to me. To Marsha, he added, "Phoebe had another bookkeeper workin' out here the last coupla weeks. I need her name and number. You can phone it to the office."

"Her name is Kate Rodriguez," Marsha said faintly. She stared at Charlie's armload. "Why are you taking that stuff?"

"Because I'm the Big Pickle," Charlie said, in a tone that meant he didn't want to be messed with. "And I'm in charge, so don't go gettin' in my way. Ya hear?"

"Because he's the firm's lawyer," I said, smoothing things over. "And this is what lawyers do when the firm's owner dies. It's all part of the routine. The sheriff knows he's taking the stuff." I looked at him. "Better get the hard drive, too."

"Don't bother yer purty head," Charlie said. "It's next on my list."

Marsha made a small sound.

Charlie leaned forward, frowning. "This is a problem, Miss Miller?" he asked, from somewhere deep in his chest. He sounded like a Supreme Court Justice. "If it is, I shall be glad to have you explain to me just why I should not take possession of these articles, on behalf of my client, Morgan's Premier Pickles."

Marsha bit her lip. She didn't say a word.

Chapter Ten

The expression "cool as a cucumber" is literally true. Scientists have demonstrated that the inside of a fresh cucumber can be up to twenty degrees cooler than the skin.

The office was an untidy room with a desk covered with stacks of paper, a conference table littered with more papers, and a table in the corner with a fax machine sitting on it, next to a computer and monitor. I looked around, wondering where the surveillance camera setup was, but didn't see it. However, I did see a three-foot plastic pickle stuck into a wastebasket, a cluster of green pickle balloons floating loose against the ceiling, and a wall covered with playful pickle posters. One of them displayed a large thermometer, an icicle-encased cucumber wearing a muffler and a pair of rakish-looking sunglasses, and the legend "Cool as a Cucumber." Vince Walton had a sense of humor. Another wall was hung with an interesting collection of sepia photographs from the old days: shots of the famous Morgan barn with its MORGAN PREMIER PICKLES sign, and shots of men standing around a wagonload of cucumbers, stirring a large wooden pickle vat, sorting pickles on a conveyor belt, and holding up shining jars of pickles bearing the Morgan label.

Blackie got down to business in his usual straightforward, nonthreatening manner, which is not at all straightforward, of course. It's a psychological trick designed to put uncomfortable witnesses at their ease, and it usually works. Not with Marsha, though, who was pale and trembling. I couldn't tell whether it was just the situation—Phoebe's death, having to confront an officer of the law—or whether she knew something that she was afraid to tell.

Blackie opened his steno notebook, put on a pair of reading glasses that makes him look like a kindly schoolteacher, and moved his chair so he could sit in the light from the window. At that moment, though, the lights came on. The fax machine whirred and clanked, testing itself to make sure it was still in working condition, and the electric clock on the wall made a curious chirping noise.

"Ah," Blackie said with satisfaction. "Looks like PEC got the transformer replaced. They work fast."

But as if to suggest that the universe was not quite ready to stop playing games, the power went off again. The fax burped, and fell silent. Blackie sighed. "Better luck next time," he said, and began the interview.

In answer to his questions, Marsha told him her name, her occupation—administrative assistant to Ms. Phoebe Morgan—and that she had lived in the garage apartment behind Phoebe's home since she was hired, three years before. She reconstructed the events of Sunday, repeating nervously what she had told me, that she had last seen Phoebe on the previous Sunday afternoon, about three o'clock. Phoebe had said that she was coming to the plant to do some paperwork, and then intended to keep an appointment.

Blackie looked over the tops of his glasses. "Who did she plan to see?"

"I don't know." Marsha frowned. "I asked, but she didn't tell me, which was kind of unusual. It wasn't an appointment I had made for her, either."

"You made her appointments?"

"Most of them. The ones that had to do with her business, anyway." A note of something like bitterness came into her voice. "And almost everything in her life had to do with business, in one way or another. Even her personal relationships. She was a user." At Blackie's raised eyebrow, she added guardedly, "Not drugs. I only mean that she used people for her own ends. Ask anybody. They'll tell you."

Blackie wrote something in his notebook. "I understand," he said, not looking up, "that somebody else lives on the Morgan premises."

"Yes," Marsha said. "Brad lives there. Ms. Morgan's son."

Blackie nodded. "He works here at the plant, I understand."

"Right." As if she had just thought of something, she sat forward and said, with greater energy, "You should talk to Brad immediately, Sheriff. I'm sure he knows things about his mother's friends that I don't know. He'd know who hated her enough to do something like this. He'll be able to—"

"I'll talk to him," Blackie said in a quietly authoritative tone. "Was Brad at the house on Sunday?"

Marsha shook her head. "He was in West Texas. Vince sent him on a scouting trip, to check out some new suppliers."

"He left when?"

"Wait a minute. I have to think." She thought. "The Wednesday or Thursday before, I believe. But you need to ask Vince. He'll know for sure. Or Brad."

"And when did he get back?"

"Yesterday. Thursday." She looked at me. "China was there when he drove up. And Pauline."

I nodded. "Brad was upset that his mother hadn't let anybody know where she was going. He thought she'd left town with Todd Kellerman."

Blackie's pencil stopped moving and his glance came up. "Kellerman?" he asked, picking up the cue. "That would be the live-in boyfriend?"

Marsha frowned, as if she were wondering how he'd discovered that bit of information. She cast a glance in my direction. I nodded slightly, and she said, with transparent reluctance, "That's ... correct. He lives in the guest house."

"He's been there how long?"

Her shrug said it didn't really matter, but the tautness in her voice betrayed her. "Since around Christmas. Todd's a painter. A friend of Brad's."

Blackie's dark eyebrows went up. "A painter? A house painter?"

"An *artist*," Marsha said, her eyes flashing scornfully. "He's very talented. Phoebe invited him to stay in the guest house while he did his work."

"Talented as a painter?" Blackie asked, raising one eyebrow.

Marsha stiffened. "Of course. What else?"

Blackie regarded her. "Was Mr. Kellerman at the house on Sunday?"

"I don't . . ." She swallowed. "Yes."

"Is he there now?"

Mutely, she shook her head.

"When did you see him last?"

"See him? On Sunday. About noon. All three of us had lunch together." Hastily, she added, "He's . . . he's been out of town for the past few days."

"Since Sunday?"

"Yes. I mean, I guess. That was when I last . . . saw him."

Blackie gave her a long look. "I need the whole truth, Ms. Miller. What time on Sunday did you see him last?"

Marsha glanced at me and licked her lips. "Can I talk to my—to China?"

"Sure," Blackie said. "Take all the time you want. I need to check on how things are going, anyway." He pushed his chair back and went out into the hall.

"I didn't see Todd after lunch," she said, when he had gone. "But I heard him. His voice. Phoebe's too. Is that something I need to tell? Isn't that hearsay?"

I shook my head. "No, hearsay is secondhand information. And anyway, the rule against hearsay evidence only applies to its admissibility in court. You need to tell the sheriff what you heard, Marsha. If you don't, and if he learns about it from somebody else, he might get the impression that you're covering up for Todd. That you think he's guilty of something." I paused, my eyes holding hers. "Do you?"

Marsha looked away. "He was guilty of being a fool," she said, anger flaring suddenly. "Phoebe was using him. She wanted to look like a patron of the arts. She didn't care about him, not really, I mean, not as a person. She didn't care about anybody except herself. But I'm sure he wouldn't—" She stopped.

"Wouldn't what?"

She gnawed her lower lip distractedly. "The thing is that Lunelle heard it, too, at least I think she did. She was behind the guest house, with a shovel and a bucket—why, I don't know, but I saw her." Her face twisted. "That woman is a damned snoop. She probably heard them, and I know she saw me."

"Lunelle. Phoebe's housekeeper?" And Janet's aunt. A snoop, huh? It must run in the family. Janet is more than a little inclined in that direction herself.

Marsha sighed. "So I guess I'd better tell, huh?"

"You damn well better tell," I said, "unless you want Lunelle the Snoop to beat you to it. Which would not be good for your credibility."

I went to the door and motioned to Blackie, who was standing in the hall, talking to one of his deputies. The deputy handed him something—a piece of paper, it looked like, encased in a plastic evidence sleeve. He looked at it carefully for a moment, then tucked it into the back of his notebook. When he came back into the room, he put his notebook on the table and went to stand at the window, his hands in his pockets, his back to us.

"Now," he said, "where were we?"

"I didn't actually *see* Todd on Sunday evening," Marsha said slowly, as if she were weighing every word for its truth and accuracy. "Or Phoebe either. I did hear their voices, though."

"Okay," he said, still looking out the window. "What were they saying?"

Marsha twisted her fingers. "They were . . . having a

discussion. Sort of an argument, I guess. It was nothing serious," she added hastily. "Just . . . a discussion. A rather loud one."

"And where were they while they were having this rather loud discussion?" Blackie turned away from the window and resumed his seat at the table, picking up his notebook.

Marsha seemed to gather herself. "In the guest house, next to the pool. I had gone for a swim—I always do laps in the evening." She managed a little smile. "It gets a little lonely out there in the evenings, and swimming gives me something to do."

"Evening?" Blackie was writing. "What time?"

"About six, I think. Maybe six-thirty. I didn't have a watch with me."

"What were they discussing? Could you hear them plainly?"

"It had rained in the afternoon, so it was cool, and the guest house windows were open. I tried not to listen, but I couldn't . . . avoid it." Marsha looked down at her hands, a painful flush climbing up her neck. "Phoebe said she thought Todd was having an affair with somebody, behind her back. He told her it wasn't true, but she said she didn't believe him. She said she had . . . evidence."

I looked at her, picturing the scene. Marsha in the water, Phoebe and Todd in the guest house not a dozen paces away, their voices raised angrily, the windows open to the evening breeze. If Marsha didn't want to hear them, she could simply have climbed out of the pool and gone back to her apartment. She could always swim later. It was my guess that she had lingered in the pool deliberately, so she could listen to their conversation. It was as plain as the nose on your face that Marsha was in love with Todd. I could just imagine how Phoebe would react to the idea that her young artist had betrayed her with one of her employees. It wouldn't be a pretty scene. It might even lead to violence.

Blackie had stopped writing and seemed to be looking out of the window. "Ms. Morgan said she had evidence," he said quietly. "Did she say what kind of evidence? A phone conversation, a photograph, something like that?"

"No." She bit her lip. "Although she did mention something . . . a letter, maybe. I couldn't tell exactly what she was talking about. I couldn't hear what he said, either." She swallowed. "There wasn't any yelling or anything like that, honestly, Sheriff. It was all very . . . civilized."

Civilized. I wouldn't bet my bottom dollar on it.

"Did Ms. Morgan mention a name?" Blackie asked. "Did she seem to know who the woman was?"

Mutely, painfully, Marsha shook her head. If she'd heard, she wasn't going to say. I wondered if the other listener—Lunelle—would report hearing a name. Marsha's name.

"And then what?" Blackie asked. "After Ms. Morgan said she had evidence."

"She told him she thought it was time he left," she replied in a low voice. "She said she wanted him to find someplace else to live."

Especially if he'd been screwing the staff, I thought ironically. Phoebe would want to get him away from Marsha.

"Did he leave?" Blackie asked.

Marsha dropped her eyes. "His car was gone the next morning, so I supposed he did. I . . . thought she had gone with him. That they had made up and . . ." Her voice faltered and failed.

"Did you hear or see anything else?" Blackie asked, when it was clear that she wasn't going to go on. "Any sounds of a struggle, anything like that?"

Marsha gave her head a hard shake. "No! Todd isn't—" She bit her lip. "No. Just what I said."

"You didn't see Ms. Morgan come out of the guest house?"

She looked flustered. "I didn't wait around. I . . . I was afraid they'd see me and know that I'd overheard. I jumped out of the water and ran back to my apartment before either of them came out."

If Phoebe had evidence of Marsha's betrayal, or if Marsha thought she did, I could understand why Marsha wouldn't want to hang around. With Todd dismissed, she must have expected that it would be only a matter of time before she got her walking papers, too.

"Have you heard anything from Mr. Kellerman since Sunday?" Blackie asked. "Has he tried to get in touch with Ms. Morgan? Phone calls? Letters? Emails? Has he tried to get in touch with you?"

Marsha shook her head mutely, and I could see the distress on her face. If Todd hadn't been on the sheriff's suspect list already, he was there now, at the top, and she had put him there, with her story about the civilized discussion that was really an argument. On the other hand—I narrowed my eyes thoughtfully. If Marsha had wanted to implicate Todd, she had chosen exactly the right way to do it: the unwilling witness, protesting a man's innocence while she made him look as guilty as sin. My eyes went to the "Cool as a Cucumber" poster. It didn't seem likely, I had to admit, but I've been fooled by the reluctant witness in the past.

"Thank you," Blackie said. He closed his notebook and put it on the table. "Can you think of anything else I should know?"

"About what?" She turned up her hands helplessly. "I've told you everything I heard."

"Yes, thank you. But I'm still curious about Ms. Morgan's accusation. You say she didn't mention a name. But do you happen to know whether Mr. Kellerman was having sexual relations with someone other than Ms. Morgan?"

A trick question, on the order of "When did you stop beating your wife?" Marsha's face flamed, and she leaned toward me. "Do I have to answer that?" she whispered.

"No," I said firmly. "You don't." But her reluctance to answer was answer enough in itself. Blackie had eyes. Now I wasn't the only one who suspected that Marsha and Todd Kellerman had been lovers.

She straightened up. "Then I won't," she said.

"Thank you," Blackie said in a courteous tone, and closed his notebook. "I have just one thing that I'd like your help with, if you don't mind." He took the evidence bag out of the back of his notebook and put it on the table. "This was found in the back pocket of Ms. Morgan's jeans. There's not much here to go on, I'm afraid. I'd be grateful if you could shed some light on it. Who do you think might have written it?"

Marsha leaned forward and I stood up to have a better look. We were looking at a fragment of the middle portion of a letter, handwritten in ink on lined yellow paper, in a small, almost obsessively neat script. The paper had obviously been torn and crumpled, and the top and the bottom portions were missing, so that the fragment began and ended in midsentence. The paper was smoothed out now, and still wet inside the protective plastic. But the words were quite legible, and as I read them, a sense of uneasiness prickled at the back of my neck. There was something familiar about some of the phrasing.

probably aren't thrilled to hear this, but I feel that you have a right to know and decide how you want to be involved. I can understand why you need to keep it a secret, under the circumstances. Nobody's going to find out from me, unless it's absolutely necessary for them to know. But given all that's happened to me in my life, I'm obviously not going to keep it a secret from

I looked at Marsha. Her face had gone white and she was biting her lip. It was my guess that she had seen the letter before. But she only said tautly, "I'm sorry, I can't help you."

Blackie's glance flickered over her face. "Too bad," he said. "I was hoping you'd recognize the handwriting. But we may be able to find fingerprints, even after a few days in the water. It's amazing what forensic science can do these days."

Marsha shivered. She was looking down at the paper. "It . . . it almost sounds like blackmail."

Not blackmail, exactly, I thought uneasily. But the writing did have a kind of urgency about it that might, under some circumstances, seem threatening. It could have something to do with Vince's under-the-table activities. Or perhaps it hadn't been written to Phoebe, but to Todd, and Phoebe had somehow managed to get her hands on it. But there wasn't really much point in guessing. As Blackie said, there wasn't much to go on here—except for the expression on Marsha's face. She knew something about that letter, I was sure of it.

Blackie picked up the evidence envelope and put it back in his notebook. "Just one more thing, Ms. Miller. I'm a little curious why you didn't mention the sale of the plant."

"The sale—" Marsha blinked. "I . . . I guess I just didn't think about it," she said lamely. "It doesn't seem very important now. Now that she's dead, I mean."

"That *is* what I mean," Blackie said. "Now that Ms. Morgan is dead, will the plant be sold?"

"I don't know," Marsha said, her voice breaking nervously. "Maybe not. The deal was only in the talking stages. Once the news got out, she knew there was going to be a lot of local opposition."

"Did anybody oppose the idea?"

She frowned. "Vince Walton wasn't very happy about it, but I don't know that he opposed her, actually." An ironic smile quirked at the corners of her mouth. "It wasn't easy to oppose Phoebe. When she wanted to do something, standing in her way only made it more likely that she'd do it."

"Why did she want to sell the plant? It's been in her family since the beginning, hasn't it?"

Marsha shrugged. "I have no idea. She didn't tell me, and I didn't ask. She was getting more involved with other things—real estate, some land development, the arts, things like that." The irony became amusement. "I sort of assumed she didn't like being the Pickle Queen anymore. It didn't suit her image of herself."

"I see," Blackie said. "Well, that's about it, at least for now. The deputy out in the hall will take your fingerprints before you leave."

"My . . . fingerprints?" Marsha asked thinly.

"Just for elimination purposes," Blackie said. "I'm sending a team to search the guest house. And I'd like you to go to the sheriff's office before you go home, and leave a statement about what happened on Sunday." He fished in his shirt pocket and pulled out a card. "Here's the address. Somebody will type it up for you, and you can sign it." He paused. "Oh, and it would be helpful if you planned to stay around until we get this wrapped up. Any problem with that?"

Marsha cleared her throat. "No," she said. She stood up and took the card. "No, no problem."

On the way out, I happened to bump into Vince Walton, who was directing the setup of a gas-powered generator. We exchanged brief nods, and I wished regretfully that I could sit in when Blackie interviewed him. I would've liked to hear Vince try to explain just how he'd managed to acquire that property on fifty thousand a year. Maybe he'd be cool as a cucumber, but I somehow doubted it.

Chapter Eleven

The Latin name for the daylily is *Hemerocallis*, which means "beauty of the day"—appropriate, since the individual flower fades at the end of the day. A single plant, though, may produce a hundred flowers. And the daylily isn't just pretty to look at, either. Its flower buds and blossoms can be eaten, and the young foliage can be simmered or stir-fried. In China, the buds, strung and dried, are known as "golden needles." In the Orient, daylilies are used medicinally, usually as an antibacterial agent to treat urinary disorders, vaginal yeast infections, and even cancers.

Since PickleFest had been called off, I was looking forward to a quiet weekend. Back at the shop, I posted a big PICKLEFEST CANCELED sign on the door and made a number of phone calls, letting people know that the next day's activities had been rained out. I didn't mention Phoebe's death, though. Hark was probably on the story already, and they'd be sure to read all about it in Saturday's *Enterprise*.

With the rain still coming down and shoppers few and far between, I decided to catch up on some indoor jobs I'd been postponing in favor of garden work. And since there wasn't enough to keep two people busy, I sent Laurel home and prepared to enjoy what was left of a quieter-than-usual Friday afternoon in the shop.

But I felt edgy and apprehensive, and although I occupied myself with some very pleasant chores—among other things, I arranged an attractive display of herbal vinegars in variously shaped crystal decanters with pretty labels, together with jars packed with pickled peppers and garlic and terra-cotta pots of rosemary, thyme, and chives—I couldn't get Phoebe Morgan off my mind. Although I had admired the woman's intelligence and energy, I hadn't much *liked* her, and I could certainly see how somebody might have been provoked into killing her, then panicked and dumped her body into the effluent tank, perhaps until there was time to dispose of her properly.

But who could have done it? After hearing Marsha's story about what had happened on Sunday evening, Todd Kellerman certainly seemed like a good candidate. And being privy to McQuaid's investigation of Vince Walton, I had to say that Vince was definitely a possibility, not to mention that he looked the part. Or it might have been one of the current or former workers at the plant, or some person with a deep-seated grudge. Art Simon, for instance, who was angry about the plant's effluent and who might have thought that dumping Phoebe into the tank was an act of poetic justice. I made a mental note to mention that to Blackie. It wouldn't be a bad idea for him to have a talk with Simon and find out the extent of his disagreement with Phoebe.

I thought back to what little I knew of Todd Kellerman, Phoebe's artist boyfriend. Judging from Marsha's description, he hardly seemed the killer type, whatever that is. But that was Marsha's description, of course, colored by her feelings about him—passionate feelings, unless I missed my guess. And while I hadn't looked too closely at the corpse, for obvious reasons, I was betting that the autopsy report would attribute Phoebe's death to blunt force trauma to the head, the generic name for being struck by anything from a brick wall to a fireplace poker. It was the sort of injury that would occur if somebody—even a usually good-tempered somebody—got mad and picked up a rock and bashed his victim with it. Or maybe the guy gave her a hard shove, and she fell against something, smacking her head hard enough to fracture her skull.

But why was I assuming that Phoebe had been killed by a man? The blow that had killed her, or the shove, could just as easily have been delivered by an angry woman. The only female in the picture—at least, the only one I knew about—was Marsha, and I hated to think that she might have killed Phoebe.

But it was possible, wasn't it? Sure it was, and it would make sense out of some of Marsha's otherwise odd behavior. Or maybe Todd had killed her, and Marsha had helped him dispose of the body. Which would certainly go a long way toward explaining why she'd been so reluctant to talk to the sheriff. In fact, now that I thought about it, it didn't seem very likely that Todd—who probably hadn't had much to do with pickles—would know about the effluent tank. But Marsha certainly did. In fact, she—

"Are you busy?" Ruby asked, interrupting my thoughts.

"I'm just finishing up," I said, stepping back to admire the vinegar display. The bottles certainly looked pretty, like tiers of colored jewels. "What's on your mind?" I expected her to come up with a new angle on Phoebe's death, since I'd filled her in on the details of Marsha's interview. But that wasn't what she wanted to talk about.

"I just got a call from Smart Cookie," she said. "Apparently this jerk on the city council is making trouble for her, big time. She sounded pretty down. I asked her to have dinner with me tonight, and we wondered whether you could come, too." She cocked her head at an angle, studying me. "The three of us haven't had a girls' night out for an awfully long time, you know. And we owe it to Sheila to stand behind her in her hour of need."

"You're absolutely right," I said firmly. "I'm sure McQuaid and Brian can get along without me for one evening. Let's not drive to Austin, though. It's still raining, and traffic will be a mess." I looked down at my jeans. "Do I have to go home and change?"

Ruby shook her head. "We thought we'd just sort of kick back. Go to Bean's, maybe. Eat chicken-fried, throw a few darts, shoot some pool." She grinned. "We can let Sheila run the rack a time or two. That ought to make her feel better."

I shrugged. "Guess I'll just have to suppress my killer instinct."

Ruby had just left when the bell on the shop door jangled and a woman came in, folding her wet umbrella. She wore a stiffly sprayed tower of tangerine-colored Big Hair, fabulously fake eyelashes, sultry orange lipstick, and extra-sized Dolly-style boobs, scarcely contained within the confines of her blue two-piece pants suit uniform, the buttons straining down the front.

I blinked at the sight. "You're brave," I said. "Is it still raining out there?" If it was, her hairdo was proof against the elements. Big Hair is like that, though. It's sprayed and pouffed and moussed to the point where it's as fixed and inflexible as barbwire. The only thing that's likely to tousle it is a Texas tornado.

"Rainin'?" she asked with a laugh. "It's a slam-bang frog-choker. A lot of roads are under water, and the radio's sayin' there's more on the way tonight. So don't put yer rowboat away jes' yet." Her voice was high-pitched and sharply flavored with her West Texas origins. "Janet still here, or has she gone home?"

"She's in the kitchen." Janet was salvaging what she could of the day's lunch for a Saturday rerun. We don't usually do that, but under the circumstances, it seemed like a good idea—especially since there wouldn't be a big crowd tomorrow, either. "This way."

The woman followed me through the tearoom to the kitchen, tennis shoes squeaking. "My stars, this is fine," she said, glancing admiringly at the empty tearoom. "Y'all sure do have a nice place here. Does do a person's heart good to look at it." She pulled in a deep breath. "Smells good, too. Janet's been makin' that vegetable soup o' hers again, huh? I'm proud to say she's some good cook."

"Aunt Lunelle," Janet said, coming out of the kitchen, drying her hands on a tea towel. "What're you doing here? I thought you were working today."

Ah, Aunt Lunelle. The housekeeper Marsha thought might have overheard the argument between Phoebe and Todd. The one who snooped.

"I *was* working," Lunelle replied, shaking her head

sadly. "But Ms. Morgan's dead, and that changes things a lot. A whole, big foot-stompin' lot." She glanced at me, one tweezed eyebrow uplifted, then back at Janet. "I guess you a'reddy know about her bein' dead."

"O'course I know," Janet said, folding the tea towel. "China and Ruby were at the pickle factory when she come up out of that tank. She popped up just like a bad pickle, right before their very eyes." She looked at me, a small frown creasing her forehead. "I'm not talking out of school, am I?"

"I don't think it's classified," I said. "But I don't remember saying that she popped up like a bad pickle." Janet's version of the truth is usually more colorful than anybody else's. I held out my hand with a smile. "It's good to meet you, Lunelle. I'm China Bayles."

"I figgered," Lunelle said, adding, unexpectedly, "T' tell the truth, you're the reason I'm here, Miz Bayles. Janet's told me about you. You bein' a high-powered ex-lawyer and all that, I mean. I got a sorta legal question I'd like your opinion about. If you got the time, that is. Wouldn't want to take you from yer work."

"Sure," I said, feeling curious about this "sorta legal" question. Anyway, it wouldn't be the first time today I had masqueraded as a lawyer. I gestured toward a table. "Would you like to sit down? Maybe Janet could make us some tea."

"That'd be real fine," Lunelle said. "Some of that zingy hibiscus stuff would be good if you got it, Janet." She sat down with a *whoosh* and took out a package of cigarettes. "Seems like it's been a long day, and it ain't even four o'clock yet."

"I'm sorry," I said gently, "but this is a no-smoking area." Lunelle rolled her eyes, but she was putting her cigarettes away when Ruby came in.

"Dinner's all set," she said to me. "Sheila's meeting us at Bean's at seven. I told her we'd let her win at the pool table if she'd pick up the beer tab." She glanced at my companion, registering recognition. "Why, hello, Lunelle."

"You two know one another?" I asked.

"Lunelle helped Janet and me with the party we did for the Seidenstickers a few months ago," Ruby said, joining us at the table. "Would you be available next week, Lunelle? We're catering the garden party at the Fergusons'—assuming that it ever stops raining."

"Betcher buns I'm available," Lunelle said promptly. She twisted her lipsticked mouth. "Figger I better start lookin' for more work. Kinda seems like my job at the Morgan's is goin' down the tubes." She paused. "Actually, I been thinkin' about settin' myself up in the cleanin' bidness. Seems like it'ud be more money, and maybe 'fore long I'd be a boss, instead of a cleanin' lady."

"I guess you know what happened this morning, then," Ruby said.

"Oh, boy, do I? You bet!" She tapped long, artfully done nails on the table, and I wondered how a cleaning lady managed a mop with such nails. No wonder she wanted to be a boss. "There's five or six dep'ties out at the house right this minute," she went on, "goin' over the place like a mama cat checking out her kitties for fleas. I didn't figger it was a real good idea to get in their way, so I left."

"Has the sheriff interviewed you yet?" I asked.

"That was another reason I left," Lunelle said crisply.

She turned her glance on me. "Figgered I'd jes' put that off for a while."

"Why?" I asked. I felt like a broken record, but I said it anyway. "If you know something that might help his investigation—"

Janet came back just then, with four glasses of hibiscus and passionflower iced tea on a tray, along with a plate of lavender scones. She was limping mightily, to show us that her knees were giving her trouble again. "Thought we might as well eat these up," she said pragmatically. "They don't hold over as good as the quiche does."

With pleasure, we all helped ourselves to the scones. "I was saying," I reminded Lunelle after a minute, "that you need to tell the sheriff anything you know."

Lunelle wrinkled her nose. "Janet, you always put so much lav'nder in these?"

"You don't like 'em, you don't have to eat 'em, Aunt Lunelle," Janet replied primly. "They're for folks who got good taste."

"Didn't say I didn't like 'em," Lunelle replied, taking another bite. She looked at me. "What I tell the sheriff depends on what you tell me," she said. She cast an ominous look, first at Ruby, then at Janet. "I reckon you ladies'll swear to keep this under your sombreros."

"Oh, of course," Ruby said quickly, and Janet nodded, her blue eyes bright.

"What I want to know," Lunelle said, "is whether I can get arrested or sued for bein' where I wasn't s'posed to be and doin' something I wasn't s'posed to be doin'. That's where I heard what I wasn't s'posed to hear." She sat back, satisfied that she had stated the problem accurately.

"I doubt it," I said, "although it might depend on the situation. For instance, if you overheard something and then tried to get somebody to pay you to keep it quiet—"

"Blackmail, you mean."

I nodded. "You could be arrested for that. Or if you stole a personal item with information in it—say, a computer file or a diary. However, if you took something and then put it back, or put it into the hands of the law, the chances are pretty good that you wouldn't—"

"Well, it ain't nothin' like that," Lunelle broke in. "It was only a bucket of daylily plants I dug out of the patio garden behind the guest house, after Miz Morgan told me I couldn't have 'em. That woman never wanted anybody to have a piece of anything that belonged to her." She sighed. "It was all hers and nobody else's, and she wasn't fixin' to share."

That was as good a description of Phoebe Morgan as any I'd ever heard. I nodded.

"Ever since I did it, though, I've been thinkin' that I might could get myself into trouble," Lunelle went on. "Then the dep'ty came around this mornin' and said that Miz Morgan was dead and Mr. Brad had told him he could search the guest house. Said he wanted to take my statement, too. I figgered I'd better find out just how much trouble I was in 'fore I went shootin' off my mouth. So I jes' waited till he headed out to the guest house, then I made m'self scarce."

I gave her a comforting smile. "Well, if it's just a few daylily plants, Lunelle, I wouldn't worry. Ms. Morgan might be upset, but she's out of the picture. The sheriff isn't going to care. He just wants to find out what you know."

"What *do* you know, Aunt Lunelle?" Janet asked eagerly. "With all this buildup, you got to tell us."

Lunelle adjusted a strand of hair. "Well, for starters, I heard Miz Morgan and that boyfriend o' hers, that artist fella, havin' a big argument."

"Okay," I said, "let's hear it."

To a point, her story matched Marsha's account, more or less. As the housekeeper, Lunelle did the household's cleaning and shopping and cooking, but she didn't usually work on Saturday or Sunday. Instead, she left food for the weekend in the refrigerator, and the people in the house— Phoebe, Todd, Brad, and Marsha—were supposed to take care of themselves. That Sunday evening, however, she had driven out to the Morgan place at a time when she thought nobody would be around, with the intention of digging and dividing a large clump of Stella d'Oro daylilies, which she wanted for her garden.

"Purtiest yeller flowers I've ever seen," she said, "purtier'n daffodils. And bloom? That bunch was a bloomin' fool, jes' kept puttin' up flowers all summer long. I had my heart set on buyin' me some, but a little bitty pot at the nurs'ry costs almost ten bucks." She made a face. "Can you believe that? Ten bucks, when there was a clump as big as a washtub behind the guest house that needed dividin'. So I thought, well, why not? Miz Morgan said no, but I figgered I'd jes' go ahead and get me a few and she'd never know the difference."

On Sunday evening about six o'clock, Lunelle had parked down the road, in front of the neighboring Simon house, and made her way through the woods, bringing her own shovel and a couple of buckets. She knew that Brad was out of town, but the doors of the three-car garage were closed as usual, and she couldn't tell whether anyone else was at home. Everything seemed quiet, though, so she thought she was safe. She went around to the secluded patio garden behind the guest house and set to work, digging and dividing. Luckily, the daylilies grew behind a large clump of agarita, and she knew she wouldn't be seen. She had filled both her buckets and was pushing the mulch back around the remaining plants when she heard angry voices. It was Todd and Phoebe, in the guest house.

"They was arguin' something fierce," Lunelle said. "She was madder'n a half-swatted hornet. Said he'd been carryin' on with some other girl."

"Some other girl, huh?" Janet blew out her breath in a puff. "Not to speak ill of the dead, but if you ask me, that's what the Pickle Queen gets for messin' 'round with a boy young enough to be her son. She looked pretty good from a distance, but up close and 'thout any clothes on, I bet she—"

"Let's let Lunelle tell her story, shall we?" I suggested quickly, before we could be treated to any more of Janet's graphic speculations.

"Right," Lunelle said with relish. "So here I was with two buckets of daylilies, and they was havin' this argument. She was mad at him for steppin' out on her and for gettin' this other girl pregnant. She'd got her hands on a letter, y'see, that told all about it. Evidence, she called it. She was mad 'nough to snatch that boy bald-headed."

Pregnant! I jerked upright, and my eyes met Ruby's. She opened her mouth to say something, but I shook my head slightly. She pressed her lips together, then gave a little shrug and subsided, probably because she didn't really believe that the pregnant girl could be Amy. After all, in any given week, there must be a dozen or more pregnant women in Pecan Springs, and Todd might have been the culprit with any one of them, maybe more. Anyway, Ruby was still convinced that Jon was Amy's baby-making partner.

But I had two important pieces of information that Ruby lacked, and I was virtually certain that the third woman in this irregular triangle was Amy. For one thing, Amy had told me that she had written a letter to the baby's father, telling him that she was pregnant. And for another, I had actually read a part of the letter itself, which a deputy had retrieved from Phoebe's back pocket and Blackie had shown to Marsha when he was interviewing her. I even recalled one of the sentences—"You have a right to know and decide how you want to be involved"—which had seemed uneasily familiar when I read it. Connecting the dots now, with Lunelle's version of the story as background, I remembered that Amy had used virtually identical language when we'd talked the evening before. It was interesting, though, that Marsha hadn't mentioned anything about a pregnancy. Had she failed to hear that part of the discussion, or decided to keep it to herself?

Janet was leaning forward. "So what happened after the Pickle Queen told him she had this letter, Aunt Lunelle? What did he have to say for himself?"

"What could he say?" Lunelle shrugged. "Ate a little half-assed crow. Said he was sorry he'd hurt her, but he had to live his own life. Said he was sorry he'd taken money from her, and the car. Said all he wanted was to do his painting in peace and quiet, not mix it up with sex and stuff, and maybe it was time he found his own place."

"Well." Janet *hmmph*'d with some asperity. "He shoulda thought of all that before he got in bed with her. Once you make a bargain with the devil, you got to pay the devil his due."

"Her due," Lunelle amended.

"The way you're telling it, Lunelle," Ruby said, "it doesn't sound like a particularly violent argument."

"*He* wasn't vi'lent," Lunelle replied. "*She* was the one fit to be tied. Yellin' about how he was a rotten SOB and a cheat, throwin' things and breakin' stuff. Sounded like a hog-killin' goin' on in there."

Another piece of information that Marsha had failed to report.

"Well, I sort of understand her position," Ruby said with a sigh. "Phoebe was my age, and Todd is how old?"

"All of twenty-five, I reckon," Lunelle said. "Which I s'pose was a big part of it. She was a jealous lady."

"Were you the only person who heard the argument on Sunday?" I asked.

Lunelle shook her head. "I thought I'd better clear out before I was spotted, so I grabbed up my buckets and my daylilies and my shovel and started to leave. When I come around the side of the guest house, I saw Marsha in the pool, jes' in front of the guest house. I ducked back so she wouldn't see me. Anyways, she jumped outta the pool, all drippin' wet, and ran up on the porch. She just stood there, all blue and goosebumpy, huggin' herself and shiverin', tryin' to figure out whether she should go in." She shook her head sadly. "That girl, she's been crazy about Todd ever since he showed up. She tried best she could to hide it from Miz Morgan, but it wasn't hard to figger out, when you seen her with him."

"How did he feel about her?" Ruby asked.

"How's any healthy young fella gonna feel when a girl

flings herself at him?" Lunelle asked rhetorically. "Marsha may look as frigid as a frosted frog, but them are the ones'll surprise you. I figger she's the one he got pregnant, which is why she was standin' there, tryin' to decide whether to go in." She pursed her sultry orange lips. "Though I don't know how come she'd write him a letter about it, them livin' not a stone's throw apart."

I had seen Marsha when she got her first look at that letter, and I didn't believe she had written it—unless she was a lot better at hiding her feelings than I gave her credit for. "You said she was standing on the porch," I said. "Did you see her go into the guest house?"

"I saw her put her hand on the knob," Lunelle replied. "It looked to me like she was meanin' to go in, if she could get up the nerve. Me, I ducked back and went around a dif-f'rent way, behind the garage."

"And you didn't see Phoebe leave the guest house?" Ruby asked.

Lunelle shook her head decisively. "By that time, I was long gone. Me and my daylilies." She looked at me. "You sure the sheriff's not gonna give me any trouble 'bout them plants?"

"If he does," I said, "you tell me, and I'll have a talk with him."

"So for all you know," Ruby persisted, "Phoebe *never* came out, at least, not alive."

Lunelle nodded. "'Fraid that's so." She looked from Ruby to me. "You think he killed her?"

"It's a possibility," I conceded, thinking with some sadness that it was highly probable, and where did that leave Amy? But there was still Vince to consider, of course. He had a substantial motive. And Marsha. Right now, there were three strong suspects, and no way to immediately eliminate any of them.

"The thing you have to do is give your information to the sheriff," I went on. If nothing else, Blackie needed to know that Marsha had gotten as far as the front door and had possibly gone inside to join the fracas—a detail she had omitted from her report. And he needed to know about the pregnancy. Unfortunately, he probably also ought to know about Amy, but that could be put off for a little while.

"There's something I'm curious about, though," I added. "Did you do any cleaning in the guest house on Monday?"

Lunelle frowned. "Well, that was the funny thing. I do up that place ever' mornin', reg'lar. Make the bed, change the towels, dust, run the vac, stuff like that. But on Monday morning, Marsha said I should leave it. Said that Todd would be gone for a few days, so there was no need to do his place until he got back. 'Course, I couldn't tell her I'd heard all that glass breaking. I didn't want to give her a chance to accuse me of bein' where I shouldn't've been."

I sipped my tea. So Marsha had kept Lunelle from going into the guest house. Another provocative little detail that she had omitted from her story. I wondered if she had cleaned the place up herself, or just left it as it was. I was betting that she'd cleaned it.

"You didn't think it was odd?" Ruby asked. "Not to do the cleaning, I mean."

"Well, maybe." Lunelle shrugged. "But Mr. Brad keeps his room locked, so I never clean in there." She wrinkled her nose. "I can smell that mary-wanna sometimes when I walk past his door. Figger he's smokin' dope and is stupid enough to think he can keep it hid. Anyway, when Miz

Morgan's outta town, Marsha is my boss, and I do what I'm told without askin' questions." She grinned, showing uneven teeth. "Mostly, anyway."

"So you thought Ms. Morgan was also out of town," I said. "Did Marsha tell you that she and Todd had gone away together?"

"Not in so many words," Lunelle replied. She took her cigarette pack out of her pocket, remembered, and put it back. "But Todd's car was gone, y'see, and Marsha said he'd left for a few days. And since Miz Morgan's car was still in the garage, what else was I s'posed to think? I figgered they'd gone off someplace together."

"After that argument?" Janet asked doubtfully.

"Folks fuss and make up all the time," Lunelle replied. She squinted at her niece. "Ain't you ever done that, Janet? That's when you get the best sex. After you both been mad 'nough to bite bullets, sex is real good. Real powerful stuff."

"Aunt Lunelle!" Janet exclaimed, horrified.

Innocently, Lunelle appealed to Ruby and me. "Well, ain't it?"

Ruby shrugged and I grinned. "I wouldn't know," I said. "McQuaid and I don't fuss much." Personally, I prefer to get good sex a different way, but each to her own.

"All I gotta say is you're missin' out on some real fine stuff," Lunelle replied knowingly. She drained her iced tea glass and stood up. "Janet, next time you make them scones, leave out some of that lavender. Y'hear?"

Chapter Twelve

BOB GODWIN'S DEEP-FRIED PICKLED JALAPEÑOS STUFFED WITH CHEDDAR CHEESE

10–12 large pickled jalapeño peppers
cheddar cheese slices
egg wash: 1 egg beaten with 2 Tbsp. water
breading mixture: ½ cup biscuit mix, blended with
    ½ cup cornmeal and 1 tsp. cumin

Slit the peppers and scrape out the seeds. Stuff with pieces of cheese cut to fit the peppers. Dip peppers in the egg-and-water mixture, then into breading mixture. Repeat. Let dry for 10–15 minutes, then deep fry in hot oil until the peppers are lightly browned and the cheese is melting. Drain on paper toweling and serve hot.

I did go home to change, after all, since I needed to wash some of the day's grit off, find a clean pair of jeans, locate my suede vest, and dig my cowboy boots out of the back of the closet. If Ruby, Sheila, and I were going to kick back, I had to have the right costume.

But I also meant to have a serious talk with Amy. I wanted to be the one to tell her about Phoebe Morgan and

ask her point-blank if she had been involved with Todd
Kellerman. I expected her to tell me the truth, too. If that
was indeed a piece of her letter in Phoebe's hip pocket,
Blackie needed to know—and she had to tell him, before
he got the information from anybody else.

From Todd, for instance. I was willing to bet that
Blackie had already gotten a warrant for his arrest as a material witness. It might take a while to locate him, but he'd
turn up, sooner or later. And when he did, he'd be brought
to Pecan Springs for questioning, and Blackie would pressure him for the name of the other woman. None of this
might have anything to do with the murder, of course—
there was still Vince, a lively candidate with a compelling
motive. But Blackie had to tie up all the loose ends, and
since Lunelle's testimony about the argument was certainly going to implicate Todd, Amy was definitely going
to be one of those loose ends.

But Amy wasn't around. The house was dark and empty,
except for Howard Cosell, who informed me in no uncertain tones how he felt about being left, lonely and abandoned, while everybody else in the family was out and
about, doing the Friday night boogie without him. His bowl
still had some food in it, but I added half a cold hot dog to
soothe his hurt feelings. He stared down at it for a moment,
then up at me. And then, managing to give the impression
that he was accepting this as a down payment and antici-
pated that the rest of the score would be settled later, picked
it up in his teeth and carried it to his basket in the corner.

While Howard comforted himself with his hot dog, I
read the note Brian had left on the kitchen table, saying
that he was sleeping over at his friend Jason's house. On
the bottom was a P.S., saying that his dad had called. He

was going to be late, and I shouldn't wait supper. Obviously, it was the right night for me to go out with the girls.

Beside Brian's note was a copy of the *Enterprise,* and I caught a glimpse of the headline: COUNCIL PRIMED TO FIRE CHIEF. I scowled, picked up the paper, and read the lead story with a growing sense of uneasiness. It was every bit as bad as Ruby had said. No doubt about it, Ben Graves was out to get Smart Cookie fired if she couldn't come up with poor old Mrs. Holeyfield's killers. I couldn't decide who should be shot first: Ben Graves for being such an idiot, or Hark for putting his idiocy into print for the whole town to read.

But there was another note on the table, and it fluttered to the floor when I put the newspaper down. I bent over to pick it up. It was written on lined yellow paper in a small, almost excessively neat hand. It had Amy's name at the bottom, and said that she was spending the night at Kate Rodriguez's house and that they were going to PickleFest. She hadn't heard, obviously, that there wasn't going to be a PickleFest.

I stared at the note, my heart doing double back-flips. I had seen that paper and that handwriting that morning. If I had needed a piece of physical evidence to prove that it was Amy's letter that had turned up in Phoebe's jeans, this was it. And now that I knew, what was I going to do about it?

I knew the answer to that question almost before I had asked it. I glanced up at the old schoolhouse clock that ticked sedately over the refrigerator, just as it had been ticking for the last eighty years or more. It was six-forty already, and there wasn't time to track Amy down and confront her before I was supposed to meet Ruby and Sheila. I went into McQuaid's office and dug around for the phone book, finally finding it on the floor under his desk, buried under a stack of old newspapers. I looked up Kate Rodriguez's phone number and address, which turned out to be on Dallas Drive, on the east side of town. I jotted the number down on a scrap of newspaper and folded it, along with Amy's note, into my pocket, feeling immeasurably sad. I didn't for a minute think that Amy herself had anything to do with what had happened to Phoebe, or that she knew anything about it. But her pregnancy might have been a factor in Phoebe's death, and no matter how embarrassed or distressed she might feel, she was going to have to explain her part in this ménage à trois to Blackie. I'd stop by Kate's on the way home from Bean's, and have a talk with Amy.

As I went back through the kitchen, I saw the newspaper with its offensive headline, still lying on the table. I folded it up and chucked it into the trash. I scribbled a note to McQuaid, telling him I was boogying with the girls and to expect me when he saw me. And then, taking pity on Howard Cosell, I gave him the other half of the hot dog.

Bean's Bar & Grill is located on the first floor of a tin-roofed stone building across the street from the Old Firehouse Dance Hall, between Purley's Tire Company and the Missouri and Pacific railroad tracks. It's a favorite gathering place for folks around here, who go there to stuff themselves on Bob Godwin's deep-fried pickled jalapeños, drink beer, shoot pool, throw blasphemous darts at an irreverent poster of a former Texas governor who has gone on to bigger and better things, and watch the sports event of the day on the giant TV set at the end of the bar. The place smells like tobacco smoke, mesquite barbecue smoke, and stale beer—a not entirely unpleasant perfume that will linger on your clothes until they're washed.

The rain had stopped for a few minutes and Ruby was waiting for me out front, a show-stopper in a red silk Western shirt with white fringe, red jeans with a flashy silver concho belt, and red cowboy boots. Together, the two of us looked like rodeo cowgirls out on the town. The noise slapped me in the face as we went into the bar, but it was a friendly kind of noise, the cacophony of jukebox honky-tonk, the chink of glasses, the clean crack of pool cue on ball, and the satisfying *thwunk* of darts against the grinning face of the ex-guv, punctuated every now and then by a loud yell and an exuberant yodel. On Friday night, the folks at Bean's are generally a noisy lot, but there's nothing ornery about them. Tonight, the crowd was a little smaller. Lots of people had stayed home, either trying to stay dry or waiting to see whether they were going to have to pack up their furniture and move to higher ground.

When you come into Bean's, the first order of business is to trade the time of day with Bob Godwin, proprietor and bartender, then you get to pat Bud on the head. Bob is the one with the coiled snake tattoo on one arm and a broken heart on the other. Bud has a red bandana around his neck and a leather saddlebag draped over his back, with leather loops stitched onto it. Bob pokes a couple of cold beers into the loops, points out the right table, and Bud delivers. The customers stick their money into the other pocket of the saddlebag, and Bud trots back to the cash register to unload his take. His full name is Budweiser. He's a golden retriever.

We stopped at the bar, where we patted Bud on the head, greeted Bob, and handed him several PICKLEFEST RAINED OUT flyers to post on the front door and in the bathrooms. Then we ordered a plate of fried jalapeños, picked up a pitcher of beer, and to the tune of "Boot-Scootin' Boogie," we threaded our way between the crowded tables toward Sheila, who was sitting in the far corner under a red neon Lone Star Beer sign. Hark was sitting with her. He got up hastily when he saw us coming.

"Don't worry," he said, picking up his beer mug and putting one hand on the table to steady himself. He had obviously started drinking at the beginning of happy hour. "I'm on my way. I'm not crashing your party."

"After that story in the paper today," I said testily, "it's a wonder Sheila hasn't crashed a chair over your head. But maybe she's too much of a lady." I put my hand on the back of the wooden chair. "In which case, I guess I'll just have to do it."

"Hey!" Hark held up one hand, palm out, plaintive. "Don't shoot the mess—mess-es-senger." He giggled, more than a little drunk.

Ruby pulled the chair out and sat down. "Who's talking about shooting?" she inquired darkly. "We're planning to scalp and skin you. And then we'll hook you up to Big Red Mama and drag your sorry carcass out of town."

"Lighten up, you guys." Smart Cookie was glum. "Hark doesn't make the news, he just reports it." She managed a tight smile. She has to worry about alienating the press.

"Yeah, that's always his defense." I gave Hark a disgusted look. "But he doesn't have to report *all* of it, down to the last slimy snarl. He doesn't have to quote that jackass Ben Graves, who doesn't know his rear from a hole in the ground." I sat down. "Get outta here, Hark. You're as big a freakin' jerk as Ben is."

Hark took a step back, blinking. "Mercy me, China. Such language, and from one of my employees, too." He looked down at my boots and giggled again. "It's 'cause you're wearin' that suede vest and them pointy-toed boots," he said. "Makes you feel like kickin' butt."

"I am not an employee, I'm a columnist," I said with dignity. "An unpaid one, at that. And if you'd watch what the hell you print, I might be less inclined to kick butt."

Hark leaned over me, and I was enveloped by the beery fog of his breath. "Have you ladies heard the latest development in the Phoebe Morgan investigation? I'm tellin' you, it's big. It's explosive. I'm gonna hafta rip out tomorrow's headline—and it was a ripsnorter." He lurched, then recovered his balance. "Wanna hear it?"

None of us said anything.

"Whazza matter?" Hark asked wonderingly. "Doncha wanna hear my great headline? You won't get to read it, since I'm gonna take it out, so—"

"Okay, Hark," Ruby said, resigned. "Tell us the headline."

Hark tipped up his mug and drained the last swallow. "MORGAN HEIRESS PICKLED IN BRINE."

I made an impolite noise.

"So what's the *new* headline?" Sheila asked.

He pointed his finger at me, sighting down it as if he were sighting down the barrel of a gun. "Not until China says she's sorry."

I crossed my arms and glared at him.

"Come on, China, apologize," Ruby said. "I want to hear this."

"Who needs a two-bit newspaper editor to tell us what's going on?" I demanded. "We've got the sheriff's true love right here, looking like a Dallas deb." Smart Cookie was wearing a turquoise plaid silk noile shirt and tee, over white pants and sandals. Her blond hair was caught up in a French braid and her skin was clear and luminous. Never in a gazillion years would you guess that she is a police chief, especially a police chief in danger of being fired. "Sheila," I asked, "what's the scoop in the Morgan investigation?"

Sheila shrugged ruefully. "I haven't seen Blackie since breakfast, China. I've heard about Phoebe Morgan's murder, but if there's any later news, I'm afraid Hark's got it. Sorry."

I stuck out my tongue at Hark. "You're repulsive, Hark." I heaved a sigh. "Okay, I apologize. Ben Graves is a bigger freakin' jerk than you are."

Hark bent over and smacked my cheek with a vulgar, sucking kiss. "Thank you, China, my love. I knew you'd see reason." He paused for dramatic effect. "So here it is, gals. Some kids looking for a place to make out found Todd Kellerman's car at a gravel pit three or four miles east of Wimberley. Kellerman was in the front seat." He hiccupped. "Dead."

I stared at Hark, the music and noise receding into the distance. Beside me, Ruby gasped.

"Dead?" I asked tersely. "How?"

"Gunshot wound in the right temple, probably self-inflicted. Gun on the passenger seat beside him. Body had been there for several days, at least. Pretty clear, wouldn't you say?" His voice became sonorous and he sketched out a headline in midair. "HEIRESS PICKLED. LOVER SUSPECTED IN A DILLY OF A DEATH."

Sheila put both hands over her ears. "Jeez, Hark," she groaned. "That's ghoulish."

"Dead right," he said cheerfully. "Life in a small town can pickle even the sharpest brain."

"If anything has pickled your brain, Hark," Ruby said tartly, "it's booze." Ruby and Hark dated each other for a while. It hadn't worked out, but I knew that she still considered him a friend and worried about his drinking.

"Maybe you're right, Ruby, m'dear. Maybe I should find me a shrink. Got any rec'mmendations?" Hark lifted up his beer mug and peered through it as if it were a telescope. "What's the difference between a pickle and a psychiatrist?"

Ruby stared at him. Sheila frowned. "What's the diff—"

"If you don't know," I said fiercely, "you should stop talking to your pickle. Now *go,* Hark! Scram, vamoose. Get the hell out of here!"

"I'm goin'," he said, backing away. "I'm gone." He stopped. "Hey, did you hear the one about the guy who ran the slicer in the pickle factory? He put his pickle in the—"

"Is this turkey botherin' you purty young ladies?" Bob Godwin asked, coming up with a plate of fried pickled jalapeños and a pitcher of beer. "Hark, go peddle your bull someplace else. These gals don't need you t' entertain 'em. They got *me.*"

With a jaunty wave, Hark disappeared in the direction of the bar. Bob put down our food. "What d'ya want after the jalapeños?" he asked, taking a bottle of catsup out of his apron pocket and plunking it on the table. "Chicken-fried steak? Barbecue? I got some cabrito kabobs on the grill, too. Butchered me a couple of real fine kids, outta my own bunch. Best organic goat meat in the whole entire state of Texas."

He pulled out his order book and beetled his furry red eyebrows at us. Bob's cabrito kabobs are very good, the meat chunks marinated in garlic, soy sauce, and lemon juice, and grilled with pineapple chunks, cherry tomatoes, mushrooms, and hot peppers. But somehow, even Bob's kabobs didn't appeal just now.

Ruby and Smart Cookie and I stared at one another, all of us thinking, no doubt, about a dead body in a closed car in the broiling heat of a Texas summer—not the most appetizing idea in the world. And I was thinking that the father of Amy's baby wouldn't be giving her any trouble—at least, not the kind she might have expected.

"The jalapeños will take care of us for a while," Sheila said to Bob. "I don't think we're just real hungry right now."

Bob shrugged and stuck his pencil behind his ear. "Don't wait too long, or that cabrito'll run out," he cautioned, and went on to the next table.

"So what do you think?" Ruby asked, frowning. "Todd killed Phoebe, dumped her in the tank, and then drove off and shot himself?"

"I don't know," I said. "I suppose it could have happened that way." I couldn't say anything about Vince, since neither Ruby nor Smart Cookie knew anything about McQuaid's new line of work or his recent investigation for Phoebe. But I was thinking about him, and wondering what role he'd played in all this.

"Marsha's in this somehow," Ruby said firmly. "I know it."

"Are you two going to tell me what you're talking about?" Sheila asked, frowning. "I gather that Todd Kellerman is Phoebe Morgan's lover. But what does Marsha Miller have to do with anything?"

I gestured to Ruby. "You tell," I said.

It took her only a few minutes to relate the little information we had: what I had learned during Blackie's interview of Marsha, and what Lunelle had told us about the argument she'd overheard.

"So you think this guy Todd got Phoebe Morgan's assistant pregnant?" Sheila asked. "That's what started the argument?"

"That's the way it looks to me," Ruby replied, daintily picking up a pickled jalapeño and biting it in half. Ruby is a confirmed chile-head. She can eat stuff so hot it melts my fillings and sends little puffs of steam out of my ears.

She chewed for a moment, and added: "And I'll bet Marsha helped him dispose of the body. After all, she knew about the tank." She looked at me. "And she knew about the security cameras, too. Remember, China? If Blackie doesn't find any pictures of Phoebe's body going into the tank, it's probably because Marsha knew how to turn off those cameras."

"And then the killer drove off and killed himself?" Sheila asked skeptically. She shook her head. "I can see a man murdering somebody in the heat of passion, and then concealing the body. But for all this guy knew, Phoebe Morgan wouldn't be found until he was out of the country. Why go to the trouble of hiding her if he was going to shoot himself?"

"Maybe he began to feel remorseful," Ruby said. "Or maybe he started to think about what was ahead for him, as far as Marsha was concerned, I mean." She snapped her fingers. "I'll bet that's it," she said excitedly. "Marsha had told him she was pregnant, and then she helped him get rid of Phoebe's body. Then he realized that he was under her power. She told him she wanted to get married for the sake of the baby, and he didn't want—"

"Stop!" I said roughly. "You're making all this up, Ruby. You don't know for a fact that Marsha is pregnant, or that either she or Todd Kellerman had anything to do with Phoebe's death."

"Well, if you're so smart," Ruby replied, with an indignant toss of her red curls, "just who do *you* think killed Phoebe and put her body into the tank? If Todd didn't do it, why did he shoot himself? What do you think—"

"I don't want to think about it at all," I interrupted. Amy's note was glowing in my pocket, hot as a coal from hell, and it was all I could do to keep from walking out and heading straight for Kate Rodriguez's place. "Let's talk about something else." I turned to Sheila. "What's going on at PSPD these days, Smart Cookie?" That was not only a stupid question but a thoughtless one, as I realized the moment it was out of my mouth.

"Nothing's going on," Sheila said flatly. "The Holeyfield investigation is totally stalled, and there's nothing new on the other break-ins."

"I've been thinking about that," Ruby said, reaching for another pickled pepper. "In fact, I went back through the newspaper and made a list of all of the victims. Do you realize that every single one of them serves on an important volunteer board?" She reached into her purse and took out a sheet of paper. "Emma Oster chairs the Nature Center board. Regina Horner is the past president of the Art League. Mrs. Carter serves on the Hospice board, and Elizabeth Drury—"

"I know all that, Ruby," Sheila said impatiently. "I've been over it a hundred times. The victims had a lot of things in common. Now, if you don't mind, let's not talk about it." She propped her chin on her hand, looked at me, and made an effort to lighten her voice. "So what's happening with McQuaid's new investigating business, China?" she asked. "Does he have any clients?"

I kicked Sheila hard under the table with my pointy-toed boot, but it was too late.

"A new investigating business!" Ruby exclaimed excitedly. "You mean McQuaid has decided to become a *private investigator?*" She clapped her hands. "China, this is wonderful! Why in the world haven't you told me?"

"Because," I said.

She leaned forward eagerly, eyes wide, expression eager. "Because why? Who are his clients? Is he doing drug investigations? Is he—"

"This is McQuaid's affair," I said flatly. "I don't want to talk about it."

"Affair?" Ruby asked, narrowing her eyes. "You don't mean that he's involved with—"

"I am truly sorry, China." Sheila gave me a penitent look. "I just didn't think."

"It's okay," I said. "She was bound to find out sooner or later." I lowered my head and frowned at Ruby. "But we are *not* going to talk about it. Okay?"

"I don't see why not," Ruby said, pouting. "I was just going to offer my services. Anytime he needs an experienced investigator, I'm available. If he wants, I could put my resume together, listing all the—"

"Ruby." I spoke through clenched teeth. "Do. Not. Go. There."

"We're changing the subject, girls," Sheila said smoothly. She turned to Ruby. "What's happening with

Amy these days, Ruby? Is she still staying with you, or has she found a new place?"

Ruby cleared her throat and shifted uncomfortably. "She . . . she's staying with China."

Sheila looked from one of us to the other. "I see," she said, in a tone that suggested that she did. "Well, it happens sometimes. To tell the truth, I don't get along with my mother. She's never liked the idea of her daughter working in law enforcement. She's always interfering in my business and telling me what to do. Not that *you'd* ever do that, Ruby," she added hastily. "I was just saying that my mother has never bothered to understand where I'm coming from or—" She stopped, seeing the look on Ruby's face. "Oh, hell," she said. "I'm making it worse."

"Yeah," Ruby said. She pushed back her chair and reached for her beer mug and the plate of peppers. "Come on, gang, let's go. I've got the jalapeños. Somebody bring the pitcher."

"Where are we going?" I asked, raising my voice over the lyrics of "Prop Me Up against the Jukebox if I Die."

"To play a game of darts," Ruby said shortly. "You're mad at Hark, I'm angry at Amy, and Smart Cookie is pissed at the council. We have to work off our aggressions somehow. And if darts don't do it, there's always the pool table."

"Yeah, right." Sheila grinned. "And if that doesn't work, we can always go out in the alley and do some target practice with the trash cans." She patted her shoulder bag, where she carries her weapon when she doesn't have it on her hip. "That'll take care of the aggression."

"Yeah, but somebody's bound to report us to the local cops," I said, picking up the pitcher. "Hark would have a lot of fun making a headline out of that one. CHIEF BAGS TRASH, SPENDS NIGHT IN CAN. If we want to work off our aggressions, it's safer to go across the street to the Old Firehouse and dance the Cotton-Eyed Joe. We haven't done that in a while."

"Since when is dancing the Cotton-Eyed Joe any safer than target practice?" Sheila hooked me around the neck with her arm and hipped me so hard that the beer sloshed out of the pitcher. "Remember last time? Ruby nearly caught her tits in the wringer, playing hit-and-run with that cowboy from Kerrville. He was all set to haul her to the nearest motel and jump her bones."

"Don't be crude, Sheila." Ruby lifted her chin. "You're just jealous because he quit coming on to you."

"He quit coming on to Sheila when he found out that she's the chief of police engaged to the county sheriff," I said, as we made our way across the room. "That bit of news hosed him down in a hurry. He didn't have quite the same fire after that."

"That's all you know," Ruby remarked, and giggled reminiscently.

Sheila laughed. "Come on, guys. First one to stick a dart in the Great One's teeth gets to spring for an order of cabrito kabobs."

I never had a sister, and maybe it's just as well. I've *chosen* my sisters. They are named Ruby and Sheila.

Chapter Thirteen

dilly, n. (5) *slang* (orig. *U.S.*). A delightful, remarkable, or excellent person or thing; freq. ironical 1935 *Amer. Mercury* June 220/1 Ain't that a *dilly* (or *honey*)! 1958 R. Chandler *Playback* xix. 159 You're the most impossible man I ever met. And I've met some dillies.

Oxford English Dictionary

I don't know about the others, but an evening of darts, pool, and the Cotton-Eyed Joe, liberally spiked with cabrito kabobs, nachos, and gales of giggles, was exactly what I needed to mellow my spirits. After our first pitcher of beer, we switched to soft drinks, so we could have a good time without getting tanked. But it had been a long day and by ten-thirty, all three of us were more than a little giddy and ready to call it a night. We splashed through another shower to our cars, traded quick hugs, and went our separate ways.

I didn't go straight home, though. I headed for Kate Rodriguez's, where Amy had said she was staying the night. Sure, it was late and the streets were flooded curb to curb, but I needed to have a serious talk with Amy, either alone or in Kate's presence, depending on how things went. If I was lucky, I might be able to kill two birds with one stone, and find out what Kate knew about the Morgan situation. Of course, Ruby would have been glad to come along if I'd asked her, and I felt a little guilty that I hadn't. But Amy's situation was complicated enough without dragging her mother into it, and she'd be more likely to tell me the truth about her relationship with Todd if Ruby wasn't sitting there, alternately glaring and making poor-little-girl noises.

I finally found Kate Rodriguez's house, located not far from I-35 at the end of Dallas Drive, where the street is cut off by Cedar Creek, which at that point runs parallel to the freeway. From the dull sound of rushing water, I could tell that the creek was already out of its banks, and I wondered how high it might get, and whether the house would be threatened. Only a few blocks downstream, where Cedar Creek dumps into the Pecan River, the land is maybe thirty feet lower and the houses flood whenever we have a sustained rain event, as the meteorologists call it these days. *Gully washer* is more descriptive, but I have yet to hear the term on television.

Amy had been right about the size of Kate's place. It looked just big enough for a living room, bedroom, kitchen, and bath. But in the glow of the nearby streetlight I could see that the house was surrounded by a large, well-cared-for yard, with flower borders along either side and across the front of the house. There were two cars parked out front—Amy's was one of them—and the lights in the front of the house were on, so they hadn't gone to bed yet. In fact, when I got to the front step, I could hear music—the heavy beat of Latin drums and a loud guitar—and smell the rich scent of fresh chocolate brownies.

Amy opened the door to my knock. "Hey, China!" she said, stepping back in surprise. A small frown creased her forehead. "Is something wrong?"

"Just thought I'd stop by," I said, evading her question. I noticed that she had cut her hair, short enough to cut out most of the rainbow. It gave her a winsome, pixie look. She wasn't wearing her Egyptian queen makeup, either. I raised my voice above the music. "I got your note."

"Oh, it's China Bayles!" Kate exclaimed. She has a pleasant voice, deep and husky, almost melodious. Through the open door behind her, I could see into the cheerful kitchen, and she had a plate of brownies in her hand. "Come in out of the wet," she said. "You're just in time to save us from a fate worse than death—eating an entire batch of brownies all by ourselves. Sit down and have some with us."

Kate Rodriquez is a tall, sturdily built woman in her early thirties, with a quiet beauty passed down to her by generations of Mexican Indian ancestors: large brown eyes and heavy lashes, ivory-satin skin, high cheekbones, a full mouth, straight dark hair cut boy-style. Her khaki shorts showed off firm, tanned legs, and her short-sleeved red shirt had what looked like chocolate stains on the front.

The living room was low-ceilinged and small, and three pieces of furniture—a futon with a denim cushion and hand-painted pillows in bright, primary colors; a leather-cushioned barrel-shaped rattan chair with a piece of Mexican weaving thrown over it; and a low wooden table topped with brightly painted Indian tiles—took up most of the floor space. The scuffed floor was covered with a large red and brown woven rug. There was no television set. Instead, the walls were hung with original art, Mexican, from the

look of it. There were bookshelves, and a triangular desk
had been built into one corner, as a computer workstation.
Beside it was a cassette deck and a stack of tapes, next to a
half-dozen framed photographs of a younger Kate and her
much younger sister. I knew that Kate's mother had been
killed in a car wreck a decade or so before. Kate had been
in college at the time, but she'd assumed total responsibility for her sister, until the younger girl had tragically died
of leukemia a few years before. I remembered seeing the
girl's photo in the stores around town, with a glass jar for
collecting money to help pay the hospital bills.

Amy went to turn down the volume on the tape, and the
windows stopped rattling.

"Nice place," I said appreciatively, looking around.
"Cozy. Everything's in scale."

"Yeah." Kate grinned. "Cozy but occasionally claustro-
phobic. I've got my eye on a bigger place, with a couple of
bedrooms and a garage, over by the elementary school. No
flooding over there." She cocked her head. With the music
turned off, we could all hear the sound of Cedar Creek.
"The water has never gotten high enough to flood the yard,
but there's a first time for everything. One of the neighbor
kids drowned in that creek the last time it flooded. It's
pretty dangerous back there."

I sat down in the chair, and Amy took one end of the futon, picking up a pillow and cradling it in her lap. Kate put
the brownies on the coffee table in front of us, and sat
down beside Amy. Driving over, I had given some thought
to how I might approach this. I'd had decided to play it
straight up, banking on the hunch that Amy had already
confided her pregnancy to Kate. I didn't think it was the
kind of thing you'd keep from your best friend.

"Actually," I said, "I came to talk to Amy. I have some news."

Amy stiffened slightly. "What's so crucial that it can't wait until tomorrow?"

"Not a problem, Amy." Kate stood up, glancing at me. "I can go in the bedroom if you want to talk alone."

"That's not necessary," Amy replied. She reached for Kate's hand, almost defiantly, and pulled her back down. "Kate knows about the baby, if that's what you've come to talk about."

"I thought she probably did," I said, unruffled. "Have you told her about the father?"

"I thought we agreed," Amy said in a guarded tone, "that we wouldn't go there."

"That was before."

Kate seemed to tense, and her arm went around Amy's shoulders. Amy gave me a blank stare. "Before what?"

"Before Phoebe Morgan was found dead, with part of your letter to Todd Kellerman in the pocket of her jeans." It was better to tell her all of it, all at once. It wouldn't be any kinder, any less brutal if I strung it out, and I might learn more if the news shocked Amy into speech. Or Kate, since it wasn't entirely impossible that she had some information about this affair.

"And before Todd was discovered behind the wheel of his car, parked at a gravel pit near Wimberley," I went on. "He died from a gunshot wound in his right temple. They found the gun, on the seat beside him. He'd been there for a while, probably since the early part of the week. About the time that Phoebe was killed."

"Todd—" Amy's eyes had gone wide, her face white. "You're making it up!" she gasped. "It's a . . . a lie!"

I shook my head. "I'm sorry," I said. "It's the truth."

"No!" she cried. "Oh, no!" Her shoulders shook and she turned toward Kate, beginning to weep. Kate put her arms around her and held her as if she were a little girl, rocking backward and forward, smoothing her hair and making small comforting noises, while Amy sobbed wretchedly. Kate's questioning glance met mine over Amy's bent head, and I nodded.

"It's true, I'm afraid," I said. "I was at the plant this morning when Phoebe's body was discovered. I heard the news about Kellerman from the editor of the *Enterprise* this evening. It will be tomorrow's headline."

Amy kept on crying. After a few minutes, I got up and went to the workstation, where a box of tissues sat on the shelf. I carried the box to the coffee table and sat down again. Kate took one out and gave it to her.

"Thank you," Amy said in a muffled voice, and blew her nose. She wiped her eyes with the back of her hand. "You're not making this up, China? He's really dead?"

"We can call the sheriff and confirm it," I offered. I looked at my watch. "Blackie's probably still in the office. He usually stays late when he's working on a case."

Woodenly, Amy shook her head. There was a long silence. "I really didn't love him," she said at last, in a tone that suggested that she really had loved him. "We didn't . . . we weren't together all that often, so I didn't know him very well, either. But he seemed like such a sweet guy, very gentle, very quiet. And so passionate about his art. I can't believe that he—" She hugged the pillow against herself, forcing the words out through stiff lips. "I just can't believe that he's dead. That he would . . . would kill himself. He was going to have a show at a gallery in

Santa Fe. He was so proud of it. He had everything to live for."

"I know," I said gently. "I'm sorry, Amy."

Another long silence. This time, it was Kate who broke it, speaking in a low, husky voice, carefully toneless. "You said that Phoebe Morgan was dead, China. How did she die?"

"The medical examiner's report won't be back for several days," I replied, "but I saw the body and it looked to me as if she was struck in the head. She was dumped in an effluent tank at the plant, probably on Sunday night."

"How did she—" Amy swallowed painfully. "How did Phoebe get my letter?"

"She didn't have the whole thing," I said. "What she had was maybe seven or eight lines from the middle, and the top and bottom pieces were torn off. Maybe Todd had it and she snatched it away from him. Or vice versa."

She looked at me, calculating. "So it didn't have my name on it? How did you know it was mine?"

"I didn't know," I said. "I guessed. And then, tonight, I found this." I took out the note she'd left on the kitchen table. "Same paper, same pen, same handwriting. So I was sure." I put it back in my pocket.

"You haven't shown it to the sheriff?"

"Not yet, but I will. He has to know, Amy. But it would be much better if it came from you, and if you could answer his questions directly."

Amy's face crinkled up again, and tears welled up in her eyes. "But my letter has nothing to do with *anything!*" she wailed, bending over the pillow. "I don't know why Ms. Morgan had it in her pocket, but—"

"She probably had it because she and Todd were arguing over it," I said, as Kate rubbed Amy's back with the flat of her hand. "Two people heard them, and both of them say that she was pretty upset. Violent, even."

"Arguing over it?" Amy's voice was strained. "Then she knew—"

"That Todd was the father of your baby? I don't think there's any doubt of it."

She sat very still for a moment, taking deep breaths, trying to calm herself. "But that doesn't have . . . didn't have any connection with her . . . with her death. Or his. It *couldn't,* China."

"That's difficult to say right now," I said quietly, "since we don't know yet who killed her, or why. And I haven't yet heard the official report of Todd's death."

"Todd didn't kill her," Amy said. Her voice was trembling. "He didn't. He *couldn't!* He wasn't that kind of person."

Kate was sitting very still. I looked at her. "Do you have any ideas? About Phoebe Morgan, I mean."

Kate's eyes went quickly to Amy, and she frowned. Reading her glance, I knew she was trying to decide what or how much to say in front of her friend. "I'll . . . have to give that some thought," she said.

I got the signal. I nodded and leaned back in my chair. Amy seemed calmer now, and I asked, more casually, "So how did you happen to meet Todd, Amy?"

"Brad introduced us—Phoebe Morgan's son." She ducked her head. "Brad and I sort of hung out together last year. We were just friends, of course," she added, too quickly. "One of those casual things. Both of us like reggae music, so we'd go places where we could hear it. Brad has lots of money, and he likes to spend it." She made a wry face. "Not always wisely, I guess—but I didn't know that then. He seemed like somebody who needed a friend. A real friend, I mean. I thought I could help him." Her voice went flat. "I was wrong."

"I guess you have to be with somebody for a while to figure that out," I said. It sounded as if Brad had been one of Amy's Lost Causes.

"I guess," she sighed. "I thought he was . . . well, entertaining, I suppose. He knew lots of cool places to hang out. We'd mostly go to Austin, to Sixth Street, to listen to live music. A lot of his friends play reggae in the clubs, and . . ." She stopped. "Well, you know. Stuff like that. That's what we did. Nothing very . . . exciting."

Her eyes didn't quite meet mine, and I knew there was more, no doubt having to do with the Sixth Street drug scene. Austin touts itself as the Live Music Capital of the World, with Sixth Street at its heart, in the same way that New Orleans boasts about Bourbon Street. East of Congress, Sixth Street is lined with bars and dance clubs, each booking a couple of bands a night. As you walk along, you're accosted by guys popping out of open doors, pulling you inside to listen to rhythm and blues, punk, grunge, reggae, rock, enough to make a music lover drool. And there are a lot of music lovers who come to Austin just to listen and enjoy themselves—and spend money, too, of course.

But this economic blessing is also a curse, for behind the lighthearted, rowdy revelry of college kids and tourists, there's a much darker, nastier scene, the private domain of the drug dealers. The Austin police do what they can to control the traffic, but it's never enough. Crack cocaine, heroin, ecstasy, designer drugs—you name it, it's available on Sixth Street. I didn't push Amy for details, though. I had the feeling that whatever her relationship with Brad had been, it was over now, and I didn't need to hear all the details of what was probably a sordid story. I segued to what I really wanted to know.

"How about Todd? When did you meet him?"

"When?" Her voice was getting stronger. "Late January, maybe. Early February. He started coming with Brad and me when we'd go to Austin. He's . . . he was different than Brad. Quieter, more reserved, and he didn't do drugs—at least, not very often. I liked him. I liked having him along. It gave me somebody to talk to when Brad was . . . doing his thing. And when he wanted to see me, just the two of us, without Brad, I said yes. Mostly, though, we didn't go out. He'd come over to my place and we'd get a pizza or something and rent a movie." Her smile was wistful, sad. "Stuff like that."

"How did Brad feel about you and Todd?"

"He didn't know, at least for a while," she said. "At the time, I didn't think it mattered to him. He's just into . . . having fun."

"How long did you and Todd see each other?"

She looked down at the tissue twisted in her fingers. "Not very long. Maybe a month. Four or five times altogether. I thought it might be—" She shook her head sadly. "When I first met him, I thought he was staying with Brad. Then I found out that he was . . . involved with Brad's mother."

"How did you find out?"

"Brad told me."

"Was he jealous of you and Todd?"

"Well, maybe a little."

Kate cleared her throat.

"A lot, I guess," Amy amended, not looking at Kate. "Brad is . . . well, he's sort of possessive about things he thinks are his."

Takes after his mother, I thought, but didn't say it out loud. "Maybe he wanted you to know the whole story before you got in over your head," I said, putting the best spin on it. Or maybe he was trying to step between Todd and Phoebe. Judging from what I had seen and heard when Brad arrived back home from West Texas on Thursday, he suspected Todd of being a con artist, and deceiving his mother. Might've been something to that.

"Well, maybe." She shivered. "I didn't stop to wonder why Brad was bothering, but of course I was very upset. The next time I saw Todd, I asked him point-blank if it was true—that he was having sex with Phoebe Morgan—and he said yes. I asked him how he could do it, her being so much older than he is, almost old enough to be his mother. It must be sort of like being a stud horse or something." She hugged herself. "But he got mad at me and said I shouldn't say anything bad about her. He said she was very sweet and generous, that she gave him all kinds of support—money, a place to live, help in getting his pictures out into the world. I think he just couldn't turn any of that down. Especially when she offered to set him up in his first big show. The one in Santa Fe."

There was another silence. Amy seemed to go away somewhere, as if she were remembering the angry scene that had taken place between the two of them. From the look on her face, the memory was a painful one. "And then what?" I prompted gently.

She winced as if I'd jabbed her with a needle. "When he told me all this, I decided I wouldn't see him again until—" She gnawed on her lip.

"Until he broke it off with Phoebe?"

"Well, of course," she flared. "Wouldn't you?" She shook her head, her eyes filling again with tears. "Unfortunately, it was a little too late." She brushed her hand to her eyes. "A lot too late, I guess, since I'm pregnant. And now he's dead."

"Thank you, Amy," I said. "First thing in the morning, I'd like you to come to the sheriff's office with me. Will you do that?"

She glanced at Kate. "We're going to PickleFest. We've been planning it for a couple of weeks. Kate's going to show me where she works and—"

"Uh-uh." I shook my head. "There was some serious flooding out that way today, and the main road is closed. Anyway, the plant itself is a crime scene, so it's off-limits. PickleFest has been canceled."

Kate gave a short, hard laugh. "Well, that takes care of PickleFest, Amy. I don't think you have any excuse."

Amy looked at me. "What does my mother know about . . . any of this?"

"Very little. She was at the plant when Phoebe's body was found, but she didn't see the letter. She knows about Todd—about the argument with Phoebe, and about his death—but nothing about the connection between the two of you." I smiled crookedly. "She's still convinced that Jon Green is your accomplice in the baby-making business."

"I'm truly sorry about that." Amy's voice was somber. "I don't know how to persuade her that Jon isn't the father, when I don't feel able to tell her the truth. She likes him a lot. I think she'd prefer that the baby was his, even if he is married. Maybe that gives it a special drama, too. You know how dramatic my mother is." Amy traded glances with Kate. "Do you—" She swallowed. "Would you ask the sheriff to keep this quiet? I'd rather not let anybody know about it, at least until I have to."

"Of course," I said. "I can't tell you for sure what he'll decide, but I know him well enough to guarantee that he'll do his level best to protect you. I'll call and let him know that you'll be available. You'll come?"

Amy's eyes went to Kate. "I think you should," Kate said quietly.

"All right, then." Amy nodded like an obedient child. "I'll come."

I leaned over and patted her shoulder. "I hope you can get some sleep tonight. You'll want to be fresh for the interview."

Kate stood up as well. "You haven't had any brownies, China. I'll put some in a bag for you, and then walk you out to your car."

Amy gave her a questioning look, and Kate bent over to drop a kiss on her cheek. "It's okay, sweetie," she murmured. "I won't be long. Why don't you jump in the bathtub and soak for a while?"

The damp air was rich with the scent of honeysuckle, and the rain had slackened to a light mist. Cedar Creek was a muted roar in the background, and somewhere close by, a chorus of frogs and cicadas celebrated the summer rain. A streetlight cast a bluish glow over my white Toyota.

Kate said nothing until we reached the curb and I unlocked the car door, opened it, and tossed the bag of brownies onto the passenger seat. Then she spoke. "I suppose you figured out that Brad was dealing."

"I guessed," I said.

"Amy says he quit a few months ago. Anyway, compared with what goes down on Sixth Street, he was very small time."

"Why was he doing it? For the money?"

"I don't think so. His mother gives him anything he asks for." She paused. "The thrill, I guess. The kicks. Some guys ride bulls or bungee-jump or free-fall. Brad sold dope. And did . . . other things. Bad things. But dope, mostly."

Bad things? Worse than dealing? "Is he a friend of yours?" I asked.

"We hung out together." A pale smile ghosted across her mouth. "For a while, about a hundred years ago, before I—" She stopped and gave me an oblique look. "I'm no shrink, China, but these crazy things he does—they've got to do with his mother, somehow. Like maybe he's getting back at her for the way she treated his father."

I wasn't terribly interested in psychoanalyzing Brad. It was Amy I cared about. I hesitated, not really wanting to know but feeling I had to. "How much did Amy know about the drugs?" The next question was harder. "How much was she involved with Brad?"

Kate shook her head. "A little involved." She looked up at the streetlight, and I had the feeling that what she was saying was not exactly the truth. "You know how she is about rescuing people. She knew what he was doing—the drugs, I mean. She thought she might be able to rehabilitate him. It took her a while to figure out that nothing she did was going to have much effect. That was about the time Todd came along, I think."

"Tough lessons," I murmured.

"Yeah. To tell the truth, I think Brad—well, he sort of scared her." She laughed without humor. "He's fun to be with, but it's crazy fun, you know? Too crazy. Dangerous crazy. Like walking a tightrope over a tiger pit."

"And what about Todd? How did he fit into all this dangerous craziness?"

She shrugged. "I don't know. But he was quieter. I think he seemed sort of safe to her, especially after Brad. She talked about how sweet he was, and how kind. And he was an artist, and sensitive to her feelings—more than Brad, anyway. She didn't see the side of him that Brad saw."

So which was it, I wondered. Sweet and sensitive, or a bastard and a con artist, out for all he could get? Or both, maybe. "She cared for Todd, I take it."

Kate kicked my front tire, not looking up. "She's been through a rough time, China. She was terribly hurt when she found out about Phoebe. She felt he'd betrayed her. She felt . . . well, like a fool. And when she found out she was pregnant, she felt even worse. Especially after the way her mother acted." Her voice became bitter. "Ruby as much as told Amy that she was a child who couldn't be trusted to make up her mind about what was best for her and the baby."

In defense of Ruby, I said quietly, "It's a two-way street, Kate. Amy hasn't always behaved like an adult—and she certainly has her own problems with trust."

"Tell me about it," Kate said with an ironic twist to her mouth. "It's a huge issue for her." She glanced up and added, without inflection, "Amy isn't responsible for those two deaths, China, but she's involved, and the more she thinks about it, the more she's going to hurt." Her eyes were on mine, her gaze straight and clear. "Inside, she's a lot younger than she looks. She doesn't have things sorted out, and she's vulnerable, fragile. She needs to be protected. I've promised her—and myself, too—that I'll do my very best to keep her from being hurt again. I hope you will, as well."

There was a resonant tone in Kate's voice that made me suddenly aware that the relationship between her and Amy had gone further than simple friendship. "Will she be moving in with you?" I asked. "When you get your bigger house, I mean?"

Kate slanted a long look at me, part acknowledgment, part defiance. "That's our plan," she said finally, squaring her shoulders with a what's-it-to-you expression on her face. "As soon as the deal goes through on the new place. I can always rent this one if it doesn't sell right away."

Far be it from me to interfere with the love lives of consenting adults. If it worked out, Amy wouldn't have to be a single mom, and the baby would have two loving parents. *If* it worked out. Ruby's wild child hadn't exactly exhibited a marked tendency toward stability in her young life, and it sounded as if she was bouncing to Kate on the rebound from her brief affair with Todd, which had come on the bounce from Brad.

On the other hand, there was something sturdy and dependable and patient about Kate that made me think that perhaps Amy had finally found someone who would not abandon her. I thought of the photographs of Kate and her younger sister that I had seen on the living room shelf. Maybe Kate and Amy had a mutual need that their relationship mutually satisfied. Amy yearned for someone she could count on after being abandoned by her birth mother and losing her adoptive parents in a car wreck. Kate craved someone to care for, as she had cared for her dead sister. It's a mistake to confuse mutual dependencies, important and compelling as they might be, with love, for dependencies can be transient and even tragic. But enduring love has been built on shakier foundations. Who am I to say how their relationship would work out?

These were not thoughts I was willing to share with Kate. Instead, I smiled. "Let me know when you're ready to move in," I said, "and I'll come to your housewarming party."

Kate visibly relaxed. "We'll be glad to have you, China. Amy thought you'd be all right about it—about us, I mean." She made a wry face. "She's not sure about her mother, though. She's not ready to tell Ruby about us yet, so I need to ask you to keep our secret."

I nodded, thinking that Ruby probably wasn't the problem. Amy's grandmother and great-grandmother—*they* would be the problem. Girl friends were one thing. Girl lovers were quite another. Unless I missed my guess, Kate would be an even bigger deal than Amy's baby. But maybe they wouldn't come out to the whole family. Maybe they'd do it on a need-to-know basis—although that doesn't work very well when it comes to Ruby's family. They all seem to feel that they need to know *everything*.

Kate was watching me with a look of sober appraisal. "Amy says we can trust you," she said. "If that's true, there's something more. About Morgan's."

"I'm listening."

She took a deep breath. "Phoebe told me that she intended to tell your husband that Vince Walton might be cooking the Morgan books and ask him to look into Vince's finances. I know from Amy that she came to your house last Sunday. Has your husband told you anything about the situation?"

I nodded briefly and noncommittally. I'd promised Mc-Quaid that I wouldn't talk about his case with anybody, but I hadn't promised not to nod.

"Then you probably know that Phoebe asked me to go through the books and see if everything was kosher." Briefly, Kate closed her eyes, shaking her head. "God, China, I can't believe she's dead. I just can't *believe* it. And yet—" Her mouth hardened. "I can believe it, too," she said fiercely. "And in my opinion, Todd Kellerman had nothing to do with it. Vince Walton did it. I'm positive. And I need to make sure that the sheriff gets the full story."

"Let's start from the beginning," I said. I leaned against the Toyota and folded my arms across my chest. "Why did Phoebe hire *you?* I mean, I know you're a whiz, but why not bring in a forensic accountant?"

Kate shrugged. "Because I'd worked out there before, as a temp, and Vince liked me. And because Phoebe was looking for somebody who didn't look like an auditor. Somebody who wouldn't scare the horses, raise suspicions in the office. Somebody who would do what she was hired to do and keep her mouth shut." She grinned. "I'm smarter than I look, China. I'm smart enough to look dumb."

"A useful attribute." I grinned back. "It also helps to look young and pretty and a hell of a lot more innocent than you are. What did Vince think you were doing there?"

"Accounts payable was behind, and she told him she'd hired a temp to help out. He accepted that. But a week or so later, he got suspicious, and decided that there was another reason—that I was there to help Phoebe get ready to sell the plant. That was the fallback cover story." She laughed shortly. "But to tell the truth, I just don't think it ever occurred to Vince that somebody might be on to him. He told me once that his mother had given him the right name. He was invincible." She made a noise in her throat. "Dumb. Heavy-duty dumb."

I stared at her. "You're saying that the plant *isn't* going to be sold?"

"Oh, Parade is interested, all right," Kate said, "but the discussion was very much in the preliminary stage. For one thing, this accounting situation has to be cleaned up, and that's not going to be easy. Only part of it is on the computer, and even there, the various pieces don't connect. For instance, there's no easy way to track a transaction all the way from the purchase order to the invoice and the payment. And even if the books are clean, you can't sell a business if you can't establish an audit trail."

I frowned. The Phoebe I knew was a controlling person. How had she let something as simple as an accounting system get screwed up? "Phoebe's always been big on modernizing the plant," I said. "I would've thought she'd take care of the bookkeeping end of things, as well."

"She modernized production," Kate replied. "She'd grown up with the business and she'd learned from her grandfather how to make pickles. When her father died and she took over the plant, she made a big change in the product line, to increase sales and lower production costs. She signed all the disbursement checks and reviewed the bank reconciliation, but beyond that, she never got very deeply involved in the accounting."

"Funny," I grunted. "I had her figured for a numbers cruncher." Somewhere in the distance, thunder rumbled.

"Well, she was," Kate said. "But she only crunched the

numbers she got from the accounting system. When she took over the plant, there was a bookkeeper she trusted—somebody who had actually been on the payroll when her grandfather was still alive—and he always gave her just what she asked for. When he retired, she decided it was time to replace his manual records with a computerized cost-accounting system. She also wanted to convert from a cash to an accrual basis, something that should have been done a long time before. But it probably wasn't smart to try to do everything at the same time."

"That's when she hired Vince?"

"Right. He was supposed to modernize the office and put all the systems on the computer to improve reporting visibility—to make it easy to track."

"Did he?" I remembered something Marsha had said about Vince not knowing everything he was supposed to know.

"Are you kidding?" She laughed soundlessly. "Actually, what he did made things a whole lot worse—at least as far as Phoebe was concerned. He bought an accounting package and installed it, but she didn't know how it worked or how the output was derived, which meant that she depended on the numbers he gave her. And since the various pieces—ordering, purchasing, invoicing, collecting—weren't integrated and the production systems weren't tied in, she was still in the dark."

"Doesn't sound good," I said.

"Yeah. The profit margin was slipping, and she couldn't understand why. In the last eighteen months, things began to look really grim, and no matter where she cut costs, the situation didn't improve. Bottom line, she began to suspect that Vince was cooking the books. She wanted me to see how bad it was."

"And how bad was it?"

A flash of lightning lit her face. "Up until a few years ago, the vendor list was remarkably stable. But after Vince took over, new vendor accounts began appearing, one at a time. Over the past couple of years, it looks like he's established accounts for maybe a dozen new vendors."

"Some of them dummies, I suppose," I said. I'd seen that kind of fraud before.

"Most of them dummies," she said, as the lightning was followed by a reverberating clap of thunder. "He'd create a purchase order and an invoice for materials that were never actually ordered or received, and when Phoebe signed the disbursement checks he deposited them into his dummy accounts."

"How much do you think he took?" I asked, thinking that the sheriff and Charlie Lipman would soon be asking her this question, since this was a matter of both criminal and civil liability.

Kate shrugged. "To be honest, I can't tell for sure. What I can tell you is that things are in a hell of a mess, and that it's going to take full access to all the records and a detailed audit to straighten everything out. But as a preliminary guess, I'd say that it's close to three hundred thousand, maybe more." She tilted her head. "It sounds like a lot of money, and of course it is. But compared to some embezzlements, it's peanuts. I read recently about a guy who practiced a similar fraud, except that he was doctoring the endorsements on the checks and got away with a couple of million before anybody got wise."

"Did you tell Phoebe what you found out?"

She nodded. "We met a week ago, and I gave her a ball-park idea. That's when she told me she was going to hire your husband, to see where the money had gone. I was supposed to have a meeting with her on Tuesday, to go over the items I thought should be examined more carefully. But Marsha phoned and said Phoebe wouldn't be available, and we'd need to reschedule." She caught her lower lip between her white teeth. "From what you said, I guess Phoebe was already dead."

I gave her a straight, hard look. "So you think Vince killed her?"

"Absolutely," she said, without hesitation. "He is an arrogant son of a bitch. People in the plant are scared to death of him. And you said she was found in the effluent tank. That's someplace he would think of. He'd stuff her body down that hole, and he'd laugh."

"But if Vince killed her—or even if he knew she was dead—why didn't he get the hell out of town? What's he still doing here, when he could be safe in Mexico or Brazil or somewhere like that, enjoying his money?"

"It's a good question," she conceded. "But it all fits together, don't you see? He's so damn arrogant, so invincible, that he thinks he can't be touched. He's probably enjoying this whole thing, and congratulating himself on getting away with it."

I could understand that. I've known people, both men and women, who were so sure of themselves that they thought they could get away with murder. And what McQuaid had dug up seemed to support this hypothesis. Vince apparently never intended to leave the country, since he'd invested at least some of his ill-gotten gains in real estate and vehicles. He was acting as if he thought he'd never be caught—which was either very dumb or very, very smart.

I touched Kate's arm. "I'd like you to come with Amy and me in the morning," I said. "The sheriff will want to talk to you. I'll pick you two up about eight, if that's okay with you."

"Sure," she said. "I'll come." Her mouth tightened. "I didn't much like Phoebe. But I'd sure like to see that son of a bitch Vince get what's coming to him."

The front door of the house opened and a figure was silhouetted against the light. "Kate?" a light voice called tentatively. "Kate, you're going to get wet out there."

Kate called, "I'm coming," over her shoulder. She turned back to me. "Gotta go. Thanks, China."

"You're welcome," I said. "Good night."

I watched her as she went quickly back up the walk to join Amy in the lighted doorway. She slipped her arm around the other's waist, and the two of them stood together, waving at me as I drove away.

Chapter Fourteen

Dill: Mercury has the dominion of this plant, and therefore to be sure it strengthens the brain. . . .

Nicholas Culpeper
The English Physitian: or, an astrologo-physical discourse of the vulgar herbs of this nation, 1642

The rain was coming down hard by the time I got home, and it was after midnight. McQuaid was still up, lounging in his big leather recliner in the living room. The lamp behind him cast a golden glow over the litter around his chair—newspapers, books, a half-filled popcorn bowl, an empty Bud bottle, and that day's dirty socks—a comfortable, masculine sort of litter, suggesting that the master of the house hung out here when he wasn't out conquering the world. An old movie (at a glance, it looked like *The Guns of Navarone*) played on the television, and McQuaid had another Tom Clancy thriller on his lap. He looked up at me over the tops of his wire-rimmed reading glasses.

"I was beginning to worry about you," he said. "You and the girls have a good night out?"

"You should have seen us dancing the Cotton-Eyed Joe. We were spectacular. A spectacle, anyway." I dropped the bag of Kate's chocolate brownies onto the coffee table. "The rewards of the chase. Help yourself, sweetie."

He reached for the bag. "Before I forget, Ruby called a few minutes ago. She asked to talk to Amy. I told her she wasn't here, so she wanted you to call."

I looked at my watch. "Maybe I should wait until tomorrow. It's pretty late, and I'm just about brain-dead."

"She sounded urgent."

I rolled my eyes. "Ruby always sounds urgent. To tell the truth, I don't want to talk to her. Sheila spilled the beans about your PI business and she got all excited."

"Figures," McQuaid said, resigned. He added, in a warning tone, "China, I'm telling you. Keep Ruby out of my cases or—"

"I understand," I said hastily. "I'll call her from the kitchen. And then you and I need to talk."

But before I spoke to Ruby, I needed to fortify myself. I opened the refrigerator, pushed aside a plate of very dead crawfish with shells and antennae intact, and took out the milk. As I poured myself a glass, Howard Cosell reminded me that he'd been left home alone and lonesome all night, and asked if he could please have something to comfort his soul. We were out of hot dogs—they weren't all that good for him, anyway—so I found one of the doggie treats he likes. I drained about half the glass of milk and then reached for the phone.

Ruby answered on the first ring. "Where's Amy?" Her voice was annoyed. "I need to talk to her."

"She's at a friend's house," I said, immediately wary. "What's up?"

"This isn't Twenty Questions, China. Who is her friend? When will she be back?"

I sighed. "Look, Ruby, it's been a long, hard day and everybody's tired. Why don't we just let things slide for tonight? I'll have her call you tomorrow."

"I don't understand you, China." Ruby's voice was strained and angry. "It sounds like you're trying to protect her from her *mother!*"

"No, of course I'm not," I said, instantly contrite. "I'm tired, that's all. My brain has turned to mush." I looked at the clock. "It's seventeen minutes after midnight, Ruby. What's so important that you have to—"

"Brad was here a little while ago, looking for her."

I frowned, surprised. "Phoebe Morgan's son?"

"Do we know any other Brads?" Ruby demanded, exasperated.

"Settle down, Ruby. Why was he looking for Amy?"

"He wanted to talk to her. He wanted to tell her that Todd Kellerman is dead. He was polite and very nice, but . . ." She paused, and when she spoke again, her voice was uneasy. "I've got an odd feeling about this, China. I'm afraid that Amy must be involved in this business somehow. Why else would Brad Knight make a special trip over here to tell her that Todd Kellerman killed himself? Does she . . . how well did she know Todd?" She took a deep breath. "What in the world does Phoebe Morgan's *boy toy* have to do with my daughter?"

"I'm afraid I can't answer that," I said evasively but truthfully. Given Amy's previous relationship with Brad, I guessed that he felt he should be the one to break the news of Todd's death. After all, Brad had introduced Amy and Todd, and the three of them had been friends—not to mention that Brad had been jealous of Todd. But I couldn't tell Ruby any of this without telling her about Amy's connection to Brad, and that would not be a good idea. It might lead to speculation about Amy's connection to Todd, and I definitely did not intend to get tangled in that can of worms.

"I guess you're not going to be a friend and tell me where she is," Ruby said wearily.

I tried to put a smile in my voice. "I'm going to be a friend and tell you to make a cup of herbal tea, run a lavender-scented bubble bath, and soak for twenty minutes before you go to bed. Everything will be brighter in the morning." Of course it would. It was pitch black right now. Tomorrow was bound to be brighter, one way or another.

Ruby sighed heavily. "I suppose you're right, China. It is awfully late. And if she actually knew Todd Kellerman, she'll probably be upset when she hears that he killed himself."

"Probably," I agreed, still cautious. "It's upsetting news." I hesitated. "Did Brad happen to say anything else while he was there?"

"I'm afraid I didn't give him much of a chance," Ruby replied. "As I said, he's very nice—a charmer, really. He has a sweet smile, although he's obviously very upset about his mother. Part of me wanted to put my arms around him and give him a big hug." She hesitated. "But I had a sort of funny feeling. I didn't really want to talk to him any more than I had to. My intuition kept telling me that there's something here that I don't understand."

Vintage Ruby, tuning in to Brad's relationship with Amy. I changed the subject quickly. "I had fun tonight, Ruby," I said. "I think Sheila did too."

"I hope it took her mind off her troubles," Ruby said. "It's no picnic, waiting to find out whether you're going to be fired. I'm only sorry that we can't help with her investigation. And speaking of investigations—"

"Let's not," I said, before she could start in about McQuaid. "Please."

She sighed. "Well, good night, then. I'll see you in the morning."

"Oops, that reminds me," I said hastily. "I've got an errand to do first thing. Will you open the shop for me? Laurel's supposed to come in at nine-thirty, and by that time, I should be there."

"You'll owe me," Ruby warned.

"Oh, you bet." I smiled, wishing I could hug her, wishing I could sit down with her and tell her the whole truth. I hate keeping things from Ruby. "Good night. Sleep tight."

I hung up the phone, picked up my glass, and went into the living room. It was time for some serious talk with my husband, although I wasn't sure exactly where to start.

I began with what seemed to be the most significant piece of business. "Have you heard that Todd Kellerman's dead?" I asked, dropping onto the sofa.

McQuaid had not only heard, he had been to the crime scene. He had happened to be at the sheriff's office, signing his statement about Vince Walton's various financial holdings, when the call came in. Blackie invited him to go along, so he'd climbed into his truck and joined the sheriff's caravan out to Simon's Gravel Pit.

"*Simon's* Gravel Pit?" I asked, the hair prickling on the back of my neck.

"That's what the sign said," McQuaid replied. "The place hasn't been worked in a few years, and the local kids go there to party and make out. The pit is full of water and the road—nearly impassable, after all the rain—ends in a beach, which is littered with the usual beer cans and condoms. The car was found by a couple of teenagers with sex on their minds." He eyed me curiously. "What's so interesting about the name?"

"It might be nothing. But Simon—Art Simon—is a neighbor who's been complaining about the quality of the effluent from the pickle factory. According to Marsha, the plant has passed all the necessary inspections, but that hasn't satisfied Simon." I paused, frowning. "I wonder if there's some connection."

McQuaid pursed his lips. "Probably a coincidence, but I'll suggest to Blackie that he check it out." He leaned forward to pick up a pencil and a pad of yellow sticky notes from the coffee table. "Art Simon, huh?"

I nodded. "Marsha knows him. She mentioned talking to him on the phone yesterday." I reached for the bag of brownies and fished one out. "How certain is it that Todd committed suicide?"

"Forensics is still working on the car, but that's certainly what it looked like. The gun was on the seat where it had fallen, and the powder burns were clearly evident." He finished writing and tossed the pad onto the table. "Why all the interest in Kellerman? Do you know him?"

I shook my head and nibbled at the brownie, which was rich and nutty. Kate was obviously as good a cook as she was an accountant. "Amy knew him quite well, I found out tonight. She's the person who wrote the letter that was found in Phoebe Morgan's pocket." Quietly, I added, "Kellerman was the father of her baby."

"The father of—" McQuaid blew out his breath. "I'm

sorry to hear that, China. This must be tough for her." He sat back in his chair. "I thought she swore not to reveal the guy's identity. How'd you get her to tell you?"

"Thumbscrews," I said, finishing off the brownie and considering whether I could afford the calories in another. Regretfully, I decided it wasn't a good idea. "No, actually, it was the note she left on the kitchen table this evening. It gave her away. Did you see it?"

"Yes, but—" He frowned. "It just said that she was going to stay at Kate Rodriguez's place tonight. What does that have to do with anything?"

The movie hit a loud patch and I raised my voice over the sound of men at war. "It was written on the same yellow paper, in the same handwriting, as the letter in Phoebe's pocket. When I heard from Hark that Todd was dead, I thought it was time to corner her. It didn't take much to get the truth. Todd's the guy, all right." It suddenly occurred to me that I should suggest to Amy that she petition for a court order to obtain and test a sample of Todd's DNA, so she would have proof of paternity. More damn complications. I scowled at the television. "Can you turn that thing down?"

He picked up the remote and hit the mute button, and Anthony Quinn was silenced just as he was about to say, "I'm not so easy to kill."

"Did Phoebe know it was Amy who wrote the letter?" McQuaid asked, dropping the remote on the table. "Was that the reason for the argument between her and Kellerman?"

"You know about that, too, huh?"

"Blackie filled me in on his interview with Marsha. And I was in the office when the Morgan housekeeper— Lunelle, her name is—came in to give her statement." He grinned. "Quite a character. She said you assured her that stealing daylilies is not a federal offence."

"Marsha calls her a snoop."

"I don't doubt it," McQuaid replied. "I didn't sit in on the interview but I read her statement. From where I sit, it looks like Phoebe and Kellerman argued over his extracurricular affairs, Kellerman hit her, dumped the body in the tank at the plant, and shot himself. Classic murder-suicide."

"Yeah, that's certainly what it looks like," I said slowly. I thought of Kate and her insistence that Vince was the killer. "But what about Vince? He has a strong motive. Does he have an alibi? Has he been ruled out?"

McQuaid shook his head. "Says he was home on Sunday evening, watching television. He lives alone, though, so there's no way to confirm what he claims. But if Vince killed Phoebe, how was Kellerman involved? Why—"

He was cut off by the shrill ring of the phone on the table at my elbow, and I picked it up, thinking that it was Ruby again. It was Amy. Her voice was somber but excited.

"China, Kate and I have been talking about Todd, and there's something she thinks I ought to tell you—tonight." Without waiting, she plunged ahead. "You said he shot himself in the right temple, and that the gun was on the seat beside him. I didn't question this at the time. I was so shocked to hear that he was dead that it drove everything else out of my mind. But I don't see how he could have killed himself that way, China. Todd was left-handed."

"Left-handed?" I frowned, as McQuaid's head came up sharply. "You're sure of that?"

"He used to say that all the best artists were lefties. Pablo Picasso and Leonardo da Vinci and Michelangelo and Raphael—and Todd Kellerman." Amy made a disconsolate little-girl whimper, as if she were afraid. "Todd didn't kill himself, China. Somebody murdered him."

"I'll pass the word," I said, and added, "Thank you for calling, Amy. If you think of anything else, just pick up the phone—no matter what time it is."

"I will," she said. "I'll see you in the morning, China." She hesitated, and her voice relaxed. "And thanks. For being such a good friend, I mean. I'd be lost without you—and Kate." In the last two words, there was an implicit recognition of the fact that I was a trusted partner in their secret. I wasn't sure whether I felt complimented or just plain uncomfortable.

"You're welcome, Amy. Try to get some sleep." I broke the connection and passed the phone to McQuaid. "Amy says that Kellerman was left-handed. He and Picasso and Michelangelo."

McQuaid swore softly. He took the phone from me, punched in the sheriff's number, and spoke to the dispatcher, a guy named Chip, whom both of us know. Blackie had gone back out into the storm—some idiot had tried to drive across a flooded low-water crossing and had been lucky enough to get hung up in a downstream tree—but Chip agreed to pass the word without delay.

"McQuaid." I held up my hand. "Before you hang up, tell Chip that I'll be in tomorrow morning about eight-fifteen with two women, both of whom can fill in some of the bigger blanks in this case. They've volunteered to make statements or be interviewed, whatever Blackie wants."

McQuaid delivered the message, then reached for another brownie and sat back in his chair. "*Two* women?"

"Amy and Kate Rodriguez. Kate has the inside dope on

Vince, to complement the outside stuff you put together." I gave him a quick rundown of Kate's story. I didn't, however, tell him about her relationship with Amy. Men sometimes take a dim view of such things. Anyway, it was Amy's secret.

When I finished, he whistled. "Three hundred thousand is more than I had estimated. It's a hell of a lot of motive." His face was puzzled. "Although if he killed Phoebe, how does Kellerman figure into it? There's a page or two missing."

"Maybe a whole chapter," I said. "What about the security cameras at the plant? Did the surveillance system turn up anything useful?"

"Not a thing," McQuaid said. "I was still there when Blackie had the tapes played, so I got a good look. The way the system is set up, there are two twelve-hour tapes for each day, fourteen tapes altogether. So a tape from Sunday night wouldn't normally be reused until the following Sunday. We viewed every nighttime tape, from Sunday night through this morning."

"Did the cameras pick anything up?"

"Somebody stuffing a body into the effluent tank, you mean? Not a chance. Nobody was on the scene who shouldn't have been there, nobody did anything they shouldn't have done. There wasn't a clue." He paused. "However, something interesting did happen on Sunday night. The tape is digitally time-stamped, in the left-hand corner. The stamp on all the cameras stopped at twenty-one hundred hours thirty-four minutes, and started up again at twenty-two hundred hours, two minutes—a full twenty-eight minutes later."

"Twenty-one hundred hours." I did a quick mental translation. "So somebody turned off the system at nine thirty-four. And started it again at ten-oh-two. Right?"

"Right. All but the camera at the front of the building, that is—the one that covers the front door. That camera wasn't turned on again until Monday morning at six-thirty, when the assistant plant supervisor—a guy named Willie—arrived and put in the Monday tape."

"Did he notice that the camera was off?"

"Yeah." McQuaid nodded. "But he figured it was just a malfunction. He ran the tapes back and checked them on fast-forward, but he didn't see anything out of the ordinary. He didn't notice the twenty-eight-minute gap in the time stamp, either. So he turned the camera back on and forgot about it."

"Sounds reasonable," I said. "So you're thinking that Phoebe's body was put into the tank during those twenty-eight missing minutes?"

McQuaid nodded. "Whoever did this knew enough about the system to know how to turn the cameras off. He dumped the body, then stopped the tape, backed it up to nine thirty-four, and started it again, and the cameras simply recorded over the incriminating evidence. To cover his exit from the building, the killer turned off the front camera." He took off his glasses and rubbed his eyes. "I'm using the masculine pronoun. I suppose it could have been a woman, although we don't have any women suspects."

"Marsha Miller isn't a suspect? She has motive, means, and opportunity. And she knows how to operate those cameras. Kellerman probably didn't."

He eyed me. "Motive? What motive?"

I parried with another question. "It wasn't clear from Lunelle's statement?"

"If it was, I missed it."

"She was in love with Todd Kellerman. She hasn't said it in so many words, but she probably slept with him a time or two."

He looked disgruntled. "I guess Lunelle left that detail out of the version she gave Blackie. You're sure?"

"Sure as shootin'. It was in the version she gave Ruby and me. And Blackie knows it, too, from his interview with Marsha this morning." I paused. "So. Marsha goes up on the guest house porch during the argument. She stands outside the door, listening to Phoebe yelling and throwing things. She opens the door, thinking that Todd is in trouble. There are angry words, maybe even a physical threat. She loses her temper, picks something up, and hits Phoebe on the head. Or maybe Kellerman hits Phoebe, and Marsha comes up with the idea for dumping the body in the tank."

"I see what you're saying," McQuaid said slowly. "Then—"

"The two of them together—Todd and Marsha—take Phoebe to the plant. Marsha, who knows very well how to manipulate those surveillance tapes, turns off the cameras while they are disposing of the body, then turns them back on again, all but the camera that covers the front door."

"It's a good theory, Counselor," McQuaid said, "but—"

"Yeah, I know." I sighed. "But it doesn't explain who shot Kellerman. *If* somebody shot him. Maybe he painted with his left hand and shot guns with his right." At his quizzical look, I said, "Some people are ambidextrous."

"True," McQuaid acknowledged. "And we still have Vince, he of the powerful motive."

I yawned and stretched wearily. "So how did that interview go? What did he say when Blackie confronted him with the stuff you found?"

McQuaid shook his head. "He refused to answer any questions until he got a lawyer, but Blackie figured he had enough for an arrest, and the judge agreed. Vince has been in the county jail on suspicion of embezzlement since about three o'clock this afternoon."

"Ha," I said. "So much for the invincible Vince."

McQuaid hit the remote again, and the TV screen went dark. "You look tired, China. What say we head for bed?"

It sounded like a very good idea to me.

Chapter Fifteen

When in a garden the mallows die, and the green parsley, and the blooming crisp dill, they will wake from their winter's sleep and return to life again, in the spring of the year. But when we die, we sleep a perpetual slumber which knows no seasons and from which none awake, not even the greatest and bravest and wisest among us.

Moschus, Greek poet, c. 150 B.C.E.

The next morning wasn't a great deal brighter, after all. Rain was falling from a leaden sky when I left the house, and since the temperature was already in the seventies, the air felt like a sauna. I was glad that Pauline had canceled PickleFest. The morning newscast had been full of ominous warnings about flooding, and River Road was closed at the Bluebonnet low-water crossing. And even if people could have reached the festival grounds, they would have been slogging through knee-deep mud, soaked to the skin and parboiled. Not one of Texas's finest days.

I pulled up at the curb in front of Kate's house and honked the horn. Amy and Kate dashed out the door and ran to the, holding hands and laughing at some private joke as they dodged the raindrops. I was glad to see Amy smiling, after her shock of the night before. While Todd's death might cast a temporary shadow, it obviously wasn't going to darken her life.

"Your mom called late last night, Amy," I said, after the girls had climbed into the car, Kate clambering into the back, Amy next to me. "Brad dropped by her house, looking for you."

A look of something—apprehension, maybe, or perhaps even fear—flew across Amy's face so quickly that I barely caught it. She turned and exchanged an enigmatic glance with Kate, then turned back. "Does he . . . does he know where I am?"

I shook my head, putting the car into gear and moving forward. "I didn't tell your mother, either. I just said that you'd check in with her when you got back later today."

Amy threw another quick glance over her shoulder at Kate. "Actually," she said, "I've decided to stay with Kate for a while—if that's okay with you, I mean."

Kate leaned forward. "We're going to take a look at that house near the school this afternoon. And in the meantime, we've decided that we can both fit into my place." She paused. "We hope you don't think—"

"That I'm being ungrateful." Amy took up Kate's sentence. "It's just that we would really rather—" Another glance at Kate, this one very easy to read. Kate put out her hand and touched Amy's shoulder.

"I understand," I said. I had heard their "we," a small word that said everything there was to say. "And of course I don't think you're being ungrateful." I chuckled. "Brian will be utterly crushed, of course. I hope you won't forget your promise to arrange a blind date for Ivan."

"Brian?" Kate asked warily. "Ivan?"

I looked up, my eyes meeting Kate's in the rearview mirror. "Brian is my son, and Ivan is his pet tarantula. Amy offered to find her a boyfriend."

Kate grimaced. "I don't think I want to hear the gory details. If I'm going to have pets, I'd prefer a nice pair of hamsters."

"Of course I won't forget about Ivan," Amy told me. "Jon's already put out the word." She sobered. "Did Mom say what he wanted? Brad, I mean."

I made a left turn onto Brazos, heading in the direction of the new county sheriff's facility, which is located out past the high school, on the western outskirts of town. "He wanted to tell you about Todd. I guess he thought it was his responsibility to break the news to you, since the three of you are—were friends."

"Oh," Amy said. "You're probably right. That was considerate of him." But her lips were tight, and her eyes were fixed straight ahead. "Would you do me a giant favor, China? Please don't tell him that I'm staying with Kate."

"Why?" I gave her a curious look, noticing that there were blue shadows under her eyes. "You're not afraid of him, are you?"

"Afraid? Why, of course not," she replied quickly, still not looking at me. "It's just that—"

"It's just that he wouldn't understand about us," Kate said, her voice low and husky. "He might be . . . you know. Uncomfortable. You know how guys are sometimes."

"You're sure you don't mean 'jealous'?"

"Jealous?" Amy turned in the seat, giving me a wide-eyed look. "Of course not. Why should Brad be jealous? He and I were never—We were friends, that's all."

Kate leaned forward. "Tell us what's going to happen at

the sheriff's office," she said, changing the subject. "Is the sheriff himself going to question us? Will we have to sign something?"

It was obvious that Brad was not on the list of approved topics of conversation. Now that I thought of it, maybe Kate was the jealous one. Todd was dead, but Brad was alive and still—perhaps—interested in Amy. Kate might be afraid that Amy would become interested in him again. But this was entirely between Kate and Amy, and none of my business. Taking my cue, I began to tell them what they might expect, adding the information that Vince had been locked up on suspicion of embezzlement since the afternoon before.

"That's great news!" Kate exclaimed. "And if you ask me, he's not just a thief, but a killer as well. I'm glad he's behind bars."

My eyes met hers in the mirror again. I wanted to ask her how Vince might have been connected with Todd, and whether she thought he was responsible for Todd's death, as well. But the question might have upset Amy, so I held my tongue.

The new Adams County Sheriff's Department office isn't nearly as pleasant as the old one, which was housed in the old library building on one corner of Courthouse Square. Of course, the old office had its drawbacks—crowded rooms, narrow halls, peeling paint, and the city council had never liked the idea of having the jail right smack in the middle of town. It wasn't good for our image of Pecan Springs as a cozy, comfortable village, where everybody played by the rules and the only criminals were people who failed to feed the parking meters or pay their library fines.

But the old office also had wooden floors, dark oak woodwork, and tall windows with stained glass panels at the top, not to mention a view of the pecan trees that shade the square and the picturesque old guys who gather on the wooden benches, relics of yesteryear. The office had a friendly, folksy, nineteenth-century feeling, as if we were still living in the old, slow times. The new building, on the other hand, is built to withstand the assaults of the twenty-first century: a car bomb through the front door, maybe, or a TOW missile attack. It's a concrete bunker with no exterior windows, and you have to show your driver's license in order to get past the guard. Once inside, the hallways and rooms have a slick, sanitary, institutional sameness: white walls, white ceilings, gray tile floors, gray steel desks with large, one-eyed computer monitors, everything washed in the blue-white glare of fluorescent lighting. It's depressing as hell, and it isn't even the jail. That's in a separate but similar building, similarly fortified.

The only thing familiar about the office was Jennie, whose pleasant, gold-toothed smile was a welcome sight. She showed us where to get coffee and pointed us to seats in the hall. "The sheriff is with somebody," she said. "I'll page him."

Blackie didn't keep us waiting long, but when he appeared, striding toward us down the hall, he was not alone. Brad was with him, and the two were engaged in conversation, Blackie listening with polite attention, Brad speaking with a somber gravity. He was dressed somberly, too, in gray slacks, a dark shirt and tie, and a navy blazer, and he wore a serious expression. I had a quick, contrasting memory of a younger, punkier kid in baggy cutoffs, untied Reeboks, and a clinking panoply of body jewelry and tattoos. This new, revised Brad was a pleasant change. He was obviously growing up.

But when Brad saw Amy, something flashed across his face, sudden surprise, mixed with a quick vexation. I turned to see that Amy, too, was startled. Her shoulders tensed and she leaned, as if unconsciously, toward Kate, as if to shield. But when Brad's mouth relaxed into a smile, she seemed to relax as well.

"Well, hi, Amy," Brad said in a mild, friendly tone. "And Kate Rodriguez. I didn't expect to see you two here."

I stood and held out my hand. "You may not remember me," I said, "but we met last Thursday, when you came back from West Texas. I'm China Bayles, Brad. I'm very sorry about your mother."

"Thank you," Brad said, with simple dignity. "Phoebe was a great lady, with tremendous energy. She'll be missed." With a despairing look, he gave his head a shake. "I keep thinking that if I hadn't brought Todd here and introduced the two of them, none of this would have happened. They'd both be alive."

"That's a natural feeling," Kate said sympathetically. "I lost my sister a few years ago, and all I could think about was what I might have done to change things." She glanced at the sheriff, frowning a little, and I knew she was remembering Vince. "But is it certain that Todd was responsible for—"

"We haven't concluded the investigation yet," Blackie interrupted smoothly. "We're not releasing any of the details." He put out his hand to Brad and the two of them shook, man-to-man. "Thanks for coming in, Mr. Knight.

We'll let you know when the autopsy's finished and your mother's body can be moved to the funeral home. It'll be Monday, most likely."

"Thanks." Brad swiveled to face Amy, his mouth tightening imperceptibly. "I stopped at your mother's to see you last night, Amy. I wanted to let you know about Todd. I didn't want you to read about it in the newspaper." He cleared his throat, and his eyes, questioning, went to Kate, then back again. "But since you're here, I guess you already know. That he's dead, I mean."

"Yes," she said in a low voice. She swallowed painfully. Her face seemed pale, and her hands were clenched in tight fists. She was looking at him as if she'd never seen him before. "I . . . heard about it last night."

"I'm sorry," he said softly. "I know that you and Todd were . . . friends. Whatever he did to my mother, I forgive him, Amy. I'll never believe that he intended to hurt her. He was just . . . well, confused. All I can do is remember the good times and think the best of him. I hope you can feel the same way."

"I . . . yes," Amy whispered. She put out her hand and pulled it back again, blinking away the tears. "I'll try."

There was a brief silence. Then Brad cleared his throat and turned to me. "Ms. Bayles, I'd appreciate it if you'd let Pauline Perkins know how sorry I am that PickleFest had to be canceled. I think it was the right thing to do, under the circumstances. Tell her I'll give her a call so we can talk about rescheduling. Morgan's wants to continue to support the community in every way it can."

"I will," I said, and watched him walk away, tall and steady. This was definitely a different Brad. It would be sadly ironic if it had taken his mother's death to straighten him out and make him grow up. I turned around and glanced at Amy. Her face looked haunted and uncertain, and I saw Kate take her hand and hold it, almost as if to keep her from following him.

"Well, now, China." Blackie broke the tension. "You said that these two ladies want to make statements."

Reminded of the purpose of our visit, I put an arm around Amy's shoulders and introduced her and Kate. "They each have a separate story to tell you," I added. "I'll wait out here. I'm their ride back to town."

"Oh, no," Amy exclaimed. She reached for my hand. "Please, China, for moral support." She threw a pleading glance at Blackie. "If it's okay with the sheriff."

Blackie nodded. "Okay by me."

So I got to hear Amy's narrative all over again, delivered more formally this time, and with the department's tape recorder operating. Blackie showed her the letter, still in the plastic evidence sleeve, and Amy identified it as a fragment of the one she had written to Todd Kellerman, telling him that she was pregnant. He listened with sympathy to her story about their relationship and to her insistence that Todd was left-handed and could therefore not have shot himself in the right temple and dropped the gun on the car seat to his right. But when he asked her if it was possible that Kellerman might have been ambidextrous—perhaps he had painted with his left hand but used his right hand for other activities—she seemed a little unsure.

"Have you ever watched him play a sport?" he asked.

"Volleyball," she said, after a moment's hesitation. "I saw him play volleyball, over at the park."

"And how did he hit the ball when he served? Right-handed? Left-handed?"

She frowned. "Right-handed, I think. But he—" She stopped, looking cornered. "But he was left-handed. I'm sure of it."

Blackie asked a few more questions, and when she was finished, he thanked her and turned to me.

"Is that it, China?" he asked. "Anything that needs to be added?"

"I think that's it," I replied, and all three of us stood. But I hung behind as he showed Amy out and asked, in a lower voice, "What do you think about this right-handed, left-handed business, Blackie?"

He closed the door behind her. "Amy is the only one who has brought it up. I checked with Marsha Miller this morning, after I got your message. She thought Kellerman could use both hands equally well, but said she wasn't sure. Brad Knight was positive that he was right-handed."

I thought for a moment. "Did Kellerman have any family? Anybody who could back up Amy's statement?"

Blackie shook his head. "Parents are dead, no siblings. It might be possible to dig into his past and find a teacher or a friend who might remember. But it's a long shot. For the moment, Amy is the only one who seems to know."

I thought how sad it was that a man could die and leave so little behind. But with that thought came also the recollection that Todd *had* left something behind, the child that Amy would bear in December. Which reminded me again that Amy had the greatest stake in proving him innocent.

"Is there any other evidence suggesting that Todd's death might be something other than a suicide?" I asked.

"Well," Blackie said slowly, "there was a duffel bag full of clothing in the backseat of his car. And several boxes of personal items stacked inside the guest house. It looks as if he was in the process of moving out of the Morgan place. But that might have been before the argument. Kellerman and Morgan could have quarreled, he killed her and dumped the body, then got to thinking about it. Suicide seemed like a better alternative than life on the lam, so he took her gun, drove out to the gravel pit, and shot himself."

"Took her gun?"

"Didn't McQuaid tell you? The weapon was a thirty-two-caliber automatic, one of two sold to Phoebe Morgan three years ago. It's got Kellerman's prints on it, and nobody else's. And I should also add—for your ears only—that we've uncovered some extensive forensic evidence in the trunk of Kellerman's car. We won't know for sure until we get the lab report back, of course, but we're reasonably certain that the dead woman's body was transported to the plant in that vehicle."

That certainly seemed to pin it down, all right, and probably exonerated Vince. It was hard to imagine a scenario in which he and Kellerman were both involved in Phoebe's murder. "Have you found the rest of Amy's letter?" I asked.

He shook his head. "The guest house had been completely cleaned. Other than some painting gear and a couple of cardboard boxes of clothing and personal items, we didn't find a thing—no letter scraps, no glass, no sign of an argument. But that's no surprise. Marsha Miller admits to cleaning the place thoroughly on Monday. She says she didn't throw anything away but some broken glass. The housekeeper, a woman named Lunelle, says it was part of her regular job, but Miller told her not to bother, she'd take care of it. Apparently, Miller wanted an excuse to be in the guest house for an extended period of time." He grinned slightly. "She wanted to have a look through Kellerman's possessions, is the way I read it."

I nodded. "It turns out that Lunelle is Janet's aunt—Janet is our cook at Thyme for Tea. Lunelle told me that she saw Marsha get out of the pool and go up on the porch during the argument. Did she give you that information?"

"Yeah. I checked it out with Miller. She said she stood there for a few minutes, trying to decide whether to interrupt the argument."

"And then?"

"And then went back to her apartment, put on some clothes, and went to a movie."

I stared at him. "A *movie*?"

"She sat through it twice and didn't get back home again until after midnight. She said she just had to get away from the house. She couldn't produce a ticket stub, though—said she'd thrown it away."

"Well, maybe," I said slowly. "I suppose it could have happened like that, but—" I shrugged.

"Yeah. Well, she gave us the name of the theater, and we're checking it out." He paused. "Didn't you tell me that Miller knew about the operation of those surveillance cameras?"

"Right. Why?"

"Because when I asked her about the system, she denied having any knowledge of it."

"That's not very smart," I said emphatically. "Ruby and Pauline and I—she told all three of us how it worked." I frowned. "Marsha might have helped Kellerman dispose of the body. But that wouldn't explain how he wound up dead—unless it actually was a suicide." I shook my head, feeling genuinely puzzled. "You know, I saw Marsha on

Wednesday night, and then again on Thursday and Friday, and she certainly didn't strike me as an accomplice to a murder. And she gave every indication of believing that both Kellerman and Morgan had gone away together."

Blackie smiled crookedly. "People don't always tell the truth. You've never been taken in by an accomplished liar, Counselor?"

I grinned bleakly. "More than once, I'm afraid. I've seen juries fooled, too."

Blackie put his hand on the doorknob. "Anything else?"

I hesitated, thinking of the handsome young man in the corridor this morning, who seemed to have grown up almost overnight. "Brad. I suppose his alibi checked out. And Art Simon, the neighbor who complained about the effluent. Have you talked to him?"

Blackie nodded. "Brad was traveling in West Texas Thursday and Friday and stopped in Abilene for a rodeo on Saturday. We checked the motel records for both Saturday and Sunday nights. He was in San Angelo on Monday and Tuesday, and on Wednesday, in the Fort Stockton area." He paused. "Art Simon . . . well, he's a different story. We're looking into the situation."

"I see," I said. "Does Simon have any connection to the gravel pit where Kellerman's body was found?"

"The pit belongs to his cousin. And apparently Simon has done more than just complain about Morgan's alleged code violations. According to Vince, he came to the plant about three weeks ago and threatened Ms. Morgan with bodily injury. Last week, he filed a formal protest with the TNRCC."

That would be the Texas Natural Resource Conservation Commission. Simon was calling in the big guns. "Bodily injury, huh? Does he have an alibi?"

Blackie lifted his shoulders and let them fall. "Nothing we've been able to corroborate just yet. Interesting thing, though—he appears to have been acquainted with Kellerman. When I dropped in to talk to him, I noticed a couple of Kellerman's paintings on the wall. He says he saw them at the bank and bought them. Kellerman himself brought them out and hung them."

"And Simon lives next door to Phoebe," I said thoughtfully.

"Right." He opened the door, giving me one of his rare, sweet smiles. "I'm glad that you and Ruby took Sheila out and showed her a good time last night, China. It got her mind off the Holeyfield investigation, for a few hours, anyway."

"That's a tough situation," I said. I grinned. "Did she tell you that she beat the pants off us at the pool table?"

He laughed. "She said that the two of you let her run the rack. She's played you and Ruby too often to believe that she could beat y'all that easily. Anyway, she had a good time."

"Yeah, we did, too."

He became businesslike again. "Well, if that takes care of it, I'll talk to Rodriguez. Thanks again, China."

Kate didn't ask me to sit in on her interview, and I didn't offer. Amy and I waited on chairs in the hall, not saying anything. When Kate was finished, the three of us went back to the car. Out in the parking lot, however, I encountered McQuaid, carrying a briefcase.

"What are you doing here?" I asked curiously.

"I promised Blackie I'd bring in the backup for the report I made yesterday. And I wanted to see what progress he's made in the investigation." He glanced at Kate and Amy, who were climbing into the car. "How did the interviews go?"

"Pretty well," I said. I chuckled. "Can't leave it alone, can you, McQuaid? Once a cop, always a cop."

McQuaid bent over and brushed my cheek with his lips. "Afraid you're right, babe. You've got to admit that there's no danger involved in this one, though—at least not in my end of it. Blackie's got Vince buttoned up tight." He paused. "Where are you off to now?"

"I'm heading to the shop. This is it for me. I've had enough of playing cops and robbers, and I'm sure that you and Blackie can handle things from here on out. Between PickleFest and these two deaths, everything's been up in the air for at least a week. It's high time my life got back to normal."

"Normal?" McQuaid grinned. "Who wants normal?"

"*I* do," I said emphatically.

Chapter Sixteen

LEMON HERB VINEGAR

If you can't get to Pecan Springs to buy this luscious lemon vinegar at Thyme and Seasons, you can make it at home very easily—and exactly as lemony as you like it.

2 cups champagne vinegar
1 cup loosely packed lemon herbs: lemon balm,
    lemon verbena, lemon thyme, lemongrass
1 tsp. lemon zest

Gather fresh herbs just after the dew has dried, when the volatile oils are at their peak. Wash and pat dry on paper toweling. Strip the leaves, place in a clean, sterilized quart jar, and bruise them with a spoon. Add the lemon zest. Pour the vinegar into the jar (you don't have to heat it) and cover the jar tightly. Place in a dark cupboard and let it steep, shaking the jar every day or so. After a week, taste the vinegar. If the flavor pleases you, strain out the herbs and pour the vinegar into sterilized bottles. If you like, you may add a sprig of lemon balm or lemon verbena and a curl of lemon peel to each jar. Cap, seal, and label. (If you want a stronger flavor, let the vinegar stand for another couple of weeks. If it still doesn't suit you, replace the herbs with fresh ones and steep for another week.)

I dropped the girls off, reminding Amy that her mother expected her to come to her great-grandmother's birthday party the next day. She made a face, but Kate whispered something to her and she smiled and turned docile, promising to be there. Maybe Kate was going to be a steadying influence.

As I drove back to the shop, I thought about what I had said to McQuaid. It was true. I was more than ready for some average, everyday, boring normality. The older I get, the more I treasure calm, quiet days in which nothing out of the ordinary happens, and I have the time to enjoy the ordinary stuff that goes on around me. A sign of approaching middle age, some might say—or maybe it's just that I've been there and done that once too often, and don't feel the need to be continually goosed into action by thunderbolts of thrills and excitement. I'll settle for taking my thrills vicariously, in books or on television.

I parked in the alley behind the shops, beside the old stone stable. A sign on the door reminded me that our annual aromatherapy workshop, Scents and Scentsations, was scheduled for the following weekend, and that Ruby and I needed to start thinking about the setup. We've been doing this workshop together for a couple of years, and I was looking forward to it. As I walked through the garden, sniffing the delicate, rain-wet fragrances of nicotiana and thyme, I began to feel much more relaxed and balanced. The ugly stuff that had been happening over the past few days had nothing to do with me, especially now that Amy had decided to move in with Kate. Of course, I cared very much what happened to the girl, but as far as Phoebe's and Todd's deaths were concerned, I could wash my hands of the situation. It was Blackie's job, anyway, and he—

"China, yoo-hoo, China! Got a minute?" It was Constance Letterman, sitting on her back step, smoking a cigarette. She stood up and waved her plump arms to make sure she'd caught my attention.

Constance owns the Craft Emporium, the craft and boutique mall located in the rambling, three-story Victorian next door on the west. Until last summer, the Emporium was in a sad and run-down state, but a new tenant moved in and Constance got busy and did some much-needed painting and remodeling. Then Ruby and I joined our front and back gardens to hers and to the garden at the Hobbit House, the new children's bookstore in the house next door to the east. There is now a continuous green space connecting the Hobbit House, Thyme and Seasons, Ruby's Crystal Cave, and the Craft Emporium. The backyards flow into each other with paths, pools, and fountains, my herb gardens adding color and fragrance in the center. People can wander from one shop to another without ever going back out to the street.

Constance was waiting for me with a barely suppressed air of excitement. "Is it true what I heard at Bobbie Rae's?" she demanded, before I had even crossed into her yard. Constance is from Nacogdoches, over in East Texas, and you can hear the sharp twang in her speech. "Phoebe Morgan went and got herself killed? *And* Pauline Perkins took it on herself to cancel PickleFest?"

"It's all true," I said ruefully. "Phoebe is dead and the sheriff has enough on his hands without half the county out there tramping around his crime scene." I looked up at the leaden sky, which promised another downpour any minute. "Not to mention that there's a lot of flooding, and more rain on the way," I added.

Constance's round face was somber as she digested my confirmation. She was wearing a loose red-and-yellow plaid cotton dress that came down to her ankles, its ample proportions outlining her top-heavy bulk. Her short brown curls looked like tight little corkscrews screwed into her scalp and stiffened with spray so they wouldn't pop up. Unless I missed my guess, she had just come from getting the Saturday Special at Bobbie Rae's House of Beauty, which is also a main switching depot on the Pecan Springs grapevine. Back in the days when Constance wrote the "Dilly Dally" column, she got most of her news from the girls under the dryers at Bobbie Rae's. What they don't know about Pecan Springs isn't worth knowing.

"I was shocked to my core to hear about Phoebe, China." Constance blew smoke out of her nostrils and pulled down her plump mouth to emphasize her distressed state of mind. "I mean, my very innermost *core*. Phoebe wasn't everybody's fav'rite person, I can sure as shootin' testify to that. But who woulda thunk that somebody hated her bad enough to kill her and stuff her into a pickle vat?"

"She wasn't stuffed into a pickle vat," I protested, although correcting Constance probably wouldn't do an ounce of good. The imagination is a powerful thing, and the image of a dead body in a pickle vat certainly added to the story's dramatic appeal. "She was in an underground concrete tank that's designed to hold—"

"Same difference," Constance said, waving her hand. "The poor thing musta been thoroughly pickled by the time she popped up on top." She shook her head sadly. "What Phoebe did wasn't bad enough for *that*."

"What she did?" I asked, surprised. "What did she do?"

"Anyway, it was quite a while back," Constance said thoughtfully. "You'd think all that old stuff woulda been forgotten by now." She sucked on her cigarette, blew out another puff, then dropped it on the ground and stepped on it. "But some folks have long mem'ries, I guess."

I studied her for a moment. Constance has lived in Pecan Springs for nearly forty years, and during that time has never stopped listening and taking notes, although her memory for names isn't always completely reliable. She is a walking encyclopedia of Pecan Springs trivia—and sometimes, what she knows isn't trivial at all. It can be hard, though, to tell the difference. She might not know herself.

"You're suggesting that somebody might have killed Phoebe because of something that happened a long time ago?" I asked warily.

"Not that long ago, I reckon." She tilted her head to one side. "About the time Ed Knight drove off that cliff and into the river, which would make it—what? Ten, twelve years?"

"Something like that," I replied.

"In fact," Constance went on, "some folks said it was the *cause* of Ed drivin' off that cliff. Sure, he was drunk, but he was drinkin' because of Phoebe and that man she was screwin' on the sly." Constance is not one to mince words.

Phoebe had been having an affair? But wait a minute—hadn't I heard something about this a few days before? Hadn't Cassie Michaels mentioned something about an affair? "What man?" I asked.

Constance opened her round eyes wide. "Why, that

neighbor of theirs, of course. Simon something." She wrinkled her button nose, pondering. "Let's see, was that his name? Seems to me that's not quite right. I can remember him, no problem—it's just his name I'm disrememberin'. Anyway, the two of them had been gettin' it on hot 'n' heavy for a couple of years when—"

"Hang on a sec, Constance," I broke in. "You're saying that Phoebe Morgan had an affair with *Art Simon*?"

"Yeah, that's right," Constance said, nodding vigorously. "That's the name. You know him, huh? A real lady-killer."

"I met him the other night," I said, remembering Simon's bronzed shoulders, his flat belly. He certainly had his attractions, if furry men strike you as sexy. In my misspent youth, I'd been known to fall for guys like him. "You're sure the story's true? It's not just gossip?"

"Oh, it's true, no question about that," Constance said comfortably, sure of her facts. "Art Simon's wife left him over it."

"How do you know that?"

"Because the Simons went to the same Catholic church as my sister Becky. When the priest told Mrs. Simon that she oughtta stick it out even if her husband was sleeping around on her, she got so mad she quit the Catholic Church and became a Unitarian."

"I see," I murmured.

"But if you want to talk to her about it," Constance continued, "don't bother asking around for Mrs. Simon. After she got her divorce, she married the Unitarian minister. She's Mrs. Fuller now, and a dang sight better off, if you ask me. The Right Reverend ain't much to look at, but nobody ever accused him of havin' an affair with his next-door neighbor."

"Mrs. Fuller!" I was startled. "Cecilia Fuller?"

"That's the one." Constance squinted at me. "You know her, too?"

"She drops in at the shop from time to time." Actually, Cecilia visited Ruby's shop more often than mine. She was a regular in Ruby's meditation classes.

"Well, there it is, then," Constance said, nodding wisely. "You just go talk to Cecilia Fuller. She'll tell you that it's all true." She paused for a moment, then added, sadly, "You know, the real loser in that deal was the boy."

"The boy? Phoebe's son?"

"Yeah. Brant or Bruce, something like that. He never was the same after his daddy died. All kinds of trouble, when he was in college over in New Orleans." Her voice became censorious. "His daddy never would've put up with those shenanigans. He would've made that boy stand up and take his medicine like a man, but all his mama did was hush up his misdeeds. And there were plenty, if half of what I heard is true."

"That's sad," I said, thinking of the Brad I had seen this morning, and reflecting again, ironically, that perhaps his mother's death had given him something to live for.

People are perverse. On pretty days, we can go all morning without a customer. But when it rains, here they come, especially on Saturdays. This Saturday, it rained off and on all day, with one shower after another, but it didn't dampen business. From the minute I stepped into the shop, I was constantly busy.

A number of people had apparently come to Pecan Springs especially for PickleFest; finding it canceled, they

went shopping instead, and quite a few dropped in at
Thyme and Seasons. They must have been in the mood for
pickled products, for my herbal vinegars were in great demand—so much so, in fact, that I had to go back to the
stockroom and find another carton of bottles to replenish
the display. The garlic and red pepper vinegar, the lemon
vinegar (particularly in the etched glass bottles), and the
purple basil vinegar, which has a beautiful rosy blush, all
moved quickly. The little jars of pickled peppers and garlic
disappeared, too, faster than I could put them out. Between
restocking, ringing the cash register, and answering the
phone, I didn't have a minute to think about what Constance had told me.

Ruby's shop was crowded, as well, and when the tearoom opened at eleven-thirty, I saw that Janet had added
chicken salad sandwiches and dilled tomato soup (which
she makes with dill vinegar) to the menu, just in case we
ran out of quiche. Ruby and I took turns helping out in the
tearoom, while people gazed out the windows and remarked how green and pretty the herb gardens looked in
the rain. Equally pretty, at least to me, was the melodic
sound of the tearoom's cash register, as we rang up our
customers' meal tickets.

By four o'clock, the big rush was over at last. Janet finished her kitchen cleanup and left, Laurel went home, and
I took advantage of the lull to perch wearily on the stool
behind the counter, eating a chicken salad sandwich and
washing it down with a glass of cool, tart rosemary lemonade from the shelf of refreshments that we put out for our
customers. As I ate, I surveyed the shop, noticing that I
needed to restock quite a few items. All the garlic and pepper braids had been sold, and several culinary wreaths.

Half of the *Herb Quarterly* magazines were gone, and some of the bulk herb jars were empty. I had plenty of work to do—happy work, because the empty spaces on the shelves meant a full cash register drawer. But maybe I'd leave it until Monday, when the shop was closed and I could spend some uninterrupted hours giving everything a good cleaning and straightening. If I was feeling really energetic, I might even do the windows, which could certainly stand a wash.

Right now, though, I had something else altogether on my mind, for the minute I sat down to relax, my thoughts had drifted back to my conversation with Constance. Now that I had a minute to reflect, I thought it might be a good idea to pick up the phone and tell Blackie what I had heard about Phoebe and Art Simon. If true, it was an important bit of information, because it suggested an even stronger and more persistent link between the two of them.

But I hesitated. For one thing, it *was* an old story, and whatever relationship the pair had had in the past had obviously not carried over into the present: witness Simon's physical threat against Phoebe and his angry protest against the plant's effluent treatment system, and Phoebe's involvement with Todd Kellerman. For another, I hated to bother Blackie with fragments of unconfirmed gossip. I'm not V. I. Warshawski, and I wouldn't presume to ask a woman I don't know to confirm a painful rumor about a sordid affair that might or might not have happened nearly a dozen years ago and that she probably wanted to forget.

But I also know that lust and hate can get all snarled up together in people's minds, and that the passion of one emotion can fuel the passion of the other. It's like a lightning strike in a tinder-dry forest. Violent feelings, lust or hate, ignite a violent outburst, and the next thing you know, somebody's dead. Maybe I should just tell Blackie what I'd heard, and let him decide whether to—

"Hey, China," Ruby said, coming through the door between our shops. "I've been thinking." She had a sheet of paper in her hand.

The sight of Ruby—a delightfully arresting vision of summer in green leggings and a filmy green bat-winged tunic, with a green silk scarf wound around her frizzy red hair—gave me an idea.

"You're just the person I wanted to see," I said with enthusiasm. "I wonder if you would do me a huge favor."

"Sure," she said. "If I can. But I want you to look at something first, and tell me what you think." She leaned on her elbows on the counter, pushing the paper toward me.

I picked up the paper and studied it. Ruby had made a list of the membership of the volunteer boards of various Pecan Springs and Adams County charitable organizations. One name in each list was highlighted with a yellow marker.

"What's this about?" I asked suspiciously.

"There are nine names marked in yellow," Ruby said, clasping her hands under her chin like a green praying mantis. She wore an eager look—the praying mantis about to devour an unsuspecting bug. "Do you recognize them?"

I sighed. "It's been a very busy day at the end of a difficult week, Ruby, and I'm nearly cross-eyed. I'm doing well to recognize your pretty face. Why don't you just tell me what this all means?"

Ruby sighed at my unwillingness to play her game, but gave in. "The names I've highlighted in yellow are the women whose houses have been burgled."

I put the paper on the counter, frowning. "I thought Smart Cookie told you last night to lay off. It's her investigation, and she doesn't want anybody meddling in it."

"I don't care what she said," Ruby replied, unruffled. "I am *not* laying off. Just look at those lists, China, and tell me what you see."

"But why—"

"Just *look*," Ruby said patiently, wrapping the fringe of her scarf on her finger.

"Okay, okay, I'm looking." I focused on the page, frowning. "Emma Oster's name is highlighted," I muttered. "She chairs the Nature Center board. Regina Horner is on the Art League board. Mrs. Carter serves on the Hospice board. Elizabeth Drury is on the nursing home board. Then there is Anne Wiggens, Senior Center board; Liz Ortega—" I stopped. "Ruby, what *is* this?"

"Read," Ruby commanded. "Just keep going."

"Grrrr," I snarled, and read the rest of the names very fast. "Liz Ortega, Friends of the Library; Ginger Taylor, Adventure Girls' Camp; Ginny Martini, the Children's Club board; Mrs. Holeyfield, the Greater Pecan Springs Humane Society board." I put the paper down. "There. I've read everything you've marked with yellow. Does that make you happy?"

"The burglars have been very busy," Ruby remarked calmly. "Nine burglaries. And one death." She sighed. "Poor Mrs. Holeyfield."

I frowned. "Ruby, I'm as sorry as you are about Mrs. Holeyfield, and I hate to say 'So what.' But so what? What are you trying to prove by putting all these names down on one piece of paper?"

Ruby had the air of a science teacher trying to coax a recalcitrant third-grader to peer through a microscope. "Look again, China. What else do you see that's interesting?"

Humoring her, I scanned the lists. "I don't see a thing," I said finally. "Except that—" I ran my finger down the page. "It looks like Phoebe Morgan was a member of each of these boards."

"Exactly, China!" Ruby exclaimed, triumphantly clapping her hands. "And while there is a bit of an overlap— that is, several people serve on three or four of these boards—nobody else but Phoebe serves . . . served on *all* of them!"

I put down the sheet. "I'm afraid I don't see the significance, Ruby. So the Pickle Queen happened to serve on the same boards as the burglary victims." I gave a short little laugh. "I hope you're not suggesting that Phoebe Morgan was Pecan Springs's cat burglar. You don't think Phoebe went around vandalizing the homes of Pecan Springs's illustrious citizens, stealing souvenirs and ladies' undies, do you?"

Ruby frowned. "Well, no, not exactly. But—" She stopped.

"Well, then, what *are* you suggesting?"

"I'm not suggesting anything," Ruby said, throwing up her arms in a flurry of green gauze. "I just think there's got to be a connection, that's all."

"There is a connection, and it's very simple," I said, handing her the piece of paper. "This is Pecan Springs. It's a small town. All these people know one another, and they feel it's their civic duty to volunteer for worthy causes. But until you can demonstrate something other than these chance relationships, I don't see how you can help Sheila."

Ruby's mouth turned down and she gave a discouraged sigh.

"But you might be able to help Blackie," I added.

Ruby brightened immediately. "Help Blackie? How?"

I related Constance Letterman's story about Phoebe Morgan's relationship with Art Simon, the former husband of the present Mrs. Cecilia Fuller. "I have no idea whether or not there's any truth to Constance's tale," I concluded, "and I'm not sure if there's a connection between something that might have happened ten or twelve years ago and a couple of deaths that occurred this week. But I definitely think it's worth checking out, if only to eliminate the possibility. Do you know Cecilia Fuller well enough to talk to her about her ex-husband's affair, if that's what it was?"

"Do I know Cecilia well enough?" Ruby asked, raising her arms with rhetorical drama. "Of course I do! Cecilia and I went to high school together. We were both on the cheerleading squad. We were both in the Homecoming Queen's Court." She made a little face. "Although it feels like a couple of centuries ago."

"No kidding," I said. I always forget that Ruby grew up in Pecan Springs. And whenever she mentions being a cheerleader, I am amazed, although I don't know why. Maybe it's because all the cheerleaders I have known were conventionally pretty and held conventional views about life, while Ruby's appearance and ideas are anything but conventional. I doubt if many cheerleaders from small Texas towns have graduated to reading the stars and teaching tarot.

"Anyway," Ruby went on, "Cecilia has been in my meditation group for going on two years now, so we've kept our friendship alive. And it's certainly true that she used to be married to Art Simon. He was a high school athletic star, and enormously popular. They got married right after college. I even remember when they got divorced, although I had no idea that Phoebe Morgan had anything to do with it." She glanced at her watch. "The Fullers live only a couple of blocks from here. If you wouldn't mind watching the shop, I could run over there right now and see if Cecilia can spare a few minutes to talk."

"Of course I wouldn't mind," I said. "You don't have to get into all the gory details with her, though." Ruby has a way of persuading people to share their life histories with her. Maybe it's because she's such a good listener. She seems to hang on every word, and she has an intuitive sense of just when to murmur "Oh, dear," or "I fully understand." If Cecilia got started, they could be there for hours. "If you can simply confirm the story about the relationship, we'll call Blackie and let him know about it."

"I'm on my way," Ruby said, turning with a whirling flourish of her gauzy green wings.

"Go get 'em, Bat Woman," I said with a grin.

Chapter Seventeen

There were many traditional rules for harvesting herbs for uses in ritual. Most importantly, the herbs must always be gathered with the left hand. It was thought that a vein in the left hand went directly to the heart, and that the left hand was wiser in ways of the heart than the right.

I spent the next few minutes tidying up the worst of the mess, reshelving books and making a list of things I needed to bring from the stockroom. I was sweeping the floor when the front door opened and a blast of rain-wet air scattered my pile of dirt and tracked-in leaves. I looked up. Amy was poking her head through the partly opened door.

"Is my mother here?" she whispered.

"She just left," I replied. "But she'll be back in fifteen or twenty minutes. Are you looking for her?"

"Definitely not," Amy said emphatically, coming in and closing the door behind her. She was wearing jeans and sneakers and a ragged, much-washed "Save the Caribou" T-shirt, with a large knitted bag slung over her shoulder. She shook her wet hair, scattering raindrops all over. "If she was here, I was going to give you something and run. When Mom sees me, she turns parental, and I don't need that right now. But since she's not here—" She opened her shoulder bag and took out an envelope, holding it up.

I leaned my broom against the wall. "What's in the envelope?"

"A couple of things. One is a picture of Todd. I cut it out of the local newspaper. It was taken in April, when Phoebe got the bank to hang his paintings in the lobby." She took it out and handed it to me, her tone pleading. "Please, China, take a look at it."

I carried the photograph to the front window, where the light was better. It showed a tall young man, easy in his body and extraordinarily handsome: dark, thick hair curling over his collar, mysteriously dark eyes, classic nose, even dimples, for pity's sake. There was something about his face, his boyishly sweet smile, that gave him a look of vulnerable innocence, at odds with his obvious sexual appeal. With ruffles on his shirt and a sword in his hand, Todd Kellerman might have been the cover model on a paperback romance, turning from the heaving bosom of the merry widow to the clinging embrace of the pure and passionate ingenue. It was no surprise that Amy had found him attractive, and that Phoebe had been willing to support him and buy him a car and be his patron. I'd probably patronize him too, if I were ten years younger and single— except that the man in the photo was dead now. He wouldn't smile that innocently dimpled smile ever again, or waken a woman to passionate desire, or feel his own passion aroused. It was a sobering thought.

I cleared my throat. "He's very good-looking."

"Yes." Amy had come to stand at my elbow. "But what I wanted you to notice is that he's holding the brush in his *left* hand."

I refocused. In the photo, Todd was posed on a stool in front of an easel displaying a large unframed canvas. In one hand he held an artist's palette, in the other a brush. Amy was right. The brush was in his left hand, the palette in his right.

"I see," I said, handing the photo back. It was strong evidence for her claim that he couldn't have shot himself in the right temple—but not irrefutable. What if the photographer had needed to get just that angle on him, and that was the best way to pose?

"There's something else," she said, taking out another piece of paper. "It's a note he left on my door once, when I wasn't home. I stuck it in a desk drawer and forgot about it until this morning, after I talked to Sheriff Blackwell. It was obvious that he didn't believe what I was telling him. So I drove to the storage locker where I'm keeping my furniture and dug through stuff until I found it."

"I don't think it's a matter of belief, Amy," I objected mildly. "Blackie's still investigating. So far, you're the only person who says that Todd was left-handed." I looked down at the note she had handed me, written on the corner of a crumpled piece of junk mail in a back-handed, barely legible pencil scrawl. *Sorry I missed you. I'll try the laundromat. Todd.* I put the note into the envelope and handed it back to her.

"Don't you think this ought to convince the sheriff?" Amy asked. "You can tell by the backward slant to his writing that Todd was left-handed. Right-handers don't write that way."

"Maybe. But the slant isn't always definitive," I said. I'm no graphologist, but I've questioned a few expert witnesses in my time and I knew what I was talking about.

People often think that lefties are the only ones who write with a backhand slant, but it's just not so. "However," I added, "between the note and the photograph, I'd say that you've made a pretty strong case for the defense."

Her mouth was firm, her eyes intent. "I'm positive that Todd didn't shoot himself, China, and I know that he didn't kill Phoebe. Whoever murdered one of them murdered both of them." She squared her shoulders and her voice took on a passionate resonance. "Somebody's got to stand up for the truth, and it looks like I'm it. I'd feel a lot better if I had your help and support."

Another cause, I thought. Amy was always happiest when she was campaigning for somebody or something that needed protection—like the whales, like the caribou, like Brad and Todd. But in this case, I knew that she had an additional motive, and a very compelling one. After all, Todd was the father of her baby. She would want to do her very best to see that he didn't leave a legacy of murder and suicide. It was going to be hard enough to explain to her child that his or her father was dead. It would be unspeakably painful to say that he had killed a woman and taken his own life. I didn't blame her for insisting on Todd's innocence, and I was moved by her passion. Suddenly, my desire to distance myself from the situation didn't feel quite so urgent.

"All right," I said. "I'll do what I can—although I don't know what." It wouldn't be the first time I had stepped up to the bench to defend someone accused of murder. It wasn't just Amy's passion that moved me, though. These two pieces of evidence weren't definitive, but if I were Todd's defense lawyer, I could certainly use them to cast doubt on the prosecution's case against him. And they were enough, taken together with things like the packed clothing and painting gear, to make me suspect that Todd might not have been the killer, but the killer's second victim. In which case, who was the killer? And was he, or she, about to get away with a cleverly staged murder-suicide?

Amy bit her lip. "Then take this," she said, handing me the envelope again, "and give it to the sheriff. You're a lawyer—you can make a better case for Todd than I can." She blinked back grateful tears, struggling to smile. "I'd just cry, and that won't impress that sheriff one bit. Anyway, I'd really rather not go out there again. That place—" She shivered. "It's cold, like a morgue or something. It gives me the creeps."

"I understand," I said, with a little smile. "It gives me the creeps, too. I'll see that Blackie gets this, along with an explanation." More than an explanation, I'd see that he got an argument. It would be unfortunate if he closed his investigation before he took a long, close look at the other suspects, including Art Simon.

Amy leaned toward me and kissed my cheek. "Thanks, China. I guess I'd better get out of here, before my mother shows up. But there's something else I really need to talk to you about." She looked nervously over her shoulder and pulled in a deep, shuddery breath. "It's Brad. I've been thinking about him coming over to Mom's house last night, and I'm afraid that—"

The door opened again and I looked up, expecting to see Ruby, back from her conversation with Cecilia Fuller. But I was wrong. Silhouetted in the doorway were two women, the elder in her eighties, supporting herself on an aluminum walker, her white hair so sparse that you could see her pink scalp through the thin curls. She wore navy

slacks and a baggy navy T-shirt with the word SCRABBLE in
large letters, and underneath, "It's Your Word against
Mine." Around her neck was a red bandana, carelessly tied.
Behind her, holding a dripping red umbrella, stood another
woman, some twenty years younger. Her stiff blue-rinsed
gray hair was carefully curled on her forehead, caplike,
and her face had been the site of a failed reconstruction effort at some point in the past. The lack of lasting success
was only partially disguised by the artful use of foundation
and blusher, lips penciled in with care, and winged eyebrows sketched on so that she looked perpetually startled.

Amy made a noise in her throat. "Grammy," she said,
without great enthusiasm, and bent over to peck at the
cheek of the older woman. She gave a casual waggle of her
fingers to the younger. "Hi, Gram."

"Look, Doris, it's our sweet little Amy!" Grammy exclaimed, her blue eyes bright. "How lovely to see you, dear.
And how pretty you look today. I do like that short hair-
cut." She glanced up at me, smiling, and held out a gnarled
and bony hand. "And China. What a pity that PickleFest
had to be canceled. You must be terribly disappointed."

Doris—Ruby's mother—wore a navy skirt, navy heels,
and a print blouse the color of grape Kool-Aid, decorated
with a chestful of shiny gold-colored costume jewelry. She
leaned the drippy umbrella against the wall, closed the
door, and turned to her granddaughter.

"I must say, this is a surprise, Amy. It's been months
since we've seen you." The clipped, slightly sarcastic edge
in her voice reminded me of my high school physical education teacher, who loved to lecture me about skipping
class before she sentenced me to twenty laps around the

cinder track. "We get a call from Shannon at least once a week," she added accusingly, "but we *never* hear from you. You could at least let us know your phone number. Or are you staying with your mother now?"

I stepped forward into the fray. "Hello, Doris," I said, with a wide artificial smile. "How *nice* to see you. And Grammy." My smile for her was completely genuine. "Are you excited about the big birthday celebration tomorrow?"

Ruby and Janet had already baked a rose geranium pound cake, and there were eighty-three candles in red plastic holders, waiting to be poked into the top. I had been instructed to bring pink and red balloons and crepe paper streamers to hang in the dining room, and an ice ring for the rose geranium punch bowl. It was going to be a gala celebration.

"Oh, yes, we are cer-tain-ly ex-cit-ed, aren't we, Mama?" Doris said. When she speaks to or for her mother, Doris enunciates with extreme clarity and raises her voice several notches—why, I don't know, since Grammy seems to hear at least as well as I do, and sometimes better. "When Ruby called last night and told us that PickleFest was canceled," she added, "we were going to wait until to-morrow morning to come. But Mama got restless so we just drove on over."

"I'm glad you came early," I said politely. "I hope the rain didn't give you any trouble on the roads." Amy didn't say anything.

"The driving was awful, but we persevered, didn't we, Mama?" Doris peered around the shop, her glance sharp and critical. "My goodness, what's been going on here, China? You need to do some tidying up."

"It was probably just a herd of bulls," Grammy remarked airily. "Somebody let them loose in China's shop."

I chuckled. Amy giggled, relaxing. "Oh, Grammy," she said. "You are *so* funny."

"What's everybody laughing at?" Grammy asked, her blue eyes innocent. "I just said—"

"Mama." In a distinct scowl, Doris's eyebrows met together in the middle of her forehead. "Once is enough. We heard you the first time."

"I think the shop looks very nice, dear," Grammy said to me, undeterred. "And I'm sure that you and Ruby do the very best you can." She leaned over and sniffed at the yellow heads of some dried yarrow and tansy that I'd tucked into a vase. "Some of your flowers are a little past their prime, though," she added. "Might be good if you'd pick some more. You got plenty out there in that garden."

"Those are dried flowers, Grammy," Amy said.

"Exactly what I said, dear," Grammy replied, pushing her gold-rimmed glasses up her nose. Her cheeks were rouged and wrinkled but her sharp blue eyes were bright and merry, her smile elfish. "Dried up and past their prime. Like me."

"You're not past your prime, Mama," Doris corrected her. "Why, you're spry as a young girl." Her artificial laugh barely concealed the bitterness beneath. Behind her hand, to me, she said in a dour tone, "Eighty-three tomorrow, and twice as healthy as I am. Why, I wouldn't be at all surprised if she outlived me by ten years, hard as I have to slave to make life easy for her. I am constantly exhausted, and she's as fresh as an April morning."

This was not exactly the truth. Grammy has her own apartment in an assisted living facility, while Doris lives in an independent living unit. Doris has to do hardly anything for her mother except, occasionally, to drive her to the doctor's. But I made a sympathetic noise, to which Doris responded, mollified, "You're planning to come to our little party, I hope, China."

"Oh, of course," I replied quickly. I smiled at Grammy. "I wouldn't miss it for the world."

It was true, actually. I'm not at all fond of Ruby's mother, but her grandmother, who is definitely not your ordinary little old lady in crepe-soled shoes, is another story altogether. I'd like to have known Grammy when she was forty years younger—except maybe I have, really. In her, I can glimpse what Ruby might become in another forty years. Anyway, I'd already assembled Grammy's present, a large herbal bath basket, stocked with packages of fizzy herbal bath salts, some lavender bubble bath, a loofah scrub, and a bath sponge, and a selection of scented herbal soaps. Grammy was going to love it.

Doris turned to Amy. "You'll be at the party, of course, Amy." It was a command.

Amy straightened her shoulders. "Yes, ma'am, I'm planning to come. I'm bringing a friend."

"Oh?" Doris's winged eyebrows took a sudden and suspicious flight, soaring up under her cap of blue hair. "Who is he? Will he . . . fit in?" Was she wondering what color he was?

"*She,*" Amy said with dignity, "is my friend Kate Rodriguez."

"I'm sure you'll like Kate, Doris," I said quickly, putting an arm around Amy's shoulders. "She's a great gal."

"Oh, well, if it's just a girlfriend," Doris said dismissively. Amy rolled her eyes at me as Doris turned and went to the connecting door, to peer into the Crystal Cave. "Where's that daughter of mine gone off to?" she demanded.

"She's running a little errand," I said. "She should be back any minute now." I looked at the clock and was surprised to see that it was almost closing time. Ruby had been gone for the better part of an hour. "Oops," I said. "Time to wind it up for today." I went to the door and put up the CLOSED sign.

"Gosh, I need to run," Amy said. She blew a kiss at Grammy and nodded at her grandmother. "See you guys tomorrow." She glanced at me. "Let me know if there are any questions about that . . . that material I gave you."

"I will," I said. I put the envelope on the counter. "I'll take care of it as soon as I finish here."

"Bye-bye, Amy, dear," Grammy said, lifting her hand. "And don't worry about bringing a present tomorrow. Just your lovely, sweet self is enough."

"Really, it's just like Ruby to run off and leave somebody else to mind the store," Doris grumbled, as the door closed behind Amy. "I can't believe that I raised such an irresponsible daughter." She picked up a bag of potpourri, smelled it, coughed, and put it down again.

"We take turns," I said in Ruby's defense. "I was gone for an hour this morning. Anyway, she's doing an errand for me." Actually, she was out doing some detective work, and probably having a blast, while I entertained her mother and grandmother. But I couldn't say that in front of Doris, now, could I?

Grammy was bent over the front of her walker, rummaging in a large green quilted fabric bag hung from the aluminum bar—her "possibles" bag, she calls it, because

anything that she could possibly need is in it. She pulled
out a ball of orange yarn connected to something that
looked like a knitted tea-cozy-in-progress, a Scrabble dictionary, a book of crossword puzzles, a hairbrush, and a
bottle of prescription pills. She dropped the bottle on the
floor. Doris noticed what she was doing and immediately
became alarmed.

"Oh, do be careful, Mama," she exclaimed crossly, "or
you'll fall over on your nose and wind up in the hospital,
and I'll have to sit with you night and day. What on earth
are you digging for? Ask me, and I'll get it for you." She
picked up the bottle.

Grammy emerged from the bag with the *Enterprise* in
her hand, and began stuffing everything else back in, the
orange yarn tangled around the hairbrush, the Scrabble
dictionary inside the tea cozy. "I only wanted the newspaper," she chirped, and turned to me. "I was so sorry to hear
about Phoebe Morgan, China. Murdered and stuffed into a
pickle barrel." She sighed heavily, but her bright eyes betrayed an avid interest. "What a ghastly way to go. Can't
even imagine what that must've been like."

Doris frowned severely. "Now, Mother," she chided,
"you know very well that she was *not* stuffed into a pickle
barrel. I read the article myself. It said that her body was
discovered in a concrete tank, which is a very different
thing altogether from a—"

The door opened with another whoosh of damp, and
Ruby breezed in, the shoulders of her filmy green tunic
dampened with raindrops. "Grammy! Mother!" she exclaimed. "I wasn't expecting you quite so soon."

"Obviously," Doris said in a huffy tone. She folded her
arms across her chest.

"Ruby, my dear," Grammy said, and pulled her grand-daughter down for a kiss. "I was just saying what a pity it is about Phoebe Morgan, ending up in a pickle barrel." Doris started to object, but Grammy went right on. "The Morgans used to be great friends of ours, you know." She shook her head sadly. "And after all they went through to keep that pickle plant in the family. It does seem a shame for her to die so young. Why, she was no older than you are."

I bent over to look at the newspaper Grammy was holding up. Beside an unflattering file photograph of Phoebe, the headline announced prosaically, MORGAN PICKLE OWNER MURDERED. Halfway down the page, in smaller print, was a second headline, equally unexceptional: ARTIST FOUND DEAD IN CAR. I was glad to see that the paper hadn't called it a "dilly of a death," after all. Most of the time, Hark's bark is worse than his bite.

"You knew Phoebe Morgan, Grammy?" Ruby asked with interest.

"Oh, good heavens, yes, of course I knew her," Grammy said. "I knew all those Morgans. My poppa and momma lived just down the road when Mick and Polly Morgan were still making pickles in that old barn, where they kept the cows and the chickens and Lord knows what all. They were dirt poor in those days, I'll tell you. Hardly had a pot to piss in."

"Mama!" Doris exclaimed. Two spots of red glowed in her cheeks. "I do wish you would watch your language."

"I'll thank you to remember that I will be eighty-three years old tomorrow, Doris," Grammy said tartly, "and I will damn well use any words I want to use." The two of them bicker like this constantly, Doris's acidic criticisms followed by Grammy's sprightly refusals to be treated as if she were six years old. I sometimes wonder how they have managed to coexist as long as they have.

To Ruby, Grammy went on, "The trouble with the Morgans was that Mick and Polly didn't have enough kids. If they'd had six or eight, there wouldn't've been a problem. But everything went to that son of theirs—Randolph, his name was. Dandy Randy, everybody used to call him, 'cause his mother always dressed him up so nice, even when they hardly had money for shoes." She rolled her eyes. "My oh my, but Dandy Randy was a dimwit. Didn't know diddly squat."

Doris's heavy sigh suggested that she had far too much to put up with on this earth.

"Well, he was," Grammy insisted, lifting her chin. "He was a sweet sort of person, but he had pickles in his head instead of brains. Why, back in the seventies, Randy would've lost the whole business—lock, stock, and pickle barrels—if it hadn't been for that nice neighbor of theirs."

"Neighbor?" I asked, intrigued by these insights. "Which neighbor was that, Grammy?"

"Why, Sam Simon, of course."

"Simon?" Ruby and I echoed in unison. We traded glances.

"Mama," Doris said in a bossy tone, "we've talked long enough. It's time for us to be going. China wants to close up her shop and—"

"That's right, Simon," Grammy said, pleased to be talking about the old days. She looked from Ruby to me. "You gals know the Simons?"

"We know Art Simon," I replied. "Is that the same family?"

"That would be Sam's boy," Grammy said. "Y'see, Momma and Poppa's place was on the north, and the Simons lived on the south, down next to the river. Sam wasn't a wealthy man, but he had some property, and his daddy had been a good friend to Mick and Polly. He was smart enough to see that you could make real money in pickles if you just went about it right. Anyway, Sam loaned Randy enough money to keep the old plant going, with the understanding that he would have a say in the way things were run. But it wasn't more than a couple months later that Randy got himself killed in that plane crash and Phoebe took over the pickle business."

"My goodness," I said. So much for Dandy Randy.

"Well, yes," Grammy replied amiably. "But it turned out to be the best thing that could've happened. Phoebe was a chip off the old Morgan cucumber, so to speak."

"Mama," Doris protested faintly.

"Well, it's true," Grammy said. "There she was, just a young thing with that little baby, but she got the business up and cooking in no time at all. My daddy thought she hung the moon, 'cause she kept Morgan's Pickles alive. He knew old Mick would've been proud of her. Others didn't much like her, though."

"Why?" Ruby asked.

Grammy shrugged. "'Cause they couldn't get out of her way fast enough and she stepped on 'em, that's why. My momma always said she was going to get herself in a whole lot of trouble." She shook her head, frowning. "Guess somebody didn't like her a *lot*. Wonder who bumped her off. Sure hope they catch the perp."

Doris fanned her glowing cheeks with her hand. "Mama

watches way too many police shows on television," she re-marked, to nobody in particular.

Ruby leaned toward Grammy. "What about the loan, Grammy?"

"The loan?" Grammy blinked at her. "What about it?"

"You said that Sam Simon loaned the Morgans some money, on the condition that he'd have a voice in the man-agement of the plant. Did Phoebe pay it back?"

"I'm sure she did," Grammy said. "That Sam knew a nickle from a pickle. He'd see to it that he got his money back, with interest." She frowned. "You're not thinking Phoebe got rubbed out because—"

"Ruby," Doris said hastily, "what shall we do about din-ner? Your grandmother needs to have her meals on time, or she gets awfully crabby."

"Crabby?" Grammy asked disdainfully. "*I'm* not the crabby one. The problem is, Doris, you've got to have your way all the time. If you'd just calm down a little and—"

"There's a ham and squash casserole in the refrigera-tor," Ruby said, stepping into the squabble in a practiced way. "All you have to do is put the dish in the oven and turn it on. I'll make some salad when I get home, and there's fruit for dessert." She fished in her shoulder bag, pulling out a key ring and handing it to Doris. "Here's the key. You and Grammy go on over and make yourselves at home. I'll check out my cash register and be with you in a jiffy."

"Come to think of it, Ruby," Grammy said thoughtfully, "I don't know about that loan being paid back. Near as I can remember, Sam Simon had a heart attack and died a week or so before Randy got killed in that plane crash. Wonder if they signed some papers, or if it was just one of those shake-hands-howdy deals that nobody happens to re-member when folks die."

Doris bent toward her mother. "Mama," she said loudly and emphatically, "we are going to Ruby's house. Come along, now, and don't argue."

"I'm not arguing," Grammy said, and began to turn her walker around. Halfway through this laborious process, she stopped. "I'm sure it had to have been paid back," she said. "Sam's son Artie was all grown up by that time, big enough to take over his daddy's affairs. And he was always careful about money, even when he was a little boy. Artie would've seen to it that Phoebe paid off that loan before she pickled her first dill."

"Mama," Doris said, in a threatening tone, "we are *leaving*. Right this minute." She picked up the umbrella.

"I'm coming," Grammy muttered, resigned. "Always rushing a body. Just get where you're going and have to go again."

"Well, *that* was interesting," Ruby said, when they had left. "It fills in the background details."

"Interesting, yes," I replied, "although it's hard to imag-ine how a loan transaction that took place a quarter century ago is connected to last week's events." I paused. "What did Cecilia Fuller have to say?"

"Plenty," Ruby said emphatically, her eyes sparkling. "It's true that Phoebe and Art Simon had an affair, and that it wrecked the Simons' marriage. Apparently, it had been going on for some time when she discovered it. She was the last to know, she said."

"How did she find out?"

"Phoebe's husband told her. He was hoping that she could put pressure on her husband to call it off. She and Art

had been having problems, and he was growing more remote all the time. She begged him to see a marriage counselor, but he kept refusing. When she discovered that he
was sleeping with Phoebe, she tried to do what she could to
hold things together for the sake of their little girls. It was
Art who insisted on the divorce."

"Tough for her," I said.

"Very tough. Art was obsessed with Phoebe and determined to marry her, come hell or high water. He just kept
after Cecilia until she finally caved in and agreed to the divorce." Ruby smiled tightly. "She said, and I quote, 'I
didn't pickle that bitch, but I'm damned glad *somebody*
did.' "

I shook my head wonderingly. "It's been what? A dozen
years? And she still feels that way?"

"It could be a dozen centuries," Ruby replied grimly,
"and Cecilia would still hurt. And I can't say that I blame
her, either." Her mouth twisted. "The two of them put her
through absolute hell."

The bitterness laced through Ruby's words wasn't entirely for Cecilia, of course. Ruby had found herself in the
same painful position some years back, when her husband,
Wade, had left her for a younger woman. She was over her
feelings of angry betrayal now and was even glad that it
had happened—that she had been released from a marriage that had ceased to nurture and satisfy her. But I knew
that every now and then, something happened to reopen the
old wound. Her bitter compassion for Cecilia was also for
herself.

The story, as Ruby related it to me, was simple and sordid, a classic of its genre. Phoebe had made a play for Art
at a neighborhood Christmas party, and by New Year's

Eve, they were spending all their spare time in bed, in Phoebe's guest house, apparently. The affair blazed like a wildfire for over a year, leaving nothing but charred ruins and devastation in its wake. Ed found out about it early on, becoming increasingly despondent and losing interest in work. He began to drink heavily, and the drinking led to the fatal accident at the cliff. In the throes of his obsession with Phoebe, Art was drinking, too, and paying so little attention to his real estate company that it tanked. Brad was a mess, as well, not to mention Cecilia and her girls.

"Brad?" I asked.

Ruby nodded. "Cecilia says he idolized his father. All of his difficulties began on the night after Ed's death, when he walked into his parents' bedroom and found his mother and Art making love. He was twelve or thirteen then—a vulnerable age."

I frowned, remembering something that Constance had said. Something about Brad getting into trouble. "What kind of difficulties?"

"Didn't you know? Brad had a lot of problems in high school, and when he was going to college at Tulane, he'd get into a new mess before Phoebe could bail him out of the old one. I don't know the details, but I do remember hearing that they kicked him out of school, and that his mother went to a lot of trouble to keep his name out of the New Orleans newspapers. That's not all of it, of course," she added. "Cecilia has been in therapy for years, and her daughters as well. They're in their twenties now, and out of control—a lot of drinking and drugs. She blames their behavior problems on their father and 'that woman.' "

"Sounds like a horrible mess," I said feelingly. "But

what happened to Art and Phoebe? Cecilia gave Art his freedom, and Ed was conveniently dead. So—"

"Not just conveniently dead," Ruby said in a meaningful tone, "but *profitably* dead. Profitable for Phoebe, anyway. The guy was insured for a half-million dollars."

"Ah," I said. "All the more reason to ask why Art and Phoebe didn't get married. It sounds as if divorce and death and the insurance payoff cleared the way for mutual bliss."

"I wondered about that, too," Ruby said. "Cecilia said that by the time their divorce was final, Phoebe had fallen in love with a high-profile Dallas lawyer. Art was just a small-time local stud, not good enough for her any longer. She tossed him aside like a worn-out boot."

"So that means that the affair has been over for nearly a dozen years," I said. "And while I don't know Art Simon, he doesn't strike me as the kind of man to carry a grudge. He—"

"Oh, but that's not the whole story, China." Ruby held up a finger and wagged it wisely. "The lawyer lasted only a year or so, and after that, there was somebody else. And *then* Phoebe got interested in Art again, briefly, and the two of them had another torrid fling. That was last year. They kept it quiet apparently—so quiet that even Cecilia didn't know until her daughters told her that Phoebe and their father had gone to Cancún for a weekend. But the romance ended when Brad brought Todd home. All of a sudden, Art was old news again. Another worn-out boot."

I did a double take. "Phoebe threw Art over for Todd?"

Ruby chuckled. "If there was anything about this whole sordid affair that made Cecilia happy, it was seeing Art hurt. The first time, he tried to make excuses for Phoebe and get on with his life, although Cecilia said he was obviously in pain. This time, though, he had to confront the truth about Phoebe—that she was nothing but a self-engrossed, manipulative narcissist who did what she damn well pleased, no matter how many others got hurt along the way."

"I see," I said slowly. I was a little surprised that Cecilia had been so forthcoming, especially when the story was so unflattering to her personally, and to the man she had once loved. Ruby has a way of squeezing information out of people who don't even know they're giving it, but she had hit the mother lode this time under difficult circumstances. "Why was Cecilia so anxious to tell you all this?" I asked.

Ruby shrugged. "I think Phoebe's death has awakened all the old feelings again. She said that she kept everything to herself for many years in order to protect her daughters. But they're in their twenties now, and she sees things much more clearly. And Art was obsessed with Phoebe—there's no other word for it. It was like a sickness with him, an addiction he couldn't break." She shook her head. "Rejection is a powerful motive for murder, China. Especially since the rejectee gave up his wife and daughters and got nothing but pain in return."

"Right," I agreed. "And not just once, but *twice*." It was difficult to understand an experienced, attractive, otherwise intelligent male being stupid enough to deliberately put his left hand into the same deadly trap that had bit off his right arm. But it happens all the time.

"Maybe there were several things going on," Ruby said thoughtfully. "Art was angry about the way the plant was handling the effluent, and even angrier about Todd. He and

Phoebe got into a quarrel. He lost control, hit her, and killed her—without meaning to, maybe."

"It's a reasonable theory," I objected, "but it doesn't explain Todd's death. Or the fact that Todd was killed with Phoebe's gun."

"Maybe Todd came to her defense," Ruby said. "And Art had been Phoebe's lover—he probably knew where she kept her gun. So he got it and used it to force Todd to help him dispose of her body. Then he forced Todd to drive to the gravel pit, where he shot him, making it look like a suicide. And then he jogged back home."

I thought of Art as I had seen him the previous week, running easily and powerfully along the road. "It could have happened that way, I guess," I said. "It certainly sounds like a plausible explanation."

"You *guess*!" Ruby exclaimed, throwing up her hands. "Just look at the situation, China. Of course it's plausible. Do you know whether Art has an alibi for Sunday night?"

"Nothing that Blackie has been able to corroborate," I said.

"There! You see?" Ruby snapped her fingers. "Art Simon is a perfect suspect. He could have killed both Phoebe *and* Todd, no problem."

"But what about the surveillance cameras?" I asked. "Would Art know how to manipulate the VCR?"

"He could have," Ruby said. "Maybe he and Vince were pals. Maybe Vince showed him how—"

"We're speculating again, Ruby." I paused. "While you were questioning Cecilia, did you happen to ask her whether *she* has an alibi for last Sunday night?" By her own admission, Cecilia had almost as much reason to hate Phoebe as her ex-husband did. And while I didn't really think that a Unitarian minister's wife would pick up a gun and kill, stranger things have happened.

"As a matter of fact, I did ask her," Ruby said, pleased to let me know that she'd thought of this. "She and her husband attended a church function in San Antonio, and stayed over on Sunday night to visit some friends. They didn't get home until Monday afternoon. So if you're wondering whether Cecilia might be a suspect, you can scratch her off your list."

"It was just a thought," I said. "We can be grateful for small favors." I glanced up at the clock. "Listen, I'll close up here, then drive out to the sheriff's office and let him know what Cecilia told you." And while I was at it, I would hand him the envelope Amy had entrusted to me, and make a few remarks. I wouldn't be delivering any major bombshells, of course, just enough bits and pieces to cast a very reasonable doubt on Todd's guilt. And Cecilia's story should make Blackie take a very hard second look at Art Simon. If the guy wasn't a strong suspect already, he needed to be.

"I'd love to go with you and tell him myself," Ruby said, "but I promised Mother and Grammy I'd spend the evening with them." She giggled a little. "Mother will probably go to bed early, and Grammy and I will drink beer and play Scrabble. The last time we played, she came up with the word *edkwele,* which turns out to be some sort of money in Equatorial Guinea." She eyed me. "Maybe you could come over and play, too."

"I was out Wednesday night and last night," I said, "and I'll be at your house tomorrow. It might be a good idea if I stayed home and got reacquainted with my family tonight." I paused. "Oh, by the way, Amy stopped in while you were gone. She said to tell you she's bringing Kate Rodriguez to the party tomorrow." I added casually, "She's decided to stay with Kate for a while, rather than at my house."

"Oh, sure, Kate," Ruby said. "I like her. I'm glad Amy's bringing her to the party. But doesn't she have a very small house? I didn't think there was room for Amy there."

"I think they've made room. The young are more flexible than those of us over forty." I grinned. "Actually, McQuaid and I will be sorry that she's moving out. We've enjoyed having her stay with us. She's a sweet kid."

"When she wants to be," Ruby said, with maternal realism. "I just wish she'd learn to be more responsible."

"Give her time. She'll be okay when she gets a few years under her belt."

"I certainly hope so," Ruby said darkly.

Chapter Eighteen

To banish ghosts or spirits, mix dill seed and mullein seed with salt. Scatter around the floor and on both sides of the threshold.

Working fast, it took me about fifteen minutes to clear out the register, tally the cash and checks, hide the cash tray under the dust rags, and make sure that the place was locked up. By that time, Ruby had finished her chores and left. I turned out the lights, adjusted the thermostat and was just heading out the back door when the phone rang.

I hesitated, my hand on the knob. The caller was probably a customer, wondering whether the shop was open on Sundays, in which case, the answering machine tape had all the necessary information. On the other hand, it might be McQuaid, wanting to know what time I was going to be home, or wanting me to stop at the grocery store and pick something up. And since I was headed out to the sheriff's office and would be a half hour late getting home, it might be a good idea to let him know what was going on. I backtracked quickly and picked up the call in the kitchen, catching it just before the answering machine clicked on.

It wasn't a customer, but it wasn't McQuaid, either. It was Janet's aunt, Lunelle. Low and fast, sounding as if she were out of breath, she said, "China, can you come out here?"

I frowned. "Where's here?"

"The Morgan place. I just found something—something you need to see. Come right *now*."

I looked out the window. "It's raining. It's after five and I still have an errand to do. And my husband is expecting me home shortly." I wanted to add, *I have a life, you know,* but thought better of it. "What is it that's so important?"

Her voice was tense. "You gotta see it. I'm not hardly believin' it myself." She paused. "When you get here, park on the road and come around to the kitchen door. Nobody else is around, but I don't wanta take any chances."

I sighed. "Lunelle, I don't have time for this. Anyway, I'm not the person you need to be talking to. If you've found something relating to the deaths, you need to call the sheriff. He'll be glad to—"

"You getcher buns in that car and get out here," she said imperiously, and broke the connection.

The rain was slanting across my windshield with tropical force, and I rejoiced that the storm system hadn't squatted out there over the Gulf long enough to graduate from a depression to a full-fledged hurricane. We haven't had one of those for a while, and as far as I'm concerned, they can stay away forever. But hurricane or not, this storm was showing plenty of muscle. The folksy announcer on KPST-FM, giving the thirty-six-hour rainfall totals, was awed.

"The governor has declared twenty-nine counties as disaster areas," he was saying. "Some areas have gotten over two feet of rain in the last thirty-six hours. The north side of San Antonio has already registered twenty-two inches, there's eighteen in San Marcos, and twelve in Austin. Here at the station in Pecan Springs, we've got eighteen inches plus in our rain bucket." He raised his voice. "Eighteen inches and still coming down, folks. That's a heck of a lot of water on the roads and in the rivers. Get a pencil and paper and stay tuned for the list of canceled weekend events. If you gotta drive, drive *slow,* y'all hear? And stay out of the low-water crossings."

I switched off the radio, not wanting to hear any more. I *had* to drive slow—there wasn't any alternative. The defrost was on high, but the windows were still fogging up, and the wind-driven water was glazing the road in treacherous sheets. While my left brain was focused on navigation, though, my right brain was sorting through various stuff having to do with this case, like scrawled, barely legible notes scattered haphazardly across a desk. Ruby's conversation with Cecilia had risen to the top of the muddle, for it offered a motive for murder—a secret love triangle—that had been invisible until now. It was easy to see why Art Simon might have wanted his former lover dead, and not very difficult to reconstruct the way the killing might have happened, precipitated by an uncontrolled storm of passion fed by angry, barely concealed torments of obsession. It wasn't hard to fit Todd's death into this ugly picture, either. That handsome, innocent-looking young man had taken Simon's place in Phoebe's bed. Having killed her, Simon might have found it very easy—and very gratifying—to shoot his rival.

It took a half hour to get to the sheriff's office. I parked, grabbed my umbrella, and splashed through the puddles to the entrance. I wanted to talk to Blackie, but he was out, supervising the evacuation of a flood-prone trailer park in a low-lying area along the Pecan River. I handed over Amy's envelope and scribbled a message to the sheriff, asking him to call me at home—where with any luck, he'd find me inside of an hour. By the time I got back to the car, my shoes felt like sponges and my jeans were soaked to the knees.

It was lucky that there weren't any low-water crossings on the way to the Morgan place. Following Lunelle's instructions, I parked on the road, out of sight of the driveway. I wriggled into my yellow poncho inside the car, then got out and made my way through the woods. The sky had lightened to the color of burnished pewter, but it was already twilight under the dripping live oak trees and the sweet smell of wet soil and damp vegetation rose like a mist from the saturated soil. As I went around the back of the house, I saw a limestone terrace, a custom-built swimming pool large enough to accomodate the Olympic swim team, a rock waterfall with a cascade of ferns, and a kidney-shaped koi pond bridged by an arched Japanese-style bridge. Nature à la mode in the Hill Country. I headed for what seemed to be the kitchen door and knocked softly.

Lunelle must have been waiting for me, for she opened the door almost before I dropped my hand. She was dressed in her blue pants-suit uniform, her Big Hair arranged exactly as it had been the day before. "I was afraid the road mighta flooded out," she said, stepping back to let me in.

"I had another errand," I said, "and driving is slow." I peeled off my poncho. Lunelle took it and hung it in the

laundry room while I untied my laces and stepped out of
my spongy shoes. "This better be good, Lunelle," I said,
when she came back.

"It's bad," she replied grimly. "I don't know what it
means, but I'm tellin' you, it's *bad*."

I gave her a reproving look. "Have you been snooping
again?"

"I wasn't snoopin' the last time," she retorted, offended.
"I was only diggin' me a few daylilies. I couldn't help what
I heard." She motioned with her head and set off through
the kitchen, noiseless in her white rubber-soled shoes. I
followed her, puzzled, wondering what the hell this was all
about.

I'd been in the office wing of the Morgan house several
times, but I'd never been in the living area. It smelled of
money, with indirect lighting, expensively tasteful rugs and
furnishings, and Phoebe's classy collection of Southwestern sculptures, textiles, and paintings, including several
that I recognized as Todd's work. But despite the beautifully artful decor, there was something inexpressibly
lonely about the empty rooms, which might have been
rooms in an art gallery, rather than a home. Whatever
Phoebe Morgan's personal imperfections, whatever her
flaws and shortcomings, she had created these nearly perfect interiors with careful attention, searching out things
she admired for their individual beauty and arranging them
so that they could appear at their collective best. The pieces
were still here, lovely, rare, valuable, but the spirit of the
collector no longer animated them. There was a pathos in
the scene, and I couldn't help feeling its sad, quiet
poignancy, and wondering what Brad would do with all of
the things that had belonged to his mother.

Lunelle passed swiftly through the living room to a wide, carpeted stairway, and I followed her up, still wondering what this was all about. To tell the truth, I wasn't very comfortable about this expedition. My stomach was beginning to flutter uneasily, the way it does when I'm somewhere I shouldn't be, doing something I'm not supposed to do. Not that I was here illegally—after all, I had come at the insistence of a family employee. But while my cool and calm left brain might be confident that there was nothing illicit about this activity, my right brain was sending a flurry of nervous messages to my adrenal glands, telling them that my body was being required to do something sly and sneaky and not quite on the up-and-up.

The upstairs hallway was another art gallery, this one more personal, it seemed. The walls were lined with narrow glass shelves that held collections of small, beautiful objects, crystal perfume bottles, ivory figures, Oriental fans, jewelry in ornate silver and gold settings. The diffused lighting came from hidden fixtures, the carpet so thick that it swallowed all sounds. The silence added to my apprehension.

"Don't like to come up here," Lunelle said, her voice low. "I'm not one to b'lieve in spirits, but I can't help but think that if Miz Morgan's ghost roams 'round anywhere, she roams 'round up here. Them little pretties on the shelves—they're hers, mostly. She was funny that way. She'd stand and look at 'em by the hour, pick 'em up and hold 'em real careful, like they was precious."

"Are we going to her room?" I asked uncomfortably.

"Mr. Brad's room," Lunelle said, her voice low. She paused in front of a closed door. "He forgot to lock it this afternoon, so I had me a quick look around." She lifted a hand, as if to forestall something I was about to say. "I don't want to hear you say it was wrong, Miz Bayles. I had me a feeling, and that's all there is to it. So don't gimme a hard time."

"A hard time?" I smiled crookedly. "Not on your life, Lunelle. I'm in this too, aren't I?" I looked toward the stairs, my nervous system jumping up and down and waving red disaster-alert flags. I asked a question I should have asked five minutes before. "Where is Brad? Is he likely to show up and surprise us?"

She shook her head. "Said he was goin' to be gone all evening, and not to expect him back. Told me he wasn't goin' to be needin' a housekeeper from now on, so I could find me another place to work." She pursed her orange-glazed lips, her eyes hard and glinting. "No sev'rance, no bonus, not even a tip. Jes' adios, bon voyage, so long." She gave me a dark look. "That's not the way civ'lized folks treat the hired help. That boy needs to learn some manners."

"You're right," I said sympathetically, thinking that Brad's short shrift had probably inspired Lunelle's snooping. She considered it payback time. But I still hung back. "What about Marsha? Is she around?"

"Miz Marsha?" Lunelle shook her head. "She packed up and went home to Houston this morning. Said her mother was havin' an unexpected female operation and needed her."

"She's gone?" I asked, startled. I remembered Blackie's asking her to stick around, and wondered if she had let him know where she was going, and why. And then I wondered if her mother was the real reason for her sudden disappearance, or whether something else was going on.

"Gone as a goose in a hurry," Lunelle said. She puffed

out a big breath. "Loaded her stuff in her car and took off. Another rat leavin' the sinkin' ship." She pushed the door open and we went in.

It wasn't a room, but a large three-room suite. We were standing in the living room, with wooden bifold doors framing the wide opening to the bedroom, where I could see a queen-sized bed, unmade, an island surrounded by shoals of dirty clothing. Glass patio doors opened off both sitting room and bedroom onto a balcony overlooking the swimming pool and guest house. Beyond that, there was a sky-wide view of the valley of the Pecan River and the tangles of cedar and mesquite on the rugged hills beyond. There was a stone fireplace in one corner of the living room, with a raised limestone ledge across the front of it, and a rack of copper fireplace tools. The room was furnished with a chocolate-brown leather sofa and chair, a square glass-topped coffee table, and a large entertainment center with a television screen almost as big as a beach towel. The place would have been terrific if it hadn't been for the drifts of dirty laundry, newspapers, overflowing ashtrays, and take-out food boxes that covered every flat surface. The beige carpet needed a good going-over with a vacuum, and over by the coffee table there was what looked like a recently scrubbed patch, where an effort had been made to clean up a spill. Ketchup, probably. There was a paper plate on the coffee table with a few scraps of greasy French fries and a half-dried puddle of ketchup in the middle. I sniffed. Lunelle had been right. A strong odor of marijuana pervaded the place, mixed with the distinctive male perfume of stale cigarette smoke, take-out food, and sweaty jockstraps.

"It's a mess, ain't it," Lunelle said, looking around with

a grunt of distaste. "All that money, and he lives like a pig." She motioned with her head toward the bedroom. "Come on."

In the bedroom, she went straight to the dresser, on top of which lay a pipe and a spill of marijuana. I thought that was what she wanted me to see, but she paid no attention to it. The top drawer was about six inches open, and she pointed to it. "Lookee there," she said.

I looked. What I saw was a jumble of ladies' underpants, all different colors and styles. The first one I pulled out was a brief and filmy bikini, fire-engine red, with a sexy frill of lace. There was also a utilitarian panty, peach-colored and sized to fit a lady of substantial bulk. Another was white and silky and somewhat old-fashioned, with a delicate border of flowers around the loose legs. I looked closer. There was an embroidered tracery of intertwined letters, *W* and *H*, laced together. I stared at it, frowning, and then suddenly the initials popped into focus. W. H. Wilhelmina Holeyfield.

Lunelle's voice had lost its springiness. " 'Fore I came to work for Miz Morgan, I cleaned for Miz Holeyfield and did her laundry, reg'lar. Them are her panties. She ordered 'em special, with her initials, and I always thought how nice it would be to have initials on your panties. I tried 'broidering 'em myself, on mine, but I couldn't make it look the way hers did." She folded her arms across her large breasts, scowling. "Something don't make sense here, Miz Bayles. I s'pose I could understand if Mr. Brad was in the habit of keepin' souvenirs of his tumbles with his young women. But somebody needs to explain to me what he's doin' with old Mrs. Holeyfield's underpants.

That don't make no kind of sense at all, no matter how you try to figger it."

"It doesn't make sense," I agreed quietly, although I was beginning to think that it did. I put the panties back as I had found them, except that the pair bearing Mrs. Holeyfield's initials were rather more clearly visible than they had been before. I stood for a moment, thinking. This required a game plan, if the evidence wasn't going to get thrown out. And it was complicated by the fact that the Morgan house was in Blackie's jurisdiction, while the burglaries, and Mrs. Holeyfield's death, had taken place in Sheila's territory. But that shouldn't be too hard to work out.

"Did you find the drawer open?" I asked.

"'Xactly like you see it," she said. "I didn't do hardly no snoopin' at all. Jes' used my eyes is all." She grinned bleakly. "And maybe stirred them panties around with my fingers a bit, to see what there was."

"Okay," I said, stepping back. "We've done what we can. Let's go."

On the way out, I paused to survey the room, my attention drawn, once again, to the freshly scrubbed patch on the floor next to the coffee table. I felt another flutter of uneasiness. Then I turned and headed for the door.

"Where we goin'?" Lunelle asked, trotting behind me as I went quickly downstairs and through the living area.

"To the sheriff's office. And no arguments," I added over my shoulder. "This is serious."

"Betcher life it's serious." Her voice was worried. "I'm not gonna get in trouble, am I?"

"You didn't get into trouble for stealing a couple of buckets of daylilies, did you?"

"Well, no, but—"

"You're not going to get into trouble for this, either," I said firmly. We had reached the kitchen, where I had left my wet shoes. "You're going to tell the sheriff that you were walking past Brad's door when you smelled something that you thought was smoke." I bent over to tie my laces. "You pushed on the door, found it unlocked, and you went in to see if something was burning and might endanger the house. You saw the pipe and the marijuana on the dresser. Then you noticed the open drawer and the panties and immediately recognized the pair that belonged to Mrs. Holeyfield."

She went into the laundry room and came back with my poncho.

"And then what?"

"And then the sheriff will ask you to tell the whole thing over again to a judge, who will issue a warrant to search this place for drugs and stolen property."

"Drugs and stolen—" She laughed shortly. "Them undies, huh? Stolen property, huh? Omigolly. That boy is gonna be in a whole lot of trouble, huh?"

"I sincerely hope so," I said. "Come on."

"You bet," she said. She patted her Big Hair. "That oughtta teach that young whippersnapper to be civil to the help."

Brad was going to pay dearly for his failure to give Lunelle a tip.

Thankfully, Blackie was back in the office when Lunelle and I walked in. It took no more than five minutes to tell him that we had seen drug paraphernalia and at least one item of stolen property in Brad's bedroom. Sheila had obviously talked over the Pecan Springs burglaries with him, because he seemed to immediately grasp the significance of Mrs. Holeyfield's embroidered underpants and to realize that Brad must be involved with the break-ins that had so upset the Pecan Springs city council. He asked Lunelle a couple of questions and, apparently satisfied with her answers, put her in a patrol car and dispatched her with a deputy to get a warrant to search the Morgan house.

When Lunelle was on her way, I took the opportunity to tell Blackie what Ruby had found out from Cecilia Fuller—the condensed version, which worked out to about four sentences—and give him Amy's envelope containing Todd's note and photograph. He look at the photo and note and listened to Cecilia's story without comment, raising an occasional eyebrow.

When I finished, he said, "That's it?"

"Isn't that enough?" I said. "Cecilia's story, taken together with the photographic evidence of Todd's left-handedness, goes a long way toward shifting suspicion for Phoebe's death from Todd to Art Simon."

"It sure might," Blackie agreed, "if we hadn't been able to substantiate Simon's alibi for the night Phoebe Morgan died."

I stared at him. "Alibi?"

"Yeah. Turns out that Simon was in Austin on Sunday night—all night, as a matter of fact—enjoying the company of a friend. A female friend, who is also prominent in Texas politics. He took her to the airport and put her on a plane to Washington early Monday morning."

"Ah," I murmured. "Is this a name I would recognize?"

"Well, it may not be a household word, but you can hear

it on television three, four times a week." He paused. "It took a while to corroborate Simon's statement, because we had to track down the woman." He chuckled at my crest-fallen look. "Nice try, though, China. And tell Ruby I appreciate her efforts to help with the investigation. Now, if you'll excuse me, I'm going to phone Sheila. She'll want to be in on the search. And then I'm heading out to the Morgan house. I don't want Mr. Knight to show up, find his rooms unlocked, and decide to destroy that evidence."

I went out to the car, feeling dejected and out of sorts. The rain had stopped and I could hear the frogs calling loudly from the banks of a nearby large ditch, usually dry, now running full of water. I had just about convinced myself that Todd was innocent and that Art Simon had killed both Phoebe and Todd, and now I had to rethink that conclusion. Amy's arguments had persuaded me that Todd wasn't a good bet, but what if she was wrong? She had no real evidence to go on, just a posed photograph and a scrawled note, both inconclusive, and a gut feeling that the father of her child was innocent. That and a couple of bucks might buy you a cup of coffee.

I unlocked the Toyota, got in, and sat there for a few minutes, letting the events of the past couple of days tangle themselves together in my mind. I used to do that when I was working on a case. Making notes on colored index cards didn't do much for me, or covering sheets of paper with squiggles and boxes and arrows, or even making lists. When I was stuck in a puzzling case, I needed to be quiet and let ideas stir themselves around in my head, like the ingredients in a big kettle of vegetable soup on the back burner of my mind. Sooner or later, something would pop to the surface, like—

I put the key in the ignition, pushing that image firmly away. Why the heck was I thinking about all of this, anyway? It wasn't my business. I'd done what Amy asked me to do: I had presented the sheriff with her documentation of Todd's innocence. I had conveyed Cecilia's information about Art Simon's motive. I had even helped Lunelle uncover evidence that pointed to Brad's involvement in the Pecan Springs burglaries, and—

I frowned, thinking of Brad and what I had seen in that bedroom, and trying to make it fit with the composed, self-possessed young man I had seen that morning. But I couldn't. It was as if there were two personalities here. Underneath that cool exterior, he must have been driven by devils, demons of anger and hatred that had urged him to break into homes and vandalize and steal the most personal of properties. Pauline and Constance had attributed his earlier misbehaviors to his father's death and his discovery of his mother's adultery. Was that what had pushed him over the edge? I tried to imagine how a teenage boy might feel, a boy just confronting his own confusing and unsettling sexuality, learning that his mother's affair with a neighbor had driven his father to the alcoholism that finally killed him. I didn't know what kind of crimes Brad had committed in New Orleans, but maybe it was no surprise that he had gotten into drugs, or that he was making a career out of breaking into houses and stealing underpants and frightening old ladies to death. Perhaps it was as Kate had said, a way of getting back at his mother, of taking revenge.

My breath was fogging up the windows. I turned the key and started the car, flicking the air conditioner to high and glancing at my watch. It was past seven now. I'd been on the go for twelve hours. I was bone-tired, and the stress of the past few days was catching up with me. What I wanted more than anything else was a cup of hot lemon tea and a warm, lavender-scented bubble bath, and after that, a nice, quiet dinner with my husband. But before I went home, I thought I'd better check and see whether he was cooking, or whether I should stop and get something. A pizza, maybe, or take-out Chinese. I took my cell phone out of my purse, punched in the number, and waited for McQuaid to pick up.

"China's Answering Service," he said cheerfully.

I laughed, loving the deep, easy sound of his voice. "That bad, huh?"

"Your fan club has been burning up the wires, looking for you. Where *are* you, sweetheart?"

"On my way," I said evasively. I'd explain the whole thing to him over dinner. "Anything you want?"

"Only thee—and a pepperoni pizza, with Italian sausage, ham, black olives, onions, and mushrooms. Double on the anchovies and jalapeños and hold the green peppers. Oh, yeah. Cheese. Lotsa cheese. I haven't had enough fat and sodium yet today, and my cholesterol level is dropping to dangerous lows."

"Gotcha. Who called?"

"Wait a minute while I consult China's answering service log." He made noises with his mouth as though he were flicking through pages in a notebook. "Your mother phoned to tell you that the Guadalupe River is lapping at their back door and that she and Sam and their dogs are spending the night at the Rest Easy Motel in Kerrville and not to worry. Ruby called to ask you to bring extra balloons to the party, whatever the hell that means. Marsha Miller called from a hospital in Houston, to say that her mother had just had an emergency hysterectomy. She'll be out of town for a few days, and she'd like you to let the sheriff know. She left a number where she can be reached in case he wants her."

"How nice of Marsha," I said. It was comforting to know that she hadn't done a flit. "Is that it?"

"One more. Amy called about five minutes ago to say that Brad Knight had just showed up, and—"

I was startled. "Brad?"

"Yeah. She's at Kate Rodriguez's place. She sounded a little nervous. I told her you'd call her as soon as you could."

The soup pot on the back burner of my mind was suddenly bubbling with images and fragments of speech. Amy telling me not to let Brad know that she was staying with Kate. Amy looking at Brad with apprehension. Amy getting cut off in the middle of a sentence that included the words "Brad" and "afraid."

"I'll call her right now," I said. "Did she leave a number?"

"Yeah," McQuaid said, and gave it to me. He paused. "Is everything okay, China?"

"I guess," I said slowly. I was trying to fit this new development into the emerging picture, which was getting more complicated by the minute. By now, Sheila was probably on her way out to the Morgan house to meet Blackie. There wouldn't be a warrant for Brad's arrest on burglary charges until they had searched the premises and rousted out the judge again, which on a Saturday night was not a sure thing. Of course, the Pecan Springs police could pick Brad up for questioning. All I had to do was punch in 9-1-1, give the dispatcher a synopsis of the story, and the cops would be on their way to Kate's house. But I was beginning to think that there were two Brads, and that one of them was at least half crazy. I had no way of knowing his current state of mind, or how he might react if a couple of uniforms banged on the door.

And then something else floated up out of that mental soup, something grotesque. Hadn't Blackie mentioned that Todd had been killed with one of the *two* guns Phoebe had bought three years ago? Where was the second gun? Did Brad have it in his possession, right now?

And as that question came up, another one, much uglier and more grotesque, surfaced with it. Was it possible that *Brad* had shot Todd? Blackie had checked out Brad's alibi for the evening of his mother's death. But if the time of Todd's death had been definitively established, I hadn't heard about it. And Brad harbored more than enough jealous hostility toward Todd to turn him into a killer. I'd seen for myself that he hated Todd for moving in on his mother. And he must have hated the way Amy had treated him— Amy, who had stopped seeing Brad at the same time that she'd turned to Todd. Fuel enough to ignite a smoldering fire of jealousy into a murderous rage.

And then something else came into my mind, something even more hideously abhorrent. What if Brad had fabricated his alibi for Sunday night? Blackie said it had checked out, but I'd known a couple of exceptionally clever killers who'd been able to make it look as if they'd been somewhere else at the moment their victims were going down, proof that it was possible to be in two places at one time. What if Brad had been *here* on Sunday night, rather than in Abilene? What if he had killed his mother, then Todd? The smoldering fire that blazed inside Brad could have burned in more than one direction.

"China—hey, China!" McQuaid's tone made it clear that he'd said this more than once. "Are you there? What the hell is going on?"

I drummed my fingers on the steering wheel. If these ugly suspicions were anywhere near the mark, it was definitely not smart for me to go to Kate's house alone. But it might not be smart to get the cops involved, either. Which left—

I took a deep breath. "Listen, McQuaid. I'm at the sheriff's office. I'm here because the Morgan housekeeper turned up a cache of women's underpanties in Brad's bedroom—among them a pair that belonged to Wilhelmina Holeyfield."

"Panties?" McQuaid said incredulously.

"Right. Sheila told me that the cat burglar was in the habit of taking personal souvenirs, and it looks like Brad is the guy. Blackie is getting a search warrant right now and is on his way to the Morgan house, with Sheila. And it has just this minute occurred to me that Brad's alibi for Sunday night may be manufactured, and that maybe he's responsible for both—"

"You are *not* going to Rodriguez's place," McQuaid cut in, his voice flat and hard. "I'm calling the cops. This guy could be a killer."

"No, wait!" I said. "We don't know what he'd do if the cops showed up. He might grab Amy and—"

"You've got a better idea?"

I bit my lip. I had to come up with something. "Well, how about this?" I asked, and sketched out a possible course of action.

"Too dangerous," McQuaid said. I couldn't see him, but I knew he was frowning and shaking his head. "I don't want you going into that house."

"But we don't know that he's there to cause trouble," I argued, "or even that he's *there*. You said Amy called five minutes ago. He may be gone by the time we show up. So how about if we . . ." I suggested a modification.

"I don't like it," McQuaid said slowly, "but—"

"Fifteen minutes," I said, and gave him the address.

Chapter Nineteen

To protect against physical danger, wear an amulet containing dill, basil, mistletoe, rue, St. John's wort, fern, and mullein.

It was close to seven-thirty by the time I parked my white Toyota on Dallas Drive, in the next block west of Kate's house. The rain was intermittent, and while there was still a good hour of daylight left, the lowering sky and the rain-heavy trees made it seem like twilight. I waited in the car for a few minutes, going over the plan in my mind and trying to calm the flutters in my stomach. Then I opened the door and got out.

I'd been hoping that I was wrong, and that Brad might have dropped in just to say hello and had already left, but that wasn't the case. His sleek red sports car wasn't parked out front, but around the nearest corner—a fact that did not bring me much peace of mind. Picking up my pace, but still trying to look like a casual visitor, I went up the walk to the little frame house, where I knocked on the door.

No answer. I waited for a moment, listening for music, for voices, for any sound inside, then knocked again, more purposefully. "Kate," I called. "It's China. China Bayles."

On the other side of the door, I heard hasty footsteps and the sound of a door closing. A moment later, the front door opened a couple of inches, and I saw Kate's pale face. Her eyes were wide and she was biting her lip.

"Hello, Kate," I said. I raised my voice, speaking loud. "Is Amy here? I have a message from her mom, about the party tomorrow."

"She's . . . out shopping," Kate said. "She's looking for a new pair of high heels," she added quickly. "I'll tell her that you were here." She began to close the door.

Amy is not the high-heels type, and both Kate and I know it. What she said was an obvious lie. Amy *was* here—and Brad, too. I pushed at the door with the flat of my hand.

"Oh, hey, that's okay," I said cheerfully. "Since Amy's not here, maybe you and I could have a little talk."

Kate took a step back. "A talk? I . . . I don't think—"

"I'm really worried about her these days, Kate," I said. "Being pregnant is never easy, and she's been having a pretty hard time of it. Morning sickness and all that." By this time, I was inside, and I took a quick look around, surveying the scene. There was no one else in the living room or the small kitchen. The bedroom door was shut, but out of the corner of my eye, I saw it open a crack.

"Pregnant?" Kate said, through stiff lips. "Where'd you get that idea? Amy's not pregnant, for heaven's sake." She took another step back, where she couldn't be seen from the bedroom door, and shook her head violently. *No, no!* she mouthed, desperate.

"Don't be silly, Kate," I said carelessly. "I'm sure she told you that she's carrying Todd's baby. She's told everybody else—me, and her mother and grandmother. She told Todd, too."

There was a muffled yelp in the bedroom, a rough

growl, and a short scuffle. Then the door was jerked open, and Amy appeared in the doorway. Tears were streaming down her pale cheeks and Brad was standing close behind her, his left hand clamped on her shoulder. If he had a gun, I couldn't see it.

There were no preliminaries. "Baby?" His voice was hard, his eyes fixed fiercely on me. "What's this about a baby?"

"Oh, hi, Brad." I was friendly and chipper, as if there was nothing out of the usual in their sudden appearance or his brusque demand. "Didn't Amy tell you? She's due—when is it, Amy? December? We don't yet know whether it's a boy or—"

"Is it true, Amy?" Brad leaned forward and spoke into Amy's ear, his grip on her shoulder visibly loosening. "If it's true, I swear I'll—"

Suddenly, without warning, Amy wrenched away from him and ran across the room to Kate. Brad was left standing in the bedroom doorway, his right hand in the pocket of his khakis. Ten to one there was a gun in that pocket, too. He took a step forward and I tensed. But he was looking away from me, his entire attention focused on Amy, her slight figure caught now in Kate's embrace.

"He's got a gun, China," Kate said, almost under her breath.

If Brad heard her, he gave no sign of it. "Is it true, Amy? Did that dipshit jerk get you pregnant?" He was distracted, caught between anger at Todd's effrontery and compassion for Amy's predicament, and he had almost entirely forgotten about me. "Well, hell, that's what abortions are for. You don't have to worry. I know how to take care of this."

There was a small noise in the kitchen, the scraping of a

door, and I spoke to cover it. "You mean, you didn't know she was pregnant?" I asked in a horrified tone. I looked from Brad to Amy. "Aw, heck. Now I've gone and spilled the beans." I stepped forward, inserting myself between Brad and Amy. His eyes left Amy and came to me. "Hey, I'm really sorry, Brad. I didn't mean to upset anybody. I just figured—"

A couple of things happened at the same time. I whirled around and lunged for Amy and Kate, shoving them both against the far wall and out of the way. McQuaid charged out of the kitchen, his gun in both hands. He spun to his left in a crouch, confronting Brad, as Kate and Amy both screamed.

"Freeze!" he barked, in his tough-cop voice.

But Brad didn't freeze. He ducked, wheeled, and made a flying leap over the bed, going headfirst through the window, glass, frame, and all. It was an unexpected, inspired move, worthy of Superman. It left McQuaid and me staring at each other.

"He's got a gun," I said.

"Stay here," McQuaid said, and wheeled, heading back through the kitchen.

"Oh, God," Amy moaned, and buried her face in Kate's shoulder. Kate's arms went around her. "China," Kate cried, "what—"

But I was following McQuaid, out the kitchen door. Since he was shot, McQuaid doesn't do the fifty-yard dash, and in a half-dozen strides, I was ahead of him, with Brad ten yards ahead of me. Just as he reached the fence at the back of Kate's yard, he turned. He raised his gun and got off a couple of shots, both very wide. I heard one of them ricochet off the kids' playground equipment next door to the left. The other one split a hunk of bark off the oak tree to the right.

Wide or not, though, that was enough for McQuaid. With a shouted "Down!" and a flying tackle, he hit me below the knees in a move he must have made a couple of hundred times on the football field, sending both of us sliding, facedown, across the wet grass.

Brad vaulted the fence, turning for one last shot. This one was closer. I heard the bullet *zing* overhead, and as McQuaid raised himself to one knee, lifting his gun and taking deliberate aim, I grabbed his arm and pulled it down.

"No!" I cried.

"Stop it!" McQuaid shouted fiercely, trying to jerk his arm away. "I'm gonna get that bastard!"

"Let him go," I cried, hanging on grimly. "Let him *go! The creek's back there, and he can't get across.*" He would have to go north or south along the bank for a quarter mile, until he came to one of the major crosstown streets. We could call the cops and have them put cars at both of those points. They'd pick him up.

On the other side of the fence, I could hear Brad, panicked, thrashing through the underbrush. It sounded as if he was blundering down the bank, headed in the direction of the flooded creek, and I suddenly realized the danger.

"Stop, Brad!" I yelled, scrambling to my feet. "Don't—"

But he probably never heard my warning over the roar of the water. There was a sudden splash and a long, frantic, despairing scream that was abruptly cut off.

Brad had gone into Cedar Creek.

Rising to his feet, McQuaid put his arms around me and held me close. I buried my face against his wet shoulder, shaking, half-crying, and his arms grew tighter.

"You okay, China?" he whispered, smoothing my hair. "I didn't hurt you, did I?"

I shook my head. I could still feel the impact of his body, but that didn't hurt as much as the sound of Brad's final frantic cry, and the haunting recollection that one of the neighbor kids had drowned in Cedar Creek the last time it flooded.

Chapter Twenty

GRAMMY'S ROSE GERANIUM POUND CAKE

 1 cup (2 sticks) unsalted butter, room temperature
 1½ cups sugar
 6 large egg yolks
 1 tsp. vanilla extract
 1 tsp. rose water*
 3½ cups cake flour
 2 tsp. baking powder
 1 cup whole milk
 2 Tbsp. very finely minced fresh rose geranium
  leaves
 1 large paper doily
 confectioner's sugar

Preheat oven to 325°. Grease and lightly flour a 10″ Bundt pan. Using an electric mixer, cream butter and sugar until light and fluffy. Add egg yolks, vanilla extract, and rose water and beat until well mixed. Sift cake flour and baking powder and add alternately with milk, beating well. Stir in rose geranium leaves. Bake for 60–75 minutes at 325°, or until a wooden toothpick inserted in the center comes out clean. Cool in pan for 15 minutes, then turn out onto a rack and cool completely. Place paper doily on top of cake, and dust with confectioner's sugar. Remove doily carefully. To serve, place on cake plate

and decorate with rosebuds and rose geranium leaves.

Rose water is available in Middle Eastern groceries.

But Brad didn't drown—although when we were all talking about it after Grammy's party the next day, Ruby pointed out that drowning might have been both deserved and ironically appropriate, given the way Brad had disposed of his mother's body.

"You girls certainly had an exciting evening," she added with a sulky look. "I wish you'd called me. I would've been glad to come over and help."

"It sounds to me," Sheila said tactfully, "as if Amy and Kate had all they could manage." She sat down at Ruby's kitchen table. "If there's any of that birthday cake left, I'd love to have a piece."

Sheila hadn't made it to the party, but had dropped in afterward to bring us up to date on what was going on. Shannon had gone back home to Austin. The Birthday Girl, happy as a clam with all her birthday loot, was on her way back to Fredericksburg with her daughter. And Kate and Amy had stayed to help Ruby and me with the cleanup.

Ruby stuck out her lower lip in a pout, probably make-believe. "But China called McQuaid."

"Under the circumstances," I said soothingly, "I thought I'd better bring in the big guns. And since it didn't seem smart to get the cops involved, McQuaid was the best alternative."

"McQuaid scared the heck out of me," Kate said, "barging through that kitchen door. I had no idea who he was." She put the last dirty plate into the dishwasher and closed the door. "He must have scared Brad, too. I guess that's why he jumped out that window." She twisted the dial on the dishwasher, but nothing happened. She turned to Ruby. "What do I have to do to make this thing run, Ruby?"

"Give the dial a good smack," Ruby said. Kate whacked it, and it obediently began to fill.

Amy was sitting at the table across from Sheila. "Brad didn't jump," she said. "He *flew* through that window! I couldn't believe what I was seeing."

Ruby finished cutting a piece of cake and put it on a plate for Sheila. "Brad's okay?" she asked. "Although I don't know why I should care."

"He's banged up," Sheila replied, "but the doc says there's no permanent damage." She grinned. "The fifteen minutes he spent in Cedar Creek last night seems to have altered his attitude. He made a full confession this morning, over Charlie Lipman's objections. Charlie kept trying to tell him to wait and make a deal, but he insisted on coming clean." She picked up her fork and took a bite. "Mmm, Ruby—this is *good* cake!"

When Brad went into the creek, I was sure he would drown. The only thing that saved him was getting snagged in the branches of a low-hanging willow tree just a few yards north of the East River Road bridge, about thirty yards from the place where Cedar Creek dumps into the river. Luckily, a couple of cops were already there, putting up barricades to keep people from driving across the flood-damaged bridge. They hauled Brad out of the water not long after they got the call from the 911 dispatcher, notifying them to be on the lookout for a murder suspect who had gone into Cedar Creek.

"So Brad has been charged with Todd's murder?" Amy asked eagerly.

"The DA will work up the charges in the morning," Sheila said. "It's a long list. He confessed to the burglaries and to Mrs. Holeyfield's death, as well as the deaths of his mother and Kellerman. But we would've got him without a confession," she added quickly. "We have those incriminating panties, plus every single one of the other stolen items, which we found out in plain sight, displayed in the upstairs hallway."

I chuckled wryly. That collection of objets d'art I had noticed on the upstairs shelves hadn't been Phoebe's—it had been Brad's.

"And of course there's the poker," Sheila went on. "And the blood that Brad tried to scrub out of the carpet in his room."

"So it *was* blood," I said, satisfied. "Given the general condition of the room, I didn't think he'd go to the trouble of scrubbing ketchup out of the rug."

"Yep, it was blood, all right," Sheila replied. "That's where Phoebe fell when Brad hit her with the fireplace poker. He didn't do a very good job of cleaning it, or cleaning the poker, either. We found both blood traces and prints. Even if he hadn't confessed, there's enough DNA and fingerprint evidence to convict him of killing his mother."

Ruby put what was left of the cake into a plastic container, stuck on a lid, and handed it to Amy. "This is for you and Kate to take home." To Sheila, she said, "So Brad *wasn't* in Abilene on Sunday night, after all?"

"No. Apparently, he drove back to Abilene after killing both his mother and Kellerman. He went back to the motel where he'd stayed the night before and paid the desk clerk three hundred dollars to change the records, making it look as if he'd never checked out on Sunday morning." She shook her head ruefully. "He went to all that trouble—and then he used a credit card to pay for the room. The charge went through the system at three o'clock on Monday morning."

"Funny, isn't it?" Ruby mused. "He could be so smart in some ways, and so dumb in others."

"It's almost as if he wanted to be found out," Kate said. She picked up a cup of coffee and leaned against the counter, looking at Sheila. "So what actually happened on Sunday night?"

"Brad says he didn't like the work Vince had asked him to do in West Texas. He decided to come back early and tell Vince he could go to hell. He was upstairs in his room when Phoebe and Todd got into the argument, which he could hear very clearly. He went onto his balcony in time to see Marsha go up on the porch and stand there uncertainly for a few minutes. Then she ran back to her apartment, and in a few minutes, took her car out of the garage and left. A few minutes after that, Phoebe came upstairs, half-hysterical, to tell Brad that she had ordered Todd out of the house."

Amy leaned her chin in her hands. "I'd have thought that would have made Brad happy," she said. "He hated Todd. He wanted him gone."

"Maybe so," I said. "But he hated his mother, too, even more than he hated Todd. He blamed her for his father's death."

"And yet he was sick with jealousy," Amy said. "That was why he hated Todd—for sleeping with his mother."

"I guess it was all mixed up in his mind," I said. "Love and hate." I sighed. "A good defense lawyer could have made something out of that. No wonder Charlie was mad."

"Shut your mouth, Bayles," Sheila snarled. "It's lawyers like you who make life hard on the rest of us."

"Don't get your knickers in a twist," I said with a grin. "You've got your confession."

"So *then* what happened?" Kate asked. "After his mother came upstairs, I mean."

"Apparently, she noticed some of the items he'd added to the display shelves in the hallway and made some sort of nasty remark about his taste in art. So he told her where he'd got them and how—a kind of taunt, I suppose. Now that Todd was out of the picture, he was going to let her have it. Let her know that he was the one behind the burglaries. He'd probably been planning that all the way along. It was the punishment he'd cooked up for her."

"Oh, God," Amy said sadly. "I can just hear the two of them."

"It must have been a real free-for-all," Sheila agreed. "The way he tells it, she picked up the poker and took a swing at him. He grabbed it away from her and in the struggle, she got hit in the side of the head. She was dead within a few minutes."

"You see?" I said. "Self-defense!"

Ruby let out her breath, ignoring me. "And then he dumped her body into the tank? But what about Todd?"

Sheila wiped her mouth on a napkin. "Todd's car was parked in the driveway, where he was loading his stuff. Brad took his mother's gun out of her room. Then he dragged her body downstairs and stuffed it into the trunk. From that point on, all he had to do was hold the gun on Todd, who did the driving and all the dirty work. They went to the plant, where Brad made Todd lash cinder blocks to the body and put it into the tank, and then Brad erased the security video. Then he forced Todd to drive to the gravel pit, where he shot him, making it look like a suicide. Then he jogged back home, took a shower, and drove back to Abilene."

"And he almost got away with it," I said. I looked at Amy. "If you hadn't insisted that Todd was left-handed. And if Lunelle hadn't been such a snoop."

Amy turned her face away. "I knew Todd couldn't have," she said. "He was too . . . soft. He'd give in before he'd resist. I think that's how he got involved with Brad's mother. She wanted him, and he didn't know how to say no."

"Did you suspect Brad?" Ruby asked.

"No, not really. But I was afraid of him. He wanted me, but—" She looked down at her hands. "But he . . . well, he couldn't." She bit her lip. "He couldn't do it."

"Do it?" Ruby asked blankly.

"Have sex," I said.

"Oh." Ruby looked at her daughter, frowning. "You mean, you—"

"That's not the point, Ruby," I said quickly. "We're talking about Brad. His mother had so thoroughly messed him up that he couldn't have normal sex."

"Which might be why he took those underpants," Sheila said. "She really did a number on him."

"Mothers and children," I said, thinking about my own difficult relationship with my mother. "We manage to make a lot of trouble for one another, don't we?"

"Yeah, sometimes," Amy said. She got up from the table and went to put her arms around her mother. "But it can usually be fixed. We just need a little time to grow up. And a little love."

I caught Kate's glance and raised my eyebrows. She shrugged, smiling, as if to say she didn't have anything to do with it. But I knew differently.

"Yeah," I said. "A little love won't hurt a bit."

Resources and Recipes

Unlike lavender or rosemary, dill (*Anethum grave-olens*) isn't an herb that you're likely to love. And yet, over the centuries of human experience, dill has proved to be one of the most useful herbs in the garden. An annual, it's easy to grow—so easy that unless you collect the ripe seeds, you'll find an eager army of dill volunteers cropping up in your garden, year after year. But you probably will want to gather the seeds, because they're so useful—in some ways, even more useful than the leaves (which are usually called, with a fine disregard for politeness, dill *weed*). Chopped finely, the fresh leaves can be added to cottage cheese, sauces, and salads. The seeds are used whole in a wide variety of dishes, most notably in pickles.

How did dill get associated with pickles? One answer, of course, is flavor—the sharp pungency of dill seed is a natural complement to both vinegar and cucumbers. But dill is also a natural preservative, and its essential oil has the ability to inhibit the growth of such ugly bacteria as staph, strep, and *E. coli.* When dill was added to the vinegar used to preserve cucumbers, the bugs didn't have a chance.

That same bug-fighting ability also made dill a popular medicinal herb. For tens of centuries and in a wide variety of human cultures, dill has settled upset stomachs and prevented infectious diarrhea, fought flatulence, and soothed baby's colic. In fact, it is this soothing quality that gave dill its name, which is derived from the Old Norse word *dilla,* "to lull." (Dill appears so frequently in the cuisine of the Scandinavian countries that it qualifies as their national herb.)

It is dill's soothing quality that probably gave the herb its reputation as a magical herb of protection. In the Middle Ages, dill was used in charms against the evil fairies and witches who soured cows' milk, spoiled the crops, or made off with the baby. The English Renaissance poet Michael Drayton recalled this tradition in his lines, suggesting that dill was so soothing that it even calmed the evil spirit in witches:

> *Therewith her Vervain and her Dill*
> *That hindereth Witches of their Will.*

As late as the nineteenth century in England, it was possible to see dill hung over the cottage door, or over the baby's cradle. Dill seeds were included in protective sachets and amulets that were worn to fend off devils and protect the mind from harmful influences. And because the plant was ruled by the planet Mercury (which also ruled the mental processes), it was thought to clarify thought and focus the attention. Altogether, an eminently useful herb.

Today, while dill may be prescribed by herbalists to soothe infant colic and ease upset stomach, we are more likely to value it for its culinary uses. The herb appears in all kinds of baked goods, especially in breads and crackers. It's a favorite with fish, and is used in sauces for poultry and vegetables. It sparks up bland dishes made with eggs or potatoes, and can be combined with parsley and chervil to poach fish and chicken.

Dill makes few demands on gardeners. It grows easily from seed or small transplants. Plant it where it has plenty of room, since it doesn't like to be elbowed by its neighbors. It has no pests, although it is beloved of the striped caterpillars who will grow up to become swallowtail butterflies. (When you see them, move them gently to a Queen Anne's lace plant, one of dill's country cousins.) Harvest the fresh leaves anytime before the plant begins to flower. If you don't want seeds, pinch off the flowers and continue to harvest the leaves. For seeds, allow several plants to flower and the seeds to mature until they are a pale brown. Then cut the head and about twelve inches of stalk and place, head down, inside a paper bag. That way, you won't have seeds scattered all over the floor. When the seeds are completely dry, store in a labeled, lidded jar, for use in your favorite recipes. The leaves may be dried or, for better flavor, frozen.

CHINA'S FAVORITE DILL RECIPES

To Pickle Cucumbers in Dill

This seventeenth-century recipe demonstrates the pickling method that was used for centuries.

Gather the tops of the ripest dill and cover the bottom of the vessel, and lay a layer of cucumbers and another of dill till you have filled the vessel within a handful of the top. Then take as much water as you think will fill the vessel and mix it with salt and a quarter of a pound of allom [alum] to a gallon of water and poure it on them and press them down with a stone on them and keep them covered close. For that use I think the water will be best boyl'd and cold, which will keep longer sweet, or if you like not this pickle, doe it with water, salt and white wine vinegar, or if you please pour the water and salt on them scalding hot which will make them ready to use the sooner.

Joseph Cooper, cook to Charles I
Receipt Book, 1640

A Dilly of a Dip

China served this yogurt-and-dill dip to the Pretty Pickle Planners in chapter four.

1 8-ounce carton plain yogurt
1 tablespoon minced fresh dill

1 to 2 tablespoons finely minced dill pickles
¼ teaspoon red pepper flakes

Combine all ingredients in a small bowl. Cover and refrigerate for several hours before serving.

Dilled Beer Bread

In chapter four, China makes Reuben sandwiches with this bread, which will remind you of a light rye bread.

3 cups flour
2 tablespoons sugar
4½ teaspoons baking powder
½ teaspoon garlic salt
½ teaspoon onion salt
1 teaspoon dill seed
2 tablespoons minced fresh dill
1½ cups (1 12-ounce bottle) beer, room
   temperature

Spray or lightly oil a 9"×5" loaf pan. Preheat oven to 350°. In a bowl, stir the dry ingredients together. Add dill seed, fresh dill, and beer, and mix well. Pour into prepared pan and bake for 40 to 50 minutes, or until a toothpick inserted into the center comes out clean. Remove from pan and cool for at least five minutes before slicing into eight slices. If you like the bread crustier, put the slices under the broiler and toast lightly.

Heavy-on-the-Dill Salad Dressing

In chapter five, China orders a German-style cucumber salad (sliced cucumbers, sliced tomatoes, and chopped green onions) with sour-cream dressing, "heavy on the dill." Here is Mrs. Krautzen-heimer's recipe, scaled down to serve four.

¼ cup sour cream
¼ cup mayonnaise
1½ tablespoons Dijon-style mustard
1 tablespoon dill pickle juice
3 teaspoons fresh dill

Mix all the ingredients together and refrigerate for several hours, allowing flavors to blend.

Dilled Tomato Soup

Thyme for Tea customers are enthusiastic about Janet's tomato soup. Dill gives it a distinctive taste.

1 pound tomatoes, peeled, seeded, and diced
3 large potatoes, peeled and diced
1 medium yellow onion, chopped
3 cups soup stock (chicken or vegetable)
⅓ cup dill vinegar or ¼ cup dill pickle juice
¼ cup finely minced fresh dill plus 1 to 2
    tablespoons for garnish
salt and pepper to taste
sour cream for garnish

3 to 4 tablespoons minced fresh parsley, for
    garnish

Place tomatoes, potatoes, onion, stock, and vinegar in a
nonreactive saucepan. Bring to a boil, reduce heat, and
simmer, covered, for about 30 minutes, until potatoes are
soft. Puree in a blender. Stir in the $\frac{1}{4}$ cup dill, salt, and
pepper. Reheat and serve with a dollop of sour cream and
a sprinkling of the remaining dill and fresh parsley.
Serves six.

Ruby's Dilled Ham and Squash Casserole

This easy recipe goes together quickly, in spite of the large
number of ingredients. Dill makes this a standout dish.

2 cups cooked corkscrew pasta
1 cup diagonally sliced medium carrots
1 cup water or vegetable stock
2 cups cubed cooked ham
2 cups chopped mixed summer squash (pattypan,
    crookneck, zucchini)
1 cup chopped onions
1 cup chopped celery
2 to 3 tablespoons tomato paste
1 16-ounce can crushed or diced tomatoes, drained
    (reserve the liquid)
¼ cup chopped fresh dill
¼ cup chopped fresh parsley (reserve half for
    garnish)
¾ teaspoon sugar

1½ tablespoons dill pickle juice
salt and pepper to taste
2 to 3 tablespoons freshly grated Parmesan cheese

In a large skillet, cook carrots in water or vegetable stock for 3 to 4 minutes over medium-high heat. Add ham, squash, onions, and celery, and continue to cook, stirring, until the vegetables are barely tender (about 10 to 12 minutes). Stir in the tomato paste and crushed tomatoes and cook on low heat for another 3 to 4 minutes. Add dill and half the parsley. Mix the reserved tomato liquid with the sugar, dill pickle juice, salt, and pepper. Stir into the ham and vegetable mixture. Add the pasta and stir. Remove from heat and pour into a large microwave or oven-proof dish. (You may refrigerate the casserole at this point.) Before reheating, sprinkle grated cheese over the top. Microwave on high until bubbly and the cheese is melted, or bake in 350° oven for 20 to 30 minutes. Sprinkle with reserved parsley. Serves six to eight.

MYSTERY PARTNERS WEBSITE

Susan and Bill Albert maintain an interactive website with information about their books, herb lore, recipes, a bulletin board, and Susan's daily (well, almost) journal. To visit, go to www.mysterypartners.com. While you're there, be sure and subscribe to their email newsletter, which is sent at least once a month. *China's Garden* and the Partners in Crime print newsletter are no longer being published.